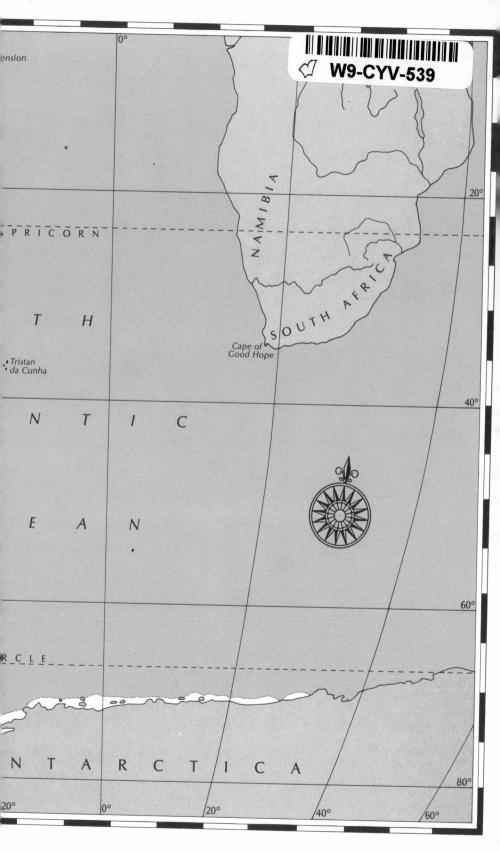

ension

NAMIBIA

20°

APRICORN

SOUTH AFRICA

T   H

Cape of
Good Hope

• Tristan
da Cunha

40°

N   T   I   C

E   A   N

60°

RCLE

20°   0°   20°   40°   60°

NTARCTICA

80°

OUTERBRIDGE
REACH

Books by Robert Stone

Outerbridge Reach

Children of Light

A Flag for Sunrise

Dog Soldiers

A Hall of Mirrors

OUTERBRIDGE REACH

—◆—

ROBERT STONE

Ticknor & Fields / *New York* / 1992

Title page illustration:
Hail and Farewell by Rockwell Kent,
courtesy of the Rockwell Kent Legacies.

———————

A signed first edition of this book has been
privately printed by The Franklin Library.

For information about permission to reproduce selections
from this book, write to Permissions, Ticknor & Fields,
215 Park Avenue South, New York, New York 10003.

Library of Congress Cataloging-in-Publication Data

Stone, Robert.
Outerbridge Reach / Robert Stone.
p.   cm.
ISBN 0-395-58781-6

I. Title
PS3569.T6418O94 1992 91-34875
813'.54 — dc20 CIP

Printed in the United States of America

Book design by Robert Overholtzer
Endpaper map by Jacques Chazaud

The author wishes to thank the American Academy and Institute of Arts and Letters for the award of a Strauss Livings, during the term of which this novel was written. Many individuals offered advice and encouragement while the work was in progress, above all Bruce Kirby and Peter Davis.

An episode in the book was suggested by an incident that actually occurred during a circumnavigation race in the mid-1960s. This novel is not a reflection on that incident but a fiction referring to the present day.

PART ONE

1

THAT WINTER was the warmest in a hundred years. There were uneasy jokes about the ozone layer and the greenhouse effect. The ambiguity of the weather made time seem slack and the year spineless. The absent season was a distraction. People looked up from their lives.

When the last week of February came in mild and spring-scented as April, Browne decided to deliver a boat to Annapolis. He passed under the Verrazano Bridge shortly after dawn on the last Wednesday in February. With Sandy Hook ahead, he cut his auxiliary and hoisted a mainsail and genoa. It was a damp, cloudy day with a gentle intermittent breeze just strong enough to raise a few whitecaps on the slate surface of the Lower Bay. Past Scotland Light, he brought her about and started for his first way point, twenty miles east of Cape May.

The boat under Browne was a forty-five-foot sloop of a type called the Highlander Forty-five, the latest and biggest representative of the Altan Marine Corporation's standard stock-boat design. Although he had written extensively about the Forty-five, Browne had never sailed one before. He had undertaken delivery on an impulse, stirred by the weather and some obscure guilt.

During the afternoon the wind picked up but stayed warm. He had a few miles of visibility; beyond it a sickly haze brought in the horizons. Close by, threads and patches of fog rolled along on the breeze, the bank unraveling. It was dull, satisfactory weather, with regular swells.

Winter's early darkness took him by surprise. He switched on the running lights and, planted on the companionway ladder, swept the indeterminate edge of sea and sky with his binoculars. There were no other craft in sight.

That evening he had a can of minestrone with crackers, cleaned the galley and settled down to listen for the marine forecast. The report was favorable. He set his radar scan for a radius of thirty miles; the scope recorded only the harbor traffic making for Ambrose Channel. For safety's sake he decided to spend the first night on deck in the cockpit. He set the radar alarm, rigged his lifeline and settled himself on a cushion beside the helm. The arctic-weight foul-weather gear he wore was too warm. He took off the top and folded it against the hatch behind him to use as a pillow. The indifferent breeze was steady all night and the sea slight. He coasted along until dawn on a starboard tack.

Around mid-morning the sky cleared and the wind freshened to twenty knots, a wind from the northeast with a proper wintry edge. The boat, with its spade rudder and deep short keel, was wonderfully fast. He went below then and set an alarm clock for two hours hence. When he woke up the wind had changed. He came about and unreefed the mainsail.

After a few hours it began to seem to him as though his boat, so fleet all night, had gone sluggish. The wind was still fresh but his speed declined and the boat seemed to wallow, pitching more than she had in the higher seas of the morning. When he went below to put on a cup of coffee he saw that water had come up over the expensively carpeted cabin sole.

"Son of a bitch," he said.

It took him a while to identify the problem, which was elemental but troubling. The Forty-five's bilge pump was back-siphoning sea water into the bilge. He set the self-steering and applied himself to the pump but in the end there was nothing he could do. And though he was not the handiest of sailors, he had no reason to suspect another man might do better. The pump had no vents and no seacock. No manner of jury rig would keep the ocean out.

For want of a nail, he thought. A hundred grand worth of Flash Gordon curves and fancy sheer — hostage to a plastic tube.

After a few experiments at the wheel, Browne found a course on which he could keep the pump outlet clear of the water. But it seemed pointless now to try for Annapolis. That would take days of nursing the boat along and he would not really be able to count on the weather in the long term. He raised his office on the radiotelephone. Ross, the branch manager, was as sanguine as usual.

"Some kind of South Korean fuckup," Ross told him. "We'll just have to fix it."

"Aren't you glad I found it?" he asked Ross. A moment later he thought he had sounded a little forlorn.

"Damn right," Ross said. "Good going. Keep it quiet, will you?"

The nearest Altan dealership with docking facilities was on the Jersey shore. He went on deck to lower his sails, turned on the engine and headed southwest.

On the way in he called his wife.

"Are you sure it's under control?" she asked him.

"I'm watching it," he told her. "I'll call you again by nine."

He made the estuary at Stone Harbor before dark and anchored off to clear the bilges. "Pump trouble," he told the local dealer. When he had packed his gear and locked the boat, he booked himself into a motel on route 121. He called the broker in Annapolis and then rang his wife again.

"I'm ashore," he told her. "So that's that."

"What will they do about it?" she asked him.

"I don't know," Browne said. "It has to be fixed somehow."

"Buzz and Teddy will be disappointed," Anne said. In Annapolis he had planned to visit with two of his old Academy classmates.

"I'm going down anyway," Browne said. "I feel the need of those guys."

"Do you know what?" Anne asked as he was about to hang up. Her voice had a false note of careless gaiety that made him realize that she had been drinking. "The market fell seventy points yesterday."

"Leaks everywhere," Browne said to her. He decided to postpone worrying about it.

That night in his motel bed, with the weekend traffic roaring by on the road outside, he could still feel the unsound motion of the new boat. Its pitching took shape in dreams he would not remember. In the morning, he took a cab to the Naval Air Station at Lakehurst and talked his way aboard a hop to Patuxent.

Buzz Ward met him at the hangar.

"Some life you lead."

"I haven't sailed overnight in years," Browne said. "I guess the weather got to me."

The unnatural weather hung over the fields of Maryland. Dogwood was budding in the wintry forest. As they drove, Browne told Buzz Ward about the boat.

"Nothing works anymore," he concluded.

"Yeah," Buzz said, "I know what you mean, buddy."

The Wards lived in a colonial house beside the Severn. Mary Ward, who did social work for the Episcopal Church, was away at a meeting in Virginia. Buzz and Owen Browne spent the afternoon walking the grounds of the Academy. Buzz was a professor of English there, with the rank of commander.

From the upper deck of the Crown Sailing Center, they watched midshipmen perform their seamanship drill aboard the mock-up warships in the river. It seemed to Browne that a third of them were women.

"Blue-collar kids," Buzz told him. "The boys are conventional-minded. The girls are the opposite."

"What's that like?"

"It's yet another form of torture," Ward said. "They march or die."

"As always."

"We try to shake 'em," Buzz said. "Also, we have the best black kids in the country."

Two of the sailing trophies on display in Webster had been won by Browne during his years as a midshipman. Buzz led him past them.

"*Sic transit gloria mundi*," Browne said, patting the glass.

"Amen," Buzz said.

The false spring and the Academy walks filled Browne's heart with ghostly promises. He and Ward went in silence past the chapel. Both of them had been married there, passing under swords into the June sunlight. It had been 1968 and the Navy at war. Both of them still lived with the same women.

Late in the afternoon, Browne borrowed the Wards' car and drove over to the Altan dealership in Waldorf. To his relief, it had closed for the day. When he got back to Annapolis, he found Ward serving bourbon to their old classmate Fedorov, who was in town for a Slavic studies conference at St. John's College, across the road from the Academy.

Fedorov was a Russian from western Massachusetts, the only son of a dispossessed kulak and his young Ukrainian wife. Two years before, he had taken early retirement and joined the faculty of a small Catholic college in Pennsylvania. He was tall and slope-shouldered, somehow priestly in his dark, ill-fitting suit. He appeared to be very drunk.

"Brother Browne!" Fedorov declared. His face was flushed.

Browne took a can of beer from the refrigerator and touched Fedorov's glass with it.

"*Na zdorovie!*" Fedorov said to him.

Browne raised the can in salute.

"Hello, Teddy."

Fedorov had always been singularly unmilitary in appearance. Now in middle age, he was jowly and bespectacled. His round, open face had an unfamiliar look that seemed to combine slyness and confusion. Brutalized by booze, Browne thought.

"*Na zdorovie!*" Fedorov repeated. In drink he became a professional Russian.

"Old Teddy's so loaded," Buzz Ward said, "he's talking Polish." He and Browne exchanged glances of resigned concern. Ward was a Kentuckian from a military family who had been a fighter pilot before taking his advanced degrees.

For dinner they went out to a restaurant in a restored colonial building near the state capitol. Their table was set by a bay storefront window overlooking Cumberland Street. The place was candlelit, herb-scented and mellifluent with Vivaldi. The wine somehow aroused Fedorov to a state of manic animation. He looked at his friends sidewise over his glasses, with a narrow-eyed crafty smile. Most of his adult life had passed in scholarly contemplation of the Soviet navy.

"Twenty years," he said, "next June. Can you believe it?"

"Easily," Buzz Ward said, and laughed at his own comment.

"I can't," Browne said.

His friends looked at him in silence.

"Well I can't, I'm sorry. It's impossible."

"All the same," Buzz Ward said, "there it is."

"Tell him," Fedorov said impatiently to Ward. "Tell Owen your plan."

Then Ward explained to Browne that he was leaving the Navy to take up religion. As soon as he retired, he and his wife were removing to northern California so that Buzz could attend a seminary there.

"That's incredible," Browne said. In fact, he was not particularly surprised at Ward's decision. "What about your fourth stripe?"

"I can retire with it," Ward said.

Browne shook his head.

"You were supposed to make flag rank, Buzz. We were counting on you."

"Twenty is plenty," Buzz Ward told him. "My kids are grown. I'm not about to divorce Mary. I need some love in my life."

Each of them had gone to Vietnam during the war and each had faced some combat. All three, as it turned out, saw their naval careers destroyed through the events of the war. Ward's fate had been particularly heroic and complicated. He had started out as one of the Navy's F-14 aces. After twenty-five missions he had been forced to eject over the Dragon Jaw Bridge. Then he had spent five years as a prisoner of war.

Fedorov rocked in his chair, arms folded, his face gross and saturnine.

"Anything to stop the clock," he said. "Extraordinary measures. Anything to break the treads of time."

Ward laughed self-consciously.

"You got it, buddy," he said. "You done put your finger on it, my friend."

"Everybody wants to be happy," Fedorov told them. "They're not happy if they're not happy. It's America. Remember the people who threw shit on us?" he demanded. He turned to look about the room as though he might find some antiwar demonstrators there. There were only a few elderly tourists. "Where are they now? Not happy, poor babies. Well, fuck them. They have their reward."

"An excellent analysis," Ward said. He turned to Browne. "Wouldn't you say, doctor?"

"I don't know," Browne said. "I'd have to think about it."

Their lives were bound in irony, Browne thought. Not one of them had chosen the Navy on his own. Each had been impressed into the Academy by the weight of someone else's expectations. In the case of Ward, it had been family tradition. Browne and Teodor were the sons of ambitious immigrant parents. If they had all graduated from high school only a year or two later they might have resisted. He and his friends had been the last good children of their time.

"Our enemies are confounded," Fedorov declared, "that's the good news. The bad news? So are we." He raised his glass of wine. "*Na zdorovie.*"

They raised their glasses with his. Both Ward and Browne were drinking soda water.

Afterward, they went back to the house beside the river. Browne decided to stay the night, do his business in Waldorf the next morning and take an afternoon train home.

In the Wards' living room, Buzz poured a small glass of wine for Fedorov, who took it without complaint. He made coffee for Browne and himself. Ward had always been a tireless coffee drinker, Browne remembered, a very naval thing to be.

"Maybe it was me who should have stayed in," he told Buzz Ward, "instead of you. Sometimes I wish I had."

"I always thought so, Owen. You instead of me. But you made a lot of money in the boat business. You damn well couldn't have done that in the Navy."

Browne shook his head quickly. "It's always risky. You can't count on anything one season to the next. Anyway," he told Ward, "I never cared about money."

Fedorov, who had appeared to be sliding into sleep, sat up straight on the sofa.

"You had better not go around saying that, Owen. You'll be locked up."

"None of us cared about money," Ward said. "That's the truth of it."

"Absolutely," Fedorov said. "Blitz was right about us."

Fedorov's reference was to an upperclassman named Bittner who had persecuted Browne and his two friends during their plebe year. Bittner had decided that the three of them were sodomists. He had gone beyond hazing, to the point of setting loose one of the Academy's periodic homophobic inquisitions. The charges had badly shaken Browne and Ward, who were not homosexual and who had been slightly more naïve about sexuality than the average midshipman. Fedorov had been driven to the lip of suicide. The experience had served to bond them. Bittner had turned out to have sodomy on the brain and been dismissed from the service. But he had been right about Fedorov.

"Well, I didn't stay in," Browne said, "and you guys did. That's one decision at least that's behind us."

"Wait until you see life in the economy, Buzz," Fedorov said to Ward. "It's terrifying! People pay for everything!"

"Speaking of which," Browne asked them, "did you guys register the market yesterday?"

Both Fedorov and Ward looked at him blankly.

"Christ," Browne said, "you don't know what I'm talking about, do you?"

"Oh," Fedorov asked, "the stock market?"

"Forget it," Browne said good-humoredly. "Never mind."

"The heroic age of the bourgeoisie is over," declared Fedorov, the naval Kremlinologist.

Ward helped him toward the foot of the stairs.

"So is the cold war, Teddy," Browne said. "We're all redundant."

Fedorov climbed like blind Oedipus, one hand on the banister, the other held out before him.

"Rubbish heap of history," he said fervently.

Ward went up behind him, ready for a fall.

On the train the next day, Browne watched the streetlighted slums of Philadelphia swing by, passing like time. The notion of twenty years gone was beginning to oppress him. In the dingy light of his shabby evening train, he felt himself approaching a new dimension, one in which he would have to live out the life he had made.

Ever since deciding to deliver the Forty-five, he had been looking forward to the sail and an evening with Ward and Fedorov. Riding home, he was discontent and disappointed. The anxiety that haunted him had to do with more than the design of Altan's latest boat and the state of the market. Old rages and regrets beset him. He felt in rebellion against things, on his own behalf and on behalf of his old friends.

As midshipmen, the three of them had been fellow stooges and musketeers. They had found each other, lost souls amid the monumental ugliness of Bancroft Hall. They had been wrongos and secret mockers, subversives, readers of Thomas Wolfe and Hemingway. They had appeared "grossly poetic," as Fedorov liked to say, naïvely literary in a military engineering school where the only acceptable art forms were band music and the shoe shine. They had survived to be commissioned by pooling their talents. Ward was a natural officer, in spite of his bookishness. Browne was athletic and, as the son of a diligent servant, skillful at petty soldiering. Fedorov tutored his friends in mathematics; they discouraged his tormentors and turned him out for Saturday inspections.

Their bohemian longings went equally unappreciated outside the main gate. However painfully Browne and his friends might aspire to stronger wine and madder music, young civilian America was having none of them in the year 1968. Midshipmen were cleaning spittle off their dress blues that year.

They had all gone to Vietnam after graduation and watched America fail to win the war there. This insufficiency was often a more remote spectacle for the Navy than for the other services, but Browne, Ward and Fedorov had all worked close to the core. They had each done their jobs but only Ward had excelled, for a while.

In the piss-yellow light of Penn Station, the hustlers and the homeless wandered into Browne's path as he made his way from the track. What did they see, he wondered, when they looked at him? A tweedy, well-intentioned man. An enemy, but too big and still too young to be a mark. Checking the scene, he thought: Yet I also am an outsider. He had left for the Academy from Penn Station on a summer morning in 1964. It had been an occasion of joy.

Riding the escalator to the upper level, he found himself wondering how, on that morning of departure, he might have imagined himself twenty years along. The image would have been a romantic one, but romantic in the postwar modernist style. Its heroic quality would have been salted in stoicism and ennobled by alienation. As an uncritical reader of Hemingway, he would have imagined his future self suitably disillusioned and world-weary. On the morning in question, he would not have had the remotest conception of what such attitudes entailed. He would have awaited world-weariness and disillusionment impatiently, as spurs to higher-class and more serious fun. Of course, not even Hemingway had enjoyed them very much in the end.

At the top of the escalator, he encountered another tier of loiterers and, for security's sake, put on his glasses. Confident and watchful, he passed unthreatened among the hovering poor. And combat, Browne thought. He would have imagined himself recalling combat. He would have expected combat to resemble *Victory at Sea*.

In the empty corridor that led to Seventh Avenue, an image of the old Penn Station came to him as he had first seen it as a child. He had tried to embrace the ponderous columns whose span defied the human scale. They had been still standing when he left for Annapolis the first time. Vanished sunlight came to his recollection, streaming through enormous windows in great beams and bursts, streaming from the throne of heaven.

Hearing his own echoing footsteps, he turned to look over his shoulder. Outside, teenagers debouching from a concert drifted along Seventh Avenue, looking covert and disorderly. Browne walked around the corner to the suburban-limousine ramp and boarded a car for home.

His house was old and outsized, a mansion on the edge of a slum in an unprestigious outer suburb. Undoing the locks, he awakened his wife. When he went into the bedroom, she smiled and raised her arms to him. On a wooden tray beside her bed stood an empty bottle of white wine, a glass and a jug of water.

"Oh," he said, "you're in good spirits, are you?"

She laughed. "Yes, I've been writing all day. And listening to music and waiting for you."

"Good," he said. He sat down on the bed beside her. "Christ, what a dumb couple of days. Between the boat and the market."

"Ross says they can fix it," Anne told him.

"You talked to him?"

"I called to give him a piece of my mind. You might have gotten wet out there."

"Poor guy," Browne said.

"I think I really gave him a scare. He thought I was calling for the magazine."

"Ross is scared of you anyway," Browne said. "You're too much lady for him."

He was suddenly moved to desire, wild with it. It was as though various hungers had combined to focus themselves on the woman beside him. He surprised them both with his avidity.

"Oh my dear," she said softly.

When they were done he lay awake listening to police sirens on the highway across the marsh. He felt as resigned to his private discontents as to the world's.

2

A GOVERNMENT marimba band was playing in the lobby of the hotel when Strickland came down to pay off his crew. The sound man and cameraman were brothers named Serrano who Strickland believed had been charged by their government with reporting on his activities. The brothers Serrano took their leave with unsmiling formality. Strickland paid them in dollars. As he walked away toward the garden lounge, he heard one of them imitating his stammer. He did not turn around.

For a moment, he stood in the doorway of the garden and watched the declining sun settle into the mountains. Then he saw his colleague Biaggio at a poolside table. Biaggio was signaling, urging him nearer, coaxing with both hands like the landing control man on an aircraft carrier. He went over to Biaggio's table and sat down.

"Eh," he said, "Biaggio." He enjoyed saying it.

His friend Biaggio was in something of a state. Normally the man reposed within an aura of lassitude that weighted his every gesture.

"I'm in love," he told Strickland.

"You d . . . d . . don't know what love is, Biaggio."

"Ha," Biaggio told him, "it's you who don't know."

Strickland shook his head with an air of tolerant disgust.

"You really have to dick everything that comes your way, don't you? You're like a fucking insect."

The languid Swiss journalist regarded Strickland with an expression of intelligent distress.

"The earth is rising on new foundations," he explained. "In the air — vitality. New beginnings. And this itself makes the heart prone."

"And the weenie vertical," Strickland said. He looked around for a waiter but there were none in sight. "Who's the lucky lady, I wonder?"

"But you know her, Strickland. She's named Charlotte. Charlotte . . . something."

"Sure," Strickland said. "Charlotte Something. The little Hun who was au p . . pairing in New York."

Biaggio shrugged and sighed. "Her eyes are pure."

"I never noticed that," Strickland said. He stood up and went to the bar to buy a beer. The bar was selling Cerveza Hatuey, a Cuban beer, at ten dollars a pop.

"You know, don't you," he told Biaggio, "that pure-eyed little Charlotte is fucking a minister of state."

"They're friends," Biaggio said.

Strickland burst out laughing. His laughter was loud and explosive. Strickland was aware that his laughter discomfited others. That was fine with him.

"They're friends!" Strickland cried happily. He mimicked Biaggio's Ticinese accent. "They are a-friendsa!"

Biaggio appeared bored with his own disdain.

"You're embittered," he said after a while. "Temperamentally you belong with the Contras."

"They're no longer worthy of my attention," Strickland said.

"You're in the Contra mode."

"Fuck you," Strickland said. "I'm a man of the left. Wait until you see my film."

"Is it finished?"

"Hell no, it's not finished. It has to be cut. But I've shot all I need. So I'm short, as we used to say in Nam. I'm so short I'm almost gone."

"Strickland," Biaggio said earnestly, "I have to borrow your jeep tomorrow. And your driver. I'm taking Charlotte to the front."

Strickland uncoiled a burst of merriment. Biaggio winced. The marimba band had stopped playing and Strickland's unsound laughter attracted the attention of people at the nearby tables.

"I myself," he told the American, "don't share this obsession to find absurdity everywhere. To find contemptible the honest impulse which —"

"Get off the dime, Biaggio. What do you mean by 'the front'?"

Biaggio looked at him uneasily.

"I was thinking of . . . thinking of going to Raton." Seeing Strickland at the point of mirth, he raised an imploring hand. "Please," he begged of his companion, "please don't laugh."

"There's a brigade headquarters in Raton," Strickland said. "There's an army airfield there. If Raton's your idea of the front, I understand how you've survived so many wars. You can have the jeep for f . . fifty dollars if you'll return it to Avis for me. You'll have to drive it yourself because I've already paid off the driver."

Biaggio slapped his forehead.

"You know I don't drive."

"Then fly. Or get Charlotte to drive. Remind her not to hit any mines."

Strickland's attention settled on the front pocket of Biaggio's yellowing white shirt. With a quick predatory gesture he removed a laminated card from it before the Swiss could intercept his move.

"Partito Comunista d'Italia," Strickland read from the card. "I suppose you're going around town flashing this."

"And why not?" Biaggio demanded. "Since it's mine."

Strickland tossed the card on the table.

"The best thing is to be known as a Mason," Biaggio said, retrieving the card. "The Masons run everything in this revolution. They are the true ruling cadre."

As the marimba orchestra took up a song of the people, a party of Americans entered the garden. Their overalls and metal-rimmed spectacles served to identify them as internationalists. Among them was a tall, dark-haired young woman whose skin had been turned the color of honey by the sun. Around her neck was the *banda roja* of the national youth movement. The two men watched her pass.

"You know who that is, Biaggio? That's Garcia-Lenz's reserve popsie. She's the backup for Charlotte."

"Bullshit," Biaggio said.

"You don't believe me?"

"Always the *sous entendre*," Biaggio said loftily. He looked away.

"I know the secrets of the heart, Biaggio."

Strickland went back to the bar for another beer. When he returned to Biaggio's table, he found young Charlotte seated in his chair. Ignoring Biaggio's impatient stare, he sat down with his beer.

"This is Strickland," Biaggio said curtly to his companion. The young woman, who had encountered Strickland in the field, gave him a wary glance. He returned what appeared to be an easy, amiable smile.

"Hi, Charlotte. What's this you have around your neck here?"

Charlotte, like the young American woman who had settled several tables away, wore a red and black neckerchief. She blushed charmingly as Strickland displayed the *banda* to Biaggio.

"I wear this," she explained, "for *solidaridad*."

"*Solidaridad*," Strickland repeated. "How about that? I'd like one of those. Where'd you get it?"

Charlotte was encouraged by his naïve admiration.

"I have interviewed Compañero Garcia-Lenz," she said with demure satisfaction. "And he has given it to me."

"No shit?" Strickland asked earnestly. "Hey, you're right about her eyes, Biaggio."

"We have to go," Biaggio said. "If you could give me the keys for the jeep. And also the papers." He brought out his wallet and found it empty of bills. He seemed to search it for secret compartments.

"Don't be in such a hurry," Strickland said. "I understand you were an au pair, Charlotte. Before you came down here? Is that right?"

"Yes," Charlotte said. "In the States."

"How was that?" Strickland asked her.

The young woman laughed happily.

"It is in Saddle River, New Jersey," she said. "They are so conservative I have freaked them out."

"Is that right?"

"And Nixon is there," Charlotte reported. "In Saddle River, yes?"

"No!" Strickland exclaimed. "Really?" He put his hand over hers on the table. "Sit tight, guys." He stood up, backed off a step and made a placatory gesture. "Don't go away."

"Strickland!" Biaggio wailed after him. "The jeep!"

Strickland went directly to the table where the party of young Americans was sitting and approached the dark-haired girl with the red bandana.

"Would you excuse me, please," he said softly, bending over her. "May I introduce you to a v . . visitor?"

Observing his defect of speech, the woman went sympathetic. Strickland expanded his smile so that it might irradiate the entire tableful of young Americans.

"I know who you are," the young woman said ironically, "but I don't believe you know me."

She told him her name was Rachel Miller. He moved back her chair as she stood up to follow him.

"Ah," he said. "Raquel!"

"Not Raquel," she said. "Just Rachel."

Although there were only three chairs at the table, Strickland insisted that Rachel sit down. Standing across the table from the two young women, he looked at each in turn.

"Charlotte, this is Rachel. Rachel, Charlotte."

Regarding Charlotte's brave ribbon, Rachel seemed to pale slightly beneath her suntan. Charlotte remained cheerful.

"And this is Biaggio," Strickland told Rachel, indicating his friend. "A veteran of *la soixante-huit*. Is he a French spy, a Swiss hustler or an Italian Communist? No one knows."

"I don't get it," Rachel said. She had become alert.

"Biaggio and I are researching the youth movement of Minister Garcia-Lenz," Strickland explained. "We're interviewing foreign members. Honorary members like yourselves. We're wondering if there's a common thread in their experience."

While not losing their good-natured expression, Charlotte's features seemed to thicken and her comprehension to fade. Rachel was staring at Strickland in cold fury.

"What's that song?" Biaggio asked cheerfully. People were singing far off, somewhere in the streets outside the hotel.

"That's a revolutionary song," Strickland said. "It's called 'A Clean Old Man Will Do.'"

Charlotte's lips moved in silent translation.

"What I'm curious about," Strickland went on, "is how foreign visitors like yourselves are recruited for the movement. Do you read his works? Does he take you to see the hovel he claims to live in?"

"What's your problem?" Rachel asked.

Charlotte appeared to have fallen asleep with her eyes open.

"My problem is the bottom line," Strickland explained. "The difference between what people say they're doing and what's really going on."

Biaggio shrugged and shook his head as though he were in conversation with himself.

"Maybe we shouldn't judge too harshly," Strickland said. "The guy was a priest for about seventy years. He's making up for lost time."

"What makes you so smart?" Rachel demanded. "Who do you really represent down here?"

"What do you care?" Strickland asked her. "You're just a tourist." He turned to Biaggio. "Next year," he said, "the old fuck will be giving them T-shirts. What would the T-shirts say, Biaggio?"

"No *pasarán!*" Biaggio suggested. He and Strickland had a giggle together. Rachel took a deep breath, stood up slowly and went back to her table. Strickland sat down in her chair.

"What the hell," he said equably. He tossed the keys to his jeep toward Biaggio. "Enjoy yourself." Then he leaned forward and spoke loudly to Charlotte, as though she were hard of hearing: "You too, *liebchen.* Drive carefully."

"You're a bad element, Strickland," Biaggio said when the keys were in his pocket. "A Trotskyite. A Calvinist."

"Goodbye, Biaggio." He raised his voice again. "*Ciao,* Charlotte! Don't run my pal on any mines!"

"Yes," Charlotte said faintly.

"Forget him," Biaggio told Charlotte as he led her away. "He cannot harm you."

Strickland turned to watch Rachel several tables over. She had taken off the scarf and she appeared to be crying. She sat in silence looking down at the table, taking no further part in conversation. After a while she got up and went toward the lobby. Strickland intercepted her just inside.

"What now?" she asked him.

"I want you to come with me."

"You must be crazy," she said.

"That could be it."

She made no move to leave but she said, "Leave me alone."

"Come with me!"

She stared at him.

"Come on," he said. He laughed. "Don't think about it, just do it. Come on!"

She blinked and for a moment she seemed about to follow him.

"Why did you do that to me just now, Mr. Strickland?"

"Because Garcia-Lenz is a hypocrite. That's why."

"No," she said. "I don't trust you."

"Actually," he asked, "what's to trust?"

"I want you to leave me alone!"

When she started past him, he blocked her way.

"I'll call someone!"

"You'll be laughed at," he said.

"You fucking bastard," Rachel said. "I know about you."

"What does that mean, Rachel?"

"I know about what happened in Vietnam. There are reporters here who were there with you."

He smiled, but she had seen the shadow pass.

"Everybody knows that story," she told him. "What the GIs did."

"If you only knew the half of it," Strickland said, "you'd eat your heart out."

"I'm sure I wouldn't," she said. "Not anymore."

"Garcia-Lenz won't remember your name, Rachel. I know who you are. I understand what you're doing down here."

Rachel's eyes were bright. She began to speak, broke off and turned her face to the artificial stucco wall.

"How can you know who I am?" she asked.

"Because it's my business. Perception. Do you understand?"

"I don't know what I understand," Rachel said.

"I'll tell you about it all," Strickland said. "My version."

"Your version?" she demanded with unhappy impatience. "Your version of what?"

"The world," he said. "How it goes. You may spend your life looking at revolutions. You should understand how to look at them correctly."

The promoters, police characters and lay missionaries in the lobby turned after Strickland and Rachel as they passed.

"I've been hyper since I got here," Rachel said. "For a while I was sick."

"Hey," Strickland said, "me too. Sick? Let me tell you!"

As he led her across the lobby, his spirits soared.

He pushed the button to summon the elevator and saw Rachel frown at him and take a step backward. He wanted to reassure her.

"Where are you from, Rachel?"

She looked at him in silence and shook her head.

"I mean, I sort of know where you're from," he hastened to say. "You went to private school somewhere. You probably went to progressive camps. Cookouts with food-from-many-lands."

Rachel raised two fingers to her brow as though her head ached.

"Folk dancing," Strickland fantasized, "interracial sing-alongs. Am . . . I right?"

Rachel leaned back against the wall beside the elevators and began to slide down it, bending at the knees.

"Hey," Strickland said to her, "be cool."

"I have to go," she said. "I have to wash my walking shorts. Goodbye."

She was sitting on the floor next to a giant aloe plant between the two elevator doors. The elevator arrived. Although they were operated by push buttons, each of the hotel's elevators carried an attendant. The attendants, Strickland had heard, were men who had served as informers under the old regime and who had been pressed into the same service by the new. The one who presented himself for service had been liberally tipped by Strickland as a basic precaution and he appeared pleased at the sight of his patron. When Strickland did not step into the elevator, the attendant peered around the corner and saw Rachel on the floor. He looked from the woman to Strickland.

"I suppose I went too far," Strickland said to the elevator attendant. None of them admitted to a knowledge of English. "I suppose I blew it."

He stepped into the elevator. It was, in fact, Strickland's last day in-country. He was bound home to New York to begin work on a film about a billionaire sailboat racer.

"*Ándale*," he told the man. "*Arriba.*"

It was almost all the Spanish he knew. When the doors closed on the lobby and the silent stares of its habitués, he felt a considerable relief.

Halfway up to Strickland's floor, the operator turned and smiled. When he saw Strickland's stormy, disappointed face his smile vanished.

"I work in the service of truth," Strickland told the old man, "which is nowhere welcome. Understand what I mean?"

The operator, seeing his passenger's disposition improved, smiled and inclined his head. Strickland took a ten-dollar bill and wrapped the man's hand around it.

"No you don't," he said.

3

BESIDE THE SOUND, under the brightening sky, Browne dug in along the shore, planting one foot in front of the other, breathing the sour iodized sea air. He ran with three-inch weights behind his fists, pumping, working the hump of sinew around his shoulders, stretching his legs. Three miles down the beach, the stack of an enormous power plant flashed a red warning beacon from its summit. The lights over the chain-link fence at the plant's perimeter were Browne's halfway mark. Panting, he strained to bind his thoughts to the plain rhythm of breath.

His chief regret had always been leaving the Navy. He was aware that this was the fair price of a rational decision, hardly more than nostalgia, a kind of luxury as regrets went. He would not have thrived there. Pushing harder, he turned his face into the breeze, saw the clean line of the Long Island shore and increased his pace. Ahead, the lights of the plant fence went out, then flashed on again as a cloud passed across the risen sun.

Running, Browne felt a pang of expectation in his breast. He felt suddenly outsized by his own hunger, by a desire that filled the new day from sea to sky. When he reached the power plant fence he ran beside it. The harsh squares of the fence and the ugly metal sheds behind it made him feel vaguely captive and violent. He turned off and went back the way he had come.

"What are you waiting for?" he whispered as he pumped over the soft sand. He could not seem to outrun the thing that had settled over him.

In the littered cul-de-sac at the end of his street, he walked off the run and tried to put his mind at rest. After a little while, the anguish and disorder he had experienced began to seem like an illusion. Running could stir things up. It was just another Sunday, he decided. He jogged down to the cigar store for the paper and trotted home with it under his arm. On the way he passed a few solitary walkers and nodded good morning to all. Each person he passed paused to look after him. Browne found himself the only one awake in the house. He tossed the Sunday *Times* on the kitchen table and called up the back stairs to his sleeping wife and daughter.

"Wake up, people! Pancakes!"

He mixed some pancake batter and diced a few Granny Smith apples in with it.

"Wakee, wakee!" he shouted.

When no one appeared he vaulted up the stairs to his daughter's room and banged on the door. Maggie was down from school for a long weekend, and it occurred to him that he should make an effort to spend part of the day with her.

"Mag! Up all hands! Time to jump off, my young friend."

When there was no answer he prepared to assault the door again. His daughter's scream arrested his hand.

"Goddam it," she cried from inside, "get out of here! Leave me alone!"

"Now listen . . ." Browne began. He was surprised and hurt. It was hard to be reasonable. "Listen here, Maggie."

"Leave me alone!" the girl shrieked. She sounded utterly hysterical. "Leave! Me! Alone! Leave me the fuck alone!"

As she had recently discovered, Browne could not abide her using such words.

"Open the door, Margaret," he demanded. He tried the door but it had been locked from the inside. He rattled the knob, resenting the absurdity of his position and quite aware of it. "Don't you use that kind of language to me!" Her adolescent wrath made him feel brutal and ridiculous. He pursed his lips in frustration.

Maggie raised a pitiable moan.

"Please! Please go away."

"No, I won't go away," Browne said. "Nor will I stand here talking to a door."

The door of the master bedroom opened and Anne came out into the hall wearing a woolen bathrobe.

"Owen, let it pass." She came up to him and took hold of his hand, referring to their tenderness of the night before. "Maggie's had some kind of social crisis. I think she may have a spot of boy trouble." She led him gently away from Maggie's door, holding him by both hands.

"I'm sorry to hear that," Browne said. "But it's no excuse. Did you hear the language she used?"

"Please let it pass, Owen. I'm sure she'll apologize. She's been in a state, the poor kid."

"For God's sake," he muttered. "I didn't know she commanded such language."

"Oh, they all do," Anne said. "She does it to get a rise out of you."

Browne let himself be drawn away.

"Look, take your shower," Anne told him. "I'll make the pancakes. You cool off and have your shower. Don't let it spoil your morning."

In the shower, Browne tried to salve his bruised propriety and ease the anxiety he felt about his only daughter, whose adventures in the jungle of young America filled him with dread. It was a difficult time to bring up children, he thought, almost as bad as the late sixties and seventies had been. Browne's expectations were high and Maggie had been an exceptionally dutiful and well-behaved child, more attuned to her parents than to her peers. All this, it seemed, was changing and the New England convent school to which, at great cost, they sent her seemed unhelpful. It had been her mother's school, but Browne had been very reluctant to send her away. Now it seemed that the other girls there were wild and sometimes unwanted at home. Drug use was more of a problem there than in the public schools. He tried not to think of it. He could not bear the thought of his daughter's pain and she did not, at this point in her life, seem very clever at protecting herself from it.

Browne and Anne consumed the pancakes. Maggie sulked in her room.

"I should take her sailing," Browne said.

"But the boat's in Staten Island."

"Well," he said, "we could go down there."

"Surely you don't feel like doing that today."

Browne was not much in the mood for sailing. He was picking at his guilt over having Maggie away at school and neglecting her.

"No I don't, really. I should have taken her along when I moved the boat in the fall."

"Well," Anne said, "she has other things on her mind."

As it turned out, he could not find much to do with the day. Anne went to work in the study he had built for her, finishing the article she was doing for the yachting magazine where she worked as an editor. Maggie hid out and then slipped away. In the early afternoon, Browne put on his mackinaw and prepared to go in to the office. On his way out he knocked on the study door.

"You should have gone to church this morning," he told his wife. "To pray for the market."

They had a laugh together.

4

IN THE TAXI from La Guardia, Strickland had the persistent notion of being followed. He rode with one knee up on the back seat, guarding the road behind. He had noticed a man in the bar at Miami airport watching him, a man he was sure had boarded his flight in Belize. Between Miami and New York he had been upgraded to first class, only to find the same tall mestizo in a seat across the aisle. As his cab mounted the Triborough Bridge his eye was on a Ford Falcon that had left the Grand Central Parkway just behind him. A dark-haired man in sunglasses was at the wheel. A second man of similar appearance sat beside him. All the way across the bridge Strickland kept watch, reflecting that there was no more sinister sight in all of the hemisphere than two tall Latinos in a Ford Falcon. It made you want to pray. When the Ford eased past them to leave the FDR Drive at One Hundred Sixteenth Street, he turned his face away.

Driving downtown, Strickland had a gander at his driver, whose name was presented on the hack license as Kiazim Shokru. He had a bald bullet head and fierce, lustrous eyes behind which burned the fires of Shia or drugs or plain madness.

"So what d .. do you think, Kiazim?" Strickland inquired. "You like New York?"

Kiazim Shokru stared at him in the mirror, apparently with rage.

"No?" They had taken the Forty-eighth Street exit and were deep in gridlock. Strickland was already weary of his new conversation. "Where do you like, then?"

The driver ignored him.

Strickland's premises were in Hell's Kitchen, just west of Ninth Avenue. He got out on the corner, took his bag from the trunk and paid off Kiazim. On his way to the building, Strickland was approached by a lost soul who had been begging from passing cars with a Styrofoam cup. He sidled past the man but then thought better of it. Pausing, he filled the man's cup with his Central American small change.

He let himself in through the metal street door, leaned against the moldering green wall of the first landing and pressed the elevator button. The elevator arrived complete with Archimedeo, the Colombian super, who, seeing Strickland, stepped back in stylized surprise.

"Hey, where you been?"

"Atlantic City," Strickland told him.

"Yeah," Archimedeo said, stepping out of his way. "I know where you been."

Strickland maintained half of the eighth floor of his building, which had been a musical-instrument factory long ago. His place consisted of two cutting rooms, a small office and a big loft space in which he had his living quarters.

Approaching his shop, he heard a radio playing inside. When he pounded on the door someone came to listen by it.

"Yes please?" demanded a nasal, impertinent voice.

"It's me, Hersey. Open the door."

The Medeco lock and the deadbolt were undone and Hersey stood before Strickland, bowing and rubbing his hands together. Hersey was an apprentice, an awkward youth of frail and scholarly appearance.

"Welcome, master," Hersey intoned. It pleased him to assume the demeanor of a freakish laboratory assistant in a horror movie, a role for which he was, in fact, well suited.

"What's happening?" Strickland asked him. "Everything arrive?"

"I think so. A hundred and eighty rolls. Thirty hours."

"Got it sunk up?"

"But of course."

"Good," said Strickland.

He went back into his quarters, showered and changed. As he dressed, he listened to his message machine. After a while he shut it off. The messages were boring and he was not in the mood to talk on the phone.

Back in the cutting room, he found Hersey at the Steenbeck, working to the creepy contemporary music the youth favored.

"Knock off, Hersey. I want to see what I have."

"The moment of truth," Hersey said. He stood up and assumed the parody of a servile cringe.

"Truth is right," Strickland said.

They sat and watched selected dailies from Strickland's Central American documentary. There were scenes of political rallies sponsored by the party in power, of religious processions and of volunteers for the harvest. There were sensitive studies of the dead. There were views from the door of a moving helicopter that raced its shadow over the savanna in a ghostly reference to Vietnam, of flamingos rising in thousands from a mountain lake, and of pre-Columbian ruins, somber and murderous. And there were interviews of every sort.

"Christ," Hersey said, watching an American diplomat attempting to explain himself, "you really open them up."

"I get them to spread," Strickland said. "That I do."

They watched the brother of a cabinet minister, sounding a little the worse for rum, attempt to explain what could not be explained to a camera.

Hersey giggled asthmatically.

"Doesn't he know you're shooting?"

"Sure he knows. And then again he doesn't."

After about an hour of film, Strickland threw the switch.

"That's about all I can take," he told Hersey. "The pungent odor of the real thing." He clapped his hands. "We're in business."

"Take a bow, big guy," Hersey said.

Strickland reflected on how often he and his principal assistant found themselves on the same wavelength. Distractingly obnoxious, Hersey was nonetheless a formidably gifted super-techie who could edit, operate the camera or take sound, enduring Strickland's proximity the while. His master prized him.

"They're so urgent," Hersey said admiringly. "And they always blow it. How do you do that?"

Strickland rounded on him.

"You don't understand, do you? Do you really think it's me

getting them to look bad? On the contrary, they piss all over themselves. Half the time I have to clean up their act."

Hersey was chastened. He took off his thick-lensed glasses and wiped them on a Sight Saver.

"It's hard to tell the good guys from the bad guys."

"Hey, I decide who the good guys are, Hersey. When you learn how to cut film, you'll decide."

"Really?"

Preparing to go, Hersey put a jacket over his black rising-sun banzai T-shirt. In the front pocket of the jacket he carried three ballpoint pens as a joke. Generally, he favored Astor Place haircuts and suits of Milanese drape.

"What about this guy Hylan?" the assistant asked on his way out. Hylan was the yachtsman who was to feature in the next project. Strickland had an appointment with him.

"Hard to say," Strickland said. "On the one hand he's our patron. On the other hand he has a cruel infantile face."

Hersey's laughter echoed from the outer loft.

Alone in his cutting room, Strickland ran another reel in sections, fast-forwarding from time to time. The scenes with the birds struck him particularly. The rising flamingos, swallows in the cactus, doves and vultures in the palm trees — he could not account for all the footage of birds he saw. Mythic and heraldic notions occurred to him. He whistled "Paloma" between his teeth. There was a way in which the birds proclaimed the country.

Most ineffable were the frames which featured the dead. The corpses in the film fascinated for reasons beyond the drama and violence they necessarily represented. Strickland pondered the way in which dead people always appeared in complicity with their circumstances, no matter how bizarre the setting or how advanced the state of their decomposition. In a way, he thought, it was almost reassuring. It made you think: If they can have *that* happen to them and look so cool about it afterward, so can I.

He went into his living loft, brought out his marijuana and rolled a joint. Then, smoking, he ran the footage he had watched earlier with Hersey. The interviews amazed him. People had no discretion. He sat at his machine, hugging his shoulders, rocking in solitary laughter. He kept imagining fade-outs that would bring birds back to the screen, a comment on the babble and confusion on the field of folk. Strickland was encouraged for the work ahead. What a piece of work is man, he thought.

Late that night, lying on his bed smoking the last of the previous summer's marijuana, he decided to call Pamela Koester. Pamela was a suburban soubrette turned occasional prostitute who had figured prominently in a highly regarded documentary on New York lowlife that Strickland had made three years before. She was his sometime connection and they had entered into a relationship.

"Hello, Pamela," he said when he had her on the line. "Big Buddy's back."

"Hey, Big Buddy," Pamela called with faint enthusiasm. "When you get back?"

"Just now," Strickland said. "Today."

"Just now," Pamela said, "and you're calling me already. What a pal."

"So," Strickland said, "come over. Bring something."

"Two, maybe three o'clock, how's that? I can't stay long. Can we watch something?"

"We'll have one of our talks. Can't you make it earlier?"

"Uh-uh," Pamela said. She clicked her tongue reflectively. "Now this is *really* embarrassing, and please don't think I'm sordid, but I have to ask you for a credit card number. Isn't that awful? For appearance' sake."

"Chrissakes," Strickland grumbled. He got out his wallet and read her the number.

He was almost asleep when the downstairs bell rang hours later, half dreaming of all the birds. He rode the elevator down to the street door.

"Hey, you're constant," Pamela said to him. She turned and signaled to dismiss the taxi that had brought her. "Calling up your first night back in town."

She was wearing a black beret, a sheepskin jacket with a woolly collar and expensive cowboy boots with fancy stitching. The beret, together with her large-framed spectacles and the leather portfolio she carried, gave her an appearance of upper bohemian wholesomeness. She had been a sensation in Strickland's movie because she was so attractive and reasonably well spoken and generally unlike the common representation of a prostitute on film. The film was called *Under the Life*, from someone's cute remark.

As they rode upstairs, Strickland asked Pamela what was new.

"I was home," she said. "I mean in Connecticut. Watching my father like prepare for death."

"Yeah?" Strickland asked. "What does he do?"

"Well, he gardens. He writes letters to the town zoning board."

"What a guy," Strickland said.

"So you were down in South America, huh? How was that? Go dancing? Score coke?"

"The birds were great," he told her.

She loved the line. She repeated it.

"The birds were great! You're unreal, Strickland. Hey, I'm really sorry about the card," she added. "I have to placate Ludmilla."

Ludmilla, a Russian immigrant, was proprietress of an escort service with which Pamela was presently employed. The service represented some advancement for her. During the period of Strickland's documentary, she had been the love slave of a feckless pimp called Junior, whom everyone had thought beneath her.

"How's Junior?" Strickland asked. "I want to hear all about it."

"Really? O.K." She laughed, being a good sport about it, and handed Strickland a two-ounce Baggie of marijuana that had been pressed flat in her portfolio. Then she excused herself to go to the bathroom. He could imagine her fingers prowling his medicine cabinet. When she came out they sat down in Strickland's office. Behind his desk was an enormous round window into which the instrument manufacturer's corporate coat of arms had been leaded. There was a similar window in the bedroom. Over the rooftops of Clinton and Chelsea they could see the towers of the World Trade Center and even a few faint winter stars. Strickland lighted a joint and turned his tape recorder on.

"Junior's terminal," Pamela declared. She spoke to the recorder with a kind of wicked excitement. "He's paranoid. He thinks everything went bad for him since he was in your movie. He thinks you owe him."

"That's funny," Strickland said.

"He's part of my past, man. He goes, 'You have no respect.'" She held her breath on the toke. "I go, 'Right on. Not for you I don't.' So it's like all over."

"Poor Junior."

"I hear he smokes crack. I hear he gets these yeast infections. His bitches say either he's taking like *a lot* of antibiotics for syphilis or he's got AIDS. They don't like it."

"Very good, Pamela."

"He's a jive nigger. He's finished!" She raised her voice and sawed the air, pulling the plug on Junior. "Yeah! He's fucked! We're talking liberation!" Pamela cried. Then suddenly she seemed to step, as it were, out of character. "How's that?" she asked Strickland.

Strickland applauded silently, palm to palm. "Wonderful," he said soothingly. "I wish I had it on film."

She looked at him sidewise, green-eyed. In the space of the moment it was possible to see how crazy she was.

"You, Strickland," she recited in a childish croon, "always looking at me. I see your ass."

"Know what I see?" Strickland asked. "I see how cold your eyes are."

She covered her eyes with her hand.

"Don't say that," she said.

Like a predatory fish, he thought. Dangerous work but he felt in control.

"How about letting me shoot you, Pamela?"

"No," she whimpered. "Come on."

"Just with the video camera."

"What would it be?" she asked plaintively. "Look at the ho? No!" she said.

"You see what is, Pamela. You take all those drugs together and your mind's a fucking omelet. I want to put you on film again, man."

She laughed and pouted.

"No."

"Maybe I should intimidate you. Maybe I should call you bitch."

Pamela clenched her teeth and shook her head.

"Maybe I should say, 'Let's roll 'em, bitch!' Yell at you. Maybe then we could work."

She looked away.

"Tie you up or something. Because you like that."

Childlike again, her anguish dissolved in a giggle. He had made her laugh.

"Strickland!" Exasperated but affectionate. "Ron, goddam it."

"What you refuse to understand, Pamela, is that I propose a flick that is you entirely. I mean, I would like to do a whole mixed-media thing. All you. To be entitled *Pamela*. Don't you think that would be radical?"

"I don't believe you."

"Ah," Strickland said, "then you're mistaken. Because I don't make jokes about my projects."

"Really?"

"Pamela, how can I persuade you?"

"Listen, Ron," she said suddenly, "I'm really sorry about carding you. I'm with these awful people."

"I'm never reluctant to pay for conversation," Strickland assured her. "It's sex I won't pay for."

She was at the stage of making faces. She put out her lip, a tragic masker.

"Don't you like sex, Ron?"

"Hey," Strickland said, "this is sex."

Then she went to the bathroom again. While she was doing whatever she did, Strickland looked through his stores for something to catch her fancy. In the bottom drawer of a file cabinet he found the ancient reel-to-reel tape recording of a radio talk show in which he had participated as a child. It was an item he had gone to much trouble to obtain the previous year. Hell, he thought, I'll squander it. He dusted the spool and put it on.

Pamela came out of the bathroom looking flushed and wet-lipped.

"I have to go," she cried. But in a moment she cocked an ear. "Hey, what's this, Strickland?"

They listened to the dulcet tones of Strickland's late mother as she described her dedication to the education of youth. The host replied in an old-time carny accent, a vanished mode of speech full of secret inflections. Strickland heard his own adolescent voice. He sounded a little like the carny and that was all wrong because he and his mother were supposed to be straight citizens.

Pamela was quite taken with what she heard.

"What is that?" she asked happily.

"It takes a little explaining," he told her.

"I want to thank all the p . . . p . . people out there for helping us," Strickland heard his own adolescent voice say.

"Who is it, Ron?"

"It's old radio, Pamela. The voice is mine. The woman is my late mother."

"Wha?" she demanded.

Suddenly he was tired of hearing it. It had not really been such a good idea. Only high had he imagined her an appropriate audience. He turned it off.

"That was made in an old studio up above the New Amsterdam," he explained wearily. "Right up the b . . . b . . block there. My mother and I were begging. We were being the deserving poor. It was *The Max Lewis Show*. People would call in one- and two-dollar pledges."

She was looking at him, mouth agape.

"I mean," he said, "what can I tell you? It all happened before you were born."

"But that's terrific, Strickland. You and your mom, huh?"

"Me and Mom."

"That's so sweet. The two of you on the radio. Who would of thought you had a mother?"

"You know, Pamela," Strickland said, "there's an old theatrical adage: Dying is easy, comedy is hard."

She stared at him. "That's a threat!" She seemed delighted. "You threatened me."

"Nonsense."

"I'm not scared of you, you know."

"Yes," he said, "I know."

Her quivering smile defied him.

"Would you really make a movie with just me in it?"

"Yes," he said patiently. "It would be my next venture."

"Just me? Long shots? Close-ups? Nothing in this picture but me?"

"They'd call it *Pamela*."

"It sounds avant-garde."

Strickland shrugged modestly.

"I don't know," she said. "I don't know what to do. Can I look at footage of myself?"

"I thought you had t . . . t . . to go."

"Please, please," she said.

So he set up a collection of outtakes from *Under the Life* which had been synched for her perusal. He left her in the office, watching herself on the Steenbeck.

Back in the living loft he took his shoes off and lay back on the bed. From the editing room where Pamela was watching herself, barks and whoops resounded, together with loud groans that rose in crescendo and dissolved in ululation.

He was wondering whether it might really be feasible to make another documentary feature around Pamela alone. He had always wanted to try making a one-person film. With her, he thought, it would be knotty work. How to penetrate that busy swarm of verbiage and gesture and find the shiny animal within? How to bring it stunned and dripping into light? But what a worthy lesson for the world to glimpse what thrived in the airless inner life of just one particular whore. It would be every bit as striking as your pet cemetery films. There would be the same uneasiness at what teemed there, under the crust. They would see its shadows cast upon her pleasant face.

The trouble was, he thought, that he might be accused of repeating himself. They might say, Whores again. Half the time they had no idea what they were looking at.

Strickland's half-stoned reverie eased him into fragile sleep. Within minutes he woke to see Pamela in his living room. She stood by the window, her face close to the glass. The sky above New York was growing light. On her face, caught perfectly by the morning's faint radiance, was an expression like a child's. Standing there, he thought, she looked for all the world as though the morning light could somehow save her. She seemed, through the homely offices of shadow and line, hopeful and expectant. It was fetching, and he thought a little about how to nail down such a look.

Pamela turned and caught him watching her.

"Look," she said, "it's light. Could we have some music?"

He looked at her without answering.

"I'm cold," she said. "Could I come and sit on the bed?"

"No," he said gently. "And it's not cold."

"Oh," she said, "you're a rat, Strickland."

She was showing him her streaked druggy face, that rapt, snotty, cotton-candy smile. All the same, he saw real desperation there. The whore in the morning, facing bed in earnest.

"You're a rat, Ron." She was playing at playing games. "Aren't you going to come and hold my hand?"

"Pamela, doll, what do you want from me?"

"I want someone to hold my hand," she said.

No doubt she does, he thought. Her eyes were vacant. She looked mournful and lost and, indeed, vulnerable, everybody's little sister Sue. It was that time of day.

"Gimme a break," he said to her.

5

BROWNE spent his Sunday afternoon at the shop, reading amid the comfortable clutter of his office. He was the local brokerage division's second-senior man and its chief literary figure. Everything the office required in the way of prose composition, from advertising brochures to dunning letters, was written by Browne. He wrote the text of promotional videos and, being particularly presentable, appeared in them. He also represented the company at expositions and boat shows around the country. He was paid a higher salary than his associates in brokerage because he made much less in commissions. Nevertheless, Browne worried. Sometimes he imagined that his work would one day appear superfluous to higher management.

The book he read was a 1920s edition of *To the Source of the Oxus* by Captain John Wood, originally published in London in 1875. He got altogether lost in it.

Early the next morning, a working day, his car was first in the parking lot. The Altan offices and showroom stood in an industrial park a short distance from the Sound. In the showroom's window, a sixty-foot powerboat with burnished brightwork was on display. Browne opened the place and went to his office.

Ross, the branch manager, was due back at noon and Browne had to take over his portfolio until then. Quite early on, he found himself running interference between the owner and the prospective buyer of a fifty-foot yawl. About eleven o'clock the calls stopped. His messages were not returned. Then the owner called to lower his price by twenty thousand.

"Why?" Browne asked. "You've already come down twenty. You don't have to go lower. I'm sure they'll pay at this stage."

"I guess you don't understand," the man said. His voice had a strange gaiety, a note of whimsy. "Well, you don't have to understand. Just move the fucking boat, O.K.?"

Browne was offended. It was profanity as an exercise in vulgar machismo, yet another yuppie playing pirate in the salty world of big boats. It disgusted him. When he called the buyer's office, the switchboard was busy and it stayed that way right through lunchtime. At one o'clock Ross telephoned to ask if Browne would keep an appointment he had made with the buyer at City Island. Browne agreed to do so. He took some notes over the phone, pulled the necessary paper and prepared to drive down. As he was putting his jacket on, it occurred to him that something might have gone wrong in the market. Friday's comeback had been so reassuring. He had chosen not to worry about it as a matter of discipline.

He put in a call to his stockbroker. The switchboard there was busy as well. Wandering the corridor, he met Dave Jernigan, one of the younger salesmen, coming from the assembly room. Jernigan's wife was a trader; Browne had once met her. He and Anne had gone to dinner with the Jernigans, and Edie Jernigan had introduced their four-year-old son. He was a nice little boy with a lisp and a staccato giggle, and Edie had asked the Brownes helplessly, "What do you do for a kid with a terrible laugh?"

The Brownes had gone home joking about laughing lessons, laughing academies, French laughing masters. But Browne was truly horrified.

"Sums up the spirit of the age," he had said to Anne.

"Heard anything about the market?" he asked the young man.

"Funny you should ask," Jernigan said. He was blond and round-faced; his reaction to every stimulus was an embarrassed smile. "It's been an interesting morning."

"Down?"

"Definitely. The tape's behind."

"That's unusual."

Jernigan's smile increased its dimensions. He looked pale and out of breath. Words seemed to fail him for a moment.

"Yes," he told Browne. "It's unusual."

At the City Island marina, Ross's customer was nowhere in sight. It was a mild, sunny winter day. A pair of soiled swans floated among the mooring buoys. He paced the deck in front of the clubhouse for an hour before giving up. Finally, he bought a hot dog from a vendor in front of the projects and drove back to the office. On the way up he listened to WQXR. The hourly news broadcast reported a drop of fifty points in the Dow, with the tapes still behind.

In the office only Jernigan remained. He was talking on the phone. When he hung up, he wandered into Browne's office.

"Your wife called."

"Any message?" Browne asked him.

Jernigan shook his head.

"Everybody's gone home. We've closed the switchboard."

"Right," Browne said. "The lessons of eighty-seven. Fear itself."

When he called his broker again the line was still busy.

That evening, Browne had been commanded to attend a seminar called "All About Sales and Product Liability," which was scheduled for six at a motel off I-95. He went straight from work to find the first lecture canceled. Browne and a bearded young man from Scotland were the only people who had appeared. The two of them went to the motel coffee shop.

The man's name was Ogilvie and he worked for Pepsico, who had brought him out for some Stateside conditioning. Young Ogilvie's face was flushed with an anger that seemed to transcend falling markets and canceled seminars.

"It's all spec-ulation," he complained as they sat at the Formica counter drinking decaffeinated coffee. His voice broke around the word as though it were some non-Covenanting heresy. "And absolutely unproductive."

The confusion and excitement of the day had inclined Browne to a slight pointless elation. He was amused by Ogilvie's sour Scottish oratory.

"Maybe," he suggested to the young man, "the heroic age of the bourgeoisie is over."

This notion further darkened the Scot's countenance.

"Socialist are you?"

"No," Browne said, "just joking."

Ogilvie looked at him critically.

"Right bastards they are," he told Browne. "They don't want to work and they don't want to see you work. They despise the productive classes."

"I couldn't agree with you more," Browne said. "I'm a salesman after all."

"I'm an engineer myself by training," Ogilvie said.

Browne considered a reply but made none. He went away feeling slighted. Driving home, he found himself thinking more about his brief unsatisfactory conversation than about the terrors of the market. The heroic age of the bourgeoisie *was* over, he thought, and socialism was finished for that reason.

When he got home, his wife and daughter were watching *The Nightly Business Report*.

"Anything new?" he asked them.

When Anne turned to him he saw that she was upset. She shrugged, disinclined to speak in front of Maggie.

"The market's in bad shape," she said. "They haven't even got the figures yet."

"Really," Maggie added excitedly. "Everybody's stock is totally worthless."

He laughed and then remembered that he and Maggie were formally estranged.

"You go finish your assignment," Anne ordered her daughter. "You're getting an early train tomorrow."

For dinner, he made himself a toasted ham and cheese sandwich. Making it reminded him of his daughter as a small girl, when she had proudly cooked such a sandwich for him from her kiddie cookbook and announced it as *croque-monsieur*. As he was eating it at the kitchen table, Anne came in and leaned against the counter.

"Maggie's on my case," he said.

"Of course," Anne said. "She's that age. You loom large in her life."

"I hope she'll apologize before she goes," he said wearily.

"She's written you a note," Anne told him. "She hates to fight with you."

"Our Maggie," he said as he cleared the table, "she's larger than life."

When the dishes were in the washer, Browne turned to see his wife tight-lipped, leaning in the same spot, twisting her wedding ring.

"You don't look happy, Annie."

She flashed a false smile, raised her hands and let them fall to her sides.

"It's only money, right?"

"Right," he said.

"Tomorrow we'll get the calls."

She had been buying stock on margin through her brother for several years, profiting where others failed. Browne thought of her as clever at business. He had stopped keeping up with the numbers.

"We've learned a few things since Black Monday," he said. "It may pass."

After a moment she said, "I'm not going to take Maggie out of school. I'll go to my father if I have to."

"Surely," he said, "it won't come to that."

"Think not?"

"The crisis passed in eighty-seven," he said. "We'd all have done better not to panic. Wait and see."

She went into the kitchen to pour herself a glass of wine.

"Are you going to say 'I told you so'?" she asked him.

"I'm not going to say anything," Browne said. "Not a word."

"Dad's going to say it."

"Let him say what he likes. Tell him it was my idea. He can't think any worse of me than he does already."

"He doesn't think all that badly of you. He said you were a good provider."

"Frankly, Annie, I don't give a shit what he said."

Anne's face was flushed with the wine. She leaned in the kitchen doorway with her forehead against the jamb. He went over and put a hand against her cheek, bidding her to look at him. She turned to face him and closed her eyes.

"I'm so ashamed," she said. "I feel so stupid."

"We agreed, didn't we? That it was only money?"

Browne was surprised at his own indifference. For some reason he could not bring to bear the emotions appropriate to disappointed speculation.

"We may lose," she said, "in a somewhat major way. We're going to have to hustle to pay it back. We're going to have to borrow and we're going to have to cut down."

"Let's tote it up in the morning," he said. "I've had enough of today."

"Never again," Anne said. "I swear."

"Forget it, Anne. It's over with. We'll proceed from here."

He went into the kitchen to get the wine. He refilled her glass and poured a small measure for himself. Ordinarily, he never drank alcohol. He touched her glass with his own.

"*Slainte*, Annie Aroon. Don't feel bad."

As he drank, she burst into tears. He touched her on the shoulder. Then it occurred to him that she might want to be alone. He put the glass down and went out of the dining room.

On the night table in their bedroom, he found a comic friendship card of the sort available from stationers, together with a smile button and a red rose. The face of the card showed a cartoon drawing of two cute anthropomorphic little animals driving a jalopy toward the sunset. "Friends to the End" said the motto inside. Maggie had signed it, "With love and apologies to Dad."

A shade impersonal, he thought, but it was as far as she could go. He went to her room and knocked on the door. A Megadeth tape was in the machine and he heard her turn it off.

"Hardly anybody sends me flowers anymore," he told Maggie when she opened the door.

She came out to him blushing, avoiding his eye, a wise guy no more.

"So we're friends again, are we?" he asked.

"Yes," she said. Teasing a little, he pursued eye contact. She kept looking away, at the point of tears. When he hugged her, she tensed into a statue of iron. King Midas's daughter, he thought, ungilded.

"When you're back next month," he told her, "we'll have a trip. Would that be good?"

She nodded, all confusion.

"Anyway," he said, "I'll see you in the morning."

In the master bedroom he watched television for a while, a documentary on public television about Cuba. In the film, Cuba's idea of itself seemed very appealing. The ideal Cuba was a place in which the ape of ego was not worshiped. People could live their lives on behalf of something more than just themselves. The ideal Cuba seemed to honor poverty and obedience with all the fervor of a Catholic boarding school.

He was still watching it when Anne came upstairs.

"Aren't things bad enough?" she asked him. "Do I have to look at Castro on top of it?"

"I'm considering life in Cuba, Annie. If our losses are too severe. Of course you wouldn't be able to play the market."

"It's not funny," she told him. "I was trying to help out. So I fucked it up. Please don't make fun of me."

"Sorry," Browne said. "I've been dealing with customers all day. I'm in a disorderly state."

He pressed the remote button and turned off the set. She sat down on the side of the bed, looking at herself in the mirror.

"What do they say? The customers."

He smiled without good humor.

"My customers are luxury consumers. They could use a little grace under pressure."

"Boy, me too," Anne said.

"Did I tell you that Buzz Ward was retiring?"

"No."

"He is. He's going to become a preacher in his old age."

"He'll be good at it," she said. "He'll look wonderful."

Again, Browne was unable to sleep and passed the early morning hours sitting up beside his sleeping wife. He thought it might have been the wine. *To the Source of the Oxus* lay open on his lap but his thoughts, for some reason, stayed on the Cuban documentary. A car went slowly by outside, cruising. With it came the sound of a rap tape played at full volume as though one of its windows were open.

The documentary had been no different from a hundred other programs that had offended Browne with their liberal humility and left-wing bias. But the vision of its imagined country, a homeland that could function as both community and cause, was one that remained with him. Browne felt his own country had failed him in that regard. It was agreeable to think such a place might exist, even as home to the enemy. But no such place existed.

The war would never be fought because the enemy had proved false. All his fierce alternatives were lies. Surely, Browne thought sleepily, this was a good thing. Yet something was lost. For his own part, he was tired of living for himself and those who were him by extension. It was impossible, he thought. Empty and impossible. He wanted more.

Ward had said, "I need some love in my life."

Ward, Browne thought, would make a good minister. A decorous man who knew the secrets of the heart. But what about me, Browne wondered. Which was the very question he had sought to elude. For a moment he felt as though he were standing at the edge of a great darkness with an ear cocked to the wind, attending silence. It was a place he dared not stay.

He remembered walking as a stranger in the ruined terminal. For a moment he became a stranger in his own house, in his own bed, beside his own woman — a stranger but without a stranger's freedom. On the other side of darkness, he imagined freedom. It was a bright expanse, an effort, a victory. It was a good fight or the right war — something that eased the burden of self and made breath possible. Without it, he felt as though he had been preparing all his life for something he would never live to see.

6

STRICKLAND had been asleep only a few hours when the phone woke him. A drab sun addressed Manhattan at a late morning slant. Pamela, his visitor the night previous, was gone.

He picked up the phone and said, "Hold on."

Hurrying to the studio door, he put the police bolt in place. He glanced about him as he went back to the bedroom, wondering if she had been pilfering. He had been too tired to see her out. Pamela had mainly learned to keep her liberated fingers under control around his property but he had once caught her with a six-thousand-dollar zoom lens.

"Yes," Strickland said to the person on the phone. He stood in the long window, pulling on his trousers, squinting in the sunlight. A bright young voice hailed him.

"I have Mrs. Manning of Hylan, Mr. Strickland."

"That's great," Strickland said. He sat down on the bed and reached for a cigarette and his Rolodex file.

"Mr. Strickland," an older woman's voice declared, "Mrs. Manning of Hylan."

The Hylan people, Strickland had observed, tended to offer their surnames as possessed by the corporate suffix. It suggested foggy glens and Celtic heraldry.

"How are you, Mrs. Manning?"

"Just fine. Will you be coming to see us today?"

"Yes I will, ma'am. I have an appointment."

"Mr. Hylan himself can't make it," Mrs. Manning of Hylan informed him. "But we've arranged a schedule."

Strickland decided he did not care for the sound of it. His annoyance occasioned him his first stammer of the day.

"But ma'am," he began, and stuck on the next sentence. "I . . .

I came back a week early to meet Mr. Hylan. We set this up months ago."

"It'll be all right," Mrs. Manning said. "We'll make it up to you."

The unusual promise intrigued him. He waited for her to go on.

"We'll show you Shadows," she said flirtatiously. "We'll give you the tour. You can look at tapes. Hello, Mr. Strickland?"

"Yes, ma'am."

"Really," she assured him. "You'll have a good time."

Strickland considered that it was early in the day for Mrs. Manning's wry alertness.

"Hey," he told her, "I'm having one already."

Strickland kept his car on the second level of a pier on the Hudson, a priceless midtown spot, convenient and secure. The car was a 1963 Porsche with austere lines and black leather upholstery. The fittings were rusty but the engine reported like a Prussian soldier on the first turn of the key. Strickland gave a little whistle of satisfaction.

At the Twelfth Avenue barricade, he paid his parking bill to an unkempt youth of Caribbean Spanish origin.

"I'm looking for storage space," he told the young man. "I don't need a lot of it. I'd like to talk about renting some."

It was desirable, Strickland felt, to rent from the same waterfront outfit who ran the garage. Their property had a way of avoiding violation. The young man gave him a card with a number to call.

On the drive upriver, he thought about Matthew Hylan, the young merchant-adventurer who had engaged him to record his next voyage. Strickland had amassed a dossier of Hylan clippings. There were pieces in *Fortune, Harper's* and *Manhattan, Inc.* There were admiring profiles in the yachting press, dippy puffs in the weeklies, poisonous anecdotes in the upscale celebrity magazines. Hylan was forty-four and supremely rich. He had inherited a North Shore Boston mortuary business worth a couple of million dollars and parlayed his legacy into a late-century colossus of fun services and real estate. He appeared vain and lippy, a millionaire vulgarian in the contemporary mode. He was single, dressy and apparently heterosexual. He liked a party. His chosen image seemed that of a sailor. There was nothing in any of the material to engage Strickland's insight. Hylan of Hylan resembled many others.

Physically, Hylan was more or less conventionally handsome. His jaw was large and emphasized in caricatures. His eyes were slightly protuberant and fleshily hooded. His mouth was large and suggestive of the appetites. Strickland had never witnessed the face in motion.

He made it up to Hylan headquarters in little more than half an hour, over the George Washington Bridge and up the parkway. Hylan Corporation headquarters occupied an old estate called Shadows, on the right bank of the river, opposite a sugarloaf-shaped hill called the Plattsweg. The main house was an odd structure, built in the middle of the nineteenth century to the eccentric designs of a disappointed matron who squandered her husband's dishonestly acquired fortune in its construction. The house was enormous, with carved buttresses and much gingerbread and a roof that curved upward at both ends with the thrusting violence of a Viking chapel. The lady founder had called it Shadows because of the way the surrounding hills abridged the sunlight. She affected to rejoice in the changing patterns they cast. There was plenty of light to be seen on the river, though; the prospects, upstream and down the Hudson, were sublime.

The old building had a modern wood-paneled reception room with a security guard on duty at a circular desk. When Strickland had been announced Mrs. Manning came promptly to claim him. She was a handsome, high-colored upper-class woman in her forties.

"Mr. Strickland," the woman cried, "I'm Joyce Manning. Welcome to Hylan."

"Thank you, ma'am," Strickland said humbly.

"Too bad about Matty. He'd have loved to meet you. He's a great admirer of your outstanding work."

"Yes," Strickland said. "Too bad."

"It just wasn't on. Things are in chaos today."

"Why's that?"

"Meetings. Arrivals and departures. Excursions about."

Strickland smiled politely.

Joyce Manning conducted him to a man called Thorne, whose name occurred often in the more serious of the Hylan articles. Harry Thorne, a hard case from the Boston construction wars, vice president of the corporation, was said to be Hylan's mentor and partner. Journalists liked to contrast Thorne's dangerous manner with the hail-fellow glibness of his younger pal.

Thorne received Strickland in Matty Hylan's office. He was ugly, vigorous and sixty-odd. There was absolutely no more to his face than function required: it was spare and brutal, with an impatient squint and a lipless pseudo-smile that emphasized the lustrous melancholy of his black eyes. Great mug, thought Strickland. Thorne's shirt was white on white, his suit funereal and superbly cut.

"How are yez?" Thorne asked with faint insolence. His voice suggested gulls over India Wharf. Strickland had no trouble recognizing his manner, which was that of a man who equated documentary films with souvenir napkins or balloons and had other things on his mind. Beyond that, Strickland thought, Thorne looked distinctly weary and irritated, as though their meeting represented a particularly unwelcome irony. He was not offended.

"Fine and dandy, sir. How about yourself?"

Joyce Manning bustled nervously, like a good witch.

"Harry," she insisted, "you've got to let Mr. Strickland see the view from Matty's office. He may want to use it."

Thorne looked blank. "Use it?"

She laughed solicitously. "In the film, Harry."

Thorne curled his lip and stepped aside. Easing past him, Strickland inspected the room. It was enormous and high-ceilinged, obviously the renovation of one of the mansion's ceremonial chambers. There were fine windows over the river, well-placed watercolors, and Navaho rugs on the hardwood floor. There were sunny boat photographs and Acoma pottery on the blond shelves along each wall.

The office's working desk was off to one side, as though put there out of indifference to the room's prodigality. It was a small desk of indeterminate wood, cluttered and mean, like that of a bureaucrat or petty accountant. Beside it, Strickland formed his very first organized impression of the Hylan Corporation: as a feverish, unhappy place, missing its master. Business might be bad. He began to walk up and down, wondering how the room might be photographed.

"Have you had the chance to see any of Mr. Strickland's films yet?" Joyce was asking Harry Thorne. "Shall we set one up for you?"

Harry watched Strickland's pacing with an air of impatience and declined to be helpful.

"No," he said. "Not for me."

Strickland turned to him.

"Too bad your Mr. Hylan couldn't make it, Mr. Thorne. It would have moved things along. It would have been constructive, if you know what I mean. I would have liked to talk t . . to . . . "

Thorne watched without sympathy as Strickland fought to complete his sentence.

"We would have liked to talk to him too," Thorne said finally. "But he didn't have any time for us today either." He turned to Joyce Manning. "Did he, Joyce?"

The secretary laughed airily.

"Now that I'm here," Strickland asked, "what have you got for me?"

"How about lunch?" Joyce Manning asked. Thorne looked at his watch.

"I don't eat lunch," Strickland said. He kept smiling. "I'm here to work."

"Show him the sailing stuff," Thorne suggested. "Show him the boat. Before you go, ask Mr. Livingston to come see me."

About a dozen men and women stood silently outside Hylan's office as Strickland and Joyce Manning emerged. Strickland thought they looked like gloomy corporate officers. The corporate dimension might be interesting, he thought, looking them over. Ten men, two women. Puffy faces, nice clothes.

Following Mrs. Manning down to the boathouse on the river, he saw cloud shadows play on the broad lawns, just the way they were supposed to.

Back in the main building, Harry Thorne was watching his executives file into Matty Hylan's office. His man Livingston was at his side — red-faced, sweaty, as full of humor as Thorne was dry.

"Step right up," Thorne told them, acting the showman. There were a few sad smiles.

"What a bunch of zombies," Thorne said. "Eh, Livingston?"

Livingston sighed.

"We go on from here," Harry Thorne announced when they were lined up in the office. "We're all existentialists here. We go forward." He pointed the way ahead with an extended arm and an arched wrist, like a lineman claiming possession of a fumbled football. "We're mobile. We're moving. We're going ahead."

A few throats were cleared. There was slight scattered applause.

"As you will soon see," Harry went on, "I have informed the press that we are very much in business and we expect things to stabilize. As I have informed the press, so I will inform the board. Tomorrow."

A deeper silence followed mention of the board.

"Questions?" Harry asked.

Questions seemed to hover. None were asked.

"We expect the board's support," Harry said in answer. "We have been led to believe we will have the board's support. Questions?"

"Where's Matty?" asked a voice from the crowd. A prankster disguising his voice. A couple of people turned to see who it was.

"Somewhere warm," Harry said. "With a broad." A moment later he said, "I apologize to the women for that remark. A function of age. Sorry."

There was nervous laughter, dental hisses, faint groans.

"What's the official story?" a younger woman asked.

"Private family considerations," he said, enunciating carefully. "Personal matters of no interest to the public."

He drew himself up and addressed the room.

"I understand your concerns," Thorne said to his executives. "I'm sure they're the same as mine. The first is — pardon the expression — criminal liability. The other is how solvent are our component organizations. Who can tell me something I don't know?"

He looked about the room.

"No one? Good. Then everyone go have lunch in the dining room. Everyone except the legal department. If you want a hot tip on the market I suggest you buy Hylan. It's seriously under-valued."

There was more dutiful laughter. People filed out until only Thorne, Livingston and the two lawyers remained.

"How's it look?" Thorne asked them.

"Matty's gone, all right," one of the lawyers said. "He hasn't sent any postcards."

"What about foul play?" Mr. Livingston asked. "Given some of his —"

"Forget it," Thorne said, interrupting.

"Why, Harry?"

"Because," Thorne said, "he's not the type."

They pondered.

"I talked to my daughter," the second lawyer said. "She's heard that the Southern District of New York is working on an indict-ment. She understands it only names Matty."

"I'm sure that little prick would like to go to trial before the election," Thorne said. "Just Matty?"

"That's what she tells me, Harry."

"The building groups in the South are going under," Thorne said. "I happen to think we can survive that. But I also think we'll have criminal proceedings there and I don't know who they'll pin it on. Maybe Hillsborough Group as such, maybe Matty, maybe us. Corporately."

"Hillsborough's numbers there are deceptive," the second law-yer said.

Harry laughed ill-humoredly. "Fuckin' right, they are. Anyway, it'll be in federal court in Winston-Salem. I wish we could fight the whole war down there."

"The bank is the biggest problem," the other lawyer said. "That's the second circuit in Connecticut. They'll have a ball with that bank."

"The bank," Thorne said bitterly.

There was a reflective silence.

"Well, let's get a bankruptcy package together for Hillsbor-ough," Thorne said. "See if we can break a few hearts."

He saw that the others were still looking at him expectantly.

"What can I say?" he asked them. "He fell in love with the game. He became the victim of his own abilities. It happens. It happens to the best and it happens to the rest — that's what they say at Suffolk Downs. Suffolk Downs is a racetrack," he informed the group. "In Boston."

"Wonder where he is," said the first lawyer.

"I told you," Harry said. "Somewhere warm with a broad. I put my foot in my mouth."

"Probably on his boat," said the man who had commented on Hillsborough's numbers.

"What do you mean?" Harry asked. "We got all his boats. Down on the river. And his big race that we're paying for. You know who that guy was — the guy that was in here with Joyce? Some asshole he hired to make a movie about the race."

"Matty's going to have to bear a lot of the responsibility for this," the second lawyer said.

Thorne turned to him. "A lot? You see that he bears it all, counselor. All of it."

The lawyers left. Livingston and Thorne stood together by the window, looking toward the river.

"Are you letting this movie thing go ahead?" Livingston asked.

"I don't want to cancel any of these Matty Hylan projects until I have to. Appearance of normalcy. When the time comes we'll pay him off."

"If you ask me," Livingston said, "we should tear down that boathouse. When this is over you'll probably want to."

"We won't tear it down," Thorne said. "We'll put a Turkish bath in there."

In the well-appointed club room of the boathouse, Strickland sat in a leather chair while Joyce Manning had an actual Filipino steward bring him coffee.

"Do you sail?" she asked.

"No," Strickland said. "But I can row."

While Joyce read yachting magazines, Strickland drank his coffee and watched various visual celebrations Hylan had commissioned of himself. Many of them featured him as skipper of his International Cup entry — studies of him at the helm in every weather, tight-lipped, osprey-eyed and born to win. There were shots of his wholesome young crew, cheering, dapping and throwing high-signs, while stirring anthems of an inspirational, competitive sort swelled on the sound track.

"Am I allowed to use any of this?" Strickland asked Joyce.

"You betcha."

Then there were talk-show appearances, news interviews and a couple of corporate cheerleading sessions. Contrary to what he had read, Hylan at close quarters appeared touchy, ill-spoken and smirking. After a while Joyce came up to watch.

"None of this does justice to the man himself," she said.

They watched an excess of Matty Hylan's seagoing home movies — tossing decks, towering waves, telltales taut against the billowing sails.

"O.K.," Strickland said finally. "I g . . get the idea."

She took him for a walk along the riverside dock, where a number of boats were tied up under tarpaulins, and through the boathouse itself, which had two vacant slips partly enclosed. The structure smelled of caulking and dank river water. Their footsteps echoed. Liquid shadows played on the walls.

"What if he doesn't win?" Strickland asked.

"He expects to win," Joyce said. "But I think he'll settle for being seen as a lone competitor."

They walked back over the lawns.

"The lone competitor," Strickland mused aloud. "Hylan agonistes."

"Man against the sea," Joyce said. "Be serious."

Strickland decided it might be amusing to see more of Joyce Manning.

En route to the parkway, Strickland pulled over and looked down at the Hylan headquarters. Dusk had come to the valley in which it stood. The last light played on the bare trees at the summit of the Plattsweg. The broad plane of the river reflected the darkening sky. Lights burned in Shadows' leaded windows.

From where Strickland stood, the absurd building with its turrets looked tortured and desolate. You could see the desperation that informed it. Its shape, he thought, must reflect the unhappy lives of those who had built it — the grafting financier, his exquisitely embittered lady. In spite of their fortune, two of their children had died there. Everything was overbusy, overdone, grasping, hysterical. It was a place without rest.

About to turn away, he saw a line of cars drawn up at the light at the corner of route 9, waiting to turn north, away from the city. Mrs. Manning was driving one of them. She put her window down.

"Isn't it great?" she called. "It's on the National Register of Historic Places."

"How about that," Strickland said.

"How do you like the project?" she shouted, shifting into gear. "Think you'll take it on?"

"It does look like fun," Strickland told her.

7

WALKING to the gate for the morning *Times*, Anne found the previous day's snow disappearing from the lawn. Though it was still a few minutes before sunrise, the air was gentle and earth-scented. She picked up the paper and stood for a moment, looking toward the light that was breaking over the Sound.

Back in the kitchen, she heard him stirring upstairs, accompanying himself with a tuneless whistling that she knew was a measure of his unease. On some days he would seem driven by a kind of shadow energy, working at home for hours over dummy sheets and manuals with a stolid absorption she found impenetrable. Others he passed aimlessly, ending up in a book or listening to music. Sometimes he would quickly, almost suddenly, fall asleep in a chair. He was wakeful at night.

Over the long weeks of winter, Anne had come to realize how little her husband had bothered to make their house really his own. It was extraordinary, she thought, after so many years. His meandering presence there seemed vaguely awkward, as though he were continually about to apologize for being in the wrong room.

The *Times*'s front page was all White House intrigue and child murder; she decided, for that morning at least, the news was more than she could bear. In the Living section she found the tidings of a good-humored and sophisticated world that seemed altogether unavailable.

"Owen," she called up to him. "Can I make you something?"

"No thanks," he said after a moment.

"You will eat something, won't you?"

"Sure," he said.

Then she had to dress for work, rushing for the eight-twenty train to Grand Central. Her work required her presence in Manhattan at least three times a week. Headed for the back door, she saw him at the kitchen table, hunched over a cup of black coffee. She could not bring herself to simply pass.

"Going to the shop?" she asked.

He looked up at her so forlornly that she wanted to cry. There was no time.

"Oh, shit," she said. "I have to go!"

"Go," he said. He made a fist and shook it in mock encouragement. "Go, go."

"Owen," she said. "Buck up, old sport."

He looked at her again and got to his feet and put a hand on her cheek.

On the train, she worried about the money. At home she forced herself not to mention the subject but it caused her considerable anxiety. They had succeeded in meeting the margin calls, cashing in some retirement accounts and some of their best investments. They had saved the house on Steadman's Island by refinancing it. A considerable debt remained to them.

One of the specters haunting Altan Marine was the state of its parent company, the Hylan Corporation. Creditors were pressing Hylan, which had owned Altan for over ten years. Its colorful and mysterious chief executive officer, Matty Hylan, was unavailable to the press. At the Altan branch, some scattered panic selling generated commissions to provide for the short run. Most owners with boats to sell could afford to wait for spring. A few salesmen were let go. Owen, the company scribe, had a fairly secure position. Nevertheless, making her way through the crowds under the starry vault of the terminal, Anne decided to call her father.

Most of *Underway* magazine's staff worked from home so there were only a few people in the office most days. That Wednesday she found John Magowan, the elderly editor, and a young woman from Kelly Girl who was filling in while the regular secretary went sailing in the Gulf of California.

"In again?" old Magowan asked her. "I hope you won't be asking for a raise."

Putting on a faint smile required all the goodwill she could bring to bear on the subject.

"We're doing some work around the house," she told him. It was true that she had been coming into the city more often, avoiding Owen's moods.

"How's your husband?" asked Magowan. The astuteness of senility, Anne thought. "Still with Altan?"

"That's right," she said.

She spent part of the morning proofing the newsletter section of the book and then made a start on an article. In it, she tried to re-create a passage she and Owen had made years before between Cape Sable and Mount Desert Island. It had been a frightening trip; they had been fogbound and becalmed in the path of the Yarmouth ferry. Running on an outboard, they had listened to the big boat sounding off in the dark, coming closer and closer until its lighted galleries slipped by them like a dream and vanished again. That night, as Anne remembered it, they had been good sailors together. Eventually she gave up on the story. The chummy gallantry with which she sought to infuse it was unavailable that morning.

At lunchtime, she went out for a container of yogurt. The springlike weather lured her down to the river, through Greenwich Village streets where she had grown up. Until she went away to school, her family had lived in a three-story red brick house on Bedford Street.

Before going back to the office she walked a few blocks of West Street, letting herself be dazzled by the sun on the water. A couple of worn female prostitutes were lounging against a warehouse at the foot of Morton Street but the day had brought out a lunchtime crowd that made the waterfront strip feel manageable. It annoyed Anne to feel like a suburbanite in her own childhood streets. Decades before her father had bought his town house, some of her people had carried hooks on the Village piers.

Back at the office, she felt flighty and bestirred by the soft city air. It had also occurred to her that she had been postponing the call to her father's office. The prospect of asking him for money — which was what it all came down to — filled her with shame and anxiety. For a while she stalled, fiddling with the wooden leads of her attempt at the Cape Sable crossing story. Finally, after four, she put the call through. It was Margaret's tuition that was on her mind and that, she decided, was what she would explain to him.

Antoinette Lamattina, who had been her father's private secretary since Anne was a child, answered at his office.

"Anne, honey!" Antoinette cooed. "He'll be so happy to hear you!"

She had not spoken to her father on the phone for several months. They had not met for over a year.

"You're in a spot," her father informed her when they were connected.

"It could be worse," she told him.

"Why don't you let me go over your accounts?"

She sat with her hand shading her eyes, staring down at her desk.

"You know," she said, "I am hating every goddam minute of this."

"You never call," he said. "I never see the Kid." It was his fond name for Maggie.

"Can you blame me, Dad? I don't want to hear the riot act. Look," she said, "I'm concerned about Maggie's tuition. Our public schools up there are not great."

She heard his bitter, self-satisfied laughter. It made her seethe.

"Do you think I'd let her go to public schools up there?"

She gave him no answer.

"I want you to come and see me," he said.

After a moment she said, "All right. Soon."

"I want to tell you something, Annie. And you can pass this along to him." Her father managed to use Owen's name as infrequently as possible. "Matty Hylan's going to get his ass in a sling. His organization is in trouble."

"Yes," she said. "We've heard rumors."

"You had better provide," her father said, "for every contingency."

"Owen's been with the Hylan companies a long time, Dad. You know how he feels."

"Sure, sure." He cut her off. "I can't stay on the line. Come for lunch one day."

Having called only made her feel more tense. Old Magowan

was standing in the corridor outside her office. She supposed he had been listening to her end of the conversation.

"Ever hear from your father?" he asked her.

"Yes," she said. "I've just spoken to him, in fact. Just now."

The old man waited for a moment and said, "Give him my best."

She fought to hold her tongue, swallowing her unpurged anxiety, her shame and anger.

"He's not a reader of ours, Mr. Magowan," she called after him. "Nor a yachtsman." The old boy was out of hearing.

She turned off her word processor, put her desk in order and found herself wondering how Owen had passed his afternoon. Putting on her coat, she walked to the office window and looked out at the waning light of afternoon on the leaden rooftops of lower Broadway. She was sorry to lose the day, the sense of the streets, the mindless promise of unseasonal weather. Suddenly it seemed to her that the last place she cared to be was in her house beside the Sound. A drink was what she wanted. Only one or two, she thought, to soften the margin between the bright day that was passing and the cares of the evening.

The young temporary secretary had gone home. Mr. Magowan was puttering around his office.

"Mr. M," she said, "would it please you to buy me a drink?"

Shameless, but she knew it might actually please him. He would be curious about the state of Altan Marine and about her notorious father. She wanted to go somewhere that was lively and pleasant but she dreaded having to hold down a table by herself and fend off passes. Magowan was often a trial but he was not without humor and his sea stories were sometimes diverting.

"Oh gosh," the old man said. "Yes, indeed." But having said so much, he seemed to lapse into confusion. He picked up his memo pad and leafed through it while she stood by.

"Maybe another time," she suggested.

"Yes," he said. "When we close the issue. We'll celebrate at Fraunces." Years before, Mr. Magowan had come within centimeters of being blown to pieces at Fraunces Tavern by a Puerto Rican nationalist's bomb but he continued to favor the place. "Have to face the docs tomorrow. Prayer and fasting."

"Ah," Anne said, "too bad."

She took the subway up to Fifty-ninth Street and walked east. Across the street from the courtyard of the Museum of Modern Art was a small hotel where she and Owen sometimes stayed when they were in the city. It had a pleasant Bar Américain and what she remembered as a good martini, and she might have one in peace there.

The maître d' took her to a table beside a window. In the lounge next door, a house pianist was playing "Send In the Clowns." The martini made her wince; she was no longer accustomed to hard liquor. For a while she sat and drank and watched the midtown crowds pass on Fifty-fourth Street. At the next table, four men in expensive suits conversed in lisping European Spanish. An elderly man in dark glasses, accompanied by a middle-aged woman in furs, hobbled slowly by on their way to dinner in the restaurant.

She had been to the same place last over the Christmas holidays with Owen and Maggie when they had come in to see *Les Misérables*. Maggie had contrived to get herself served a whiskey sour. In all, the holidays had not been particularly pleasant. Maggie and Owen had found every possible occasion to quarrel. A few nights after Christmas Maggie had gone into New York to a Grateful Dead concert at the Garden. She had stayed overnight with her friends, not calling home until after three in the morning. That had been thoughtless and selfish but he had absolutely refused to let it rest. He had made it the central event of the season.

Finishing her first martini, Anne ordered a second. With her gaze fixed on the street window, she was aware that one of the Spaniards at the next table had an eye on her. When she took a blank, chastening look in his direction, he turned away discreetly. It made her feel gratefully inclined toward him.

Anne had always taken her good looks for granted. Since adolescence she had been used to modestly altering the valence of a room. When she paid and rose from her seat, the man was watching her again. Anne glanced at him briefly, kept her eyes down, her expression pleasant. It gave her a lift to be admired. If it mattered to her, she thought, the time had come to work at maintenance. She would be forty in the spring, although some people she knew would have been surprised to hear it.

She walked quickly down Fifth Avenue, flushed, buoyed by a vague, hopeful confusion that owed everything to gin. Rockefeller Center and Saint Patrick's were places charged with fragments of her girlhood.

At the ramp leading down to the train, she bought a nip of Gordon's and soda. It was a seedy thing to do. She sipped it on the ride home, looking out at ringed track lights in the fog and the last of the previous day's soiled snow.

Owen was asleep in her study when she got home. He lay in her leather padded desk chair with his feet up on an adjoining couch. Three books and a *National Geographic Atlas* were stacked beside the chair. She picked them up. One of the books was Melville's *White-Jacket*.

She stood over him for a moment, regarding his long-jawed face at melancholy rest. Sleep lay lightly there. On the desk were the specifications for a stock boat called the Altan Forty, some pictures and a dummy ad. The copy he had begun to write was in the typewriter.

"With any Altan product your buying power commands the finest engineering, styling and craftsmanship in the industry. The Altan name is itself an emblem of quality . . ."

So he had fled from that to Melville. She left him sleeping. He rarely brought advertising copy work home; whenever she saw it, its paltriness made her feel ashamed for him. She experienced a glancing, barbed notion: He has wasted his life with me.

Upstairs she felt soiled and dry. Alcohol's no use to me, she thought, if all it can do is serve up little morbid conceits. She was not used to thinking of herself as drunk. She had been Peg-leg Annie at school, outdrinking the mere Irish. After she had changed into jeans, she went downstairs again and turned on WNYC in the kitchen. Vivaldi's "Winter." Whirling. She took an aspirin and a glass of water and planned a take-out order from the local Chinese restaurant.

Owen had always been a better writer than she. She felt as convinced of that as that she had always been the better sailor. It was altogether unfair that he was consigned to filling blocks of type in color brochures. The pieces and essays that caused her so much labor came much more easily to him. He enjoyed doing them but never had the time. Hers were trivial, she thought. His were serious and elegant.

There was a bottle of Entre-Deux-Mers in the refrigerator that she had opened a few days before, almost full. It might be as well to have a little and go to bed early. Without it, the cocktails might keep her awake.

As for her, she liked persuading people. It would be easy for her to turn to copywriting, to organizing presentations, maybe even to organizing deals. The idea of action, of moving product and turning cash, seemed not at all uncongenial. In the world of boats, she could never sell directly. Women didn't. But indirectly — by skill, by guile, by stealth — that was another story.

She drank her wine and began to spin a fantasy of how she might make time for him to write. He could do travel pieces that were as good as anyone's, surprisingly sly and funny. Together they could sail anywhere.

If only there were some way. She had tried a little wheeling and dealing through her brother and his friends in the stock market and it had gone badly. Sometimes she thought about the commercial possibilities of bringing women into sailing, teaching, making videos. Owen hated public performances. He would soon have to face the boat show with his sales package. He would hate it and complain. Whereas she, she was sure, might thrive there. If only there were a way.

After a while, Owen woke up and walked into the kitchen rubbing his eyes. A Bach adagio played on WNYC.

"Are you all right?" she asked him.

He shrugged. They listened to the news headlines and the weather report. More springlike weather was predicted for the next day.

"I should have wakened you. You'll be up all night."

He laughed at her solicitude.

"I'm all right, Annie. How are you?"

"I stayed in New York and got addled. I went to the American Bar on Fifty-fourth Street."

"Alone?"

"I couldn't find anyone to take me."

"I should have taken you."

"You're no good," she said. "You don't even drink." She was silent for a moment. "Ladies used to go to Schrafft's and drink old-fashioneds. I wonder whatever happened to that." Have I no friends? she was asking herself. Is it that other women dislike me? "And anyway, you had to work on the brochures."

"Right," Browne said.

They called out for dinner and ate in the kitchen, the radio turned low. Anne had another glass of wine.

"Do you have to go in tomorrow?"

"I don't know." He seemed to think about it. "These days I'm afraid to turn my back. I mean," he said, "there may be layoffs."

"They need someone who can write," Anne told him.

"I wouldn't mind taking a couple of days off before too long," he said. "We could sneak off to the island."

"Ah," she said, "the island."

A little after nine she went to bed, quite weary. Owen stayed downstairs, listening to the program of 1930s jazz and swing he enjoyed.

For a while she lay awake, restless and dizzy. The band music drifted up to her, truly old and far away. When at last she went to sleep, it sounded across the dark water of her dreams, all tremulous tenors, naïve syncopation and loss. Dreaming, she understood that its syncopation was not really so naïve. It was Owen's music. It mourned some dream of his.

8

OWEN BROWNE had met Matty Hylan, his ultimate employer, only twice. On each occasion he had either been slapped on the back or punched ceremoniously on the arm. Not being one to dissemble heartiness, Browne did not remember the meetings as having gone well. He had never been asked to Shadows, the corporate headquarters on the Hudson. He was surprised, as a result, when one morning Ross dispatched him there to appraise a few of Hylan's boats. The boss himself was said to be in Europe, preparing for a single-handed sailing race. Business was not thriving. Although the market had come back, the fortunes of Altan Marine had not risen with it. The spirit of recreation had somewhat folded her wings.

Ross was a shy man a few years younger than Browne, with steel-rimmed spectacles and a brush mustache. He had a way of emphasizing his statements with a dental grimace that lent his person a touch of Bull Moose enthusiasm and made him appear older than he was.

"It'll do you good," Ross said. "You ought to get to know the folks over there."

Since his visit south, Browne had been having trouble with his moods. His dreams were troubling. Sometimes he had violent fantasies of a frighteningly vivid quality. Occasionally he flashed scenes from the war. At other times, pieces of music or half-remembered scraps of poetry would send him headlong into a fond reverie, without much content but vaguely religious and sentimental. Inevitably it ended in anger, sleeplessness and fear. His sexual life seemed to be progressing by extremes, periods of indifference alternating with much desire. The summons to Shadows was interrupting one of Browne's better days. He had been in the throes of composition, writing copy on the company's new stock boat, the Altan Forty. It was said to be based on the boat Hylan would take to sea later in the year. Browne had convinced himself of its high quality.

"I'll go," Browne said resignedly. "I don't expect I'll like it much."

He drove the icy back roads over the Taconic ridge and crossed the river at Peekskill. Going up the right bank, he thought he could hear a military band playing on the parade ground at West Point. The river was icy gray and the trees along the high slopes still bare with winter. Driving down toward Shadows, he was thrilled with the grandeur of the old house. He had grown up around a large estate, although not one so fanciful and grand. The sight of the place filled him with a sad nostalgia, a mixture of disappointment, hope and pride.

In his office, Harry Thorne was chatting with Livingston. They were waiting for Joe Duffy, the representative of the public relations firm Matty Hylan had retained.

"I think I'll write a book," Thorne said. "Have I material?"

"About what?" Livingston asked. "Yourself or Matty?"

"Matty," Thorne repeated. "What a story that would be, huh? Not the story he liked to put out. But the real story of the real Matty Hylan. Some story it would be."

Livingston sighed and nodded.

"I've known him from when he was a kid," Thorne said. "I made the man my science. What happened? He dazzled me."

"Everybody understands," Livingston said. "Believe me."

"The fucking gutter press . . ." Thorne began. Anger prevented him from finishing.

"Everybody knows it was Matty," Livingston said. "They'll say: Harry loved the guy."

"I was a fool."

"Everybody will say the same, Harry. That you're a man of your word. That your word is your bond."

"You know what I think?" Harry asked. "I think a lot of them would like me out the forty-fourth-floor window. Like Sam Spencer."

When Duffy arrived they listened sadly to his efforts at exculpatory prose. He was a red-faced, pot-bellied chap in a checkered English sportcoat. Livingston had told Harry that Duffy was smarter than he looked. As Duffy was reciting from his handouts, Joyce Manning came in to announce that Owen Browne had come to look at the boats.

"The guy from the Altan yard," Livingston reminded Thorne. "To do the appraisal."

Thorne waved the notion away like an unpleasant odor.

"Matty's race was going to be an important part of your public picture," Duffy pointed out. "Cancellation is going to be bad. I mean, I think you're going to have to pay for the whole thing anyway. Maybe something can be done with these boats."

"You're the artist," Livingston said to Duffy. "Know anything about sailboats?"

"The wind makes them go," Duffy replied. "Let me have a talk with this guy."

Stepping into the outer office where Joyce Manning presided, Duffy saw Browne pacing in the corridor.

"Looks like a sailor, doesn't he?" he asked the confidential secretary. "Suntanned. Square jaw."

"Yes," she said. "Isn't he lovely?"

Duffy went and introduced himself to Browne and they started walking along the lawn to the river. Browne explained that he wrote copy for Altan and appeared in the company videos. The chilly day warmed as the sun rose higher.

"You like to sail?"

"I like nothing better," Browne said.

In the echoing boathouse, Browne conducted Duffy on a tour of the boats moored there.

"This is a Concordia yawl," he told Duffy of one handsome vessel. "Mahogany hull, built in the late 1930s. Bronze fittings and winches. Designed by a man named Hunt, the best."

"Jeez," said Duffy reverently. They moved along.

"A Tayana Thirty-seven," Browne explained. "Designed by Robert Perry. Teak decks. She's heavily built and traditional."

They looked at two Wright boats, Newports, Dickersons, Farrs. At the end of the dock were three of the Altan stock boats.

"You have over two million dollars' worth of boats here," Browne told Duffy. He walked over to the stock boats at the end of the line. "Next year we'll have the new racer-cruiser out, the Altan Forty. A beauty. Finnish design."

"I've heard," Duffy said. "The one your boss is racing." He studied Browne for a moment. "Come up to the office for a minute, Owen. I want you to meet some people."

At Shadows, they sat in Hylan's office after Duffy had introduced Browne to Thorne and Livingston. He had asked Joyce Manning to come in as well.

"So will Altan sell Matty's new boat?" Livingston asked Browne. "Even in a bad year?"

"In a word, yes," Browne said. "A forty-footer, thirty-six feet at waterline? We would price her at a hundred and a half. She's going to be a fine vessel. I can sell her, I assure you."

"Owen does sales videos," Duffy pointed out.

"We'll have a look at them," Livingston said. "Get us some," he told Mrs. Manning.

"I understand you went to Annapolis," Harry Thorne said.

"Class of sixty-eight," Browne said.

"Sixty-eight," Thorne repeated. "What a year. I was in the Navy too," he told Browne. "During my war, I was a gunner's mate aboard the cruiser *Northampton*."

"Owen's a great sailor," Duffy said. "Sails alone, like Matty."

Browne had once sailed alone from West Palm Beach to New Bern, North Carolina. It was the only solitary sailing he had done.

"That right?" Thorne asked.

"Yes," Browne said, "I've done some."

"What's so good about this boat?" Thorne asked him.

"It's sound," Browne said. "It's beautiful."

"Yeah?" asked Thorne.

"It's something to be proud of," Browne said. "For what that's worth."

The people in the room watched him, unsmiling.

"You know," Livingston said, "Mr. Hylan proposed to sail the prototype of this boat around the world alone."

"Why not?" Browne asked.

When Browne had gone, Thorne, Livingston and Duffy walked along the riverbank. A gravel path led through an old apple orchard whose trees were beginning to bud. The rain held off.

"I've never been down here before," Harry said. "It's restful."

"Matty's touch," Duffy said.

"Matty's touch," Harry repeated. "So it keeps our minds off federal indictments and bad paper. Better we had a cement plaza in Fort Lee."

"Amen to that, boss."

"How about the young guy?" Thorne asked.

"He's not so young," Duffy said. "He was in Vietnam."

Thorne nodded.

"If we shitcan Altan Marine," Harry said, "let's find a place for him."

"Now you got your eye on this guy," Livingston told him. "You're always falling in love."

"That's me," Harry said. "It's nearly spring. I'm romantic."

Browne was halfway back to his office when, on impulse, he turned south on the parkway and drove home to change his clothes. Anne was out, in town. Showering, he began to think about his days at sea, between Florida and Cape Fear. Fantasies of solitary voyages occurred to him. He had enjoyed his lone blue-water passage, although he had suffered from fatigue and some hallucinations.

When he had changed he called the Altan repair yard on the north shore of Staten Island where he kept his own boat. The telephone was answered by one of the émigré Polish shipwrights the company had hired during the previous summer.

"It's Browne from Altan Sound View," Browne told the man. "Can you get the *Parsifal II* in the water for me? I want to take her out."

The Pole, to the best of Browne's understanding, assured him it would be done. Browne got in his car and headed south. It was nearly four when he pulled into the Altan yard in New Brighton. He parked against the chain-link fence and started walking toward the office. As he went, he saw one of the Poles securing a sheet metal grate over the shed. In the office he encountered a burly red-headed man whom he recognized as one of the company's old hands.

"I want to take my boat out," he told the man. "I telephoned earlier."

"I don't know about that," the big man said. "We're about to knock off." He spoke with a Down East accent. Browne's officerly sense sniffed contentiousness.

"Look, all I want to do is rig the sails," he explained. "Just let me get my sail bags out."

A second boatwright wandered over from the shed, a sallow man with a long face and a bony, prominent nose.

"The season ain't started yet, fella."

Together, Browne thought, the two of them embodied the spirit of No Can Do. It was everywhere lately, poisoning life and the country. He was not in the mood to be accommodating.

"Look," he told the yardbirds, "I telephoned early this afternoon. I asked you people to put my boat in the water. I was told it would be done."

"Like I told you," the red-headed man said, "we're closing."

Then he saw his catamaran through the open door of the office. She was set with her hulls resting on the rails of an elevator at the end of a dock, her mast and standing rigging in place.

"Christ," he said, "I'm looking at the goddam boat. I can get my own sail bags. How about a hand with the elevator?"

The pair regarded him with sullen contempt. It occurred to him that he had raised his voice. Browne liked to think of himself as extremely, even excessively polite. But the world was no longer safe for good manners. He looked from one man to the other, angry to the point of violence.

"Something wrong?" someone asked.

Browne turned to see a man in the doorway. The man was stocky and hard-faced, with curly gray hair and a dark jaw. He was wearing a camel's hair coat and tweed gillie's hat. Browne had seen him before but failed to place him.

"Maybe you can help me," Browne said to the hard-faced man. In his excitement, Browne had adopted his father's peremptory manner without being altogether aware of it.

"Mr. Browne, isn't it?" The man came forward and extended his hand. "I'm Pat Fay. We met in Newport Beach last year."

"Sure," Browne said, still not remembering him. He gave an embarrassed laugh. "Say, I'm trying to get some help with my boat. But it seems to be closing time."

The big man regarded him in a smiling, not unfriendly manner. "Yeah?"

"I wanted to take her out for an hour or so. Run down the checklist."

"You'd have to leave her in the water overnight then. Tied up to a mooring."

"Well, I'd lock her up," Browne told him. He saw the man exchange looks with one of the yard workers behind him.

After a moment Fay said, "O.K., you men go home. I'll help him."

"If you're gonna stay, Pat," the Down Easter said, "we'll stay too."

Fay took off his hat and his camel's hair coat and set them down on a desk.

"I'm sorry to trouble you," Browne said. "I thought the boat would be in the water." It seemed to him that there was something sinister in Fay's manner.

"No problem," Fay said in a distantly cheery voice. He turned to the boatwrights. "This is Mr. Browne, fellas. One of our salesmen." Browne did not correct him. Then Fay introduced the boatwrights, who were named Crawford and Fanelli. Browne nodded without looking at them. Fay's air of patient virtue was getting on his nerves.

"We know him," Crawford said. "He keeps his boat here."

"Right," Fanelli said.

"See, Mr. Browne," Fay said. "They know you."

He and Fay went down to the dock. Crawford and Fanelli sauntered along behind. The evening was charged with everyone's stifled anger.

When the catamaran was in the water, Crawford, the Maine man, let him into the shed to get his sails.

"Guess you don't know who Pat is," Crawford said as Browne lifted the sails out of a locker. "Just the damn chief designer of this company."

At that point, Browne recalled meeting Fay in California. He was a former Navy mustang who had gone to work for Altan as an engineer.

"Glad to have his help," he said to Crawford. "Yours too."

The three men stood around as he cleared his outboard. They watched him pick up the motor and heave it into the brackets. The effort of hauling it himself left him breathless and sweaty. When he climbed into the boat, he saw that Fay had stripped to shirtsleeves and that there was a broad grease stain across the front of his white shirt and striped tie.

"Better check your running lights," Fay called to him. Fanelli untied the boat's stern line, flinging it into the water with a disgusted motion.

"Thanks again," Browne called to them.

After several pulls, he got the Evinrude to turn over. With his sails still bagged, he motored off into the twilight shadows of the Upper Bay. Waterborne at last, he had to laugh at the absurdity of his own situation. He had come out on the merest impulse. Then the yardmen's resistance had provoked him into following through. Left to himself, it seemed, he might have changed his mind entirely. Now he was riding the swells off Staten Island with absolutely no purpose in mind.

For a while he headed for the lights of Manhattan island, dodging around Robbens Reef with Katie's Light to port. The city lights reminded him of the summer after his plebe year. His ship had steamed up the harbor and anchored in the Hudson. Out on the town, midshipmen had been less well received than they expected. He had fallen in love with Anne that summer.

He heard the throbbing of a diesel and turned to see a lighter coming up behind him at a good ten knots. The craft swung around him, passing to starboard. A bearded long-haired man in the wheelhouse looked down at him in astonishment. Browne was amused at the idea of how strange a spectacle he must present to passing craft. A butterfly in the gasworks, an ecological commando in a boat full of limpet mines. He waved to the lighter's pilot. The man put his hand out the wheelhouse porthole and made the horned sign against the evil eye.

In mid-harbor, he turned his back on the lights and Liberty's statue. Hard by the Bayonne shore, he skirted a nun buoy and passed under the lighted fantail of an enormous container ship riding at anchor. Three Filipino crewmen leaned against the rail, smoking, looking silently down on him. On an impulse, he brought the helm around and steered for the Kill Van Kull.

Ahead of him in the roadway, a Moran tug was steaming unencumbered toward Port Newark. Browne fell in line behind her. When the tug peeled off into Newark Bay, Browne increased his speed, heading down Arthur Kill. The channel lights drew him on. Passing Prall's Island, he saw a night heron take flight and sail over the oil storage tanks on the Jersey side.

The gathered night was starless and soiled by the glow of the harbor. Red and white refinery lights dappled the surface of the water. The wind carried the stench of the Fresh Kills dump. Browne laughed to himself. He ducked below and jammed a tape into the machine. The voice of Russ Columbo wafted into the sour-smelling darkness. "I Couldn't Sleep a Wink Last Night" was the song. With his tape at full volume, he eased past the Island of Meadow. His lights caught a rat running along the oily bank of the Jersey shore. Then he saw another. He shivered in the wintry breeze that had come up with darkness.

Ahead of him were the lights of the bridge that spanned the Kill. When he saw the black derelict shapes of a salvage yard on the Staten Island shore, he turned in and cut the motor.

In a still backwater off the Kill, ringed with lights like a prison yard, wooden tugs and ferries were scattered like a child's toy boats. Some lay half submerged and gutted, their stacks and steam engines moldering beside them in the shallows. Others were piled on each other four and five high, in dark masses that towered above the water. Browne knew the place. It was the property of his father-in-law, Jack Campbell. The wooden boats that rotted there, floodlit and girded round with electrified fence and razor wire, had been working harbor craft eighty and ninety years before.

Browne's father-in-law, a Yale man, was the presiding chief of a race of water ruffians — Irish and Newfie by origin — who had lorded it over certain sections of dockland since the last century. Rich from rum-running, bootlegging and two world wars, the Campbells owned odd lots of wharfage and real estate all over the harbor.

Parsifal's port float ran up the hull plates of a decaying tug, raising the shriek of fiberglass on metal. Under the awful sound, Russ Columbo's seamless crooning sounded on. The tug lay so far over that Browne could step out onto her topsides. He threw a line around a bitt on the tug's fo'c'sle and secured it. Then he walked along the rust-flaked hull to the wheelhouse and hunkered down to look around him. Somewhere ashore, a dog began to bark.

On Browne's left, the hulks lay scattered in a geometry of shadows. The busy sheer and curve of their shapes and the perfect stillness of the water made them appear held fast in some phantom disaster. Across the Kill, bulbous storage tanks, generators and floodlit power lines stretched to the end of darkness. The place was marked on the charts as Outerbridge Reach.

In the week after their wedding, Anne had brought him to the place as a joke. "This is what comes with me," she had said. "This is the family estate."

"Well," he had said. "We need a picture." So they had taken a picture of Anne's brother Aidan in his racing coracle among the hulks. Sheltering from the wind against the pilothouse bulkhead, Browne remembered the afternoon as though it were the day before. He laughed at finding himself there again. The tape ended and the marshes of Outerbridge Reach received the soiled tide.

He remembered scraps of the place's history. Thousands of immigrants had died there, in shanties, of cholera, in winter far from home. It had been a place of loneliness, violence and terrible labor. It seemed to Browne that there was something about the channel he recognized but could not call to mind. On the dark shore, the junkyard hound kept barking as though it would go on forever.

9

WHEN a few weeks passed without any further word from Hylan, Strickland began to brood. He had no other project in reserve. He passed the time cutting his Central American documentary with Hersey.

One day he and Hersey spent twelve straight hours splicing footage of foreign volunteers, *internacionalistas* who had gone south to assist the revolution. Among the internationalists Strickland had two particular favorites.

His favorite male internationalist was a man from Oklahoma, a tall, sepulchral Methodist minister with a nasal drone and a wandering Adam's apple. His favorite female was Charlotte, Biaggio's freckled, buck-toothed German girlfriend, the one who had been an au pair in Saddle River. Charlotte had a wide, unvarying smile and bobbed her head from side to side as she spoke to the camera. To specify footage he and Hersey had given some internationalists nicknames. They called the earnest minister "Homer." Hersey referred to Charlotte as "the Daughter of the Regiment," abbreviated to "the DR." She was so earnest and fatuous that the sight of her tempted Strickland to the obvious. He had to resist the impulse to intercut her merry palatal observations with corpses, parrots and amputees. Hersey imitated her relentlessly in Dutch-comedy German.

"*Up*tight! Ich bin *up*tight! Sie ist *up*tight! Wir sind *up*tight!"

"Saddle River is right," Strickland told him. "That little broad went down on the whole Sandinista army. She went crazy for T-shirts. She has like five hundred T-shirts with slogans on them and each one represents a d . . different blow job."

"Don't be *up*tight!" Hersey said. He clenched his teeth in a demented grin and batted his eyes and rolled his head from side to side. Finally, Strickland sent him home.

Later he called Pamela, who arrived with a bag of take-out salad from the corner Korean. They discussed the Hylan project.

"I swear," Strickland said, "the whole thing's fixed. I think it's being staged for Hylan."

Pamela ate cole slaw with her fingers and laughed at him.

"You're so sordid, Strickland. How can you think that! I mean, those people are so pure!"

"Yeah?"

"Hey, I know all about boats," Pamela insisted. "I used to sail."

The next day Strickland's partner and business manager called him in. His partner was a woman named Freya Blume, whose offices were on the fourth floor of the Brill building, a five-minute walk from his studio.

When he arrived at the office, Freya came out and kissed him. She was a tall handsome woman a few years older than he. Her gray hair was short and attractively styled.

"Beautiful as ever," Strickland told her.

Freya put a hand to her heart.

"Why, how flattering!" she said archly. Her voice had a trace of old Europe. "How nice."

He saw that she had put on some weight. She dressed very carefully. Freya and Strickland had been lovers many years before. Almost all the attractive women Strickland knew had been to bed with him.

"Everything's signed," Freya told him. "Apparently Hylan's in Finland working on his boat. Can you go over there?"

"Christ," Strickland said. "That was sudden."

Freya shrugged.

"I thought they had forgotten about it," Strickland said.

"Yes? Well they haven't. Been to Finland?"

"Never."

"Lovely country. Forest and sky, lakes and sea."

"I have yet to set eyes on this guy, Freya. He won't give me the time of day."

She put the contract down in front of him.

"You have better than the time of day. You have his signature."

Strickland had a look at the last page. A signature had indeed been scrawled under the name of Matthew Hylan.

"I haven't even finished cutting the Nicaraguan stuff."

"You're lazy," Freya told him.

"Think so?"

"Yes. Very talented but very lazy." She gave him a quick fond smile.

"I have two questions," Strickland said. "One is: what about budget? Two is: do they have to approve a final cut?"

"We'll have to submit an itemized budget. It won't be a problem because I happen to know they'll go to a million."

"What if they don't like what they see?"

"They're not paying you a fee. So they have no control."

"Is this on paper?"

"No. But that's the way it works."

"V-very generous," Strickland said. "Very easygoing. What if they're not satisfied?"

"You mean what if Hylan and his company come out looking like assholes?"

"Yeah," Strickland said. "Something like that."

Freya laughed. "But Hylan likes you. He liked *Under the Life.* He loved *LZ Bravo.*"

LZ Bravo was a film Strickland had made during the Vietnam War. During the filming bad things had happened to him, and although it contained some of his best work he did not care to be reminded of it. He stood up and walked to the window and looked down at the mid-morning *paseo* on Broadway.

"I really won't know if this is possible until I meet the guy," he told Freya. On the street below, the wayward individual to whom he had given his cordobas and lempiras was attempting to beg from a Greek hot dog vendor. The vendor showed his teeth. Two Sisters of Charity in knit sweaters and saris walked by. "I have to rely on Hylan himself to shoot the footage at sea."

"That should be good," Freya said.

"Yes," Strickland said. "If he's the man I take him for, it should be good."

They looked at each other and laughed.

"I think you can count on him," Freya said. "I've met him. He's a young putz."

"So I hear," Strickland said. "Pretentious and self-promoting. Which is how I like them."

Freya shook her head in fond reproach.

"But the shore stuff is important too," he added. "The corporate creeps."

"He makes no bones, this fellow," Freya said. She was speaking of Strickland. "You make no bones of your perspective."

"No bones whatsoever," Strickland said.

That evening he got out his Olympus and took Pamela on the town. They started with a drink at the Lion's Head and then went on to Fran's, a club below Houston Street on the Lower East Side. Fran's was no longer in vogue and required a seven-dollar entrance fee but Pamela favored it because she could buy cocaine at wholesale prices there. Strickland took care of it all. He had no use for cocaine himself, but the price of admission and the cocaine together were cheaper than dinner at one of the stately French restaurants Pamela favored.

They went down to the basement where there was a small bar and, in an adjoining space, a dance floor. When Pamela had scored from the dreadlocked Martiniquais barkeep, she wanted to dance.

"Go ahead and dance," Strickland told her. "You don't need me."

That night, a smooth Los Angeles band called Low Density Babylon was performing and the band had brought some of the regulars back to Fran's. Strickland took his camera out as Pamela kicked into her solo. He had really come to watch her dance. After the first few numbers, she withdrew into the ladies', only to emerge renewed. Presently she had a would-be partner, a small French magazine correspondent with a balding pate and shoulder-length hair. In general, she ignored him.

Strickland could hardly take his eyes off Pamela as she hot-cha'd it across the floor. She was a fine dancer with true animal grace and an agreeably eccentric style. The Frenchman could not get with her. Pamela had seemed to thrive on the street. She had advanced her station from that of runaway waif to star ho-dom to virtual courtesanship, leaving ruin and wreckage in her train. She was only beginning to run out of energy.

He sat drinking beer and watched her. Her face was long and keen; she had a fey expression and huge green eyes. Panic was the word for her, panic from the Greek, a crazy smile, sudden fear in lonely places. Her eyes were a caution, warning away the faint of loin, the troubled and the poor. She looked capable of anything, at the point of becoming either the perpetrator of a major felony or the victim of one. Looking into the future, Strickland saw the Tower ahead, blood and flaming curtains, slaughter.

Low Density Babylon ground on; the dancers splayed their hands and boogied. It was a weeknight and the weeknight crowd had turned out: a few blacks who could dance, a few of Hersey's fellow students, a contingent of English media scum. The English imagined themselves and their schemes invisible and danced with abandon, looking goatish and soiled. For some reason, Strickland had observed, they were always the best dancers in the place. Lights played on their toothy faces.

Strickland raised his camera and clicked away. Like the English in the room, Pamela thought nobody saw her tinker's shuffle. But I do, Strickland thought, and he did. The reflection afforded him poor comfort. He had to wonder what good it did him.

What good does it do me, Strickland asked himself as he peered through the lens, that I see and understand so thoroughly? That my camera never lies? If I'm so smart, why am I not richer, in works, in wisdom, whatever? He had little to learn about the field of folk and its bellyaching and its feeble strategies. He supposed he lacked the will to enjoy it all in solitary splendor. To understand so well had got to be enjoyed for its own sake. Otherwise it was its own punishment.

Fran's that night suggested the end of the century, the cunning of dice play, the destruction of someone's world. He raised his camera. In its eye, he framed the dancers. Horrible instrument, he thought, it never lied.

Someone grabbed the camera from him. He slid off the stool and turned angrily to face a skinny bouncer with a shaved head and a dangling earring.

"We don't need no insurance," the bouncer explained.

"Don't put your dirty fingers on that lens," Strickland told him.

The bartender with the dreadlocks came around to join the bouncer.

"No pictures in here, mon."

Strickland stepped back and raised his open palms as though

someone were pointing a gun at him. It was the stance he always assumed, anywhere in the world, when confronted.

Over the bouncer's shoulder, he saw Billie Bayliss, the club's proprietor, rushing toward him. Billie was a short cockney woman whose pancake makeup tinged her face the color of lemon peel. Costumed in a red hunting jacket and an antique hobble skirt, she approached in short angry steps.

"Oy!" she shouted.

Billie was panting and puffy-eyed. In her perturbation she resembled a fat youth done up for drag comedy in the school play. Her left arm was in a sling.

"People get all funny about cameras, darlin'," she told Strickland.

Strickland noticed for the first time that there was a scar that ran along her jawbone, disappeared beneath her jowly chin and emerged on the side of her neck. The flashing lights from above the dance floor caught it.

"How about telling your waiters to give me my camera back," Strickland said to Billie.

"Paparazzos don't make it, motherfucker," the young man with his camera said.

"Do take it easy, will you, Ron?" Billie said to Strickland. "These lads are too young to know who you are."

Strickland had gotten to know Billie Bayliss a few years earlier when he was researching *Under the Life,* and the sight of him, camera in hand, would have annoyed her in the best of times. The best of times, for Billie and her club, were over.

"They don't," she told him, "go to films at the museum."

"So tell them to give me back my c . . c . . ." Having said so much, Strickland failed of the next word. Billie Bayless watched with satisfaction as he struggled to complete his sentence. A dirty smile lit her thick features.

"Give him his camera back, Leon," she told the bouncer.

Pamela had spied the encounter from the dance floor and hurried over in a state.

"How can you think he's a paparazzo?" she nearly shrieked. "He's only the greatest fucking film maker of our time!"

"Course he is," cooed smiling Billie.

Leon shoved Strickland's camera back at him.

"If you're going to come here," Billie said sweetly, "go ahead and come here. But don't bring a camera, there's a good lad." She waved a hand toward Pamela without looking at her. "And don't bring her, will you?"

In the taxi on the way uptown Strickland told Pamela he was going to Finland. The news seemed to make her unhappy. When they were up in the studio, she was still pouting. Finally she said, "Oh, Ronnie, I would love to go to Finland."

"Don't call me Ronnie."

"Strickland," she said urgently. "We could have such a bitching good time."

She was sprawled on his bed. Strickland was in the next room, making a list of the equipment he would have to bring.

"You wouldn't like Finland, Pamela."

"The fuck I wouldn't," she replied. "I'd adore it."

"Nonsense," he said.

Coming into his sleeping quarters, Strickland saw that her eyes were flooding, her lips compressed with anger.

"Don't be silly," he said to her. "You don't want anything to do with a country like Finland. You'd find it . . . *up*tight."

"I wouldn't," she insisted.

"Come on," he said, sitting down beside her. "You want to go to the islands, don't you? Maui? Aruba? You want the sound of the sea and the s-sun on your golden hair, right? So forget about Finland."

"Please," she sang to Strickland, "please, please."

"O.K.," Strickland said. "If you come for free."

His words seemed to increase her anguish.

"You know I can't do that," she said bitterly. "How can I go places for free?"

"Pamela," Strickland said patiently, "I can't have you on my credit card ticking away like some kind of crazy taxi meter. You don't really want to go to Finland anyway."

"I do!" she declared. "And you could make it all expenses. If you made that movie about me you could have a Finland sequence. That would open it up."

Strickland found himself wishing he had her antic mood on

film. Her tantrum amused him and made him feel strangely indulgent. He sat down on the bed beside her.

"Look, baby," he said softly, and took Pamela by the hand, "you don't want to go to Finland. It's the land of the noon moon. There are wolf packs. People go insane from the cold and dark."

She closed her eyes and clenched her fists.

"But that's just why I would adore it there!" she cried. "Because it would be so wild and interesting!"

"Out of the question," Strickland told her.

Pamela burst into tears. She eased her legs off the bed and slowly crumpled to the floor where she curled in a fetal position and sobbed as though her heart would break. Strickland turned onto his stomach, reached down and stroked her hair. His gaze was on the city lights beyond the great window.

"There, there," he said softly. "You see, it has nothing to do with Finland."

Pamela moaned.

"It's your life, Pamela. It's very disorderly. It lacks cohesion."

"I know," she whispered.

"If you look into the center," he asked her, "what do you see?"

"I don't know," she said.

The thought of it made him shudder.

"Visualize, Pamela. What's in there?"

Infantile reprobation, he thought. A Third World of the mind, full of snakes and fever. He had almost gotten that much on film, for those who knew how to look.

"Nothing," she insisted. "Me."

When she stopped crying he let her do a line and put her in a taxi. As it drove off, she turned her pale pretty face toward him through the rear window. She had said nothing to the driver in Strickland's presence. He had no idea where she would go.

Back upstairs, Strickland sat before the Steenbeck and looked into its blank monitor. He had no regrets about solitude, of that he was certain. It was the only way to get things done and loneliness was an illusion. He had surrounded himself with a requisite silence and within it he could thrive. Outside was the swarm, the birds and the confusion. He had no serious connections there. All the same he was quite at home. Even strangling on his own words in that contaminated air, he could make them spread, make them dance. There were those who trusted him for the stammer, as though it should somehow keep him honest, and there were those, the stupider ones, who patronized him as a half-wit. His infirmity seemed to encourage people toward boasting and indiscretion. He had noticed it even as a child. It was they who came to him and impaled themselves.

But he had to admit that in the weeks since his return from Central America he had experienced a wavering of confidence. It had come out of nowhere, dogging his decisions on the Central American footage, making him increasingly wary of the strange Hylan project. Hardly since adolescence, it seemed to him, had he felt that hateful quiver of the gut, that tremor in the good right hand. But how familiar it was all the same, instantly recognizable over time. It waited, he supposed, for everyone. And perhaps there was such a thing as knowing too much. He was fast to his perception like some flying creature to its paralyzed wings. Once tiring he could never rest.

He had an urge to play the tape he had found of himself and his mother on the fifties Times Square radio show. He picked up the spool and turned it over. He could only wonder what had possessed him to play it for Pamela. What had he been trying to prove?

Strickland put the spool aside. He took a beer from his refrigerator and walked to the great round window to smoke a cigarette. The Hylan job was a good thing, he decided. It would allow him to let the Central American material settle so that he could cut it at his leisure. Moreover it was interesting. And the people involved were just like all the others. Pilgrims. Sleepwalkers.

Two days later, Strickland received a Hylan press kit and a set of travel agency vouchers. He spent the afternoon arranging to air freight his equipment. On the following day, he was in another taxi on the way to the airport. Passing Flushing Meadow, he let his eye fall on the detritus of the old World's Fairs. It was a place he often went by in his comings and goings. Most of the time, he passed it with hardly a thought.

Strickland understood that his mother had worked back of Eat Alley during the 1939 fair, with some attraction the city had closed down. He could remember her cursing the mayor, La Guardia, years after — also a picture postcard stuck in a mirror somewhere. The mirror would have been in their ancient Willys trailer, a prewar wonder they'd had when he was small. The postcard showed the totems of the fair, the Trylon and Perisphere.

Years later, living in New York and having taken New York as his subject, he came to read a history of the 1939 fair. War had broken out in the course of it. One by one, nations whose pavilions stood along the main concourse had passed under enemy occupation or even out of existence. In the end, the Trylon and Perisphere, the fair's symbols of progress, had been reduced to scrap — melted down, in effect, for weaponry. The fact had afforded him some vague satisfaction, a sensation completely divorced from reason, that had to do with his mother's rage. Strickland had become skilled at detecting and recording his own dumb reactions. About them he was not sentimental. His made no more sense than anyone else's but, unlike many people, he felt no compulsion to deny them. Your own shit, he thought, that sort of thing. It could be useful.

His cab shot by the tattered globe of the 1964 fair. Every inch of chrome had been stripped; ribbons of wire frame rattled around the supporting stanchions. Vietnam had been gathering around that one. Fairs were obviously bad luck and also bad business.

One day, he thought, he might make a film of the fairgrounds and its ghosts. He had never used old photographs and the music would be fun. No one would claim he was repeating himself. When his taxi pulled up in front of the Finnair terminal, he was deep in contemplation.

Stepping up to first class check-in, he found himself reluctant to part with the fantasy of a different film. The ones unmade were always pure. But in his heart he knew that there would never be such a venture, that he would never celebrate old fairgrounds or migrating salmon, threatened rain forests or Ojibway pictographs, or any of the other worthy subjects that sometimes occupied his daydreams. Strickland was devoted to the human factor. It was people he required.

10

"YOU HAVE an Academy ring," the woman at the stall opposite said to Browne. She was dark and slim, wearing sneakers and jeans. Her booth advertised a patented star-finder for the northern hemisphere.

Browne turned the class ring on his finger.

"Yes. Class of sixty-eight."

It was opening day at the Maritime Exposition at the 42nd Regiment Armory in New York. The crowds were sparse. All day he had been sitting beside a screen on which he himself appeared, extolling the virtues of Altan boats. He was heartily tired of hearing himself.

"My ex-husband graduated from the Academy. His name is Charlie Bloodworth. Ever run into him?"

"Never," Browne said.

"He's at Green Cove Springs now. That's where they make the old ships into razor blades."

"So I've heard," Browne said.

"We lived in Atsugi," she said. "Guam, too."

Looming above them were the hulls of two Altan stock boats. One was the Highlander Forty-five, which from his own experience Browne knew was badly made. The second was the Altan Forty, which he regarded highly. Before sailing south, Browne had actually made a tape on which he praised the Highlander Forty-five. He did not play it. Instead he played his pitch for the Altan Forty. A stand-up sign beside the Forty proclaimed it to be the stock version of the boat Matty Hylan would sail around the world. There was a picture of Hylan on the stand-up.

"I like your tape," the slim dark woman said. She was deeply suntanned. "I'm really hung over."

In the stuffy, humming air of the armor, he could not be sure he had heard her correctly.

"Too bad," he said politely.

"Know any cures?"

"No," he said. "I don't drink much."

The woman laughed.

"How about watching my booth?" she asked.

Browne agreed and she walked away, still laughing.

As the afternoon wore on, the crowds became even smaller. The woman did not return to her star-finder booth. Browne had brought along a volume of naval history. That afternoon, he read about Trafalgar, Nelson and Collingwood advancing in separate columns toward the Franco-Spanish fleet, breaking the line.

At some point, he decided to get up and take an aspirin. Well over an hour had passed since the woman at the stall opposite had disappeared. Browne set out in pursuit of a drinking fountain.

Searching for water, he passed through the wing in which the powerboats were displayed. It was much more crowded than the sailing section. There were overweight matrons in yachting caps and couples with matching tattoos. There were cabin cruisers and sleek cigarette boats with gleaming fins. Model interiors blazed with chrome and tiger-striped upholstery. Browne walked through it all feeling light-headed. When he came to the beige curtain that divided the displays from the storage and receiving section, he slipped past it into the gloom.

The storage area was a wilderness of crates and cardboard boxes piled to the forty-foot ceiling. Beyond the crates, on a buffed concrete floor, stood two armored personnel carriers of the New York National Guard. Near them was a drinking fountain.

On his way to the fountain, Browne heard something like a sensual moan from the area behind the crates. Looking more closely, he saw the balding head of a middle-aged man above one rank of boxes. Extending from the boxes along the floor was a woman's foot with a tanned ankle and sneaker. Between one thing and another, Browne formed the impression that a sexual act was taking place. Drinking from the fountain, downing his aspirin, he felt angry and revolted. He avoided the area on his way back.

The woman from the star-finder booth returned fifteen minutes after Browne got back to his own booth. She seemed pleased with herself and he thought somehow it must have been she he had seen sporting among the stacked boxes. The exposition could be a wild scene, the top of the year for certain people. Browne had heard stories about the casual sex but he had never seen any evidence of it before.

A little before six o'clock, Pat Fay, the designer whom Browne had pressed into service at the Staten Island yard, came up and looked at the stand-up ad for the Altan Forty that had Matty Hylan's picture on it.

"You might as well take it down," Fay said.

"Why?" Browne asked. He could see that the designer had been drinking.

Fay handed him a copy of the *New York Post*, open to page three. The headline over a three-column story inquired, "Where's Matty?"

There was a metal chair handy at a table piled with Altan brochures, so he sat down to read the story. Its substance was that in the face of bankruptcy and mounting scandal, Matty Hylan, bon vivant and captain of commerce, had vanished.

"They might have that race," Fay said. "Matty won't be in it."

"What I'm wondering," Browne said, "is what does this mean to us?"

Fay shrugged and walked away.

Browne stayed seated at the table for a while, trying to ponder the results of Hylan's disappearance. All at once the idea came to him of volunteering to enter the race on his own. If he could not sail the boat Hylan was having made in Finland, he might sail the stock model on the floor in front of him. He was sure it was a good boat. He felt a surge of confidence in his own abilities as a sailor. Immediately he began composing, with a pencil on a sheet of lined yellow paper, a letter to Harry Thorne.

He had finished the letter and pocketed it when he saw the woman who sold star-finders still lounging before her stall. She sat on the ledge of industrial carpeting at the corner of the booth with one leg folded under her. Browne thought she was watching him suggestively.

"Matty's gone," she said. "How about that guy?"

"Off for more congenial climes," Browne said.

"I guess he won't be sailing."

"Too bad," said Browne. He began to gather up his papers. There were very few show-goers about. "It was a good boat."

"If I was Matty," the woman said, "I would have disappeared during the race. I'd vanish at sea."

"Guess he couldn't wait," Browne said.

The dark woman looked at him with a kind of affectionate insolence. He thought she must be on something.

"Or I'd give them something to bellyache about. I'd not sail around the world but say I did. Hole up in Saint Barts and let the other guys sail and cross the finish line first."

"I don't think that's possible anymore," Browne said.

"Matty could do it," the woman said.

Browne told her good evening and went home.

11

No word awaited Strickland in Helsinki. Hylan was not booked into any of the major hotels. Since it was the weekend, he called Joyce Manning at home to leave a message on her machine. No reply was forthcoming. On Sunday, he arranged a meet with a local cinematographer and a sound man. They met a few blocks from Strickland's hotel, in a place called O'Malley's. As an earnest of their seriousness, everyone ordered soda water.

The Finns were called Holger and Pentii. They had recently worked on location in Florida for a Finnish-language TV thriller; they read *Variety* and were conversant with the picture business. Strickland explained his needs to them; he was charming and hesitant and they were patient with his stammer. Once satisfied with his assistants' bona fides, he became more composed. Everyone relaxed and called out to the Irish girl behind the bar for Harp lager. Her name was Maeve and Holger said she worked for the Marxist-Leninist wing of the IRA.

They spent the rest of the evening talking movies. Pentii was a Russ Meyer fan and his favorite among the master's oeuvre was *Faster Pussycat*. For Holger, who seemed the more thoughtful of the two, it would always be *Heaven's Gate*. When they broke up, Strickland told them to meet him in Sariola the next evening. He would drive himself there in the morning for some preliminary conversations with the boatyard management.

After breakfast the following day, Strickland telephoned the yard in Sariola. The man with whom he spoke was very polite but cautious to the point of evasion. It was all very odd. Around mid-morning, he piled his gear into a rented Saab and took off down the *autobajn* for Sariola.

The town lay deep in scented oak forests along the Gulf of

Finland. It was an old place, with a Swedish cathedral, cobbled squares and rambling wooden houses that suggested Chekhovian Russia. The air was clean and dry and the skies overhead as blue as June in California. The dark woods around the town were losing their winter silence but a surprising cold lurked in the groves and shadows.

At his new pastel plastic hotel, Strickland changed into clothes which he hoped seafaring types might find congenial: Topsiders, khaki slacks and a bulky naval sweater. Then he shouldered his camera case and set off on foot for the boatyard. Before he had gone a mile, he was light-headed with the sun and the smell of warm evergreen, his eyes dazzled, his nose and forehead reddening.

At the sign of Lipitsa Ltd., he followed a dirt road off the highway. Bird calls of a mystical complexity seemed to announce his passage. He walked out into the seaside meadow in which the Lipitsa yard stood to find three men waiting for him. Behind them a freshly laminated boat with a sexy curved transom and a shark-fin keel lay up on blocks. Beside it stood a graying, flaxen-haired man with the build of an oak stump and eyes the color of wild grapes.

"I'm Strickland," Strickland told him. "I've come to film."

"Lipitsa," the man said softly. He seemed to hesitate for a moment before extending his hand.

"Is that the boat?" Strickland asked. They looked at the shiny creature in its perch.

Lipitsa nodded.

"I've been trying to find Mr. Hylan," Strickland explained. "He doesn't seem to be available."

The old man's eyes twinkled over his high cheekbones, alight with boreal suspicion.

"I was hoping to ask you about that, sir. Can you come inside?"

Lipitsa's offices were on the second floor of a converted farmhouse, a solemn exercise in wood whose silent varnished spaces held a churchly resonance. There was an oak desk, some ancient photographs that appeared to represent the age of sail, and a long line of model boats in token of the ones he had designed. Strickland took a chair and faced the old man across the stern surface of his desk.

"Tell me what you want to do," Lipitsa said.

Strickland explained that a documentary film had been commissioned by the Hylan Corporation and that he was there to shoot it.

"Do I understand you to mean," old Lipitsa asked him, "that you have been paid?"

"I've been paid a retainer. And I've been given expenses."

"And you have no idea where our Mr. Hylan has gone?"

"Absolutely none," Strickland said. "I didn't know he was missing."

"You last saw him when, please?"

Strickland began but had to start over.

"I . . . I've never seen him. Now that you mention it."

"Ho," old Lipitsa said gravely. They looked at each other in silence for a moment. "I'm ahead of you," said the Finn. "I saw him in London two months ago. But you have been paid and I have not. So there you are ahead of me."

"What," Strickland asked him, "do you think is going on?"

"Don't think me impolite," Lipitsa said. "But I'm very curious and you are coming from over there. What do you think?"

"Quite honestly," Strickland said, "I have no idea what to think."

Old Lipitsa passed him a copy of the *Financial Times*. There was a story on the front page which reported growing concern as to the whereabouts of the youthful tycoon in question. The story contained, as rumor, a report that a number of grand juries in the United States had also expressed interest. Strickland did not bother to read the details. He realized that there would be decisions to make.

"What did he say? When you saw him in London."

Lipitsa curled one of his considerable eyebrows. "Wonderful things only."

Strickland folded his arms and looked at the floor. Abandoning the project now would cost him nothing. At the same time, it bothered him to abort something under way. There was also the possibility that little by little a film might come together for him that was more interesting than the one conceived. Disasters fascinated. It might just be worthwhile, he thought, to shoot until the money ran out and then see what manner of film was taking shape.

"What about the boat?"

"It's not paid for," Lipitsa said. "Barely half."

"Then," Strickland said, "I suppose he can't race."

"He has stolen our design," the Finn said solemnly. "This is what I think."

"Tell me the story," Strickland said. "Let me film it."

Old Lipitsa shook his head.

"We shall have to go to court in America. American courts are strange. I have nothing to say."

Strickland understood that he would not yield on the issue. In the end he persuaded Lipitsa to allow them to film the boat and the interior of the old man's office the following afternoon. The office walls were hung with photographs of Lipitsa as a young seaman aboard one of the grain ships that plied between northern Europe and Australia before the Second World War. They were the last four-masted sailing ships in commercial service.

On the walk back to town, Strickland was passed by a young woman in leather on a motorcycle. He went back to his hotel and put in a call to Duffy. It was still early in New York. Later in the afternoon he walked down to the main square of Sariola. One of the cafés had put a table out and it was just warm enough, with an ample sweater, to sit outside. The sun was low over the treetops and the Gulf of Finland.

He was sipping a lemonade when the door of the adjoining establishment opened and the leather-clad young woman he had seen on the road came out. In one hand she held a hefty stein of beer. The other held a sausage which she was endeavoring to eat on the fly. The sight of Strickland occasioned her a hasty swallow.

"Is it Mr. Hylan?"

"I'm afraid not," Strickland said politely. He rose. "Would you like to sit down?"

The young woman took a seat and gestured at him with the sausage. "I would like to ask questions but first I must finish."

Strickland was tempted to ask whether he should look the

other way. He stood by with a pleasant expression as she annihilated the wiener and washed it down with a long draw on the brew. The young woman's name was Mari Hame; she was, as Strickland at once suspected, a journalist.

"And Mr. Hylan," she demanded, "where is he?"

"No one knows. Not in America and not here."

"But this is strange," Mari said.

"Yes, it is strange," Strickland agreed. "He's missing."

Strickland found himself somewhat fascinated by the young reporter. The word for her, a word that graphically insinuated itself, was homely. She had long dark hair; her face was extremely pale and a little too full. Much of its character attached to the huge horn-rimmed glasses she wore, the lenses of which appeared as thick as the February ice on Lake Ladoga. But behind them her eyes were a treat, dark blue and utterly fanatical.

"Everyone is interested," she confided to Strickland. "An American millionaire disappears."

"I understand," Strickland told her. "An American millionaire is a significant contemporary figure."

As things turned out, Strickland spent the night with Mari. She told him of her adventures in Africa as a foreign aid worker. She reminisced about her first trip to Paris in the course of which she had consumed fourteen Pernods in succession at a sidewalk café. She asked Strickland if he knew a person named Charles Bukowski.

Next morning his telephone rang. Joyce Manning was on the line.

"We've had a change of plans, Ron. Come back as soon as you can."

"Where's Hylan?" he asked.

"Nothing on the phone, please. Just come back, O.K.?"

"Tomorrow," he promised. "If I can finish up today."

"Soonest," Joyce told him.

That day, he hired a plane to overfly the Lipitsa yard and filmed from the air. Mari went along. In parting she gave Strickland a picture of herself at the Evangelical Mission station on the banks of the Okavango. Strickland thought it a marvelous photograph. Drawn and pale beneath a thorn tree, she faced down all the ironies of the Third World. Haunting her blue stare was the silent, unappeasable rage of the Lutheran God, His utter incomprehensibility, His furious impatience with the contradictions of inferior beings. Back in New York, he pinned Mari's picture to his bulletin board, beside his pictures of starveling cattle, birds and the dead.

12

One day they went up to Stonington to get the ferry for Stead-man's Island. The day was as warm as predicted but drizzly and gray. Anne started out in fair spirits, favoring her mild hangover. Owen drove in silence.

During the crossing, they sat together atop a gearbox on the lee side, eluding the listless rain. The fog was heavy and the horn sounded at three-minute intervals all the way across.

Years before, in a different world, they had met on the island. She had been a counselor at a sailing camp and Owen an instructor. They had started dating the summer after his plebe year and the ferry had figured in their courtship. Often they had gone back and forth to the mainland for the ride, only to be alone in each other's company. In those days a band played for dancing during the summer months. She had taught him to dance, after a fashion. They had spent whole crossings necking on the same gearbox, starboard aft.

Now side by side, not touching, they seemed to be avoiding each other's eye. Secretly she glanced at him as he looked over the local morning paper. His silent, indifferent manner made her suspect him of being embarrassed at all these reminders of their old love. For a moment she felt the remnants of that breathless romance strewn around her, demystified and ironical with time, exposed to the gray rain.

Their house was two miles from the village, set above clay bluffs, a rambling Victorian relic surrounded by wind-dwarfed dark pines. Next to the house stood an old gazebo, its broken latticework rattling in the breeze. Immediately they set about the tasks of occupation. Browne lit the furnace, stripped tape from the seaward windows and made a fire in the fireplace. Anne opened the water and the gas.

When they were finished she put water on for coffee.

"Christ," he said, "there's so much to be done around this house."

"For God's sake, Owen, don't start tinkering or I'll be sorry we came. You're going to do the brochures, aren't you?"

"Sure," he said. She watched him obsessing and rebelled.

"Well, you can't do everything at once." She went around the table at which they had been sitting and put a hand on his shoulder. "Why don't you finish them off and then keep company with me?"

Her touch seemed to liberate him from his own stony state. He took her hand.

"Good idea," he said. While he was setting up on the dining room table, she put on her raincoat and went outside to walk beside the cliffs.

The rain had stopped and fog was gathering to take its place. Following the sandy trail through stands of bayberry and wild roses, she could not see the ocean two hundred feet below nor much of the way ahead. The break of the waves sounded muffled and distant. On a misty promontory a half mile from the house, she bent to gather winter weeds and grasses for the house. She had a sense of the fog reflecting her own inwardness. She felt drawn to old obvious questions that had been put aside. Who inhabits me? What do I feel?

The unfamiliarity of the place and the weather out of season combined to produce in her a vertiginous confusion. She stayed where she was, afraid of falling. The fall she feared was deep and dark, more frightening than the empty space between her clifftop and the sea. For a moment she was paralyzed with nameless dread.

She walked in the fog for the rest of the morning. Back at the house she made some toast and read the Stonington paper. There were stories about a suspected cat poisoning, about a movie being filmed in the next town and about a proposed amendment to the village laws governing the sale of liquor. The paper also carried a syndicated story about Matthew Hylan's disappearance and the impending collapse of his corporate network. Anne skipped over it. She had followed the story in the *Wall Street Journal* and the *Times*.

An hour later, she was curled in a living room chair reading *Middlemarch* when she saw Owen get up from the table and head for the door. She put the book down and went after him.

"Owen?"

He looked at her blankly, getting into his lumber jacket.

"Are you finished?" she asked him.

He shook his head.

"Where are you going? I thought we had a date."

"I'm not finished," he said. "I want to walk and think."

"Well, really," she said, unable to keep from saying it. "What is there to think about, writing that crap?"

"It's my job," he said. She had to admit he had her there. She had been more angry than she realized.

"I'm sorry," she said. "I guess I resent the time it takes you. I wanted to walk with you before dark."

"I'll be back," he said, "before dark."

She returned to the living room, broke out her Smith-Corona portable and started work on her article about their Cape Sable crossing. Around three, a call came from a secretary at the Hylan Corporation. Harry Thorne wanted to speak to Owen. Anne told her to call back later.

When it came time to light the lamps she was still alone. She paced for a while and then went out to gather up more logs for the fireplace. The fire burned high and bright. Eventually she found herself in the cellar where the old furnace was rattling away, looking through the stored wine. She chose a 1978 Rioja with the vague idea of making steak. Before long, she had opened it and poured herself a glass. She took the bottle and sat down beside the fire. *Middlemarch* failed to hold her. She kept remembering the ferry ride. That made it impossible not to think of the past.

An ocean eternally blue. Lost summer sunlight, love, youth and laughter. The land of lost content. She thought they were drifting apart physically. Something was missing. He seemed unaware of it.

"Oh, shit," she said aloud. "Goddam it."

Inevitable tears. The bottle of Rioja was half empty at her feet. She felt so ashamed and foolish that she picked up the wine and took it into the kitchen with the intention of pouring it down the sink drain. At the point of doing so, she thought better of it. She put the bottle on a shelf above the toaster.

She went upstairs to the guest bedroom and turned on the old black-and-white television set that lived there. Dr. C. Everett Koop was on camera, delivering a quiet homily of which Anne understood not a word. Sitting propped on pillows against the brass bars of the shiny antique bed, she felt less anxious than angry. When she heard the kitchen door she got up and went downstairs. He was standing in the kitchen looking out at the fog.

"Why didn't you come back?" she demanded. "I was waiting for you." It was too late for her to digest her own anger. "I waited all afternoon for you."

He looked at her without expression.

"What is it?" she asked. "What's going on? What's wrong with you?"

"Sorry," he said. It was not the answer she required.

"Why didn't you come back?" she insisted. "I was waiting." She took a tissue from the kitchen table, wet it and held it against her cheek. She was past caring whether he saw her cry. Then the telephone rang and she folded her arms and turned away.

"It's for you," she said. "They called before."

He looked at the phone and let it ring again.

"For God's sake," she said, "answer it." Then she went into the living room, sat down at her typewriter again and stared in dumb incomprehension at the text of the story on which she had been working.

Unable to make out Owen's end of the conversation, she could tell from his voice that he had gone into his public, salesman's mode. Then, after he had been on the phone for a few minutes, she heard something in his tone she barely recognized, a measure of suppressed excitement, of brisk conspiracy that brought her back in time. It was how he had often sounded in their first years together and it reminded her somehow, perversely, of the war. When he came out of the kitchen she was on her feet waiting for him.

"They want me to race Hylan's boat," Owen said to her. "In the Eglantine Solo."

She said nothing.

"What do you think of that, Annie?"

Finally she said, "You don't have the experience."

"I can't say no," he told her, laughing. The same note was in his voice. "I won't."

She felt a wave of panic.

"You've never sailed alone," she told him.

"Yes I have. To Cape Fear."

"And you saw things. You told me that you saw things."

"Everybody does. It's like being in the woods."

"Come on, Owen," she said, as though it could be laughed aside. "Be realistic."

Suddenly he seemed angry.

"This is what isn't realistic," he shouted. "This!" He raised his arm to include the two of them and the room in which they stood and things beyond it.

Fear struck her again, a tremor like pain.

"What do you mean, Owen? Do you mean us? Do you mean me?"

"No, no," he said impatiently. "You're taking it wrong." She was not reassured. "It's me," he told her. "Sometimes I feel like I'm in the wrong life."

"The wrong life," she repeated coldly. "I don't understand."

"I mean," he said, "that I've never done the things I ought to have done years ago. I took a wrong turn."

"Would you like a glass of wine?" she asked him.

Owen looked at her in surprise. He smiled and shook his head. When Anne went into the kitchen he followed her.

"Sometimes," he said, "it's as though whatever I'm feeling is completely artificial. I have these highs and lows and I don't think they attach to me at all. That isn't life."

No? Anne thought. Isn't it? She poured herself a glass of Rioja, the correct amount into the correct glass for red wine.

"This," Owen told her, "is a chance for me to get a hold on things." He showed her his fists, his hands gripping an imagined helm. "To make it up."

Anne sipped her wine and looked at his grasping hands. She had not heard him. The wine made her feel much better.

"You're thinking about the war," she said.

"Don't be ridiculous," Owen said. He went warm with a patronizing sort of kindness. It terrified her to feel so separate from him, so seemingly outside the range of his desires.

"I don't want it said I drove you to sea, Owen."

He seemed to think she was joking.

"Poor old Annie," he said. "You're shitfaced, aren't you? Shellacked, right?"

"Maybe," she said. She had not been joking about driving him to sea. She had to admit it was an odd thing to have said. "You have responsibilities," she told him.

"This is the way to discharge them."

"It's not."

"Yes," he said, "this is the way to recoup. A good way. A clean way."

She put the wine aside and went to him and leaned her head against his shoulder.

"Are you sure, Owen? Are you really sure?"

"In a word," he said, "yes. Absolutely certain."

Then she rebelled and tore away from him.

"It isn't the right thing to do," she insisted. "It's crazy."

"You're wrong," he told her. "It *is* the right thing."

"You'll be alone."

"Why not?"

"Owen," she said, "I don't want you to. You really don't have the experience." Having said it, she realized that he was altogether serious and that only her will stood in his way. She was certain she could prevent him from trying it, if she dared. But then there would be the rest of life to get through.

"These people at Hylan don't know anything about sailing," she insisted. "If they did, they wouldn't ask you. They'd find someone more experienced."

"You're right," he said cheerfully. "But they did ask me. I'm going."

She must have looked forlorn; Owen took pity on her.

"I'm going to persuade you," he said soberly. "If I can't persuade you, I won't go."

"No," she said, "that's not fair."

He laughed. "Why?"

"Because you'll persuade me."

"Damn right," he said happily. "I'm a believer."

She clung to him a little drunkenly as they went upstairs. He jollied her along to bed. When the lights were out she said, "I can't imagine what it would be like."

"For you," he wanted to know, "or for me?"

"For both of us."

"At the worst," he said, "like the war."

"We were young during the war."

"We're still young, Annie."

She shook her head without answering.

"Do you know what it could mean?" he asked her. "In the business? It would make us, Annie. It could move us from where we are into something else altogether."

"What's the matter with where we are?"

"Are you kidding?" he demanded. "Are you satisfied with things?"

"No," she said.

"Well," he said, sounding a shade surprised, "I finally got you to admit it."

"I mean," she said, "I would be if you were. I don't know what I mean. I mean what if you die on us out there?"

"You don't go through life with that attitude."

For that she had no reply. She turned over on her stomach and rested her throbbing head on her folded hands.

"Remember?" he asked her. "Remember how it was?"

Anne tried to remember how it was during the war. Her memories seemed distorted and even immoral. Somehow the anxiety, the weight they had both borne, the constant sense of being in trouble, had vanished and whatever traces remained had long ago been bonded in the blood and was part of them. Now, absurdly, she remembered the beach at Pattaya and mai tais at the Halekulani and all-night loving at the Navy's Waikiki Beach hotel. At dawn, his whispering, *Lente lente currite noctis equi.* They had been adolescents. She remembered the deliciousness of youth and the feeling of fuck the world, the proud acceptance of honor, duty and risk. In spite of everything, they had proved life against their pulses then, beat by beat.

In her inebriated state, she understood his thirst for life and youth. And, she thought, he was capable of bringing great strength to bear, a strength that people like her father could not understand. She had always believed him a much underestimated man. There was a part of her that, day in day out, would always remain his secret admirer. She had seen hope in his face that night and it was beautiful. He was not the only one who needed to be a believer.

13

A WEEK LATER, shambling and red-faced, Duffy the public relations man arrived at the house above the Sound. Anne was surprised at his unprepossessing appearance. Seated on their sofa with a cup of coffee on his knee, he philosophized.

"Some people are lucky," he explained. "They can afford to come across as themselves."

Owen and Anne shared a quick glance. Very shortly, Duffy commenced to address Anne in a collegial fashion, as though they were partners in PR. He discussed Owen as though he were not present.

"I look at Owen," Duffy said, "and I think: Lindbergh! See what I mean?"

Anne smiled because the association embarrassed her. In the circles in which she had been raised Lindbergh was much admired. Anne Morrow Lindbergh had been her mother's favorite author.

Duffy was crestfallen. "You don't think so?"

Owen muttered something under his breath. His irritation struck her as comical. Duffy persisted. "You know what I'm saying? Clean-cut but serious. Serious but not weird. See what I mean?"

When Duffy left, he took their family photographs with him to leaf through for inspiration.

"Christ," Browne said when the man was gone, "what an utter asshole!"

"Don't you think they're probably all kind of like that?"

"Remind me to call up Thorne tomorrow," Owen said. "They're going to have to send me someone else."

The next day Owen forgot about calling Thorne and Anne did not remind him. Duffy would do, as far as she was concerned.

On the following Friday, the Southchester Yacht Club held a cocktail hour to introduce the entrants in the race to the press. An hour before it was scheduled to begin, Duffy came to the Brownes' door wearing a tweed checkered cap. "God save all here!" he called cheerfully, hurrying inside. Anne made coffee for the three of them. The publicist sat down at the kitchen table and began spooning sugar into his cup. His face had an unhealthy radiance.

"You're gonna be asked a lot of questions about Hylan," he told Browne. "Refer them to me. Maybe we can get it all over with today." Then he addressed himself to Anne. "Do you know these other guys?"

She understood that Duffy was asking her about the three other contestants in the race that the club had managed to assemble: Dennis, Kerouaille and Fowler.

"I've met them all," Anne said. "Owen knows Fowler. He's a broker down in Virginia Beach."

"I know him all right. He's the last of the oyster pirates."

"Ready?" Duffy asked the Brownes.

Browne finished his coffee and said, "Sure, let's go."

On the drive, Duffy regaled them with old-time newspaper stories. The day was cloudy and warm, the Sound's surface heron-blue. A sultry light seemed to hang over the far shore.

Duffy turned out to have worked on the long-lost *New York Journal-American*. He had a wife who was chronically ill. The previous week he had taken her for a drive up the Hudson to Boscobel mansion and it had been very pleasant. Halfway up the stone steps that led to the club's front door, he turned to them breathlessly.

"You two stay close together. We want Anne in the pix."

Southchester's club was set on a bluff over a salt marsh, an enormous timbered Tudor manor attended by ancient, wind-stripped sugar maples. Candles were burning in its windows. Voices and music drifted down from inside.

They found the club premises a mob scene. Bars had been set up; the place smelled of whiskey, perfume and leather. Owen and Anne followed Duffy across the trophy room through the press of the crowd. At the door of the club library, a tall man with a graying nautical beard appeared to be expecting them. Duffy briefly attempted to make introductions but the bearded man paid no attention to him.

"Browne, is it?" he asked Owen. "I'm Captain Riggs-Bowen, club secretary." Browne shook his hand. An aged man in a blue blazer appeared and was introduced as Mr. Whitney, the club commodore. Members of the press had begun to shout questions at Browne. Duffy interposed his person.

"If you have questions about Mr. Matthew Hylan," he announced at the top of his voice, "let me have 'em. Mr. Browne has no information for you."

About two dozen reporters followed Duffy into an adjoining room. Riggs-Bowen, who had come alert at Anne's presence, conducted the Brownes to the back of the library where the three other entrants in the race were waiting. They lounged somewhat defiantly in captain's chairs beside an antique oak table on which stood an enormous vase full of daffodils. Everyone stood up as the Brownes approached.

Ian Dennis was a foxy-faced, introverted Australian who had set his name to a book that recorded his adventures during sixty-seven days adrift in a rubber raft. He was in the United States to promote it and was attempting to do so in nearly total silence.

Patrick Kerouaille was an amiable Breton schoolmaster and also an author. Kerouaille's books were written by himself and recorded the mystical ruminations toward which life at sea inclined him.

The third sailor was the Virginian, Preston Fowler, who had a reputation as a shady character and a soul-withering false smile.

"How's business?" he asked Browne.

"Things are tight," Browne told him. "What with the market."

"Where's your big boss at?" Fowler asked. "Ever hear from him?"

"Nope," Browne said.

"I didn't know you were a single-hander, boy," Fowler said. He winked at Anne. He had a pug-dog face with a faintly swinish turned-up nose. "When'd you take it up?"

"I've been single-handing for years," Browne told him.

"I never knew that," Fowler said.

"Sure," Browne told him. "A couple of trips to Bermuda. And the Azores. A couple of transatlantic deliveries." He felt Anne kick him in the ankle.

Fowler laughed. "Hiding your light under a bushel, were you, Owen? And you call yourself a salesman."

"Selling's an art, Preston," Browne said. "Sailing's recreation."

Riggs-Bowen began to shepherd them toward the trophy room for pictures. As they went, Anne grabbed his arm.

"How could you say that?" she whispered urgently. "I've never heard you not tell the truth before."

"I don't really understand it myself," Owen told her. "At that moment — it was what I wanted to say."

She looked around the room in sudden alarm.

"Good God," she said, "will it all be like this?"

"Yes, I think so," Browne said.

14

STRICKLAND moved alertly among the salty revelers with a smile for everyone. Attempting invisibility, he had sought to disguise himself as a sort of waterman, in a blue windbreaker and Top-siders. As it happened, most of the people at the press party were wearing dark suits.

Strickland's attention was taken by the richly tanned young persons in tuxedos who functioned as menials at the party. Male and female alike, they exuded vitamins and sunshine. Their cheeks were smooth and their teeth bright; they were the club's children. So taken was Strickland that he could hardly conceal his interest. When a young person's gaze met his, Strickland held it until the poor creature looked away in confusion. Their untroubled faces represented a newfound land for him.

In the center of the library, three bearded young men in striped jerseys were playing jigs and hornpipes on a banjo and tin whis-tles. Strickland sauntered up to the service bar, where an ice-cream-blond girl was waiting to take his order.

"You a sailor?" he asked the girl as she prepared his vodka and soda. She had large friendly brown eyes.

"Yeah," she said. "I teach at the sailing school during the sum-mer." She laughed a toothy mock-rueful laugh. "But today we're all serving."

"You're n . . not . . ."

She waited politely on his stammer.

"You're not old enough to fix drinks," he managed to tell her.

Her smile became slightly fearful.

"Just kidding," he assured the youngster.

As Strickland stood drinking beside the bar, a tall, good-looking man in a Brooks Brothers suit approached for service.

The man had a long youthful face and hair that appeared to be prematurely gray. His eyes were mild. He ordered two glasses of white wine and a Coke.

"Hey, Mr. Browne," the young bartender chirped happily, "the Coke for you?"

The man only smiled. A second tuxedoed young woman of similar appearance came down the bar for a look at Mr. Browne.

"You in training for the race?" the bartender asked.

"That's right," Browne said.

"Yeah?" the young woman said. "Too bad."

The other girl laughed explosively at her friend's effrontery.

Browne gave them a sad smile and went off with the drinks.

The barmaid made a show of calling after him. "Hey, Mr. Browne! You're jammin'!" In fact she called only loud enough for Strickland and her friend to hear. The two girls laughed together.

"Like him?" Strickland asked.

She acted out a moment's reflection.

"Uh, yeah," she said, and laughed with her friend. Then the other girl went back to her serving station and she was alone with Strickland.

"Think he's going to win?"

"Definitely," she said.

"Why?"

"Well," she said, "because I like him."

"Because he's jammin'?"

"That's right," she said.

"You mean," Strickland asked, "you find him attractive?"

The corners of the young woman's mouth began to turn down.

"How'd you like to be in a movie?" he asked her. "A movie about the race."

She looked at him unhappily without answering.

"What's your name?"

The girl swallowed and, under his stare, recited her name, which was Carol Cassidy.

"Stay loose, Carol Cassidy," Strickland said. "This summer we'll be filming and I'll come back and we'll talk some more, O.K.?"

The girl nodded.

"Now tell me," Strickland said, "who's in charge of all this?"

"Well," the girl said, "Captain Riggs-Bowen, I guess."

"And which one is he?"

A reporter with a plastic press card hung around his neck came up to the bar. Carol Cassidy took a quick look around and started making the reporter's drink.

"I don't see him," she told Strickland. "But you'll find him. He's English. And like very distinguished?"

Setting off around the room, Strickland regretted not having brought his camera. As it stood, he would have to retain the essence of the place in his mind's eye. But surely, he thought, there would be other such scenes.

The single-handed sailors had been gathered for photographs in the middle of the trophy room. Amid the buzz, Strickland detected a Briton's upscale, mellow tones. Homing in on the signal, he saw a man he presumed was Captain Riggs-Bowen in conversation with two admiring ladies. He stood by until the ladies drifted off.

"Excuse me, Captain?"

Riggs-Bowen turned an insolent stare on him. He had a brick-red blood-pressure mask around his eyes, which resembled those of a raptor. The irises were light blue and oyster-shaped. Gotta get him in the flick somehow, thought Strickland.

"Who's g . . going to win?"

"Well," the captain said, "we don't know, do we? They'll race and we'll see."

"Any favorites?"

Riggs-Bowen scanned Strickland's person for some clue to his identity. Strickland wore none.

"Press, are you?"

"Media. Will it be close?"

"Hard to say," Riggs-Bowen said. "Impossible."

"Are they all good?"

"Not necessarily. We don't vet them, you know. If they have a sponsor, they're in."

"How about Browne? What do you think of him?"

"Nice fella. As far as I know."

Strickland looked at the posing sailors.

"Who are the two people with him?"

"His wife," Riggs-Bowen said, "and his press agent."

"Really?"

Riggs-Bowen assumed the patient, patronizing tone with which he was most comfortable.

"It's not unusual for them to have press agents, you know. Sometimes they have literary agents as well. That's how these things are today."

"His wife is nice looking," Strickland said. The captain's keen glance widened slightly. "And," Strickland went on, "he has the eyes of a poet."

Riggs-Bowen favored him with a dark smile.

15

STRICKLAND introduced himself to the Brownes over the telephone. It was arranged that he would join Owen and Anne on Steadman's Island for a brief weekend.

He arrived early Saturday morning by chartered plane from New York. He brought along videotapes of two of his films: *Under the Life,* which was about a prostitute named Pamela Koester in New York, and *Kid Soto,* which recorded the morning, afternoon and fight night of a club boxer in Riverside, California. While the Brownes watched his documentaries, Strickland prowled the house and the grounds outside. Once Anne came out and found him examining the bookshelves. Most of the books in the summer house were naval histories or travel narratives.

The film maker took lunch with them but he had little to say. Strickland believed in withholding himself from the subjects of his films, at least at the outset. Eventually, he reasoned, they came to you.

Over coffee on the porch, the Brownes sought to bring him forth a little by talking about the films.

"I never thought," Owen said, "that people like that could be so sympathetic."

Anne joined in. "Really! They're so funny! You feel for them."

"Oh," Strickland said haltingly, "thanks. They're just folks."

He had brought a small Olympus camera with him and over the afternoon he took a lot of photographs. The idea was partly to accustom them to the sight of him with a camera, partly to collect their images and pin them to his walls. Every time Anne turned around, she seemed to find him there, at an odd angle to the place she occupied, commanding a long view.

Once she was bold enough to ask him, "Have you always stammered?"

He showed her a sunny, forgiving smile.

"Since I was eleven. There was a kid in sixth grade who stuttered. I was imitating him. Making fun of the kid. They told me it would stick. And it did."

"Oh no!" Anne cried. "Really?"

"I wouldn't make it up, would I?"

"Well, I don't know," she said. By then she obviously regretted the question and was trying to keep it light and distant.

He took a great many pictures of Owen working in the study, assembling charts, making lists. Anne lent him some family snapshots. Shortly before dinnertime he announced his intention to go back to New York. Owen was upstairs in the shower. Anne had opened a bottle of wine.

"Oh dear," Anne said. "I was counting on your staying for dinner."

He was uncertain whether she was relieved or disappointed. He suspected something of both. In any case, she made no immediate move to drive him. Owen Browne came downstairs in a bathing suit and T-shirt. He was well built, long-legged, with big shoulders and without flab. It was a conscientious preppy's body.

"Didn't you make a picture about the Vietnam War?" Owen asked Strickland.

Strickland nodded quickly.

"What was it called?"

"*LZ Bravo*," Strickland said.

"I haven't seen it," Browne told him. "I've heard about it."

"What have you heard?"

Browne was embarrassed. "To tell you the truth, I can't remember. Only that I've heard of it."

"One time I'll run it for you," Strickland said to them.

"Good," said Owen.

"Owen was there," Anne said.

"Yes," Strickland said, "I know he was."

It turned out that Anne drove Strickland to the small island airport. She had taken three glasses of wine and she watched the yellow line with her jaw set.

"So," he asked her. "Why's he doing it?"

She laughed and tossed her head. Proud of her old man, Strickland thought. It would be necessary to record that one.

"Don't you know why?"

"I don't sail," Strickland informed her.

"Imagine what kind of a feeling it is," she said to Strickland. "Making your way across all that ocean. Making your way across the whole world. All on your own savvy and endurance."

"Sure," he said. "I guess I can understand that." He sneaked a look at her and saw that she was basking in the glow of her own words. Her eyes were bright. "You'd like to do it yourself, wouldn't you?"

"Who, me?" she asked. "I'm an armchair sailor."

"So you approve of his going?"

Her confident smile tightened. "Oh yes," she said.

"Who's he doing it for?" Strickland asked. "You or the rest of the world?"

She looked straight ahead at the road and shook her head slightly, as though she had not understood his question.

They drove up to the Quonset hut that served Steadman's as an airline terminal and Strickland got out of the car. Before Anne could pull out he leaned in the open window.

"I like to try out a couple of basic questions at the beginning of a project," he told her. "I need to find out the questions that work, understand? I need to know which questions I'll be asking. I hope you don't take it wrong."

Anne favored him with a quick impatient smile and put the car in gear. He stood and watched her drive away.

The next day, while he worked on the Central American footage, he had Hersey develop the pictures he had taken on Steadman's Island. He was in search of a title for the film and in that effort had invested in two volumes of Pablo Neruda with facing English and Spanish texts. The film taking shape would have the left-liberal coloration required to justify a reference to that poet. It would also contain a few home truths for the private delectation of that tiny band of perceptual athletes whom Strickland regarded as his core audience.

Hersey put the shiny new Steadman's Island prints on Strickland's desk. Strickland turned off the Steenbeck and rolled his chair over to inspect them.

"Hey, Ron," Hersey said. "These look like nice people."

Strickland picked up a picture of Anne Browne on her porch and inspected it.

"What do you mean, Hersey? What are you talking about?"

"Well, I mean they don't resemble our usual run of scumbag."

Thumbing briefly through the rest, Strickland felt the quickening of an old familiar appetite.

"Trust me," he told Hersey.

About ten o'clock that night Pamela arrived. She had forgiven Strickland for not taking her to Finland. When she came in he was lying on the sofa in his office smoking a joint. He had pinned his Steadman's Island pictures of the Brownes on the bulletin board, along with that of Mari in Africa and those of the war in Central America. Pamela went to them at once, aglow with enthusiasm.

"Oh wow," she exclaimed. "This is like the nuclear family, right? Mommy and Daddy and Sis. Shit, I wish my family looked like that."

"I thought they did," Strickland said.

She took a print from the board and settled beside him. "Oh my God! She has the khaki skirt. And the little plaid belt. And the little black sleeveless blouse. I can't stand it."

"You know what they said about you, Pamela?" He cleared his throat, preparing to do Browne's voice. "They said, 'I n-never knew people like that could be so sympathetic.'"

"Oh no!" Pamela cried. Giggling, she folded her arms and shuddered, as with a dread delicious thrill.

"They subscribe to *The American Spectator*," Strickland added. But this further *frisson* was not available to Pamela, who went to the desk for more pictures and began leafing through them.

"Lookit this! Her hair is getting a tad gray. Prematurely, right? And she's not doing anything to it." Pamela breathed an admiring sigh. "How tall is she?"

"Taller than me. Almost as tall as him and he's over six feet." He took the picture from her hand. "The two of them look alike, can you see it? She has a sort of square jaw."

"Like her?" Pamela asked. She looked him in the eye and ran the tip of her tongue along her upper lip.

Strickland shrugged. "I don't know. I look at her and I think of a hundred and twenty-five pounds of pound cake. Of course, I kind of like pound cake."

"Get real," Pamela said impatiently. "She's the handsome prince I've always dreamed of. And the guy is a hunk."

"He's a hero, too. A pilgrim."

"Oh, Ronnie, you'll have such fun."

"I believe I will have fun," Strickland said. "Please don't call me Ronnie."

"Can't I meet them, Ron?"

"Nah," Strickland said.

"Come on!"

"Sure, why not? Sometime maybe."

He took the pictures from Pamela and looked at them. Pamela, who was watching him, shivered again.

"What's the matter with you?"

"I don't know," she said.

"Look at her big Republican butt," Strickland said fondly.

"She has a *derrière poire*," Pamela declared.

"Yes? And what's that?"

"It means her bum is pear-shaped."

"Yeah? Is that good?"

"I think they like it in France. I got it from a Frenchman."

"And who did he say it about? You?"

"Actually," she told Strickland, "he said it about Kim Basinger. The actress."

But Strickland was less interested in the answer to his question than in the photograph before him. It was a shot of Owen, Anne and their daughter, Maggie, together, taken by some houseguest the year before, a shot so theatrical and portentous it was hard to believe it had not been contrived. All the same, Strickland understood that it could not have been. It showed the Brownes against a stormy horizon, facing the dark gray ocean. Their gray slacks and sweaters matched the tones of sea and sky and gave the picture a monochromatic feeling. Stoutly, the three of them faced the gathering storm. Anne Browne and her daughter shared the same vocabulary of features and, in this picture, the same exalted, fateful smile. Browne seemed to have thrust himself between his women and the elements.

"Jesus," Strickland said.

"I love the kid," Pamela said. "I'd like to lick her."

"God," Strickland said, "I've got hold of something here. Let me not blow it. Because if I pull this off it will be something."

Pamela waved an imaginary flag.

"Yay, Ron! Go for it!"

16

ONE MILD spring afternoon, Strickland took lunch with Captain Riggs-Bowen on the premises of a Manhattan club of which the captain was a member. Amid the mellow clutter of books, faded oil paintings and antique statuary they raised their drinks to each other. A pleasant breeze stirred the long lace curtains. Evian water was Riggs-Bowen's chosen *aperitivo*.

"I thought that was good about Browne," the captain told Strickland. "Your 'eyes of a poet' line. I had to laugh at that."

"Thanks," said Strickland modestly. "And what do they think of him at the Southchester? Browne, I mean."

Riggs-Bowen was dismissively puffy. "Don't know that they think anything, really. The commercial interests are part of today's world, aren't they?"

"Sure," Strickland said. "That's Browne? The commercial interests?"

"Well, he's a salesman."

According to Strickland's information, Captain Riggs-Bowen had found a snug harbor as the husband of two rich American women in succession. He carried two handkerchiefs, one in his breast pocket and another up his sleeve.

"But I've seen the Southchester's m-membership. There are a number of people whom you could call salesmen."

The captain grew impatient. "Don't misunderstand, please. We're in the New World here. It doesn't matter what people do for a living or whether they do anything at all, if you see what I mean. Commercial is a state of mind."

Strickland nodded thoughtfully. "An attitude?"

"Yes, exactly. I mean Matthew Hylan, really. And Mr. Harry Thorne." He gave Strickland a guileless stare across the starched tablecloth. "Come on," he said, gently suggesting the parody of a New York accent.

Smiling, Strickland watched him.

"Harry Thorne is all over us these days," the captain went on.

"Is he?"

"Yes, altogether. He's discovered us. Discovered the world of yachting."

"Really?"

"Oh yes. And we're getting the benefit of his energy."

"He's probably a guy who likes to win," Strickland said.

Captain Riggs-Bowen seemed at the point of a remark which he visibly reconsidered. A young Irish waiter took their glasses away. For lunch, Strickland ordered the Salisbury steak. The captain chose horsemeat filet.

"Speciality of the house since the war," he explained to Strickland. "Reminds me of a vanished France."

"Do you think there's much support for Browne?"

"No idea," Riggs-Bowen said.

"Doesn't it appeal to you that his parents were English?"

Then it was the captain's turn to stammer. He appeared slightly embarrassed.

"Oh yes, I forgot. They were in service. Out on the island. Of course."

"What does that mean?" Strickland asked. "What service? What island?"

"Long Island. They were staff. At a house out there. Actually," he told Strickland, "I'm a U.S. citizen. Have been for twenty years."

"Who," Strickland wanted to know, "would you like to see win?"

Riggs-Bowen chortled. "Who, me? Neutral! Completely. A jolly good race is what we want."

"How is Browne's attitude commercial?"

The captain appeared to have trouble understanding Strickland's question.

"Well," he said after a moment or two, "look at the kind of stuff they're putting out. Do you read the Hylan press releases?"

"They're high-minded," Strickland said.

"They're bullshit," the captain said. "Hype."

"Why's that?"

"Look," Riggs-Bowen said, "it's all Thorne's way of turning ruin into prosperity. Or trying to. The club's being used."

"Wasn't Hylan a member?"

"Yes," Riggs-Bowen said. "Alas."

"I wonder," Strickland asked the captain, "if you'd consider being interviewed on camera. Sort of put your two cents in."

"Glad to," the captain said.

Strickland, who was altogether surprised at his readiness, tried to be cool.

"What I'd like you to do, see, is to tell us what you're telling me now."

"Really? What am I telling you?"

"Well, interesting things," Strickland said with all the mild-eyed sincerity at his command. "What you have to say about Thorne and the Hylan company is very insightful."

"Oh good," said Riggs-Bowen. "I'm jolly pleased you think so. Is that what I should talk about to your cameras?"

"Absolutely," Strickland said reverently. "It puts everything in perspective."

"Oh good," Riggs-Bowen repeated, and laughed in Strickland's face. "But I think not." He chuckled warmly as though thoroughly satisfied by the wine and his club and the view of Central Park.

"Really," Strickland said, "you'd provide a unique perspective."

The captain continued to bask in his own glow.

"Club history *is* fascinating. We're one of the oldest in existence on either side of the ocean. Oh yes, Mr. Strickland. We have tales to tell. Ha-ha, yes. But comments on the race? On present members? Better not, you know."

Inwardly, Strickland grew very angry. He resolved that if he could not use Riggs-Bowen's droll remarks as commentary on Browne's race, he would nevertheless make the captain regret his own willingness to appear.

"Whatever you want to talk about," Strickland said, "would be fine with us."

"We always oblige media when possible," Riggs-Bowen said. "We like to shine. But discreetly."

"Well today, understand, we're talking strictly for b . . b . . . ."

"For background," the captain pronounced, as though happy to be of assistance. "I do understand." He poured the last of the wine. "Well, the background is this: Hylan wasn't a bad sailor. He was an unreliable little Irish bastard. From Peabody or Saugus or somewhere. Still — not a bad sailor. Had the Finns make him a great boat. Which he never paid for."

"I think I know all that," Strickland said.

"You know all that. Now Thorne — who knows fuck-all about boats — has a bug up his arse for victory. So he's presented us with this Browne person whom no one ever heard of, never competed, never belonged to a club — one of his salesmen. And the theory is they take the Hylan so-called their new stock boat, Altan Forty or something, and win the Eglantine Solo with it."

"And you think that's unlikely."

"If I were you, Strickland," the captain said, "I'd look into that boat."

"What about Browne?"

Riggs-Bowen laughed good-naturedly. "But Strickland, you know about Browne. You said it yourself. He has the eyes of a poet."

"He has a certain quality," Strickland said. "It's hard to tell about him." He was hoping the captain might volunteer an impression of his own. "If you think he's not qualified, why are you letting him race?"

"Look, if they're duly sponsored, they're in. Anyway," he demanded of Strickland, "what's unqualified? Chay Blyth didn't know a sail from a bedsheet when he got into his first Golden Globe. Beginners circumnavigate all the time now. And the press love it. So if he wins, I'll be the first to shake his hand. I'll even do it for your cameras."

"You don't believe he can win?"

"The sea selects," Riggs-Bowen said, "God bless her. Hype doesn't float. And of course he may decide not to go."

"Ought he not to go?" Strickland asked with a smile.

"I wouldn't," Riggs-Bowen said. Then his eyes wandered away

from the table and an expression of singular tenderness came over his even, rosy features. He mouthed a greeting and called for the bill. Strickland followed his gaze to the exhibition room. A handsome lady of a certain age stood hesitantly among the etchings, one hand half raised in a timid greeting.

"Not me," the captain told Strickland, handing the waiter the signed bill. "Not in a Hylan stock boat." He stood up to indicate that lunch was over.

"What if he does win?" Strickland asked.

"Then good on him," Riggs-Bowen said. "You'll have a happy ending for your film. Which I'll be in, I hope. On behalf of the club. I'll talk about the race then, you wait and see. We'll all be in clover."

Captain Riggs-Bowen turned and marched toward the exhibition room with a sprightly step. "Dear lady," he crooned to the woman waiting there, "was the lunch dreadful? And how are our friends at the Urban League?"

Strickland left quietly. Walking across the park in the spring sunshine, he pondered the captain's usefulness. Riggs-Bowen was cagey but vain, a scurvy, overconfident politician. My meat, Strickland thought. Yet he had none of it on film.

On his way west, he found himself at the Mother Goose playground and, on an impulse, cut through it. Once he had picked up a young nannie there. The recollection guided his steps, a half-formed notion to check out the nurses and young mums.

An aged pigeon lady was scattering crumbs for the birds by a broken drinking fountain. As Strickland passed, a toddler ran headlong for the fountain from the bank of swings, scattering the feeding pigeons. When the flock settled down, the child charged them again and this time they took wing and made an aerial circuit of the playground. Their flight and flutter fascinated Strickland at a level beyond words. Some unspoken, unspeakable truth there, he thought. Central America. He felt ready to work again, to edit, for the first time in days.

17

HE CALLED the boat *Nona* after a boat of his father's. His father had named that boat after the sloop Hilaire Belloc sailed in the Irish Sea. After *Nona*, Browne's father had acquired a schooner of twenty-four feet and fearlessly christened it *Don Juan*. The original *Don Juan* was the schooner that failed Shelley in the Gulf of Spezia. Shelley's boat had been a hot dog, stripped for maximum speed. He and his friends had died running before the storm, billowing sails up, in imitation of the west wind. Browne's father, in his cups, could recite long bits of *Adonais*. Browne himself supposed he knew more about Shelley's boat than about his prosody.

Early in the summer, he began spending nights at the boatyard on Staten Island, sleeping in one of *Nona*'s finished compartments. He had conceived the idea of testing her living space and accustoming himself to her interior.

Each evening, at the dead end of a street on a low bluff overlooking the yard, neighborhood teenagers would gather to drink beer and sometimes to smoke marijuana. Browne would lie in his makeshift rack, listening as their mean, barren laughter drifted across the water. Later in the night, crack smokers arrived, cackling and howling like night creatures of the jungle. Some evenings he turned on his radio to drown it out. He was used to being outside other people's laughter. After a while he came to cherish his own dark solitude at the edge of the city and its voices. It was as though he were preparing a new, secret life for himself.

Browne's favorite music had always been old jazz and blues numbers from before the Second World War. He had found a station that played them several times a week and sometimes he would stay awake through most of the night with Russ Columbo,

Buddy Bowen or Bessie Smith. He started keeping a radio log, alert for pieces of any sort that might engage his ear. Certain music had particular associations for him. His father had liked Wagner and Elgar, whose full knightly title he had never failed to pronounce.

During the day, *Nona* was hauled up on chocks for her refitting. The work was loosely overseen by Fanelli or Crawford. Browne's relations with the two yardmen had stabilized at the point of awkward correctness. They allowed him to understand that they had not forgotten his out-of-season voyage up the Kill. As a result, he tended to supervise their work with a mixture of intrusive zeal and diffidence. Browne was aware of his own inconsistencies but he could not seem to break the pattern. He tried not to comport himself like a naval officer. Yet that was the only public style he had.

In spite of the tension at the yard, Browne found himself spending more time there. The nights were what he enjoyed. From *Nona*'s cockpit he could look across the harbor to the lights of Manhattan and ease back into memory. The skyline had lost some of its magic since he was a child. There were square, brutal buildings whose rectangles of light diminished the soaring, triumphant towers above them. But he could remember standing on the Staten Island ferry, holding his father's hand and seeing the pinnacles of Wall Street lit like cathedrals in midair.

It would have been a Wednesday in summer, his father's day off. His father would be slightly drunk.

"The American dream, old son," Browne's father would say. He had seemed to be laughing and crying at once, or at least his voice suggested that. Browne's father disliked the Statue of Liberty, which he associated with low immigrants as opposed to tragic exiles like himself. He disliked Charlie Chaplin films for the same reason. Chaplin was the only thing English he would not defend utterly.

Browne was aware of the variety and intensity of the moods that beset him. Part of his preparations for sea consisted of self-observation. Eventually, he believed, he would develop an interior voice, a commanding self able to cope with sea and solitude. The barometer of his inward state was finding a fair level. At the worst of times he felt much better than he had during the past sickly winter: that had been very bad, a season of paralysis and despair.

Since Maggie had come back from school, he and his daughter seemed to be coexisting. It also seemed to Browne that spending some time away from the house added to his pleasure in Anne. He believed the intensity of his marriage bed had been somehow renewed. The prospect of the voyage seemed to create a salutary state of nerves that resulted in frequent arousal. Browne had even begun to mystify his sexuality, trying to read the future, like a haruspex, in the turns and duration of their love.

One day at the yard, he fell to talking with a cabinetmaker who was building a system of lockers and shelves into one compartment of *Nona*'s wooden interior. Browne had hired him through one of Altan Marine's customers, who had advised that the man was the best in the business but independent-minded and best left alone. Browne had devised a basic weight-distribution plan and the man worked according to it.

The cabinetmaker was named George Dolvin and he altogether justified his reputation for thorough and conscientious work. Browne was well pleased with him. His tight, ingeniously fitted woodwork gave *Nona*'s interior the beginnings of a sound, ship-shape aspect that was good for morale. Dolvin wore steel-rimmed glasses and an old-fashioned green eyeshade. His hair was gathered behind his head in a graying ponytail. He was a music lover and kept the radio tuned to WBAI.

On the day in question Browne had brought over a thousand dollars in cash to the yard as an installment on his fee. Dolvin was customarily paid off the books; his employers located him by word of mouth.

"I'm really pleased with what you're doing," Browne told him when he had counted the bills out for Dolvin. Dolvin put the money at the bottom of his toolbox and smiled slightly. He was generally unforthcoming. On that occasion, though, he seemed prepared to chat with Browne.

"I'm glad to have my wood circumnavigate the globe," he said. "You can give me a testimonial."

"Got a boat of your own?" Browne asked. He was curious about Dolvin and wanted, vaguely, to continue the conversation.

"Used to have a beaut," Dolvin said. "Government got her."

Browne assumed Dolvin's boat had been confiscated as a consequence of the drug wars and said nothing further. But Dolvin's episode of extroversion continued.

"Feds took her for the taxes I withheld. After the Vietnam War."

"I see," Browne said.

"I had her up in Yarmouth, Nova Scotia, see. I'd moved up there when I was drafted but I kept working for the same contractor. Got married. Built her from keel up. Then I brought her down to Cape Ann in seventy-seven. Somebody must of turned me or something. Ex-wife, maybe. I got the amnesty but the bastards grabbed my boat."

"Bad luck," Browne said. And then, without much thinking about it, he said, "I was over there myself."

After a moment Dolvin asked, "Vietnam? No kidding?"

"No kidding," Browne said. "For four years."

"You must have seen some awful things," Dolvin said.

Browne thought the man sounded a little driven. He only shrugged.

"What did you do there?" Dolvin asked him. Then Browne had a sudden sense their conversation might take a difficult turn.

"It doesn't matter now, does it?" he said. "It's all over."

"Yeah," Dolvin said. He had adopted a tone of mock innocence as though to spy out transgression. "But what was it you were doing?"

"I'm not supposed to say," Browne told him with a laugh. That was true enough, although the electronics involved were no longer so secret.

Dolvin was sanding the edge of a drawer with sandpaper. "That's funny, ain't it? You're over there doing stuff you can't even talk about and I'm the one got to have amnesty. I'm the one loses my boat."

"I wasn't doing anything unspeakable," Browne said. "It was just classified."

"Didn't involve killing?"

"There was a war on."

"And money to be made by the corporations," Dolvin said. "And promotions for the officers."

Dolvin, Browne reflected, was a Yankee character and a first-rate worker. It was absolutely necessary to put up with him.

"The way I heard it," the carpenter said, "it was wholesale murder."

Dolvin's voice was mocking and distinctly unmusical. It was easy to see why people kept their distance from him.

"You heard it wrong," Browne told him.

"I doubt that," Dolvin said. "I doubt it very seriously."

The sight of Dolvin's unearned gray hair outraged Browne. An impulse toward explanation overcame him.

"There were supposed to be rules," he said coldly. "There were Rules of Engagement. They were sometimes violated, either in the heat of battle or by criminal behavior. But they were part of everybody's orders."

Dolvin put his tools down and threw back his head as though he would break into song. "The Rules of Engagement," he crooned in smiling mockery. It seemed to Browne that Dolvin was even imitating his inflection. "The Re-yewls of Engagement. What a crock! You sound like Nixon. I suppose you think it was a noble struggle! You sound like Ronald Reagan! The Rules of Engagement, my ass."

"You don't know what you're talking about," Browne told him. "You don't know any more about the Vietnam War than a pig knows about Sunday. You don't have a right to an opinion."

Dolvin appeared astonished. After a moment, Browne jumped down from the scaffold and walked over to buy a Coke at the machine that stood beside the yard office. He drank the soda standing at the edge of the dock, squinting across the harbor toward Jersey City. It was a hot, hazy day with hardly a breeze off the bay. They never wanted to hear that about their opinions, Browne thought. They prized their opinions, which were all they had. It was not the first time he had recited the same line. People didn't like to hear it.

Above all, Browne wanted his vessel launched without ill will. Before going back to *Nona*, he bought a second Coca-Cola for Dolvin as a kind of peace offering. Essentially, he had a low tolerance for conflict. He found the carpenter still frozen in his tracks among *Nona*'s timbers. The cabin space stank of their anger.

"Why don't we talk about something else?" Browne suggested.

Dolvin only stared into *Nona*'s bilges. Browne shrugged and left the Coke on the scaffold. He was a little embarrassed at having invoked the Rules of Engagement. They had not really counted for much. And in spite of himself, in spite of the provocation, he felt a compulsive, superstitious need to heal the quarrel.

Browne spent the evening at a Mets game with Maggie and her boyfriend, a shortstop for Portsmouth Priory of whom he and Anne approved. When he arrived at the yard the next morning, Dolvin's van was not in the lot. He climbed the scaffold, looked down into the cockpit and then saw the naked ribs and plywood of *Nona*'s skeleton. The mahogany cabinets were utterly stripped and gone, with not an anthill of sawdust remaining. At first, Browne could make no sense of what he saw. Stepping down into the desolate compartment, he found his money lying unconcealed on a folded tarp. There was five hundred dollars there. Underneath it was a check for two thousand dollars, the amount he had given Dolvin earlier for retainer and materials. He left the money where it lay and climbed out of the boat. Crawford and Fanelli were waiting for him, arms folded, deadpan.

"I guess he quit," Crawford said.

Browne gave him a long slow look. "Looks like it."

All at once he realized that Dolvin had returned the whole sum, and that the yardmen had stolen five hundred dollars of it. He felt certain of this. It was as much as they had dared to take.

"You must of hurt his feelings," Fanelli said with labored seriousness. "You must of criticized him, am I right?"

"No," Browne said, "you're not."

"He was into last night gettin' everything together," Crawford volunteered. "He had his old lady out here. They put it all in his van."

"What do you think you're gonna do?" Fanelli asked innocently.

"I don't know," Browne said. "What would you do?"

"Jeez," Fanelli said. "Shit if I know. So," he asked Browne, "you argue with him or what?"

"I told him I was in Vietnam," Browne said. "That seemed to bother him a lot."

For an instant, Crawford and Fanelli looked genuinely surprised.

"George Dolvin," Crawford said. "He's a hotheaded guy. People used to say he was a mad bomber. Been in jail." He turned to Fanelli. "What was it about? Abortion?"

"That's right," Fanelli said. "Abortion and the bomb and stuff."

"I think he's like religious," Crawford said. "Seventh Day or something. His wife's the same."

"He better fucking pray," Browne said, "if he's damaged that boat."

When Browne and Crawford examined the interior, however, the frame was quite intact.

"The guy's like a Seventh Day or something," Crawford assured Browne over again. "One of those things."

"Well, we'll do it over," Browne said. "Maybe I'll do it myself."

"Yeah?" Crawford asked. "You work with wood? Cuz I got this friend, he's a carpenter. He's good, the guy. He might do it for the same price."

Browne declined to answer.

Half an hour later, he drove to a Sears off the Garden State Parkway and spent an hour or so pricing woodworking equipment. Dolvin had taken his receipts with him so Browne had no idea where he had obtained his wood. On impulse he bought a set of books on carpentry and brought them over to Staten Island with him. Then, just before lunchtime, a Federal Express truck delivered some of the electronic gear he had ordered. He spent most of the afternoon taking inventory of parts and arranging to stow them. The compartments in which he had planned to place the major equipment no longer existed.

For a few minutes, late in the afternoon, he found himself completely overcome with rage. It bore down on him so violently that he was afraid to so much as reach out a hand. He hid from the yardbirds in the innards of his boat. Motionless, sweating in the close space, he tried to will it away. But the anger seemed capable of crushing him, will, intellect and all. With his arms folded, his eyes closed, he sat trembling at the bottom of the companionway and made himself eat it. Swallow it whole.

Driving back that evening, he began to worry about money again. It began to seem to him that Thorne's guaranteed eighty thousand might not be quite enough to cover the trip. He was determined not to cut corners.

Once home, he cooked a quick stir-fry dinner for himself and Anne. Somehow he could not bring himself to tell her about the business with Dolvin. It was too bad, he thought, because he knew the story would engage both her indignation and her sense of the absurd. He wanted her company in the business. But he said nothing.

Anne had been buying books and making lists. From book-shops, chandleries, maritime museums and libraries she was acquiring checklists, texts on meteorology and the journals of solitary sailors. At home, she continually revised her own inventory of necessities for *Nona*. At the office, she worked on old Magowan, trying to worry him and *Underway* magazine into an arrangement for a series of articles about Owen's voyage. She had determined that a book must come out of it, a book they would write together. The study that Owen had built for her had been converted into their headquarters.

After dinner, the Brownes lingered over the table, Anne sipping white bordeaux. She could see that he was in the grip of a storm.

"Maybe you should have stayed with *Nona* tonight," she said.

"It's you I'm after tonight," he said, "not *Nona*." He said it in a way that was not at all lighthearted.

"Maybe you've forgotten, Owen. Maggie's having a sleepover party. We'll be up to here in squealing fifteen-year-olds."

He shrugged.

"I suggest you keep a low profile," she said to him. "I hope you won't get annoyed."

"This time," Owen told her, "we'll all have to put up with each other."

From the kitchen they could hear Maggie on the phone; she sounded eager and happy. Home from boarding school, it was a thrill for her to have her own company. Her school friends visited infrequently because of the neighborhood.

"She told the same thing to Alison Moran," Maggie was saying on the telephone, "and she repeated it! That girl is such a loser. A total loser!"

Anne raised her eyes heavenward. They went upstairs.

In the bedroom he took his shoes off and settled on the covers, trying to make himself read the manual that had come with his satellite navigation equipment. Anne turned on the bedroom TV set to a special program from Lincoln Center, a performance of the Verdi *Requiem*. She lay across the bed with her chin on her hands, her glass on the floor beside her. After a while the funereal Latin began to make her uneasy. When she saw that Owen was paying no particular attention to the music she got up and turned it off. The music sounded on from somewhere else in the house.

Anne got up, went into the hallway and followed the sound. She traced it to the attic, where Maggie and four of her friends were gathered around an old set, lounging on mattresses on the floor, convulsed with laughter at the Agnus Dei. Maggie, the house comic, was holding forth at the expense of the singers and musicians over whose unlovely countenances the camera roved. Anne stood concealed at the top of the steps that led up to the loft.

"Look at them," Maggie cooed with malign delight, "they're all losers! They meet every week to cheer each other up with music. They're gross. They're absurd. They're losers, losers, losers."

This interpretation of the performance reduced Maggie's friends to a helpless, mirthful tangle of pubescent limbs. Not wanting to spoil the fun, Anne crept back down the attic steps and called up from the floor below.

"Please keep the sound down, kids."

Her intrusion produced a stricken silence that reverberated through the house.

Sitting up in bed, Owen had put the manual aside. He watched her come in and finish off the wine.

"What's wrong?" he asked.

"Nothing's wrong," Anne said. "They're having a ball."

She sat down on the bed and looked at the floor.

"Maggie has this thing about losers," she told her husband.

"Yeah," he said, "I heard her on the phone before."

"It's a word I dislike."

"Hell, it's just a word," Browne said. "They don't mean anything by it."

"It's vulgar and cruel," Anne said. "It makes her seem crass. I'm going to have to talk to her."

"You're pretty high-toned," he said, "aren't you?"

"I particularly dislike that word."

Owen laughed to himself.

She looked at him sharply. "Yes?"

"Nothing." Then he said, "I know why you dislike it."

"Really? Why?"

"Never mind," he said. He stuck a pillow against the bed's headboard and lay back.

"I mean," Anne said, "I don't know where she gets it from."

"It's in the air," Owen said, "these days."

"The kids have this false sophistication. It's repulsive."

After a moment, Browne leaned up on his elbow. "Is it such a bad thing that they know the difference between winning and losing?"

"I wasn't suggesting they shouldn't," she said.

"I don't think kids should be taught that somehow winning is morally suspect. Or that losing is a nobler condition."

"Owen, you aren't listening to me."

"Sure I am," he said. "Sure I am and I'm concerned with the deeper meaning."

"Oh, bullshit," she said, somewhat to her own surprise. She was mildly drunk again.

He looked at her blankly, a little scandalized by her insolence. "Don't you tell me bullshit, Annie. I'm concerned with the message that gets across. Life has winners and it has losers."

"Life?" she asked.

"Losing stinks," he insisted. "Kids should know that. They should have a horror of losing!"

"I suppose you have to take that attitude," Anne said. "To prepare."

"You sound as though it was all something I invented. But I know why it bothers you so much. Shall I tell you?"

"Sure," she said, "tell me."

"Because the prospect of losing at anything scares the bejesus out of you. It's not me that's the compulsive winner around here. It's you."

"Do you really think that?" she asked.

"Yes, I do. You hate not winning so much you can't stand the sound of the word 'loser.' But you were brought up not to let on. You're very aggressive and competitive, in fact."

She stared at the floor for a while, thinking about it. Then she lay back beside him and covered her eyes with her hand. "I don't think I like it," she said, "when you tell me about myself."

"No," he said, "you like it the other way around."

They made love. He thought it went well and that he felt her rejoicing. It made him smile in the darkness. His heart was high. He could see a sun-dappled ocean, a suitably azure sky, pennants flying. The lesser forces giving way before the strong.

"Is that winning?" she asked, laughing at him. "Did you win that one?"

It was a long time before he went to sleep. Although they said nothing further he had the sense that she remained awake beside him.

18

"GREAT HOUSE," Hersey said. They parked across the cul-de-sac from it, on the highest slope of the terrace. When they had carried their equipment across the road Strickland rang the bell at the gate.

It was not a large house but clearly an old one. It had been painted white, although not recently, and its green shutters were attached with rusted fittings. There was a balcony over the front door and an uneven portico supported by squared pillars. The whole front had the charm and incongruousness of ancient, hand-hewn carpentry.

"George Washington slept here," Strickland said.

"No shit?" asked Hersey.

The house was set in a disorderly garden with hedges and arborvitae. There were two large oaks on either side of it and an iron spiked fence around the whole enclosure. Planters full of pansies hung beside the front door.

Strickland turned and looked behind them at the town that sloped down to the Sound. Between the hill on which they stood and the water's edge lay the rooftops of a city housing project daubed in black graffiti and a few disused skeletal mills.

Turning again, he saw that a fair-haired young girl had come to the door. The girl was frowning; Hersey was giving her an artificial comic smile. From the pictures he had seen, Strickland recognized the Brownes' daughter, Maggie. The pictures had not captured the girl's extraordinary resemblance to her father.

"Hi, Maggie," Strickland said. "Can we come in?"

"Nobody's here," she said.

"You're here," Strickland told her. The girl blushed and looked grave. "We've come to put your house in the movies. Didn't your parents tell you we were coming?"

She shook her head. "I didn't think they were expecting anyone. Mom went riding. Dad's speaking at a yacht club down in Tarrytown."

"Well, we'd like to shoot your terrific house if that's all right. And you too."

Maggie groaned and grimaced. "Oh, no!"

Strickland and Hersey walked around the house to the back garden, which was thick with fallen leaves and riotous with ivy.

"Are these people preppy or what?" Strickland asked his assistant. "Mom went riding. Dad's at the yacht club. Tennis anyone?"

"Real class," Hersey said. "How we gonna fuck 'em?"

Strickland appeared indignant. "What's the matter with you? You don't like my work?"

"I love it," Hersey said. "In the dark, anyway."

"That's good enough," Strickland said. "But you persist in not understanding. My subjects often fuck themselves. They discover themselves through me. In this case I'm quite sympathetic."

Strickland preferred to work with film rather than videotape and he had decided to use it for the footage taken ashore. He would then provide his solitary sailor with a Betacam and Hi Band videotape for the voyage; later, the tape and film might be married. Tape had a wiggy sincerity that appealed to humanists.

Out in front again, on the edge of the hill, Strickland considered the ways in which he might make use of the shabby neighborhood in the film. On the way up they had passed a street corner on which a number of ragged black men were gathered. It might be nice to bring them in. And to bring in also the worn frame houses in need of paint, the boarded tenements, the projects. It might be nice, he thought, to have the eye ascend in a spiral and achieve the house and the squeaky-clean world of the Brownes, Mom, Dad and little Sis, self-absorbed, oblivious on the hill. There was scope for experimentation. It was Hylan's money after all.

They set up outside the front gate and Strickland prevailed on the girl to come out of the front door and walk to the gate and open it. Solemn, self-conscious Maggie advanced with all the breezy informality of a sacrificial maiden opening the gates to fate itself. Hersey hand-held the camera.

Then she let them inside and everyone went into the kitchen, the only room in the house that was not piled high with gear.

"What a great kitchen," Strickland said, inspecting the bare brick wall on which Anne had hung omelet pans from Brittany.

"It's where we hang out," Maggie said.

"Who hangs out?"

"Well, us," Maggie said. "My mom and my dad and me."

"Your mom," Strickland repeated. He took the camera from Hersey and sighted it at Maggie. "And your dad and you. The trio."

Another one of Maggie's comely frowns obscured her face.

"How old are you, Mags?"

"Fifteen," the girl said. "I'm surprised you didn't know that. You knew my name."

"Ah, touché," Strickland said. Hersey was standing by with the Nagra recorder. Strickland turned toward him and blinked. It was an eye signal they had worked out. Hersey gave him the sound beep.

"So tell us about this house," Strickland said, and stammered as he said it.

Maggie blushed and swallowed and looked away. "Well, it was built in, umm, 1780. And it was a captain's house. The owner of the house was captain of a clipper ship that went to China in 1785. It carried ginseng." She took a quick panicky look at the mike Hersey had thrust in front of her. "And it brought back porcelain. And silk."

"You don't say," Strickland said. "And where do you go to school?"

"I go to Mount Saint Clare," the girl replied mechanically. "I'm a sophomore."

"Is that a convent?"

"It's just a regular school," Maggie said. "There are some nuns teaching there but mostly regular people." She looked around her in distress. "Would you excuse me now?" Without waiting for a reply, she hurried from the kitchen.

"Sure," Strickland said to the empty room she had left behind. "This time."

"You scared her away," Hersey said reproachfully. "You're confrontational."

"I engage," Strickland said. "That's my method." He shook his head. "She's high-strung. Like her dad. And her mom." He pronounced the household words with an edge of disgust. "The Browne Package. It's very fragile."

The two of them listened to her run upstairs. Then Strickland got to his feet. "Here's Mom now," he told Hersey. He had seen Anne drive up outside. She was out of the car, opening the driveway gate that led to a garage at the back. When she had parked the car she started for the front door. Before she could reach it, Strickland went out to her.

She was wearing fitted rust-colored breeches and black boots, a short-sleeved polo shirt and a riding hard-hat. She had a pair of tan gloves in her hand. The sight of her rocked him.

"How'd you get in?" she asked him.

"M-Maggie let us in. Are you annoyed?"

"I guess not," she said. "But we weren't expecting you."

"I spoke to your husband yesterday," Strickland said. "He must have forgotten."

Anne pursed her lips and shrugged. Strickland was trying to remember their most recent conversation. Which aspect of himself, he wondered, had he last left with her? As he faced her in the front yard, his thoughts were not of pound cake. The slow pain of desire assailed him, musk in the throat.

"What's he doing?" Anne asked.

She meant Hersey, who had gone into the back garden and was looking over the roofs of town toward the Sound.

"He's looking for shots," Strickland said. "You know, checking it out."

While she was looking at Hersey, he ran his eye over her. When she turned back toward him, she raised a hand to the braid behind her neck. It made him think she might have sensed his attention.

"Owen should be back in midafternoon," she told him, "if you can wait until then. I can give you some lunch."

"Very kind of you," Strickland said. "We have lots to occupy us. And we bring our own lunch."

When she started for the door, he called her back. "You're not going to change, are you?"

Anne failed to understand him.

"You're not going to take those clothes off, are you? Because we'd like to get you like that. It says something about your life."

She stayed by the door for a moment as though she were thinking about it. Then she smiled slightly, tossed her head and said, "Sorry, but I think I will change." She laughed nervously. "Sorry."

"All right," Strickland said. He watched her go inside and strolled over to where Hersey stood admiring the view.

"She has a nice body," Hersey said. "Should we emphasize that?"

"She's a big creamy bitch," Strickland said. "Let's emphasize *that*."

"Hey," Hersey said, "I think you're in love, boss."

Upstairs, Anne found Maggie in her room with a rock video on TV, trying to write a letter.

"That man is so ghastly," Maggie said when she saw her mother. She put a hand on her stomach and turned the corners of her mouth down in a parody of nausea.

"Was he asking you questions?"

"Sort of. Well, he asked me where I went to school. And I told him about the house and stuff."

Anne folded her arms and leaned in the doorway of her daughter's room.

"That sounds reasonable enough. But he *is* a strange guy, isn't he?"

"He's gnarly," Maggie said. "He's repulsive."

"I wonder how they chose him," Anne said. "I wonder what your father thinks."

In the master bedroom, she found herself drawn to the mirror on the inside of her closet door. She had been aware of Strickland's insolent inspection. Standing in profile, she drew herself up and studied her reflection, hands on hips. Her breeches were skintight. The ride had left her feeling stiff and tired. She had gone out on a whim, to rent a mount and ride a trail in upper Fairfield County that she remembered from her high school days. As a girl she had learned to jump at a stable there.

Anne was not altogether pleased at the sight of herself. She felt slack and ill-conditioned, a little overweight from days at a desk and wine in the evening. She sat down on the bed and struggled with her boots. When they were off she lay back and turned on her side, feeling utterly fatigued. Without taking her top or breeches off, she clasped her hands between her thighs, drew up her knees and went to sleep.

Later, coming out of the shower, she heard Owen's voice from the kitchen downstairs. She dressed deliberately, reluctant to give up the dim silence of her bedroom to face the male presences below. At the same time, she thought the interview might be worth watching. Owen was very articulate but he was also forthright and uncalculating. It would be better, she thought, if she were there when things took, as they just conceivably might, a wrong turn.

Before she went down, she looked at herself in the mirror again. She had chosen slacks that were schoolgirl plaid, a white blouse and pearls — a chaste and impregnable outfit. At the last minute she decided to put up her hair and wear her pendant earrings. The earrings were a double touch of theater in defiance of Strickland and his cameras. She was coming to understand the amount of public performance that would be required of her. Sometimes she was able to enjoy it. In any case, she was determined to bring it off, to be and to appear worthy of Owen's enterprise.

She found them in the living room among the stacked provisions. Her husband was seated in an armchair by the window, awash in light. Strickland lounged on a sofa across the room from him. They had lighted Owen indirectly with a standing lamp and umbrella. The setup was familiar to Anne, who had modeled as a teenager.

As soon as Strickland saw her, he stood up.

"Hey, c'mere."

"Not me," she said. "I don't want to be in it."

Strickland raised his arms in an imploring gesture and then let them fall to his sides. "You don't want to be in it? Then we have a major misunderstanding here."

"I only mean," Anne said, "that when you're filming Owen you ought to concentrate on him."

"I welcome your input," Strickland told her. "But let me worry about what I'm filming. I'd like you both here."

Blushing slightly, she took a seat on her husband's left. Owen winked at her as she sat down.

"Don't let her push you around, Ron," he said to Strickland.

"Your wife's impossible," Strickland said. "She won't even wear what I want her to wear."

"Christ," Owen said, "are you going to tell us how to dress next?"

"Of course," Strickland said.

He had been filming Browne for nearly an hour, trying to uncover him. It was what he did with everyone and Strickland liked to say that they were all the same to him. Browne seemed possessed of an enormous confidence in his own presence. It would naturally be useful in selling yachts to suburban mariners. Whether this happy-go-lucky savoir faire reflected inner certainty was another matter. Probably, Strickland thought, Browne had always found himself the smartest, most articulate person in any given room. Strickland thought it was not much of a trick, considering the rooms in which Browne had passed his time.

Idea-wise, Strickland found that Browne had a few nuggets for the camera:

"I think most of us spend our lives without ever having to find out what we're made of. Our lives are soft in this country. In the present day, a man can live his whole life and never test his true resources."

And also: "The sea is the bottom line. Out there you have the elementals. You have day and night. You have ocean and the sky. Your boat and yourself. It's a situation of ultimate self-reliance."

"The great American virtue," Strickland said. He was not averse to helping out.

"I have no shame about invoking patriotism," Browne declared. "There is a tradition of American seamanship."

"Great," Strickland said, and gave him the superbo sign, touching thumb to forefinger.

Browne went further: "I think we have to work at keeping the qualities that made us strong. I think we have to reach back and touch the past in a way. Long ago we had to fight the forces of nature. They were unforgiving of mistakes. So in winning out over them, we had to win out over ourselves."

"Those are the hardest battles, aren't they?" Strickland asked obligingly. "The ones we fight against ourselves?"

"No question about it," Browne said. "And I'm not ashamed of achievement. I'm not ashamed to prevail."

Strickland thought it interesting that Browne had referred to shame three times in a few minutes. He declared a break and called Hersey into the next room.

"I'll take sound, you shoot it. I want Little Momma in a straight-backed chair, upright, *up*tight, got it? Let's get some of her reactions. Can you handle it?"

"Sure," Hersey said.

When they went back to the living room, Strickland brought a dining room chair for Anne to sit on. She accepted it without question.

"Will you win?" Strickland asked Browne.

"I'm supposed to say yes, I suppose. So I will. Yes, I'm gonna win it."

Strickland turned to Anne. Hersey panned to cover her. She was stiff-upper-lipping it with a strained smile. As Strickland watched her, their eyes met.

"Won't this come out a little unconnected?" she asked.

"We clean up the transitions," Strickland assured her. "Don't worry about it." He turned to Browne. "What does winning mean to you? As a man."

Browne laughed. He seemed to find the question embarrassing.

"As a man? Hell, what would it mean to any man? It's better than losing." He turned to Anne as though for confirmation. Perhaps, Strickland thought, it was something they had talked about. Anne kept smiling, doing her best to look proud of him.

"What about the prize, if you get it?" Strickland asked. "What will you do with it?"

"Christ," Browne said, "that question fills me with superstitious dread."

"Then don't answer it," Anne said.

"I don't know what I'd do," Browne said. "No idea."

"Think about it."

Anne and Owen looked at each other. Hersey filmed them in turn.

"I think I'd like to write if I had time. I have a few things to say."

"Go on," said Strickland.

"I like teaching people to sail," Browne said. "It was something I really enjoyed when I was young."

Strickland looked at Anne. "Did he teach you to sail?"

She only shook her head.

"Annie was a salt when I met her," Browne declared. "She knew more than I did."

Strickland nodded and smiled appreciatively. "Whom would you teach to sail, Owen?"

"Whom? Well anyone. Kids, maybe." He looked from the camera's eye to his wife and then to Strickland. "It might be great for handicapped kids, don't you think? It would build self-confidence. And it would help train them to overcome."

No one answered him.

"So," Strickland suggested, "you have a sort of program in mind."

Anne spoke up before he could answer.

"Absolutely not."

"We have a few dreams," Browne said, "that's all."

"Let's talk about the prize," Strickland said. "How much is it again?"

Both Brownes appeared uncomfortable.

"Fifty thousand dollars," Browne said. "But there's more to it than that."

"Talk about that," Strickland said.

"There are opportunities," Browne said, and faltered.

"I really think it's bad luck to talk this way," Anne said. Then she saw that Hersey was still shooting. "Why is he filming this?" she demanded.

"Take it easy," Strickland told her. "We won't use everything we have. I told you we would clean up the transitions." He saw her turn a reproachful look on her husband. "How about letting me ask him one thing more?" he said with the parody of a guilty smile.

"Hey," Browne said to him, "you don't have to ask her permission. Address yourself to me."

"No offense," Strickland said. "It's all in a good cause."

"I hope so," Anne said.

"How important is the money?" Strickland asked Browne. "In the great scheme of things."

"It's important. I mean," he said, "money is honorable. It's an honorable goal. I'm not ashamed of racing for money."

"If there were no prize money would you enter all the same?"

"I don't know," Browne said. "The prize is definitely an incentive. Definitely." Anne Browne was watching her husband with an unhappy expression. "I mean," he went on with a laugh, "some of history's great voyages were undertaken for money. In the hope of eventual wealth. Even Columbus, actually. And Magellan."

"N . . n . . names," Strickland declared to Anne, "that I haven't heard since high school."

She looked away.

"I don't believe that anything as serious as a world race should be entered into for trivial reasons," Browne said. "Money is a rational goal. An acceptable token."

"So you're not just an incurable romantic?"

"I don't know," Browne said. "Maybe."

Then the phone rang and Anne rose — gratefully, Strickland thought — to answer it. A moment later she was back, plainly relieved at an excuse to leave the session.

"New York Nautical has the Admiralty charts I ordered," she told the men from her kitchen. "This would be a good time to pick them up."

Strickland began to stammer an objection but Browne cut him off. "Good," he told his wife. "Pick them up now and I'll make dinner when you get back."

"Fair enough," Anne said, and gave everyone a wintry smile and went out to her car.

On the way home she was surprised by darkness. A light was on upstairs in Maggie's room. Owen was in the kitchen reading.

"Good," he said, "you're back. Can I fix you something?"

Anne shrugged and took a bottle of chablis from the refrigerator.

"I don't know why," Browne said, "but I have a bad feeling about today."

"About the filming?" she asked, pouring the wine.

"I have the feeling," Browne said, "that I acted like a complete ass."

"I don't think that," she said quickly.

"Thanks," Browne said. He sounded unconvinced.

"I think it was him."

"I don't know," Browne said. "All he did was ask questions. Pretty routine questions, really."

"It was him," Anne said. "Something about the way he questioned you was off."

"I think I said some dumb things. I may live to be sorry."

"I'll talk to him," she said.

"I don't want you to," Browne said. "I'll know better next time out. Are you sure you don't want anything to eat?"

She shook her head. "You did surprise me with one thing," she said after a moment.

"Really?"

"About the money," she said. "You don't really care about it, do you?"

"No," he said. "I don't give a damn about the money. Of course I don't."

"Well, you more or less told him it was your motivation for the cruise." They had taken to calling his undertaking the cruise, Navy-fashion.

"I thought it was the right thing to say. The right answer."

She put her glass down. "But why, Owen?"

"I guess I wanted to be a regular Joe."

"But you aren't a regular Joe. Not in the least."

Browne laughed. "You're an elitist, you know. That's not considered a good thing to be."

"I don't care," she said. "You mustn't vulgarize yourself before a lot of inferior people. Publicity or not."

They sat in silence. Anne finished her wine. If the time had been right, she thought, she would have set out then and there to convince him once again of his own excellence and of her unqualified love. But the time was not.

I will give him a letter, she thought, to read at sea.

"There's no reason Strickland should want to make me look bad," Browne said finally. "The better everything goes, the better for his film, right? If I win, if I look like a champ, it's all to the good."

"I don't know about him," she said. To herself she thought, He's a snake, is Strickland. Thinking about him, she could picture a snake slithering across bright grass toward a dark cistern. "We'll see."

19

OVER THE SUMMER, they got used to frequent calls from Harry Thorne. One day Thorne called to suggest that Owen visit a person Harry called the coach. She was a kind of trainer and a kind of therapist, Harry said, and Browne might find her useful. Browne decided it would be politic to go.

The coach's name was Dr. Karen Glass. Her office was on West End Avenue in the Seventies, on the ground floor of a gray stone mansion older than the tall apartment buildings around it. When Browne arrived for his appointment thunderheads were gathering over Manhattan and, although it was only six in the afternoon, streetlamps flashed on along the avenue. The impending storm cast an expectant light.

The front door was glass, curtained and barred with iron grillwork. When he rang the bell, a light went on inside. A female voice addressed him through a speaker in the vestibule. Browne identified himself and was admitted.

Dr. Glass was a very attractive blond woman in a paisley dress of the sort that had been popular in the sixties. She came to the doorway of her office to greet him. A bicycle was propped against the wall beside it. On the left, a flight of carpeted stairs led up into darkness. On one step, halfway up the flight, a child's Masters of the Universe doll lay against the balustrade.

"Hi, Mr. Browne," she said.

Her office had three big windows opening on the side street. The room was earth-colored, decorated with landscape photographs, Indian blankets, an abstract oil painting in desert tones. Everything seemed positive and upbeat, although the effect was somewhat subverted by the light outside. Just as they settled down to talk, lightning broke and then thunder, and the rain came down.

"Do you like white noise?" she asked him.

"I don't know what it is."

"It's like the rain," she said, gesturing toward the window. "It's good for you."

"Oh," said Browne. He saw that the white noise came in a machine, with attached earphones.

"Can you relax a little for me now?" Dr. Glass asked.

"I doubt it," said Browne.

He declined the white noise but before long she had him talking. They talked about his parents and about life on the Long Island estate his father had managed. His mother had been Catholic, his father a fallen-away member of the Plymouth Brethren. She wanted to talk further about that. Browne declined. He explained that his father had taught him to sail.

From time to time, she would throw in some outrageous question designed to detect pathology. He had the right answers. They talked about the Academy and then a little about the war. She was trying to bring out the raconteur in him.

"I started out in Tactical Air Control," Browne told her. "Then I went to the Naval Advisory Command."

"You advised their navy?"

He shrugged.

"What did you tell them?"

"Red sky at night is the sailor's delight," Browne declared. "Red sky at morning is the sailor's warning."

"Oh," she said, "you're funny."

"The navy of the Republic of Vietnam never produced many naval heroes," Browne explained. "It did produce a number of amusing anecdotes."

Karen Glass kept smiling.

"We had these people and we dressed them up and fitted them out as a navy. They pretended to be one. I didn't advise them," he told her. "I was a public affairs officer for NavAc-V. The advisory command."

"But you did some fighting?"

"I wouldn't call it fighting. I was fired upon."

"Is sailing like being fired upon?"

He was twisting his Academy ring. She glanced quickly at his hands.

"It's the opposite," Browne said.

"Really?"

"Sailing is harmony." He hoped she would write it down. She didn't.

"Why sail alone?"

"Alone it's perfect." As far as he could tell that was what he believed.

"Do other people make things less perfect?"

"Of course," he said. They smiled at each other.

"But there's a whole other way of looking at things," Karen said. "Where something's less perfect because it's solitary. It's incomplete."

In the end they agreed to split the difference.

"Come back if you like," Dr. Glass said as he went out. "Tell us what's on your mind. Try the white noise."

He thanked her with the excessive politeness to which he was prone. On the train home, after a brief period of elation, he became very depressed. Anne met him at the station in the car.

When she went upstairs, he stayed down to read in her study. The entire lower story of the house was piled with provisions; there were stacks of canned goods and plastic jugs, heaps of new underwear in cellophane, and propane cylinders. The whole house smelled slightly of the beef jerky Anne had been making in the kitchen, drying strips of meat on the oven racks. The local butchers had come to recognize her as the person who bought several pounds of sirloin tips at a throw, sliced as thinly as possible.

From the study he could hear Maggie in the laundry room off the kitchen. He put his book aside. When she went past the study with the clean wash gathered in her arms, he called her back.

"How are you, Maggie?"

"Fine," she said. He asked her if she might put the laundry away and come back to talk. She behaved as if the request puzzled her. "Sure," she said with a shrug.

After five minutes or so she came back down. She entered the study almost furtively, brushing her sleeve across her face like the original snot-nosed kid. She could always manage a few unlovely mannerisms for his disapproval.

"What does 'fine' mean?" he asked.

"I dunno," she said. "I mean, I'm O.K. and all."

Browne realized suddenly that he had no idea what to say to her and no words to frame the questions he wanted to ask. The session with Karen Glass had left him somehow in pursuit of communication, hungry for something beyond language.

"It's been a crazy summer, I know," Browne said. "Everything's upside down. I'm sorry we couldn't get to the island. I really wanted to." Maybe, he thought, it was love he was after. The thing itself.

"That's O.K., Dad."

"So how are things on the job?" She had taken a summer job stocking shelves in a supermarket on the Post Road. Browne had not allowed her to work at the local McDonald's, where she could have made more money. The neighborhood was bad; he worried about bandits, abductors, impulsive crackheads.

"Fine," she said.

"I think it's a better arrangement," he declared. "Your mother and I don't have to worry all the time. That's better, don't you think?"

"Sure," she said. "I guess so."

"We have to talk," Browne told his daughter. "We'll go out to dinner one day before you go back to school. You can pick the place. We might even go to New York."

"O.K.," Maggie said.

"Where," he asked with grim persistence, "would you like to go?"

Maggie swallowed and pursed her lips. Her shrug turned into a shudder. She gave him a desperate smile.

"I don't know."

"No particular preference?"

"Anywhere," she said. "Wherever you want."

Before he could take it any further, Anne called down to them from the top of the stairs.

"Owen? Coming up?"

He and Maggie held each other's eyes for a moment, complicit in their secret struggle.

"Yes," he called back. "Right now."

"I don't know what the problem is with her," Browne said to

Anne as he undressed. "My presence seems to strike her deaf, dumb and blind. She behaves as if I'm her enemy."

"She'll get over it, Owen. Really."

"I read a piece last week," he said, "about sustained marijuana use. Apparently kids lose their vitality. They become passive. I can't help but wonder if that isn't the problem."

Anne only laughed. "It isn't. Believe me."

"I don't know how you can be so certain. The stuff's all around her at school."

Anne shook her head, climbed beneath the covers and closed her eyes. Then she asked, "How did it go with the shrink?"

"I think it was pretty bad," he said.

She kept her head on the pillow and looked straight at the far wall. "Why?"

"I don't know," he said quickly. "I think I made a fool of myself. I have a very strong feeling of that."

He went into the bathroom to brush his teeth.

"Why?" she asked him when he got into bed. "What did he ask you? What did you say?"

"It was a young woman," he told her. "The session was very short."

"I'm sure it went fine," she said.

"No," he said. "I couldn't relax for some reason. I said the wrong thing sometimes. I felt as though I wasn't telling the truth."

"Owen," she said with a laugh, "you must be the only man in the world who gives himself such a hard time."

He shook his head gravely. Anne got up on her elbows.

"Do you think other people demand so much of themselves?" she nearly shouted. The passion in her voice surprised them both. "Do you think anyone but you cares so much about things like the truth?"

He laughed and then realized that she must have been drinking. "Don't they?"

"Not in this country," she said. "Not in this day and age."

20

RUNNING ALONG the beach at the end of summer, Browne breathed a thinner, drier air. In the cooler mornings, mists rose like smoke from the Sound. Time grew shorter by the day.

The house to which he returned after each morning run had taken on the aspect of a chandlery. Half the rooms were filled with electronic gear, line and sailcloth, canned goods and charts. The reek of smoked meat, as they continued their experiments with jerky, varying the marinade to suit his taste, had seeped into the very woodwork. Its increasingly disagreeable presence left him disinclined to bring the stuff at all.

Anne had set up a computer system through which they could track the state of equipment and monitor orders and purchases. She spent most of her time in the office ordering charts, fielding requests for interviews and offers of sponsorship. For transport between the house and the yard in Staten Island, they bought a used Dodge van. Maggie had gone to a ranch in Colorado for the last weeks before school opened.

Ten days before the date set for *Nona*'s shakedown cruise, Anne took a call from Mary Ward. Mary and Buzz were going to a fishing lodge in Minnesota that belonged to Mary's brother. They wondered if Anne would care to come along.

"In case you wanted to get away," Mary said.

"Absolutely not. It's too exciting. I'm working around the clock."

"I told Buzz I thought you would be. He made me call."

"Call me after Owen goes," Anne said. "That's when I'll want company." Then she added, "Maybe Owen should go for a few days. I think he's overtrained."

"We'd love that," Mary said at once. "Ask him."

When she asked him, he declined energetically but by evening he had changed his mind. The next afternoon he was in a commuter plane, flying north from Minneapolis, watching cloud shadows drift across the forest.

Buzz drove him from Ely airport. At the road's end they climbed into a canoe and motored across to the west shore of a narrow lake bounded by dark pines. Night had fallen by the time they arrived at the lodge and it was cold. Mary, waiting for them, had made a fire.

The first evening went strangely. At dinner, it was as though he tried to tell them too much. Their deepening silence made him feel garrulous. He began to fill it with his own speculation — that he had offended them in some way, that they were critical of his preparations or thought him boastful or boring. He regarded them both very highly but in the past he had always been able to relax in their company. After dinner, there were embarrassing silences. Buzz had two bourbons and water, claimed fatigue and went to bed, leaving Browne and Mary together.

Mary's brother was a cardiologist affiliated with the Mayo Clinic and his lodge was the house of a sensitive outdoorsman. There were antique stuffed birds and sheepskin rugs and Sierra Club books on the coffee table. Over the mantelpiece was an enormous grayling he had taken on a self-tied fly in the Northwest Territory.

Mary sat knitting in a rocker before the fire, her eyes lowered, a leftover smile on her face. She was exactly the same age as Anne but she had gone gray and her small-boned figure had waxed matronly. Browne watched her secretly but she caught him at it and widened her smile a moment for him and looked away.

"Mary," he said, "what's the matter with us?"

She laughed without looking up.

"You're not angry," he asked, "are you?"

Since the Wards had taken up religion, Mary's politics had sheared leftward. She and the Brownes sometimes found themselves on different sides during the age of Reagan.

"Owen," she said, laughing again, "what should I be angry about?"

"I don't know," he said. "Why should things be so awkward between us?"

He watched her blush like a teenager.

"You're very tense," she said. "It's natural. Anne says you're overtrained."

"So you think it's me, do you?"

"Yes, I do," she said without looking up. "You need to relax. That's why you're here."

Browne sighed and took himself off to bed. On a shelf in the guest room he found Stanley Karnow's history of the Vietnam War and began to read it. Though he had read it before, he found himself unable to put it aside. When Ward came to wake him just before dawn, he was still reading.

They went east with a light outboard powering the cardiologist's North Star wooden canoe. In mid-morning, Ward, who was fishing with unbarbed hooks, caught a northern pike. Wearing rubber gloves, he seized it by the eyes and removed the hook. The fish shimmied to shake off the touch of humanity and dived free.

"Tough love," said Ward.

They talked a little about their friend Teddy. Teddy was alone. He had been arrested after a drunken automobile accident. They had no ideas.

In the late afternoon, near the mouth of a stream, they caught four brookies for dinner. For the night's camp they chose a small island, pitching the tent in a level place close to the water where they would see the sunset and get wind enough to discourage the mosquitoes. A pileated woodpecker came down to drink not twenty feet away from their camp. When the fire was going, Ward drank bourbon while Browne cleaned the fish.

"Have a drink, Owen," Ward said.

"It's wasted on me."

"Have a drink, goddam it."

So after he had finished with the trout and washed up, Browne sat down by the fire and had a cup of bourbon and lake water to oblige his friend.

"I think Mary's pissed at me," Browne said when he had drunk the bourbon. "Damned if I know why."

Ward grunted. "Pissed at you? Goddam, man, Mary's not pissed at you. Quite the contrary."

Browne was flushed with the whiskey. He took a handful of water from a cooking pot to cool his face.

"So you're well known now," Ward announced. "You're in the magazines." *Sports Illustrated* had run a feature on the race with the contestants' photographs in a box. "I suppose the women will be after you."

"Better believe it," said Browne.

"Well, I hope you'll have the wherewithal to turn them away."

They cooked the fish in batter and ate them with fried canned potatoes. After dinner they washed up and slung their gear over a high limb in case there were bears out bathing. Ward kept the whiskey beside him.

"It was hard to talk last night," Browne said as they watched the fire. "Hard to relax."

"The pressure of great events," Ward said. "Great deeds."

"I almost forgot about it," Browne said. "I put it out of my mind."

Ward nodded silently. A loon cried on some distant lake.

"This is changing my life," Browne said.

"I would think so."

"The way it came about is so peculiar."

"I guess that's right," Ward said.

"If I believed in providence . . ." he began, and let the thought drop. "Listen, Buzz — I'm getting something I want. It doesn't always happen that way for me."

"Feels good, I guess."

Browne leaned sleepily back against a log. "Good is right."

"Sure it does," Ward said. "I know it does."

"The only thing I ever wanted like this was Annie."

"Owen," Buzz Ward said, "I think you're naturally good at getting what you want. Once you find out what it is."

"That's the trick, isn't it?"

"That's the trick, buddy."

They looked into the declining fire and Browne said, "Sometimes I'm not sure I can pull this off. I don't have that much experience."

"You better decide," Ward said.

"Do you think I can do it?"

"I don't know," Ward said. "If you doubt yourself, maybe you shouldn't go."

"It's too late," Browne said, and laughed.

"You have commitments," Ward said. "You have a responsibility to Anne and Maggie."

"Yes, I know." He poured a little more of the bourbon into his cup and drank it, grimacing. "I have responsibilities in every direction. Never mind," he said. "I'll be fine."

"Drunk again," Ward muttered, and stood up a little stiffly.

"Wait a minute, Buzz," Browne said. Ward leaned back against a tree trunk. Browne was looking up at him across the fire. "You got through five years of those camps in Nam. How'd you do it?"

Ward eased himself back down to the ground along the tree trunk. "You're such a goddam romantic," he said to Browne. "What do you want me to say?"

"Just tell me how. I've never asked before."

"Well," Ward said, "I always had a stick to clean my teeth with. I believe that was a large part of it."

"It made you," Browne said.

"Aw shit, Owen. What the hell you mean by that?"

"You know what I mean."

"You don't understand," Ward said.

"You always had something. People admired you. We did, Teddy and I. But you came back from over there and you had taken on a power. It was unbelievable."

"Is that the way it looks to you?"

"Not only to me, Buzz."

"I lost it all there, buddy," Ward said. "I didn't die. That was my only power. Most people don't realize what not dying can entail."

"You have no idea how shitty my life has been," Browne said suddenly. "How fucking pedestrian and dishonorable. I would like to command such a power."

Ward sighed. "Owen, you're just the same as you've always been, buddy. You haven't learned a thing in twenty years."

"I haven't given up hope," Browne said, "if that's what you mean."

Ward fixed an eye on him. "Want me to tell you the secret of life, goodbuddy?"

"Damn right I do, preacher."

"Value your life. Shitty as it may be. Value your family. The war's over and you're alive. Do it in honor of the men who aren't." He stood up again. "That's it. That's all she wrote. I hope you don't think it's too pedestrian."

"Buzz," Browne said quickly when Ward started away, "what should I do? Should I go on this voyage or not?"

Ward looked away from him.

"I'm asking you that because you know the outer limits," Browne said. "And you know me."

"I wish you hadn't asked me that," Ward said.

"What's your answer?"

"I won't answer now," Ward told him. "I might be wrong. If I think I know, I'll write."

"Thanks, Buzz."

"Ask Annie," Ward said.

Browne shook his head. "I don't ask Annie questions like that. She expects me to know my mind. She doesn't want to hear my chickenshit doubts and ponderings."

"I'll tell you one thing I'm sure of, fella. Your wife knows you better than you think."

Browne laughed.

Late in the night, Browne woke to a strange chilling sound, a howling close by. He realized almost at once that he was alone in the tent. Then he heard it again, an agonized baying somewhere along the lakeshore. He climbed out of his sleeping bag, grabbed a flashlight and crawled out of the tent.

The fire was reduced to faint embers but the risen quarter-moon had light enough to reflect on the water and outline the far shore. When the sound came again, Browne saw that his friend Ward was making it. Standing ankle-deep in the lake, Ward turned his face to the sky and crooned.

"What the hell are you doing?" Browne demanded.

He knew that Ward had turned to face him. He could only see the man's outline, not his face.

"Shut up!" Ward said sternly. "Shut up and listen."

From far across the lake, from some unmeasurable distance, came the cry of a wolf — first one, then others. It was a sound out of time, pale and haggard as the moonlight.

"Thank you, Lord," Buzz Ward said. He stepped onto the shore unsteadily, and at close quarters Browne could see that he was grinning with pleasure. "What do you say to that, my friend?"

"Amen?" Browne asked.

The next morning they paddled south.

"I'm really sorry about last night," Browne told Ward. "I seem to have come unglued. You know I'm not much of a drinker."

He heard Ward's engaging guffaw from the stern of the canoe. "I shouldn't have insisted. Don't know why I did. Anyway, you didn't say anything out of line."

"I don't know about that."

"You spoke your heart, man. You can do that with me."

"I've spent so much energy being positive about this thing. The minute I took a day off and broke the rhythm I started to unravel."

"I understand, buddy."

"A weak moment," Browne said. "There must be a way to utilize negative energy."

"Well," Ward said, "you could be on to something there, Owen."

On the morning Browne was due back in Connecticut he helped the Wards cut winter logs for the doctor's house. He had first turn at the saw. When Buzz took over, he and Mary carried the cut wood to the woodshed. Once Mary waited for him in the doorway of the shed.

"Buzz said you thought I was angry."

"I did. I guess I was wrong."

"It would be very hard for me to be really angry at you, Owen. You were such a good friend to me."

He understood that she was talking about the time during the war when Buzz had been in the camp and Browne back in the States. As she spoke to him, he realized suddenly that she had been in love with him then, and he with her. They had been people of principle together.

"I guess we did the right thing," he said.

"Absolutely the right thing," Mary said. "And it was really up to you. I'll always be grateful."

"I'll always have a few regrets," he said.

She nodded and put her hand against his face. Her look had such tenderness it took his breath away, although it had all been twenty years before and she was no longer, as she had been, beautiful.

At the airport, the Wards told him love to Annie.

"You be sure and tell her to call us," Mary said. "We'll be in the East through the winter."

"You know," Browne said, "it's incredible how positive she is about this. I think she wishes she was going instead of me."

"She was always a good sailor," Mary said. When he started for the gate, she looked at him again as she had that morning. She did not reach out to him this time.

Walking across the runway toward his plane, Browne saw the Wards at the terminal window and gave them a quick thumbs-up sign. Buzz Ward, though he smiled and waved, did not return it.

21

ONE DAY Strickland was trying to concentrate on his Central American film when some footage he had taken of the Brownes came back from the lab. It was a humid drizzly afternoon, with a wet mist over the rooftops that obscured the buildings of lower Manhattan. He stacked the cans in his work space. In the next room, where Pamela lay sleeping, a radio played softly, tuned to WBAI. An announcer with a mild speech impediment was imperfectly reading the wire copy from Sri Lanka. A great many villagers in one part of the island had been cut to pieces, the corpses and odd survivors set alight. "More than one hundred," declared the leaden-tongued broadcaster. He had a touch of the Elmer Fudds.

Strickland had no choice but to imagine the scene on film. He had once spent two weeks in Sri Lanka, the most beautiful land on earth. The people there were intelligent, humorous and kind. The event described was one of those from which the viewing public required protection.

"Nice day for something," Strickland said aloud. He felt at the point of inward riot.

On the bulletin board, he had pinned a row of photographs of Anne Browne. He walked over and inspected them. Some of them were contemporary shots he had taken around the Brownes' place or in the boatyard. Some were the prints of pictures that had appeared in advertising supplements over twenty years before when she had been a teenage model. Her body then had been striking, with a behind that was about as hefty as a model's could be and the slimmest of waists. Her hips now were a little broader and her waist a little wider but she had managed to maintain the principles of her construction. She had wonderfully long legs. Between her knees and her navel, Strickland thought, she was sublime.

His reflections were interrupted by the downstairs bell. Looking out the window, he saw Hersey and Jean-Marie, Hersey's girlfriend from film school, waiting outside. He went down and brought them up in the elevator.

"Just in time," he told them.

"I love your place," Jean-Marie said. "I've never been here." She was a petite Italian American from Jersey. She had never been there, Strickland suspected, because she despised his work and dreaded him.

When his guests were seated before the monitor, Strickland went to wake up Pamela.

"We have company."

"Who's here?"

"Hersey and Jean-Marie. Now do me a favor and don't try to sell them any drugs. And keep your hands off them."

Everyone settled in front of the monitor to watch the new footage.

Pamela passed a joint around. Everyone smoked it. Hersey and Jean-Marie had brought wine and some salad from the corner Korean.

"I don't get it," Hersey said. "What are we seeing here?"

They were seeing the Brownes' daughter, Maggie, pacing beside her garden wall in Connecticut. She walked frowning, arms folded, eyes downcast. Her lips moved. She was speaking.

"Does she know you're there?" Pamela asked.

"She believes herself alone," Strickland said. "She's addressing herself."

"Sneaky," Jean-Marie said. "Poor kid."

Next they saw Browne himself, walking along a chain-link fence against a waterfront background.

"When did we get this?" Hersey asked.

"I filmed it myself."

"I get it," Pamela said. "They walk the same."

"Pamela," Strickland said, "there isn't always an *it* to get."

"You always have an it," she said.

"That doesn't mean I always know what it is."

"Yes you do," she said. "You know everything."

"But should you be filming them without their knowledge and permission?" Jean-Marie asked with affected innocence. "It seems unfair."

"What are you, Jean-Marie, a lawyer? I thought you were in film school."

"I am," she said.

"Well, tell me," said Strickland. "Should I? Pudovkin set a cow on fire. Should he have done it? I mean, who knows?"

"Shit," Hersey said, "the entire cow?"

"It's the Siberian equivalent of lobster," Strickland said. "Seals in the flavor."

"I don't think it's right," Jean-Marie said.

They watched Browne on the monitor, looking lost in thought, gazing out over the Lower Bay.

"He looks like Irving Pichel," Hersey said, "in *Dracula's Daughter*."

Everyone was amused.

Next they saw Browne groping through what appeared to be the curving stairway of a duplex apartment high over the city. He held his hand out in front of him. What appeared to be a huge red brocade curtain across the window closed out daylight.

"I call it," Strickland said, "The Blind Orion Searching for the Rising Sun."

"He doesn't know you're filming?"

"He thinks he's in the dark. It's Matty Hylan's apartment. We managed to get in. I put infrared bulbs in the light fixtures."

"So," Hersey said, "he thinks he's invisible but he's lit up like Disney World."

"What's on the walls?" Pamela asked. "Is it blood?"

"Now he looks like Bruce Cabot," Hersey said. "How come you didn't let me in on this?" he demanded of his mentor. "What am I, some fool from the real world?"

"What did you tell him was happening?" Jean-Marie asked. "How did you get him in there?"

"I told him I wanted to try something. He went along. He's an educated man. He appreciates the arts."

"That's so unethical," Jean-Marie said.

Strickland was still pondering his previous notion.

"This is a guy," he told the young people, "who understands art. He just doesn't know what he likes."

"You have to have sympathy," Jean-Marie said almost tearfully. "I mean, don't you?"

"Sympathy of a kind, yes. Sympathy is funny. It's various."

Pamela suddenly began to tremble.

"Who here saw *Lost in Space?*" she asked. "They had like this Aryan fascist family. In a nice way. There was this one show. It had a robot and a gay man. It was about an echo. From a cavern. It was like *soo* frightening. Does anyone remember?"

The people in the room ignored her.

"I mean," Jean-Marie said, "is that how documentary works? Is it really all right to impose an arbitrary context on your subject? And trick them? And blind them?"

"Jean-Marie," Strickland said, "all this time I thought you were this nice little dumb guinea."

Hersey took the plastic bowl of cole slaw from her right hand before she could throw it at Strickland. Disarmed, she bit her thumb at him instead.

"When I'm filming people, Jean-Marie, I see it this way: They're the town, I'm the clock. Get it?"

"You think you're the clock," Jean-Marie said bitterly. "Someday, man, someone's gonna be the clock on you."

22

Very early one morning Browne skipped his customary run and went to Staten Island. Sunrise found him driving past the spoiled salt marshes of the Bronx and the towers of Co-op City. At the yard he let himself in with his electronic key and went aboard the *Nona*.

The afternoon before, a letter from Buzz Ward had arrived. Browne had not had the courage to read it. He put the letter, unopened, in one of the study's desk drawers. During the night, he had awakened every few hours, thinking himself back at sea. He and Anne had planned to spend the day driving in the country and it had been necessary to leave her an apologetic note. It seemed important that he go back to *Nona*.

Once aboard, he had little to do. The boat stank of the past days' mistakes, or misfortunes or malfunctions or whatever the unrelenting fuckups of *Nona*'s maiden voyage might rightly be called.

All around him were the gauges and grids of his expensive performance equipment, stuff which even after three days at sea he had not begun to understand. It had been installed the previous week by a couple of former Navy electronic technicians. The ETs had been no help; ETs never were. ETs, as Browne knew well, were always science-fiction-reading autodidacts who tended toward Maoism, neo-Nazism or the philosophy of Ayn Rand. The two who had installed *Nona*'s performance equipment commanded no diction other than that of New Age mysticism and computer-babble.

In fact, there was no one to whom he could turn for technical advice. Now and then, Harry Thorne would dispatch a few of the company's engineers to Staten Island and Browne would have to make notes on the run and try to hold their interest. Crawford and Fanelli had performed reasonably on the shakedown cruise but he had determined not to let them see the limits of his knowledge.

It was also true, Browne had discovered, that the intricacies of marine dynamics bored him. He was used to using technology as a selling point, building syllogisms out of gadgetry for people who knew less than he did.

Sitting at *Nona*'s navigation station with a cup of cold coffee in his hand, Browne was compelled to reflect on how much he had discovered about himself since the beginning of the adventure.

The shakedown had started out in cheerful confusion. Strickland and his obnoxious assistant had filmed Anne repeatedly failing to break the champagne across *Nona*'s reinforced bow. Duffy had huffed and puffed among such of the media as he had managed to assemble. There had been a youth from the *Times,* some yachting-press stringers, a woman from the Brownes' hometown paper and a photographer from the *Staten Island Advance.* A Channel Seven Eyewitness News team had appeared, taken some footage without interviews and disappeared with it forever.

"It's on the cusp of sports," Duffy had explained. "They haven't learned how to handle it."

But the morning's wind had been a true inspiration, the wedge of a cold front whipping from the northwest at eighteen knots. Browne, Crawford and Fanelli had clambered aboard. Strickland had handed over a video camera for Browne to practice with. Then they had raced out of the Narrows on a broad reach and he had played moviemaker, crouching amidships to capture the spray across the weather bow and the web of the big bridge overhead. It was fun. It turned his head; he could imagine his own fine narration. After a while he let Fanelli take the camera.

He had used the bell buoy over Cholera Reef as a downwind mark, cut it close and headed for Ambrose Channel. Within an hour they were reaching along the south shore of Long Island in a moderate sea. From the start, he had not been able to use his electronic gear to good advantage. He suspected it had been imperfectly calibrated. Still, its automated wizardry seemed to be functioning, reading out the arcana of wind speed, boat speed, and polar curves. His own impulse was to simply watch the luff and feel for the wind, and that was what he did.

Browne was so pleased with it all that he began to imagine he might somehow win his two pressed crewmen to the cause — the day was so bright, the vessel so responsive, the sails setting so nicely. But whenever he took time to notice, he only felt their eyes on him, as though they were strangers on some subway platform in the dead of night. He had to wonder if they would ever forgive him. Fanelli, as ordered, took pictures.

The night watches passed. They did four hours each. Browne had hoped that being aboard together overnight might ease his relations with the yard workers but the two men kept their distance. He decided he preferred Crawford to Fanelli, or at least disliked Fanelli more.

On the first day, they had averaged a glorious seven knots on a steady port tack. On the morning of the second day, they kept finding holes in the wind, which would rise, gust for a while and let them down. Browne tried using his racing computer to find out the optimum sailing angle, an uncertain business in a shifting wind. It was so much easier to just read the telltales. Toward evening, with the Mohegan Bluffs of Block Island in sight, he practiced trimming sail from inside the plastic bubble that had been fitted over the cockpit for heavy weather.

That night they beat around the island's North Light. At dawn the wind changed again, shifting northeasterly and bringing rain. They spent most of the day testing the boat in Rhode Island Sound. *Nona*'s behavior had a certain consistency: very fast reaching, to windward, uncertain. Toward evening they were tacking broadly, hurrying to pass through the Race on a favorable tide. Browne forbade any use of the auxiliary.

"I think we're gonna be out here all fucking night," Fanelli told Crawford, quite within Browne's hearing.

"Just do your job, mister," Browne told him. He couldn't keep from saying it.

Off Long Sand Shoal in the dark, they came close to passing over the cable of a tug and barge, Long Island Sound's specialty disaster. Barge running lights were always hard to see.

The next morning off Stratford Point, Browne went aft to ease the backstay with the hydraulic ram and took a fall, banging his wrist against the gunwale. It hurt enough to make his ears ring and it kept on hurting. Below deck, gear had shifted overnight. He had never properly replaced the mad pacifist's woodwork.

"Gonna have to move that generator," Fanelli said happily. His eyes shone with spite. Browne was learning to hate him.

Next the plastic of his cockpit bubble began misting and could not be cleared. Eventually it would mean harassing the manufacturer for a better plastic. Even through the streaks, though, he could see the self-steering vane working itself loose aft. Trying to fix it was what landed him overboard, clutching in the last dreadful minute at the rail and sliding over, the sea rising over his eyes like disgrace.

Snorting and swallowing to catch his breath, he had turned over on his back and arm-rowed into the swells. Browne was an excellent swimmer. He had the leisure to observe Crawford bringing the boat about while Fanelli filmed him helpless in the water. Looking down at him there, the two men seemed transfigured in their joy, a pair of angels in some Last Judgment, a couple of justified slaves whose fallen master was blessedly afloat in shit.

From Norwalk, *Nona* motored home on her auxiliary. Browne remained on deck with a Navy foul-weather jacket over his wet clothes, ignoring the cold useless wind, ignoring his pain.

The somber landscapes of New York went by, the penitential islands of Hell Gate, the industrial flats of Queens and finally the towers of Manhattan. From *Nona*'s deck, the city looked utterly impregnable, thrusting up its walls against them, every building monstrous and brutal. The cable car to Roosevelt Island passed above them as they came down the East River, scurrying overhead with insect vitality. They passed, reduced to insignificance, beneath the Brooklyn Bridge.

Anne was waiting on the dock when they arrived at the yard, together with Duffy and Hersey. As they tied up, Duffy and Anne applauded.

On the drive home, she asked him how it had gone and he had said, "Pretty good. She's very fast. Handles well."

The same night they had planned dinner in New York with Harry Thorne, Strickland and Duffy.

"I can easily cancel," she said. "We'll go later in the week."

"Good idea," he said.

He was afraid of what he might tell her. He thought he might say something negative, something to make her afraid.

Browne put his coffee cup in the galley sink and went out on deck, nursing his taped wrist. Over the city, the sky was clear, the wind brisk and westerly. The yard was still with Sunday silence. After a while he went ashore and started walking along the waterfront, hands thrust into the pockets of his windbreaker. He kept thinking about rolling overboard. "What dreadful noise of waters in mine ears! What ugly sights of death . . ." He knew that one.

At the end of the yard property was a metal gate topped with razor wire. He let himself out and followed the shore along a private street of neat wooden houses. There were Neighborhood Watch signs on the telephone poles. A garage door displayed the colors of the Italian flag. Where the street ended, he eased himself around the sunburst spikes of an iron barricade and onto the cement sea wall that continued beyond it. Beside the water, a slope of littered, balding parkland rose to the squat brown rectangles of a city housing project at the top of the hill.

He met no one on his walk. Farther along, ringed with dying maples, was a deserted playground. A huge herring gull sat atop a children's slide that was slashed with black curling graffiti. There were chipped crack vials and broken glass underneath the ruined benches. Beyond the project was a cemetery, and beyond that the Veterans' Hospital and then, across a cove, the Bethlehem Steel shipyard. In that yard, Browne had reported aboard the only ship of his naval career, an attack transport called the *Mount McMurdo*. He had gone to her straight from the Academy and before leaving for Nam, a temporary billet. His first watch as officer of the deck was on her quarterdeck, returning the drunken salutes of men staggering back from the gin mills of New York.

Browne found himself among the gravestones of the cemetery.

There were rusted VFW markers and beside some of the graves small flags were stiffening on the westerly breeze. On his walks he had passed through the same cemetery many times before. Most of its fellowship had died of influenza while being mustered out of the First World War.

He leaned against the cemetery wall. Are you languid, are you weary? An old hymn. He knew the nature of his lassitude. It was fear.

Fear, he thought, was something he had come to terms with. He believed himself as capable as any man on earth of putting the spongy stuff aside and getting on with the day's business, no matter how bad the day's business might be. Still, the thing had such variety. It could change temperature and color, taste and odor, hit you high or low. Sensations of an indeterminate nature so often resolved themselves into fear.

Fear of death, he thought, no. Nor of pain, nor of other people's anger. Hardly. Neither snakes nor the cries of your well-motivated oriental infantry, startling and demoralizing though they had been one dark night, had paralyzed his hand. Still, such variety.

He was no great shakes of a sailor but of course that was not necessary. Inexperienced adolescents had single-handed around the world and the winners always looked good after the fact. It was a question of what was inside. He had begged all his life for such a chance and all his life done what had to be done and never once regretted risk or contest. Quite the opposite, he had always regretted the lost chances, played safe and been sorry. It seemed to him he was dying of the last of his youth and strength as day after gray day they went untested and his blood thickened. Now the action had come for him and he was afraid. Such variety, he thought, had fear.

On the harbor, a lighter shot past, its decks piled with coils of wire. Across the lighter's wake stood the Lady and the exotica of Ellis Island. Suddenly he thought of his conversation with Strickland, his interview given dead into the camera. Utter crap, absolute drivel! He cringed recalling it. Strickland must think him a complete fool.

On the way back, he walked through the streets of the project.

People at the yard were warned against it but there were only a few drunks and middle-aged black women walking back from church and children, little girls in taffeta, big-eyed little boys in bow ties.

It was as though, he thought, some rat lived around your heart. But not a rat — a child, a brother. Your late brother, the infant reprobate, beaten senseless by the rod, by the drill sergeants and the good nuns of life. Smacked proper but always back for more, always appearing in the clutch, the stretch, the shadow of the goal, to ask who you think you are. So insistent, so persuasive, and above all innocent, a choirboy who didn't do it, snitching on you to yourself. Terrified and enraged by the threat of accomplishment. All childish urges, excuses and despairs. No rat, no other, but snotty, weepy, fearful self, the master of most men. The contemporary God.

Had he not, babbling to that film maker, said something about all the big battles being with yourself? Something of that sort had got said. It was true enough of him. That was at the heart of his fear. In his nightmares he was powerless and craven. The sensations were so familiar that even though he had behaved well enough up against the real thing, his weakness and cowardice in dreams were more real to him than the courage he had actually mustered. When you were good and scared it could never be undone.

His fear was not of being overcome but of *failing* from the inside out. Discovering the child-weakling as his true nature and having to spend the rest of his life with it.

It all made him think of his father. Good-naturedly. Yes, he thought, I remember him fondly now. In spite of everything he was a friend to me.

23

STRICKLAND opened the street door of his building to find Harry Thorne waiting for him, offering an umbrella against the rain. Thorne had a complacent expression. He seemed eager. All spectacles, testicles, wallet and watch, Strickland thought.

"Mr. Strickland, my good friend," Thorne inquired, "how are you?"

Strickland was taken with Thorne's good-humored, patronizing manner. He stammered a half-reply and let Thorne conduct him to the limousine, a Lincoln Continental. When they got to the car, a chauffeur in dark glasses hastened out from behind the wheel, anxious to display his readiness to stand uncovered in the rain.

"Relax," Thorne told the man, and opened a rear door for Strickland. Strickland murmured his faltering gratitude and settled down in the back seat for a look at Harry Thorne. Thorne caused Strickland more difficulty in his speech than was usual. He was so avid.

"How's it going?" Thorne asked. He oversaw Strickland's attempt to reply. Some people endeavored not to stare at Strickland when he stammered. Not Harry.

"Fine," Strickland managed at length. "How's business?"

The counterquestion provoked a tight bitter smile.

"Never better," Thorne said, and kept his eyes on Strickland. "What's the matter, don't you believe me?"

"Sure," Strickland said. "I was wondering if you could give me some time in the next week or so. Before Owen sails."

The limo prowled the streets of the theater district. Thorne removed his attention from Strickland and eyed the dinner crowds.

"Pose for you, you mean?"

"Well," Strickland began, "n .. not pose, necessarily, but —"

Thorne interrupted him. "I don't want to be in your movie, Ron. Sorry, but I don't think it's appropriate."

"You have to be," Strickland said. "I'll have to convince you."

Thorne returned his attention to Strickland's person. "Why's that?"

"Because your presence is necessary," Strickland said. "Without it the story can't be told."

"What story?"

"You'll see."

"I will?" Thorne asked lightly.

Strickland swore an inward oath. He would make Harry Thorne sit in the dark and watch himself.

"Well," Thorne said, "maybe I can give you five or ten minutes on a weekend."

"Five or ten minutes won't do," Strickland told him. "Two afternoons might."

Thorne nodded. "We'll see." Strickland understood that his forthrightness had claimed Harry's attention. "When do I get to see some of it?"

"It's too soon. When he's under way I'll edit what I have."

"Good," Thorne said. "I look forward with interest."

Outside the restaurant, the chauffeur escorted them through the rain. The place was a steak house with red banquettes, racing pictures and sawdust on the floor. Its downstairs dining room adjoined a bar at which a great many boisterous and competitive New Yorkers were gathered three deep. Strickland saw Browne and his wife at a table that was only a few feet from the crowded bar. The din was considerable.

"Welcome home," Harry said to Browne, and shook his hand. He kissed Anne attentively. Then he gestured abruptly to the waiter. In hardly any time a maître d'hotel arrived. Thorne drew him aside. Strickland hovered close to hear.

"Why are my friends at this table?" Thorne asked. The man inclined his head, taking his medicine.

"You know what they say about these tables?" Thorne asked Strickland when he saw him eavesdropping. He gestured toward the banquettes over which the racing watercolors were hung. "They get the horses." With an identical gesture he indicated a horizontal intersecting the bodies of the customers at the bar. "And they get the asses. That *is* what you say, isn't it, Paul?"

"I'm very sorry, Mr. Thorne," Paul, the maître d', said. The Brownes seemed unaware of the exchange. Paul led them to a different room in which the lights were softer and the conversation more subdued. Harry walked between Owen and Anne, arms linked.

The house sent over a bottle of wine and Thorne offered it for Anne's inspection.

"But that's wonderful," she cried. "Obviously," she said archly to Thorne, "you've been here before."

Over the appetizer, Strickland watched her flirt with Harry. Her presence made him feel irritable and frustrated; he had to consciously resist looking at her all the time. It was not usual for him to be reticent with women. Generally, he was happy to let them notice his attention and figure things out for themselves. Browne himself was very quiet, Strickland observed. He was sunburned and apparently very tired, which was likely enough after a few days on the ocean. Watching him, Strickland tried to measure the bias between the man himself and the image he left on the screen.

On the screen, Strickland thought, Browne looked pretty good, a tame tiger. His features were strong but so regular that the effect was of overhandsomeness. That, together with his mild eyes, gave him a soft appearance, at least on first glance. His good looks caught one's attention but their blandness did not inspire the proper measure of respect.

In person, he did not seem so easygoing. His moves were full of anger, something the camera could not convey in the absence of perspective. At rest, his face could look quite haunted and unsound. There was something violent about Browne, Strickland decided. It was a quality he was good at spotting.

The wine was so good that Strickland, lost in his own observations, found himself smiling on Browne like a doting patron on a protégé. All at once he understood why Browne, in spite of his clean-cut aspect and beautiful wife, had been given a bad table in an establishment like the one in which they sat. His physiognomy was unlike that of a winner, Manhattan-style. In one quick look he could be seen as naïve and anxious to please and remotely dangerous.

"Younger people should understand," Harry was telling Anne, "that private commerce does not have to mean selfishness. Because you can't live and work in the name of self alone, not any more than you can live and work in the name of nothing. Do you know the phrase 'the moral equivalent of war'? Politicians use it but they don't know what it means."

Duffy arrived at their table from the bar, where he had apparently been rallying some of his fellow publicists. Owen seemed at the point of going to sleep.

"You know," Duffy announced, largely, it seemed, for Thorne's benefit, "when I first saw Owen I said right away: Lindbergh! I said it right away."

Thorne broke off his conversation with Anne by putting a hand on her shoulder.

"Duffy, does anyone but you under the age of seventy care about Charles Lindbergh? Or even know who the dickens he was?"

Having said it, Thorne looked at Anne to see if she was amused. They ordered another bottle of the same wine.

If Thorne seduced her, Strickland thought, he would have to find a way to get it in the film. The notion displeased him. He decided he thought it unlikely.

"What I mean is the personal quality," Duffy said. "The way one man can exemplify the best of America."

At that point Browne — to his credit, Strickland thought — rebelled and roused himself.

"Give me a break, Duffy."

When he saw that everyone was waiting for him to go on, Browne began to tell them about the shakedown. Together with Fanelli and Crawford he had sailed *Nona* to a point east of Block Island and back, a three-day voyage. At one point, Browne told them, he had fallen overboard.

"Where was that, Owen?" Anne asked him.

"Off Bridgeport, I think."

"Where else?" Harry asked, and everyone laughed.

As Browne told them the story of his shakedown cruise, Strickland found himself watching Anne again. She had put away quite a lot of wine. Though she continued to play the coquette with Harry Thorne, it seemed to Strickland that she avoided *his* eye. Perhaps, he thought, an interesting sign. The sight of her responding to Thorne's charm made him impatient.

"And what will she do," Harry asked Browne playfully, "while you're at sea?"

Anne hastened to answer for herself. "I think I'll read *War and Peace*. A little every night."

"You sh .. should both read it," Strickland said helpfully. "Then you could discuss it when he got home." He smiled to indicate that he spoke in fun. The company ignored him.

When coffee was finished, Owen declared that he'd had all the celebrating of which he was capable. Anne stood up at once.

"Yes," she said, "we'd better go." Strickland thought he saw a shade of hesitation and regret.

"Take my car," Harry said. "I'm staying in town."

"Thanks, Harry," Browne said. "Can we drop anyone?"

"You can drop me," Strickland said. He was slightly drunk. He should at least, he realized, have asked which way they were going.

Once in the car, they headed for the Triborough Bridge by way of Hell's Kitchen. Owen Browne apologized for his fatigue and went to sleep in a corner seat with his head thrown back against the cushion. For a while, Anne rubbed her husband's shoulder blades.

In the near-darkness, Strickland felt that she was wary of him. He regretted coming along now and being at such close quarters with her and so outside her life. He was taken with the thought that he might never, ever get any closer. The thought made him feel both lonely and angry.

Once, when they were stopped for a light on Thirty-fourth Street and Tenth Avenue, he managed a long secret look at her. Her bright silky hair was braided behind her head. The color of her eyes was nearly Viking blue, but with a Celtic shadow. Her face was strong, willful and austere, wonderfully softened by her smile. It was a brazen, faintly androgynous pre-Raphaelite beauty, daunting, almost more than he thought he could handle.

It was unclear to Strickland how she had worked her way into the scheme of his senses. Generally, he favored the mysterious and perversely turned and, on the face of it, Anne Browne was neither. No one had ever instructed her in concealing her intelligence or moderating her enthusiasm. Nothing about her spoke to his particular desires. But somehow everything about her did.

They talked a little, about the wine. When they got to Strickland's loft, she got out of the car and came with him to the door. It had stopped raining.

"I wanted to talk to you," Anne said to Strickland. Her face was flushed and she was at the edge of unsteadiness. "We must talk when we get a chance."

"Sure," Strickland said. "We must."

"I've been thinking about your Vietnam film," she said. "You definitely weren't on the team, were you?"

"Definitely not."

"Some of it's very funny. I mean tragically funny. You're a very persuasive film maker."

"Yeah?"

"Yeah. You're on our team, though, aren't you?" she asked. "You're not making fun of us, are you?"

Trying to answer, he found it impossible. Out of the question. But he had actually begun to speak and he could not make himself stop uttering the arrested consonant or put his teeth around the end of it.

"Oh, I'm sorry," she said. Then she laughed at him. Actually simpered and put a hand to her mouth, laughing at his stammer. "I'm really sorry."

"It's O.K.," Strickland said.

"We really must talk," she said, trying to bend her laughter to a polite smile.

"Absolutely," Strickland said.

Upstairs, he poured himself a drink and stood by the round window, leaning his forehead against the glass. When he had finished his drink he dialed Pamela and left a message on her machine, asking her to come over. Then he poured a second drink and dialed her again and said, "Forget about it."

24

KEITH FANELLI, his wife, Silvia, and their three-year-old son, Jason, lived in a single-family house in Tottenville on the south shore of Staten Island. The house was modest and painted yellow with aluminum siding on its front. There was an extra apartment over the garage. Behind the house was a comfortable back yard in which stood a portable gas barbecue and a redwood picnic table.

Silvia, Strickland found, was a fierce little brunette who spoke the pure and uncorrupted Brooklyn *poissard*, a diction almost extinct in its home borough. They were teaching Jason to chew gum and talk like his mother.

"I think he's crazy, the guy," Silvia declared. She meant Browne. "He wants to sail around the world? Never happen!" She turned to invoke her husband's witness. "Right, honey?"

Fanelli nodded faintly without looking at her.

"He's a fruitcake," Silvia added. "I mean, c'mon."

"Why don't you go to the park?" Fanelli asked her.

Strickland was visiting the Fanellis on a balmy Indian summer afternoon. Fanelli's fellow yardbird Jim Crawford had driven over from his house in Jersey. Strickland had brought a bottle of unblended Scotch and two six-packs of Colt .45. He had also brought a tiny Maxell tape recorder, which was concealed under his shirt. Both men had refused to speak on camera. Strickland decided to examine the legalities involved from some future perspective. He therefore proposed an off-the-record conversation and that, Fanelli and Crawford believed, was what they were having.

The three men sipped their whiskey and watched Silvia lecture Jason with mock sternness.

"Jason, don't you swallow it. No, no, no!"

"Hey," Fanelli said, "Silvia, eh?"

"Yeah," she said crossly, "yeah, yeah. He's never home," she said to Strickland. "He comes home and *we* gotta go out."

When Silvia and the tyke had departed for the park, Strickland poured more Scotch into everyone's glass.

"The thing is," he said to them, "can this guy win?"

Fanelli and Crawford exchanged a quick look and drank their whiskey.

"He's a phony," Fanelli said. He looked at them as though he were ready to fight about it. "That's all he is."

"Don't mean he can't win," Crawford said. Crawford had a Maine accent, which Strickland much admired. He could only hope the recorder was doing its number.

"Nah," Fanelli said. "He's just a fuckin' hype artist."

Crawford shrugged.

"Hey," Fanelli insisted, "c'mon man. Browne? He ain't gonna win."

"Could surprise," Crawford said.

Fanelli turned up his lip. "Nah."

"Why do you say that?" Strickland asked Crawford.

"I think he really wants to win. I mean wants to a whole lot."

"Fuck, man," Fanelli said. "He's a pussy."

Crawford shrugged.

Fanelli turned on Strickland, appealing to reason.

"He's a preppy!" Fanelli insisted. In his excitement, his voice went shrill. "He's a fuckin' salesman and he's not even a good salesman. That's what I heard. I heard it's Harry Thorne who's putting him in this race. Harry Thorne, man, Harry Thorne don't know boats. Harry Thorne started out in the glass business. He don't know shit either."

"He's like a bad officer," Crawford said, "Browne is. The kind you don't want over you. Gung-ho do-or-die bullshit. Sometimes they do, sometimes they die. Take you with 'em, too."

"You sound like you're speaking from experience," Strickland said.

"Yep," Crawford said.

"You know what it is?" Fanelli demanded. "They're hyping this boat. This piece of shit."

"Piece of shit?" Strickland asked. "His boat?"

"Never mind the boat," Crawford said.

Fanelli appeared chastened into something that might pass for silence. He folded his arms and rolled his eyes and muttered under his breath to indicate the measure of insight he was sacrificing to discretion.

"With a little bit of luck," Crawford said, "he might just take her around."

"Thorne is queer for him," Fanelli said.

"They want to sell boats, all right," Crawford said. "No question about that. He wins, we'll be seeing his picture."

Fanelli shivered with disgust.

"Me, I thought he was a total pussy too," Crawford said. "Since we went out, I ain't so sure. He's accident prone. There's a bucket on deck, he'll step in the fucker. But he might get lucky."

Fanelli appeared scandalized. It was as though he could stand no more.

"Fuck you! You wanna bet? I'll give you fuckin' odds."

"What odds?" Crawford asked.

"Fifteen to one."

Strickland rejoiced at the turn the conversation had taken.

Crawford was silent for a moment. "Tell you what," he said. "My bet would be this — either he wins or he dies. You pay me either way. If he quits or runs behind, I pay you. You give me the odds. Ten to one."

Fanelli went stock-still as though frozen by some kind of stroke. He stared at the sky.

"Fuckin' A," he shouted. The two shook hands. "You're a witness," Fanelli told Strickland.

"Absolutely," Strickland said.

25

On a Sunday afternoon, with the yard quiet, Browne looked up from his labors and saw Duffy the publicist standing on the dock beside *Nona*.

"Maiden voyages always go badly," Duffy told him.

"Who says?"

"That's just what they say," Duffy explained. "It's a proverb of the sea."

"Who says it went badly?"

"Just kidding," Duffy said. "Anyway, you owe me an interview. Anne said you'd come down here."

"Sorry," Browne said. "Not today."

"Jesus, chum, you have to talk to me sometime. You have to give me something to work with."

"Not today, Duffy."

"I have to tell you, Owen, it's not supposed to be this way. We're supposed to be hyping you to the limit."

"I know," Browne said. "One day I'll find the time for it."

Duffy studied him for a moment and nodded toward a bench on the end of the dock.

"Come with me, will you, Owen?"

Browne followed him to the bench and they sat side by side.

"Are you O.K.? I mean off the record. Bullshit aside."

"I'm perfectly fine."

"You're such a Yankee, fella. I can't tell what's on your mind. I don't even think your wife can. And she can if anyone can."

"I'm not really a Yankee, Duffy. My parents were immigrants like yours."

"No kidding? From where?"

"From England."

178

Duffy guffawed.

"That's not emigration, Owen. That's colonialism. I mean, you grew up on the North Shore of Long Island. You went to Fessenden School. I mean, it's pathetic."

"I grew up on the estate of John Igo," Browne said. "That's where I learned to sail. My father was basically a servant. My mother definitely was."

"But you went to Fessenden."

"Mr. Igo had no sons. He thought, incorrectly, that my father liked and admired him. He sent me there. Or caused me to be sent. I went to Fessenden to please Mr. Igo. I went to Annapolis to please my father."

"How about that!" Duffy exclaimed.

"Mr. Igo believed his family came from Gloucestershire. Maybe they did. Anyway, he hired all his help over there. His millwrights, his stable hands. He hired my parents."

"Your folks alive?"

Browne shook his head.

"My father grew up in a temperance household and took to drink at forty. My mother died young."

"What were they like?"

"Like gnomes," Browne said. He laughed at Duffy's astonishment. "Mother's family were exceedingly small. She had an album. Her parents had huge eyes and tiny bodies. She came from a town where everyone looked that way."

"Shit," Duffy said, "this is interesting. Only I don't think we can use it."

"Annie doesn't put it on the résumé," Browne said. He looked toward the Manhattan towers. "And my father? What can I say? On a certain level he was an English servant."

"Like in the movies, you mean?"

"I always found movie servants very puzzling. They weren't anything like my father. My father was very smart. Very well read. A big boozer once he started drinking. He taught me wine. How to taste it. How to order it."

"But you don't drink."

"No," Browne said. "That's probably why."

"How come he took a job out here?"

"I never really knew," Browne said. "He never really told me exactly. There was some secret. Or some scandal. Something got stolen. He was accused of something. He'd get loaded and complain about the unfairness of it all and my mother would hush him."

"That's a familiar story."

"Right," Browne said. "*Silas Marner*."

"Never mind *Silas Marner*," Duffy said. "It's every immigrant family's story. Every goddam one of them. It's my family's story, it's your family's. Every child of immigrants I ever met had the same family story. The big secret back in the old country. The one thing the Americans must never, ever know. It's a fucking archetype."

"He didn't think of himself as an immigrant," Browne said. "Didn't care for the term."

"Did he talk about England a lot?"

"He told me I was lucky we didn't live there. He said the English live in fear of each other. An Englishman is always spying out the high ground, he said. People like to compare themselves favorably. With anything. A log, a passing cloud. He said that here the more intelligent people are, the nicer they are, and in England it's just the opposite."

"Too bad they're not around to see you win," Duffy said.

They sat in silence for a while. Then Browne said, "Tell me something. Who should I be? Who's the irreplaceable man the public requires?"

"Somebody better," Duffy said.

"Better than me, you mean?"

"Better than them. The public."

"But there aren't really any heroes."

Duffy shook his head. "You gotta have heroes, Owen." After a moment he stood up and looked toward the soiled clouds over the Jersey marshes. "Know whom I'm thinking about?"

"Lindbergh?"

"No, man. Vince Lombardi."

"A great man," Browne said. "What about him?"

"Wrong," Duffy said. "Vince Lombardi was not a great man. Vince Lombardi nearly destroyed this country. A first-generation guy, right? Ex–Fordham football player. Not a great man at all."

"I happen to disagree," Browne said. "I think he was a great coach and a great sportsman. A good example for the kids."

"He was a fucking monster," Duffy declared. "He caused the Vietnam War."

When he got home that night, Browne told Anne about Duffy's carryings on. She laughed.

"Duffy adores you," she told him.

"Really?"

"Oh, but absolutely," she said. She had been drinking a bit. "We all do."

26

THAT NIGHT, in Hell's Kitchen, Strickland, Hersey and Pamela smoked dope and watched the footage Fanelli had taken of *Nona*'s maiden voyage. On the screen, Browne, gasping for breath in the Sound, commenced his rowing backstroke.

"What's he doing in the water?" Hersey asked. "Is he supposed to be there?"

"I don't think you're supposed to be in the water, Hersey. I think that's why you have the boat."

"You mean he like *fell off*?" Pamela asked.

"So it would seem," Strickland said.

There was a sequence in which Browne stood somewhat heroically at the helm. Strickland played the tape of Fanelli and Crawford's conversation behind it and the effect was supremely funny. Hersey grinned. Pamela was undone. She tilted over backward in the lotus position until her knees were pointed at the ceiling. Her screechy laughter filled the studio.

"So you like that," Strickland asked, "do you, Pamela?"

"Oh God," she said, panting.

"Great stuff, boss," Hersey said.

"It's time," Strickland told them, "to consider the framework here. He may win. He may not. He may die out there. We have different possible outcomes and we should be ready to cover all of them."

"You lose some of the humor if he dies," Hersey said.

Strickland regarded him with injured innocence.

"Why?"

Hersey's grin grew brighter.

"Things don't lose their humor, Hersey, just because somebody dies. Humor goes on and on. So do things. But if he does — if he actually sinks with my priceless Sony Betacam — we'll have to go with what we've taken here and offshore."

"Can you make a picture out of that?"

"I'm sure I can," Strickland said. "If he makes it we'll have a mix of tape and film which could be interesting. Intimacy matched against articulation. If he sinks we'll do a sort of *Riders to the Sea.*"

"Och, aye," Hersey declaimed in a keening proto-Celtic lament, "the sea, the sea, ochone. The cruel grave o' the sea."

Pamela started to cry.

"I don't want him to die," she said, sniffing. "I want him to win."

Strickland turned to her.

"Right," he said. "It sort of figures that you would."

"Don't you want him to win?" Hersey asked Strickland. "I mean, he's *ours.*"

"I want the picture," Strickland said. "That's all I want."

"Anyway," Hersey said, "you should worry. You got him fucked regardless."

Strickland abruptly turned off the projector and stood up. He turned on the overhead light, one that was hardly ever used.

"I'm t . . tired of it!" he shouted at Hersey. He paused and closed his eyes until he could say the rest of it. "I am fucking tired of you suggesting that I'm fucking him in some crazy way. I don't think it's funny anymore."

Hersey and Pamela regarded him with dread.

"I'm after the truth about this guy," Strickland said. "Maybe he thinks I'm his personal fucking press agent but I'm not. There's a way things are. There's a way he is. This guy, this family, they say something about how it is now. That's what I'm after. I don't give a shit about his feelings or your feelings or anybody's. Understand me?"

"Sure," Hersey said.

"That's enough for tonight," Strickland said. "Let's break it up. We have a lot of work tomorrow."

Pamela was having trouble in her life which required a considered absence from her suite at the Paramount. Strickland let her camp in his studio. When Hersey was gone and Pamela out of the way, he started running the film again. Browne coming aft over the hatches, ducking the boom. Browne in the galley making soup, glancing morosely at the camera. Browne asleep. Fanelli had a nice instinct for the right shot.

Strickland watched Browne squint into dawn — haggard, sensitive, Browne agonistes, representative of man the measure. Pamela had cried for him but it was Pamela she mourned for. If Duffy were any good at his job, Strickland thought, he would have been selling Browne to the masses. The polite yachtsman, out there for the insulted and injured, the losers and the lost. They could track him in their atlases day by day, the disappointed, the misled, the self-sacrificers, as he bore their wounds away and washed them in salt. They should all feel for Browne, Strickland thought, the soft, wet people of the world. They should all honor and admire him, the Handsome Sailor, their charioteer.

You could play a clever game of inside and out, Strickland thought, and divide humanity between those who were of Browne's constituency and those who were not.

Do I understand him as well as I think? Strickland asked himself. And if I do, why? It was a question he scarcely dared consider. He smoked a joint and had a drink and a Halcion and lay in bed awake until his thoughts were scattered.

27

THE NIGHT before sailing, Browne stood in his garden watching the lights go on in the terraces of the town below his house. Along the shore, the illuminated cars of an Amtrak train raced by. It was a clear cold evening. Venus, forty degrees over Long Island, was the evening star.

For a while he lingered among the blanched grapevines in the arbor, looking at his own house. His daughter was in her room, studying to Megadeth. Anne was in the kitchen sipping wine as she cooked dinner. *All Things Considered* was on the radio. Maggie's room and the kitchen showed the only lighted windows. The homely comforts which the sight of his house suggested made Browne feel somewhat forlorn. Before going in, he took a quick look at the sky that would be waiting for him.

For the first time in many weeks, the downstairs rooms and hallways were clear of his supplies. Everything had been put aboard *Nona*. He found Anne at the kitchen table.

"How are you?" she asked. The red bandana she had worn around her hair when they were loading *Nona* was folded on the table beside her.

"A little restless," Browne said.

A difficult silence descended on them. He cleared his throat. They had been straining every nerve to avoid portents.

"I have a feeling," he said, "that I'm going to appreciate things a lot more when I get back."

"Yes," she said, "it could be the beginning of a beautiful friendship."

They laughed.

"I think this is the way to live," he told her. "Taking hold of it."

Somehow he could not quite succeed in saying what he meant.

For months they had talked about a night-before-sailing celebration. In the event, they had simply let the idea drop. Anne and Owen had steak and salad at the kitchen table. Neither of them ate much. Maggie had a sandwich in her room under the pretext of finishing the book she was reading for school. She had come home with special permission because of his departure. After dinner, he decided to go up to her.

On his way upstairs, he kept thinking that he owed them both some kind of further explanation. He was haunted by a sense of estrangement not only from his wife and daughter but even from the familiar house in which he found himself. Things had a peculiar novelty that was both invigorating and unsettling.

He knocked on Maggie's door and went in. She was sitting on the window seat among her stuffed animals, looking out at the darkness. Her tuna fish sandwich was uneaten on its plate right in the middle of her bed. Beside it was the book she was supposedly hastening to finish, *The Bridge of San Luis Rey*.

"For God's sake," he said, "do you want your bed full of tuna fish?"

She jumped to get it and put it on her night table.

"Sorry, Daddy."

"Listen, my young friend," he said. He wanted to touch her but he could not quite bring himself to do it. "This isn't goodbye, because we'll be seeing each other tomorrow. But tomorrow is going to be sort of chaotic."

She sat on the side of the bed and looked at the floor.

"There are some things I'll need you to do for me," Browne said. "Help your mother as best you can. Keep yourself out of trouble and study hard. I'm relying on you."

She nodded and cleared her throat.

"I don't think I'll come to the boat," she said. "I have tons to read. I'll be up really late."

The fact was that he preferred her not to come. He knew it would make things easier for both of them. Nevertheless he felt compelled to stand up for convention.

"But you came home to see me off."

She gave him a trapped look.

"You're right," he said. "So be good."

A quick frightened smile crossed her face and she picked up the book, fleeing the moment. He had always found her physical resemblance to him an impenetrable mystery. Someday, he thought, the two of us will be able to speak. He bent to kiss her and she froze as she had done since the age of twelve or so, went rigid in the presence of his affection. Touching her cheek with his lips, he could feel the tremors that beset her. Outside her door, he was struck by a wave of regret.

All that evening, he prowled the house like a stranger. Odd old things turned up: his dress sword, a record of the Blackwatch Pipe Band that he had bought in his last year at the Academy and taken with him to Vietnam. He found an album that had pictures of their wedding at the Academy chapel and Maggie's baby pictures and pictures he had taken during the war. One showed the officers of Tactical Air Control Squadron Nine in their tin cylindrical officers' club. Another was of sunrise over the A Shau valley, the mists and mountains like the pattern on a Chinese screen. The sight of his youthful self preserved made Browne uneasy. It made him feel, he thought, a little like his own ghost.

On an impulse, he put his bagpipe music on the phonograph in the study. The skirling made him smile. It was his oldest record, part of the process he had developed to raise his spirits in times of danger, along with night-before-battle scenes from Shakespeare and cavalier poetry.

> Now thrive the armorers and honor's thought
> Reigns solely in the breast of every man.

It was all completely adolescent; still, it helped.

Anne came in laughing, drawn by the pipe music. "God," she said. "How long since you played that?"

"A long time," he said.

She sat down in the study's worn leather chair, took up the album and began to leaf through it.

"I often think of those times, Owen. The war. Do you?"

"Yes," he said. "Lately."

"Those were not bad times," she said. She had been drinking again; wine sometimes made her seem cool and dispassionate, mysterious. "I shouldn't say it."

"Say it," Browne said. "We had some of our best times then. We knew the difference."

Later, she prepared herself for him, did herself up in the perfumes and lingerie he favored. His feeling of estrangement persisted and somehow it increased his desire and gave her a certain intriguing unfamiliarity. They made love for a long time and finished wet and exhausted. Like swimmers, Browne thought. By the standards of his sexual haruspication, it augured well. He woke briefly, thinking he had heard her in tears. She appeared asleep. He thought it must have been a dream.

He could not sleep for long. He woke up again in the dead of night, a little after two. There were more dreams of salt water, the ocean and tears, full of anxieties he could deny in the light. He found himself lying awake and trying to remember the way in which he had dealt with fear during the war. It was as though he had known some special system then and since forgotten it.

As he lay trying to summon up his youthful courage, a thought came to him, suddenly and with a dreadful clarity. The thought had the shape of an insight and its core was the message that he was not sailor enough to make the trip. That he lacked the experience, the patience, the temperament, the qualifications entirely. As an insight it was very convincing.

In the wake of this reflection, a long-rejected possibility occurred to him. In spite of everything, he thought, he did not have to go. It would be quite possible for him to simply not do it. There were any number of sound reasons to claim: his health, the boat, considerations of family. There were a thousand alibis.

Thinking of the boat made him recall the electronic equipment uncertainly assembled in the cabin, the snaking lines and turnbuckles, the stiff, store-new canvas in his sail bags. He felt helpless at the prospect of it all. It was more than he could handle.

Lying in the dark, he wanted more than anything not to go, wanted it with an intensity that made him feel like weeping. His heart raced. Anne stirred beside him and he was tempted, in his black panic, to awaken her. Then he realized she was awake. She reached out a hand and touched his forehead.

"You're soaking wet," she said. "Are you O.K.?"

"Yes," he said. "I thought of something I want to read up on. Last-minute research."

"What?" she asked.

"Nothing worth waking up for," he said. "Get some sleep."

He got out of bed and at once felt cold. Shivering, he put on his bathrobe, went down to the study and laid a new fire in the grate. When it was burning, he sat down in the leather chair beside it, unconsciously rubbing the damaged joints of his right hand. Though his fear remained, his thoughts were clearer. He understood that he must go. He would have to distance himself from the terrible panic and go in spite of it. Within twenty-four hours everything would be resolved and he would be at sea. He remembered the cold night sky he had looked into that evening, an infinity of time before. Then he thought of Buzz Ward's unopened letter. He got up and took it from the desk drawer in which he had secreted it.

"Dear Owen," Buzz had written, "I will treat your question as a serious one. I have written down what I think are your reasons for going and also some good reasons for you not to go. I think, on balance, that you ought not to go and that you have gotten yourself into this and ought to get yourself out. Still, I know that you will choose to do the honorable thing."

Browne smiled. Buzz was a sound man and had covered the angles. The message was that he ought not to go but that he had to, now. Exactly what I would have said myself, Browne thought. He read no further but crumpled the four pages of the letter in his hand and aimed a shot at the fireplace. At the last minute he decided not to toss it. He was curious about its length, about what there would be in four pages of Buzz's veteran counsel not to venture, to eat the bread of quiet desperation instead. He decided to take the letter with him to sea.

She had awakened from alcoholic dreams to drunken regrets. Half sick and thirsty, she lay in the dark trying to place the sound that had awakened her. It was a sound, she thought, like weeping. She thought it might have been herself, crying in her dreams. She remembered reaching out and finding him bathed in sweat.

Owen was in the downstairs study; she heard him crumpling paper for a fire. Finally she gave up on sleep, got up and pulled an Irish sweater over her nightgown. When she was halfway down the stairs, she saw him in the small study, sunk in the big leather chair, looking into the fire. She realized at once that he was considering whether or not to go. She drew a sudden breath of hope and freedom.

Hurrying down the rest of the stairs, she was possessed of certainty and resolution. Of course he must not go. Of course his experience was insufficient and his preparations jury-rigged. She had always known it. It was time to say so, in spite of everything.

When she got to the doorway of the study, he looked up at her. He was desperate, she thought, that she ask him not to go. She was sure she saw it in his face. He would not abort the race on his own. It was up to her to ask him.

"What are you doing up?" he asked her.

That he considered such a thing at all, she thought, was a measure of how lost they had become. Changes, yes, but not this terrible adventure thrust on him by others, this folly, this delusion.

"I heard you," she said. "You woke me."

"Is something wrong?"

She stared at him, wanting to speak.

"Are you O.K.?" he asked.

If I ask him not to go, she thought all at once, it will be with us the rest of our lives. He will regret it forever. She would always have stood between him and the sky-blue world of possibility. She would be responsible for every boring, repetitive day as things went on and the two of them grew ever more middle-aged, disappointed and past hope. Their lives would be like everyone else's and it would always be her fault.

"You'll be starting out exhausted," she said. "You should be resting."

The weight was more than she dared carry. And, in spite of everything, she wanted him to do it, wanted him to win.

"I'll be O.K., Annie. Don't worry."

"What are you reading?"

"A letter," he said. "An old letter from Buzz. Go on back to bed."

Obediently, she turned away. She got a bottle of mineral water from the kitchen and three aspirin and took it all up to bed. Then she lay awake, heavy with fear, to wait for the morning light.

28

In the morning, Strickland and Hersey arrived before dawn and waited in the van until the first light went on in the Brownes' house. Anne let them in without a word.

For a while they filmed Browne drinking tea in the kitchen.

"His voice sounds funny," Hersey said when he and Strickland were alone.

Strickland declined to reply. He had recognized the inexpressive quality in Browne's voice as fear, that old softener of the palate and misaligner of the jaw. Fear's peculiar melancholy reminded him of the morning fog at Phu Bai. There were several kinds of sweat, Strickland recalled.

When everything was ready, Owen and Anne stood holding hands in the living room, exchanging pale smiles. They leaned forehead to forehead until Browne said, "O.K., folks, let's go."

"What about Maggie?" Anne asked. "Isn't she coming along?"

"She was up late. We've said our goodbyes."

Anne looked as though she might protest but in the end Maggie was left to sleep, or the pretense of it.

"Great stuff," Hersey said when he and Strickland were back in the van. They were driving the Merritt Parkway headed for town.

"When you're shooting it," Strickland told his assistant, "remember that he may fuck up. We have to be ready to go both ways with this."

"How much of a difference do you think it makes," Hersey asked, "what you're thinking when you shoot it?"

"I don't know," Strickland said.

In the yard office on Staten Island, Crawford told Browne that a replacement set of solar panels he had ordered late had not arrived.

"So be it," Browne said. He did not seem chastened or alarmed. Then they filmed Crawford and Fanelli getting *Nona* on the elevator and into the harbor. Fanelli kept flashing knowing looks at the camera. When *Nona* was afloat, Strickland and Hersey helped the Brownes carry cardboard boxes filled with books and music tapes aboard. There were more pieces by Elgar than Strickland had ever heard of and some nautical hearty-har by folkies such as Gordon Bok. There was some Sinatra, which Strickland assumed would have been the height of sophistication at Annapolis in the middle sixties. The rest was proper highbrow uplift, much Beethoven, the best-known baroque pieces. Among the books, Strickland spotted a Bible and the poetry of Frost, John Donne, Garrett Mattingly's biography of Columbus and some histories by Samuel Eliot Morison. Hemingway's stories. *Look Homeward Angel. A Treasury of American Humor* in case laughs were hard to come by. Your basic Great Books for that desert island.

Putting the last box aboard, Browne lost his balance. His foot slid off the end of the floating dock and down the slimy edge of a rotting piling that looked as though it might have supported a prison hulk from the Revolutionary War. When he brought it up, Strickland saw that there was blood on his white tennis shoe and on the leg of the gym trousers he wore.

"You're cut, man," he said to Browne.

"It's all right," Browne said quickly. He looked around to see that his wife was on the pier above, out of earshot.

Strickland peered into the murky water into which Browne's leg had briefly disappeared. He could make out a rusted and jagged-edged half-chock, a foot and a half or so below the water line. Browne bunched the cloth against his wound and limped aboard. He used a rag to wipe the blood from his sneaker.

"Don't you think you should have it looked at?"

"Fuck it," Browne said.

Before they cast off, Crawford shook hands with both Brownes.

"Good luck, Captain," he told Browne somberly. An exchange of forgiveness seemed to be taking place. Fanelli merely smirked and nodded. Then Browne, Anne and Strickland got aboard and they set off across the harbor, powered by a fifty-horse Evinrude borrowed from the yard. On the way over, Strickland sat with his back against the mast, shooting Ellis Island and the Statue of Liberty. They passed Governors Island close enough to inspect the Coast Guardsmen's children, lining up for class outside P.S. 109. Anne, sitting beside the Plexiglas dome over the cockpit, waved to them. Only one child waved back, a girl of eleven or so, a head taller than the others.

"Well, bless her," Anne said.

At the mouth of the East River, Strickland shot the Brooklyn Bridge looming large overhead. He remembered seeing it as a child on the Sea Beach express, kept pigeons from the Brooklyn tenements wheeling against the city sky. As a kid he had spent a few winters out at Coney Island, living across the slot from Steeplechase and the gypsies. He put his camera aside and zipped up his jacket. Obviously, he thought, the day was going to be difficult, full of time trips and empathy. Fear was contagious. Such a tender emotion, truly the mother of sensibility.

From the cockpit Browne began to recite Hart Crane. He kept one hand on his leg where he had cut it.

"O harp and altar, of the fury fused,
How could mere toil align thy choiring strings!"

Strickland neglected to film Browne reciting. He watched Anne listening to her husband. Must be love, he thought.

"Go on," he said when Browne stopped.

"It's all I know," Browne said.

"Ah," Strickland said. "Well, we don't have good sound out here anyway." He turned his attention to the mast. "What's the round thing up there? I don't remember seeing it." He was pointing to the transponder housing. "Is it radar?"

"It emits a signal," Browne told him. "The signal is picked up by a satellite and sent to a dish in Switzerland. It records my position. That's how people know where I am."

When *Nona* tied up at the South Street Seaport dock, Strickland gave Browne some instruction in the use of the videotaping equipment. Then Strickland went ashore and Hersey met him on South Street with the van. A few banners proclaiming the race fluttered on poles around the seaport complex but it was too early for crowds. They drove uptown to get the rest of their equipment.

After eleven, Strickland came back with Hersey and Pamela. They found a parking space on Peyster Street. Strickland and Hersey humped the equipment across South.

"Oh shit," Hersey said, dodging a taxi, "a carnival atmosphere."

It was so. The morning had ripened into a fair, blustery Sunday suitable for wholesome high adventure and at South Street Seaport a carnival atmosphere prevailed. In its Sports Monday section, the *Times* would call the crowd at five thousand plus. The attending public was an exercise in gentrification; there were infants backpacked onto Daddy, colorful Finnish caps and tall slender women with prominent teeth. A beer company's brass band, uniformed in red and gold, played "Columbia, the Gem of the Ocean." The fife-and-whistle mariners who had entertained at the Southchester Yacht Club, peacoats unbuttoned over their striped jerseys, stood ready to fill in during band breaks. Along South Street vendors sold hot sausages, franks and roast chestnuts.

Hersey and Strickland moved among the crowd; Hersey had the camera and Strickland took sound. For a while Pamela followed closely, trying repeatedly to insert herself into the shot. She was drinking methamphetamine and grapefruit juice from a miniature plastic bottle that said "Spanish Fly" in pink letters. Only drugs could raise Pamela at such an hour. She had become a woman about town and gone out of the life. She had an apartment in Battery Park City, a no-show job with a foundation newsletter and a weekly cleaning lady.

"Please, I want to meet them," she begged Strickland. "Really! Can't I?"

Beside the vessel, secured to the New York Yacht Club's float, Pamela got her wish. She blushed like a schoolgirl.

"Really," she said to Browne, "you're like so *brave*. I mean, that's really an incredible thing to do."

"I haven't done it yet," Browne reminded her modestly.

"But you really can't miss, right?" Pamela asked breathlessly. "Everything that goes around comes around."

Everyone smiled thoughtfully.

"Well," Browne said, "I wonder where Harry is? Anyway, I should go see the other guys."

As he started off, Pamela put her arm in his and went with him. Anne and Strickland were left together on the float.

"Is she your significant other?" Anne asked.

He laughed at her. "My what? Are you kidding me?"

"No," she said, "I'm not kidding."

"She's a whore," Strickland explained. "She's in *Under the Life*."

"Yes," Anne said, "I recognized her."

"P-Pamela doesn't have any significance," Strickland said. "She's a child of the universe."

"Is she really drinking Spanish fly?" Anne asked. "I didn't think there really was such a thing."

"Speed," Strickland told her. He thought her particularly attractive and courageous at that moment. The force of her self-control both aroused and challenged him.

Browne and Pamela, a pleasing but incongruous couple, were making the rounds of the other entrants in the race. Hersey was signaling to Strickland across the crowded concrete plaza.

"Gotta go to work," Strickland said. He walked up the gangplank from the yacht club float, leaving Anne alone beside *Nona*.

A local television station was filming Browne together with the Virginian, Preston Fowler. Fowler had taken hold of Pamela and was hugging her close. Hersey and Strickland set up and began shooting.

"I see your boat over there, buddy," Fowler said to Browne. "Looks like one of your regular forty-footers."

"It'll be our special after next year," Browne said.

"Yeah," Fowler said. "I know all about it. Well, you have the courage of your convictions, old shoe. Gonna stop and see Matty on the way around? Where is he? Down in Nassau, somewhere like that? Havana?"

Pamela made herself comfortable in Fowler's embrace. He was drinking champagne from a plastic glass, sunburned, unshaven, wearing a dirty, yellowed wool sweater. His eyes were sleepy and his speech slurred.

"Yeah, we got him tucked away, Fowler." Browne walked over and extended his hand. "Anyway, good luck."

Fowler shook his hand, avoiding his eye, pretending infatuation with Pamela.

"He's loaded, right?" Strickland said to Browne when they had left her in Fowler's keeping. "Is he going to sail around the world that way?"

Browne laughed. "He's probably been partying all week. He'll lay offshore somewhere and get himself together. Then he'll be out to win."

With Strickland and Hersey following after him, Browne sought out each of his competitors in turn. Ian Dennis was in the cockpit of his gleaming aluminum cruiser with a young woman from his publisher's office. When he saw Browne he stood up quickly.

"Best of luck, Dennis," Browne said.

"Cheers," Dennis said. "You too, mate."

The young woman, whom he did not introduce, gave Browne a thin smile.

Next he went to Kerouaille's boat, a teak-scented beauty in which the Frenchman had spent most of the past twenty years. He stopped to chat with Massimo Cefalu, an Italian naval commander who was sailing an Italian stock boat, and Martin Held, a builder from Saint Croix, who was setting out in a boat of his own creation. There was a Pole named Stanislaw Rolf, who kissed Browne on the cheek, a Dane, two Englishmen, four more Americans. If a man was not aboard his craft, Browne would seek him out in the galleries of the seaport. After a while, Hersey and Strickland stopped trailing him.

"He's really got to shake everybody's hand, doesn't he?" Hersey said. "What's his problem?"

"Maybe he's superstitious," Strickland said. They set up on the plaza among the crowds to film the banners and signal flags that fluttered on halyards over the seaport's piers. Strickland kept thinking about Browne's progress among the contending sailors. Suddenly it struck him that there might be some dimension to the thing of which he was not altogether in charge.

Later he found himself on the float dock with Anne and Owen. Hersey was dozing in the van while the band played. Pamela, as far as anyone could tell, had gone off with Preston Fowler. Out in the East River, Captain Riggs-Bowen and a young assistant were puttering up and down in a little round-bottomed motor launch flying the Southchester Yacht Club's burgee. A procession of escort and tow boats was forming up between the seaport and the Brooklyn Bridge.

"Almost time," Anne said.

"I should leave you two alone," Strickland said.

"No need," Browne said.

"It's all right," said his wife.

They both demurred so earnestly that he suspected they were anxious at the prospect of finally finding themselves alone together.

Then Anne said, "Oh my God, the panels."

Strickland looked at Browne. His face was set and pale.

"Never mind," he said.

"But Christ!" Anne said. "My God! How could I have forgotten?"

"I had to let them go," her husband told her. "They were ordered late."

"But all this time I've been buying tapes and varnishing eggs. I should have seen to it."

"It was my fault," Browne said. "I'll make do with what I have."

"I'll leave you," Strickland said quickly. "Keep an eye on my equipment."

In the plaza, he saw a man wearing a police press pass and accosted him.

"What t . . time do they go?"

He had stumbled over the words and the man looked at him with condescension.

"On the tide." He glanced at his watch. "Less than two hours, I'd say."

He went over to the van and woke up Hersey.

"They're saying their goodbyes. Let's go."

Just before they locked up, Strickland paused.

"We ought to give them something," he told Hersey.

"What do you mean?"

"Go buy a bottle of champagne," he said suddenly. "So he can drink it at Christmas. Drive over to Chambers Street or somewhere and buy one."

Hersey knew his rights.

"Bullshit! We'll lose our parking space. Anyway, it's Sunday."

"I have to give him something," Strickland said.

"Why?"

Ignoring Hersey, he rummaged through the back of the van. It was loaded with the detritus of old projects and locations: ruined stills, film cans, fast food containers, plastic bags of marijuana seeds, paint-spattered tarps. From under one of the last, he pulled out an oversized book of his Vietnam War photographs that had been published as a companion piece to *LZ Bravo*. The book was stained with coffee rings and its jacket photograph was faded but he decided to take it along for Browne.

"Let me tell you," Hersey said helpfully, "you appear a little fucked up."

Strickland ignored him.

When they got back to *Nona*'s space, Strickland saw that Duffy and Harry Thorne had arrived. Everyone stood on the float admiring a pair of binoculars that Anne's father had sent Browne for *Nona*'s journey.

"Too bad he couldn't come himself," Harry said.

"All the same," Browne told them all, "it's quite a gesture."

Anne had the same tense, almost stricken look she had worn before.

Duffy announced that he had a plan.

"You'll love this, Ron," he told Strickland.

According to Duffy's plan, Browne would spend his last minutes ashore in prayerful meditation in the chapel at the Seamen's Welfare Association farther down South Street.

"It's five minutes from here. The room is terrific — it's white wood, original glass. They have a big bell, a steering wheel, all shit like that. Has to be a great picture, as even I can tell you."

"But it's bullshit," Browne said amiably, "because I don't happen to be a churchgoing fella."

"That's true, Owen," Duffy said quickly. "It's bullshit but that's no reflection on you." He turned to Strickland for support. "He'll bow his head in manly silence. They'll put it on calendars. What do you say?"

"Why not respect his beliefs?" Thorne asked.

"C'mon, Harry," Duffy said. "Don't be so Jewish."

"Let's do it," Strickland said.

"Yes," Anne said. The men on the float all looked at her.

"No," Browne said. "Forget about it."

Aboard *Nona*, Strickland gave Browne more videotape and his last instructions. He sat at the top of the companionway, watching the lone sailor burrowing among his gear to find the last fraction of space. Browne had jammed the camcorder and tape between two two-hundred-centimeter diving cylinders.

"You planning on diving?" Strickland asked.

"I might have some underway repairs. I thought about it and decided it was worth the space."

"Right," Strickland said.

"Well, I guess I'm set," Browne said, looking up at Strickland with a smile. "It's been a long haul."

Strickland found himself unable to speak, which in itself was not unusual. He felt a sudden desperate reluctance to let Browne go. Part of it was merely technical anxiety. How to supervise a documentary whose subject was seven thousand miles away? But he felt also the blade of some intense, elusive emotion. It might be pride, he thought, in the degree to which he had occupied Browne's space with his own observation.

"How's your leg?" he managed to say at last.

Browne shrugged without answering.

"Too bad about your solar panels."

"Let me worry about that," Browne said.

Strickland felt himself shudder. He began to speak but failed again, at first.

"Don't go," he told Browne. "Don't."

"How's that?"

"Just kidding," Strickland said.

"Maybe I should not do it," Browne said, "and say I did."

Strickland scrawled his signature on the title page of the book of Vietnam photos he had brought from the van and tossed it on the navigation table.

"Good luck."

As he got up and turned away, Browne was still smiling up at him.

On the dock, he joined Duffy and Thorne. Anne went aboard *Nona*.

"Well," Thorne said, "a new phase."

"This guy is gonna burst on the scene," Duffy said. "Mark my words."

"They're deserving people," Thorne said. He turned smoothly to Strickland. "They're the kind of people this society doesn't put forward. But it ought to recognize them, don't you think? It might learn something from them."

"There's always something to be learned," Strickland said, "from people."

Thorne gave him a long and not altogether respectful look. He walked away and went to stand by himself. After twenty minutes, launches chartered by the Southchester club began towing the entries out into the East River and across the Upper Bay. Strickland had hired a lighter from which to film the departure as far as Fort Hamilton, the starting line. At the last minute he decided to let Hersey cover it alone.

"Make sure you get the city behind him," he told Hersey.

Thorne, Hersey and Anne rode in the towing launch. Duffy went aboard the lighter. Strickland stood on the dock and watched *Nona*, under bare poles, hauled out on the tide. The musical tars performed "The Leaving of Liverpool." Out in the roads, two Department of Marine and Aviation ferry tenders sounded their whistles. A city fireboat played its hose in salute. A layer of high gray cloud closed off the bright weather and the wind picked up.

As Strickland stood on the end of the pier and watched *Nona* head out, Pamela came up and stood beside him.

"Where were you?" he asked her. "I thought you were going around the world with that redneck."

Pamela shook her head and gathered the collar of her leather jacket closer.

"I didn't like him," she said. "He said lousy things about Owen."

"Like what?"

"The usual shit guys like him say."

"I understand," Strickland said.

Shivering, she looked bleakly out at the harbor. Her eyes were red. She appeared worn out, rheumy and pale.

"My God, I hope he wins," she said.

"Do you really?"

"Yeah," she said. "Don't you really?"

"I haven't approached it in those terms," Strickland said.

"What do you mean?" she asked. "It's a race, isn't it?"

It occurred to Strickland that he might want to use Pamela in the film after all, in spite of the confusion it might occasion the public.

"Indeed. Indeed it is," he said, and laughed and put his arm around her.

29

WHEN ANNE was a little girl, her father's office had been in a nineteenth-century building on the corner of Broadway and Rector Street. Visits there had always been treats, often at Christmastime, so that she remembered his chambers as decorated and cheerfully lit against the gloom of late December afternoons. Outside, there had been holiday crowds and Trinity Church and a walk to Schrafft's across City Hall Park in the winter's first exciting flakes of snow.

At Schrafft's she would have a Broadway soda and her father would tease the Irish waitress and drink whiskey. His drinks had always appeared rich and festive, an elixir, the stuff of adult happiness.

During the early seventies, Campbell and Olson had moved its offices into the sky, occupying a suite on the ninety-first floor of the World Trade Center. Whereas the old offices had been filled with ship models, company pennants and brass nameplates, the new place, as Anne still thought of it, might have been a bank in some shopping mall in space. Clouds dissolved against its sealed windows. Impossibly far below, the new landscape — gentrified North River and sleek condominiums along the Jersey Palisades — spread out like a conceptual rendering of itself.

Yet, as ever, Antoinette Lamattina, who had been her father's secretary for thirty-five years, was waiting for her in the outer office. Antoinette was old times and good times personified, Anne's gift-giving fairy godmother.

"Annie, honey," Antoinette cried. "It's been so long we haven't seen you!"

Looking into the secretary's shrewd, kind black eyes, Anne nearly choked up.

"Oh, Antoinette," she said as they embraced. She had never called Antoinette Lamattina by her first name until she herself was out of college. "You look wonderful."

So Antoinette did at nearly sixty, gray, slim and elegant, as though she thrived on chaste bereavement, frequent communion and the occasional excursion to Roseland Ballroom. She was a childless policeman's widow. Glowing, she led Anne toward her father's inner office.

"Captain! Look who's here."

Watching her father rise to meet her, Anne was at once impressed with his quickness and apparent health. He was just under six feet tall, only an inch or so taller than she. All that remained of his notorious good looks were slimness and a smooth face. His handsomeness had been of the softer, youthful sort. His regular features and fair skin had grown a little roseate.

"Hello, Dad."

"Have a look at you," Jack Campbell said to his only daughter. Smiling Jack, they called him around the harbor. Bitterly.

She had been halfway toward embracing him when he stopped her for his inspection. Blushing and self-conscious, she stood her ground.

"You look fabulous," he said. "Want a drink?"

"Absolutely."

Jack had Antoinette summon one of the illegal Irish girls the firm employed. The colleen brought them a single-malt, as irregular as herself. It was tanked across the Atlantic in barrels and bottled, a few dozen measures at a time, in Halifax. This private stock was the last vestige of the family's rum-running days.

"I watched," Jack Campbell said. He inclined his glass toward a telescope on a tripod beside one window.

"We thought your eye was on us. Thanks for the binoculars, by the way." She took a sip of the old malt. "Why didn't you come down to the boat?"

"Ah well," Campbell said. "I couldn't take the time. I get a lot done on Sunday. I don't like the crowds at the seaport."

"All good reasons," Anne said. "But your not being there was noticed."

"By Harry Thorne, you mean?"

"By Harry. By Owen. By me. When I got home Maggie asked me if Granpop had come down. I lied and told her you had."

"You shouldn't lie to her. She'll stop believing you."

She sighed and looked away.

"So," Smiling Jack said smugly after a moment, "he's on the bosom of the ocean."

It was the sort of observation to which she had learned not to reply.

"We're keeping a map of his progress," Jack went on. "Antoinette is keeping it in her office. Did you see it?"

Anne shook her head.

"Great fun if he actually won, eh?"

She contemplated her drink.

"Yes," her father said. "That would confound the whole damn world. Love to see it happen."

"You know," Anne said, "we may end up in very good shape. We could come out of all this very well."

"Think so?"

"Harry's been great."

"Has he?"

"Owen might get his own operation out of this. Maybe a dealership."

"That's great," Jack said. "Win or lose?"

"What do you mean?"

"I mean, will Harry stake him win or lose? If the Coast Guard fishes him out of the drink tomorrow, does he get his dealership?"

She sipped her drink. "Harry's a good guy."

"You realize, don't you, that Harry and his whole operation are holding the bag for Matty Hylan? He may be in no position to help you. Regardless."

"Owen will get a book out of this, Dad. He's a good writer. A video. Everyone knows him in the boating world."

Campbell got up and went to his telescope and looked down at the harbor. On the wall nearest him was an oil painting of the waterfront at night, an unsentimental balance of shadows and harsh light, painted by an East European émigré.

"Maggie's doing well in school," Anne said.

"We'll keep her in school. Don't worry about it. And your highly strung husband need never know the source."

"Please, Dad."

"Sorry. But I know how proud he is. His concept of honor and so forth."

He sounded like an anthropologist, she thought, describing, with a touch of humor, the denizen of some exotic alien culture.

"Obviously," Jack went on, "the man's got you buffaloed. You even had to wait until he sailed to see me."

"We didn't come up," Anne said. "You didn't come down."

"I take it Harry and the Hylan group are supposedly paying for this mystical voyage?"

"Yes."

Campbell turned to the window and folded his arms.

"It's such a fantasy," he declared. "By God, I can't believe it! Even of him. Around the bloody world!"

"You're just not a sailor, Dad."

"Let's say," Jack suggested, "that I'm just not a yachtsman."

Jack Campbell was a little too well spoken to pass for a true proletarian around New York harbor but he liked to think of himself as a working man. He had graduated from Yale at twenty-five, just after the Second World War, having interrupted college for the Merchant Marine. There he had advanced from able seaman to deck officer, with eight trips from Davisville to Liverpool and ten to Murmansk from Scapa Flow. Before that he had been out between college terms, as ordinary, messman and wiper, in the grimmest billets, fighting for his virtue against convicts with a bunk chain. He was not given to nostalgia about his youthful adventures.

His own father had been an even harder man, a Newfie from Kings Cove turned ship's engineer. Old Jack and his brother Donald had imposed Campbell tugs on the harbor by serviceability and terror. They had finally put it all together when Old Jack had married Anne's grandmother, a wealthy chandler's daughter whose people had once lived in shanties along Broad Channel.

"If Owen had gone to work for you," she said, "it probably would have been worse. It's a good thing he didn't."

"Too good for us," Jack said. "Too high-minded."

"I'm very proud of him, Dad." She said it with a smiling complacency she knew enraged him. "And Maggie will be."

"I suppose," the old man said, "it's an excellent way to get away from it all."

"We could all use a little of that."

"What is it they say?" Jack asked. "Get in touch with your feelings? Be your own person? Sweet self-awareness and all that malarkey? By Christ," Campbell said, "I've wrung more salt water out of my socks than that man of yours ever looked at."

"He's not trying to compete with you."

Jack laughed, as if at the very notion.

"I have guys who like to sail that work for me," Campbell said dismissively. "They're very taken with what he's doing."

"He's not like the guys who work for you," Anne said.

"Meaning what?"

"He thinks there are more important things than money."

"Am I missing something?" Jack asked. "Isn't money what you're here about?"

"He believes there are other standards. Harry Thorne understands that, if you don't."

"I understand Harry favors him for your sake."

She stared at him. "What do you mean? Where did you hear such a thing?"

"Around," Jack said.

"You guys are a stitch," she said after a moment. "You macho high rollers."

"Your husband doesn't make himself respected," Jack Campbell said.

"What passes for respect around town lately?" she asked. "If I wanted to find out about human respect" — she made a gesture that took in his office and the world it overlooked — "would I come here?"

"You have a lot of nerve, kid."

"In this place full of flunkies? Where no one knows the meaning of the word? Don't you tell me about my Owen, Dad."

"You're a couple of assholes," Jack said. "The two of you. You deserve each other."

Playing by their own rules, they sat and sipped their good whiskey and waited to calm down. She had been at the point of threatening to keep him from Maggie. Eventually she walked to a south-facing window and looked out. The sight of the Narrows, through which Owen had passed, filled her with dread. Her father's words about getting away from it all had stayed with her. She thought of Owen away from it all, lost to her.

"I can't understand your attitude," she said to her father at last. "I never could. I've been with him twenty years and I've never seen him do a cheap thing. He could have gotten out of combat. He could have gone to work for you in some overpaid no-show job like certain people I won't mention. Why are you always putting him down?"

She had spoken facing the window. She heard her father's laughter over her shoulder.

"It's not fair, is it?" he asked. "Well, I don't know."

"I know he makes some people uncomfortable," she said.

Jack laughed again, to her irritation.

"I know he's a pretty good provider, Annie. And he doesn't drink and he doesn't beat you. But" — he looked at her in slight confusion as though he feared he would be unable to explain — "you know around the docks — how can I say this — a man had to carry himself a certain way. There was one way to walk the street. One way to handle yourself in a saloon. Christ, I don't know, a way to handle yourself. He's got it all wrong."

"And that's it?" she asked.

"I know he has good qualities," Jack said. "But his best qualities don't speak to me."

"I hope you understand," she said, "that I encouraged him every step of the way in this trip." Saying it, she felt a flutter of panic in her throat. "It's something he needs to do. For himself and for us."

"Not something I would have chosen."

"Look, he loves boats. He loves the sea. Those are clean, simple things. I love him because he loves those things."

Jack's tolerant mood seemed to contract slightly.

"Romance of the sea? Christ, the ocean is a fucking desert. Nothing out there but social cripples and the odd Filipino. You don't find Americans out there anymore because we've come beyond that."

"Yes, well," Anne said, "Owen has a few things to say about the state of the country in that regard."

"Jesus," Campbell said, "spare me! I yield to no one in my

patriotism. But spare me your husband's reflections on the state of the Union."

In a moment they were both laughing.

"Is he really that good a sailor?" Jack asked gently. "Does he have the temperament?"

"He has the smarts and the strength, Dad. Believe me."

"Christ, he's really put himself on the spot, hasn't he? Do you really think he's doing it for you?"

"Yes, I'm sure of it, Dad. To make us proud of him. That's how he is."

Content she had what she'd come for, Anne embraced Antoinette on the way out. Doing so, she suddenly imagined something predatory about the woman's sympathy. She felt the suggestion of a waxen, widowy twilight the two of them might share, with windowless rooms for ballroom dancing in the afternoon. It made her straighten up abruptly.

Descending alone in the express elevator, she understood for the first time the nature of the solitude she would have to endure in the coming months. It would really be the two of them, each alone against the world, as it had been during the war. There was no support and no sympathy she could altogether trust. No one shared the risk finally.

Above all, the thought of having to endure encouragement filled her with disgust. It was too much like consolation. Winning was all, she thought. It was the only revenge on life. Other people wanted reassurance in their own misery and mediocrity. She required victory.

PART TWO

30

JUST AFTER SUNRISE, forty-eight hours and over two hundred miles off Ambrose Light, Browne sat in *Nona*'s open cockpit and looked at the western horizon. Astern, the last fat white clouds of home were falling away. A northwest wind whistled in the rigging, force 5 and steady.

Months before, on the night of Harry Thorne's first phone call, he had gone straight to the Admiralty charts and begun to plot his way around the globe. But he was not inclined now, watching the morning's white horses roll by, to chart courses. In the last hours of darkness he had dozed off and then awakened to find himself on a sunlit ocean of sultry blue — the Gulf Stream. For such a long time, he thought, he had been promising himself unfamiliar skies. Leaning over the side, he dipped his hand in the quarter wave and felt it warm. The sensation made him smile.

At some level he felt involved in an escape. His impulse was simply to head out and put the land behind him. Beyond that, it made sense to keep on easting while the wind held and get across the Stream as quickly as possible. The first weather fax had carried nothing but sweet assurance; there were no tropical storms on the prowl and no threatening northers.

Browne had slept very little since clearing the Narrows. Propped up in the cockpit against a stack of foul-weather gear, he had drifted in and out of consciousness, fighting to outlast darkness. His radar alarm was set for a fifteen-mile radius. Through two nights in the coastal shipping lanes, he had stayed on deck, scanning the dark horizon. A few hours on the sky-bright waters of the Gulf Stream inclined him to rest easy. In the afternoon he went below, cleared the last-minute gear from his bunk and stretched out.

When he went on deck again, the sun was low and the pastel water overlaid with a puritan October light. The wind was steady and he kept *Nona* eastward. In the last daylight, he checked the screws in the self-steering vane and eased the lines against chafing. According to his knot log he had come 154 miles since the day before, a speed of close to seven knots.

For dinner he cooked a can of chicken broth and poured it into his usual coffee cup, a Navy mug in the Navy pattern. Anne had packed it for him in tissue with a blue ribbon. Inside was a note detailing the boat's stowage plan. He needed only to glance around the main cabin to realize how much of the stowage she had overseen. Tossing the homely red and white Campbell's soup can in the scraps gave him a momentary flash of incongruity. Home away from home.

On deck at dusk, he sipped his soup and listened to the accommodating wind. The loneliness he felt rather surprised him. Except for Anne's presence, he thought of himself as a solitary. In his deepest recollections, it seemed to him, he was always alone.

Browne's last solo passage over blue water had been five days spent between Florida and Cape Fear. It was a passage he had trouble remembering. One time at sea blended into another when things went well, and that one had gone well enough. Some of the time, mainly at night, his mind had played tricks. It had been easy to get the wind in tune and start it singing. On the open sea, the eye tended to impose form on random patterns of wave and light. The same thing happened in deep woods. It happened to everyone.

After a while Browne found that trying to recall the Cape Fear trip made him uncomfortable. It reminded him of the lie he had told Riggs-Bowen about sailing around Queen Charlotte Island. Alone in his cockpit on the dark ocean, he rapped the heel of his hand against his forehead. The thing was so outrageous it made him laugh out loud. Of all the godforsaken fog-shrouded coasts on earth to claim, he thought, bound in killer rocks and floating fir trunks, of all outrageous lies! But there was no unsaying it. It had been a primitive spasm from some morally underdeveloped area of the nerves. Remembering it was very painful and strange.

A clear sky burned overhead, appropriate to the west wind.

Altair shone radiant over the continent behind him, Betelgeuse and Orion over the farther ocean. It was a childish pleasure to have the stars to himself again. Before midnight, he went below. He woke up dizzy. Rising, he had to cling for a moment to the overhead bar. On deck the wind was warmer and tasting of rain but still steady from the northwest. The steering vane was carrying on, heading *Nona* due east on a port tack. The circling beam of his radar showed a clear horizon.

At the chart table, he idly opened his copy of *Ocean Passages for the World*. In the morning, he decided, he would take a sighting and set a provisional course. *Ocean Passages,* for the time of year, directed him to 34° north, 45° west, from which point he might set out against the northeast trades. Browne thought he might east it even farther if the wind held. For the first time, he turned on the monitor of his satellite navigation device. Then he switched on his Icom receiver, tuned in the Naval Observatory time signals and set his watch and the boat's chronometers. At the edges of the cabin, all the wizardry, the electronic telltales with their knobs and gauges, sat dark and dusty. Browne suspected he might never even try to use them.

After a while, he felt thirsty. He went to the galley, helped himself to a few cups of water and lay down in his rack. When he closed his eyes, the dizziness returned. Browne had been seasick only once in his life, bouncing up and down off Little Creek in the beachmaster's boat during a mock invasion nearly twenty years before. It seemed perverse of things to visit the condition on him now.

He got up and dialed some progressive jazz on shortwave and turned off all the cabin lights except the one over his chart table. Then he settled back to listen to the music and tried to sleep. Shortly he was sweating. When he pushed his sleeping bag aside he felt cold. Then all at once he became aware of the wound in his leg where he had cut it on the dock at the boatyard. He sat up and turned on his overhead light.

The sight of the cut, just above his ankle, gave Browne a rush of alarm. It was covered with a scab the color of New York harbor and the skin around it was a bright red that faded by inches. Pressing beside it, he felt a dull muscular sort of pain from ankle to thigh. The wound appeared to be deep although it had not bled much. At the yard, when he had cut himself, the tide had been at ebb. So the spike that had caused the wound was one set below the low-tide line, never exposed to air. It was a classic example of the sort of puncture wound that developed tetanus. Over five years had passed since his last shot and it had not occurred to him to get a new one. Cuts were usually clean at sea.

"Bloody hell," Browne said.

Gathering himself under the down bag in his rack, he read from *The Complete Home Medical Encyclopedia,* which was part of his medical kit:

"Onset usually begins with headache, low-grade fever, irritability, apprehension, and restlessness. The first real sign of tetanus is a stiffness of the jaw and difficulty in opening the mouth. Muscular stiffness can develop in the neck and elsewhere. Most agonizingly, the patient remains alert. He cannot open his mouth or swallow; his eyebrows become raised; the corners of his mouth become upturned, giving the appearance of a perpetual grin . . ."

The radio faded out as Browne sat down on his bunk. It was extremely unlikely, he thought, that he had tetanus. But not out of the question. He got some aspirin and penicillin from the sick chest and took them with water. The more he thought about his jaw, the stiffer it seemed to him.

He slept for a while after that. When he awoke, he was sicker than before. His mouth tasted foul, his neck was sore and there was a band of pain around his temples. He felt so plainly feverish that he never bothered with a thermometer.

"Early hospitalization is essential," said the *Home Medical Encyclopedia.* "Much depends on the early administration of tetanus antitoxin."

Even if it was not tetanus, Browne thought, there were other deadly dangers. Gangrene. Botulism. He looked up each one in the medical text. Later he felt too sick to read or even get out of his bunk. Each time he moved, his body was racked with chills. Eventually, he forced himself up to check the radar screen. All was still clear. He staggered out on deck and looked into the dark haze of his own sickness. The wind was dry and cool again and blowing from the same quarter.

When he went below, his gaze fell on the radio transmitter. The obvious course, it seemed, was to turn around and head for land. If it got worse he might raise the Coast Guard. As soon as he pictured himself being rescued, he felt a moment's certainty that aborting the trip was the right thing to do. He was plainly too sick to go on. The image of his own illness overpowered him. He sat on the bunk with his chin on his chest, too sick to see straight, wanting to start back but too addled to commence coming about. All he was aware of in the cabin was the transmitter. He had the urge to ring up his wife. He wanted to recruit her into his dilemma, but still more he wanted to hear her voice. He felt whipped and frightened. In the end, he simply took more aspirin and more penicillin and went back to sleep.

When he awoke again it was still dark. A cloud of fever dreams had held him down, each one depicting some anxiety. It took him a moment to remember what the actual trouble was supposed to be. Then he could only lie there, pondering his condition, meditating on symptoms. To be sure, his neck was stiff, his jaw ached; he was still very feverish. But this time the accompanying panic failed to strike him. It was as though he had not the energy for panic.

If I die of tetanus, Browne thought later, or gangrene or botulism or whatever else, then I will simply die of it. I will lie here as long as it takes to die and call no one. I will not run puking home to her or the Coast Guard or anyone else.

He realized then that he would have to relearn, in soft, advancing middle age, the sense of suspended fortune that had been mother wit and second nature when he was young and in the war. Such things did not simply come back. In spite of all the conscious preparation, he was unprepared for sea.

It was so much in the mind, Browne thought. The logic of ordinary life was the logic of weakness and fear. The imperatives of weakness and fear were persuasive. His helpful medical book was a busy encumbrance. The time to treat the cut had been before the race began and he had chosen to ignore it. He would live with his own decision, excused from further responsibility. There were ways of coping with everything, even despair.

And it was useful to think of the dividing world overhead, the gates of Altair sliding closed, Orion leading on. He was in a zone of transit between his lost world and the one beginning to take hold. He swallowed another penicillin tablet and turned over.

Just before first light a strange signal came in on shortwave. A man with a West Indian accent was reading aloud:

". . . a man riding a red horse an' he stood among de myrtle that were in de bottom

"And behind him were dere red horses, speckled and white.

"Then said I, Oh" — and here the man moaned softly and in such a sad way that Browne would never forget it — "oh, my Lord, what are dese?"

Browne opened his eyes in hope of daylight but there was none to see. He was still sick enough. The signal faded out then. Browne pulled the bag close around himself. He had enough trouble, he thought, without mystery sky pilots.

Later on, he awoke to a sound that cheered him. The sun was high in the sky and Morse code was coming over the Icom, loud and clear at over thirty words a minute. As a midshipman, in the autumn before he was commissioned, Browne had spent some months at the Navy's radio school in Norfolk. He had been taught to receive at the typewriter; typing a sentence still brought ghostly electronic echoes to his inner ear. Trying to follow the Morse on his receiver, Browne sat up and realized he felt better.

Hand-transmitted Morse had practically disappeared from the sea lanes in the days since Browne had been a midshipman. Nearly everything was faxed or automated. Listening more closely to the signals, he understood that there were two operators on the line repeating each other's signals. The sending speed was incredibly fast for hand transmission but distinctly that. Then it came to Browne that what was being sent back and forth were variations on the phrase BEN'S BEST BENT WIRE. In Morse the words were pure rhythm and used by old-time operators to demonstrate the quality of their fist, their skill with the key. After about five minutes of electronic syncopation, the operators signed off.

"GL, OM." Good luck, old man. A marine operator's sign-off from Conrad's time. Roger. Out.

"Bless you, Sparky," Browne said aloud. "Both of you."

He climbed out of his bunk and felt his sickness had passed. It was early afternoon and he was hungry. Later, he decided, he would take a sighting.

He made himself a cheese omelet for breakfast and ate it with fried ham and, as things did at sea, it tasted marvelous. When he had washed the dishes he went on deck.

The day was fine, the wind steady and the ocean still and blue. As a bonus, four gray bottlenose dolphins were leaping with *Nona's* bow, as good an omen as could be. He hurried back below to get the camera Strickland had given him. For whatever reason, the dolphins disappeared, declining to be recorded. Just for practice, Browne focused his lens on the horizon and shot the empty sea.

When the wind picked up, he buckled on his safety harness and leaned his back against the mast. It was a bad night that he had put behind him. He found it difficult to imagine his way back into the depths of fear and helplessness that had assailed him. Kneading his sore leg, he found it quite serviceable. End of alarm.

It all had to do, Browne thought, with the zones of transit he had crossed. Within them, what was human met with what was not. Over there, the continent, with its frantic egoism, millions of ravenous wills. Here the sea, serene and unforgiving. Out of such places, interior storms arose. He settled back against the mast with Strickland's camera on his lap and waited for the dolphins.

31

WITH Owen securely at sea, Anne had started working for *Underway* magazine again. The week before Thanksgiving, she spent one morning in the office alone reading the January issue's proofs. When they were ready, she walked them to the printer's herself and took an afternoon train home from Grand Central. She was expecting his call that evening, via the marine operator.

Riding home, she found herself a little high with anticipation. She had gotten the magazine out ahead of time, using the prospect of his call as a treat and incentive. At the same time she knew perfectly well that the telephone link was an ambiguous pleasure.

Driving from the station, it occurred to her that she might sign up as a volunteer at the Veterans' Hospital in Bristol. She had worked there during Maggie's first years in grade school. During the Vietnam War, she had volunteered at the Naval Rehabilitation Center in Kaneohe. Her memories of that were more pleasant than otherwise. If only she could summon back the tricks that had worked for her in those days. But they were lost in time and their memory drowned in nostalgia. To wish for those old tricks was to wish youth back.

She stopped at Gemma's Exxon on the Post Road to fill up on gas and get a quart of oil. Since she was in the neighborhood, she took the opportunity of running next door to Post Liquors for a quart of Finlandia.

That evening, as the time for Owen's call-in approached, she sat in the study drinking vodka and orange juice and thinking back on the years of the war. She could not altogether suppress the guilty pleasure she felt recalling them. How impossible it would have been at the time to imagine she could ever look back on them with pleasure. And with more than pleasure, she thought: with longing. It was partly, she supposed, a longing for him and for things to end well.

From the day after his departure, she had been running into the residue of things done wrong. There was the matter of the solar panels. Then she discovered that she had made a miscalculation in the amount of cooking oil he would need. He was almost certain now to run out of it before the race was over. The rubber for a reinforced casing around the mast step was shown by its invoice to have been the wrong sort. A letter for his birthday she had put aboard in a briefcase with the boat's papers had somehow ended up back in the car. There were many, smaller things. Besides them, there were the telephone calls at night. For some reason she did not understand, she connected these calls with the errors. They were the standard silent harassing calls in the night: a pause and the receiver replaced. Of course, the race had been much publicized. She was known to be alone. She said nothing to anyone about either the calls or the mistakes.

Three quarters of an hour before his call was due, she gathered up her charts and rulers and went upstairs to change clothes. She thought it might be fun to dress up for him, and before long she had laid a considerable variety of clothes on the bed for her slightly addled inspection. Then, in the depths of the closet, as though it were meant to be, she found a leather miniskirt that she had bought in the late sixties, too dated to wear, too nice to throw away. When she tried it on she found it fit, although barely. It was what she had worn to meet him at Oakland airport when he came home from the war.

"Far out," he had said, feeling her up in it. It was hard to imagine him saying that now.

She ended up putting on an old knit leotard of the sort that went with leather miniskirts and a pair of old boots and a purple turtleneck sweater that she had once worn with an ivory pendant on a silver chain. Then she sat down at the dressing table to fuss with her hair, a drink at her elbow. It was permitted, she thought, to drink while you talked to your husband at sea. And she had been cutting down.

The sight of herself in the mirror startled her. She saw that the fantasy for which she was dressing had less to do with present games than with past time. Her hair was the same length it had been in the late sixties. Fascinated, she combed it out. When other girls in college had ironed their hair, hers had always been straight and fine. Calmly, although not altogether soberly, Anne faced herself in the mirror. All flesh is grass, she thought. A helpful notion from the old country.

Her beauty, such as was left to her, was the old man's. His was the striking look that caught the pulse of its victims. Also the false angelicity and kindly eyes. From her mother she had received long, sound bones. *An honest countenance,* one of her teachers, a droll old nun, had used to say. Aging, she would resemble her father more and it would all catch up with her. And now? Not bad, she said, hardly daring to smile at herself there.

She put her hands to her hair and old shards and shimmers of the past came back to her. Songs and old cars. The married junior officers' housing with its snot-colored walls, suggestive of crooked government factors, the Philippine insurrection, the Seminole wars. Eucalyptus, San Diego, sandalwood, Hawaii. Always the war, the news, the war, the demonstrations. *Girl we couldn't get much higher. Gonna set the night on fire.*

Of course, they had no right to the songs. The songs belonged to the marchers, the epicene young creeps, but she and Owen had made a few their own. There were naval couples who smoked marijuana in those days; it was not unheard of. There were a few among the enlightened or the corrupt. The young Brownes had not. Mai tais had been their aphrodisiac and high.

What did we know? she thought. The Notre Dame fight song. The words to "Dover Beach." She put the drink aside and relaxed on the bed. Stacked on the night table was some of her chosen winter reading. *Brideshead Revisited,* for the first time since college. The New Jerusalem Bible with its Tolkien translation of Genesis, a gift from her brother Dermot, ardent Christian and recently unemployed broker. Nien Cheng's *Life and Death in Shanghai.* Minna Hubbard's memoir of crossing Labrador, a present from Owen. She picked up the Hubbard and reread Minna's adoring dedication to her lost Leonidas, the strenuously living, doomed, obedient Spartan.

32

AT NOON on Tuesday, Browne took a sun sight and located himself northeast of the Cape Verde Islands. The fix did not conform well to his satellite reading. At the same time his compass was shifty, as though some countermagnetic force were in the air. The wind was moist and intermittent; he was riding the Canary Current, making about two knots under the mainsail and a light drifter.

In midafternoon, he sighted an island off his starboard bow that was black but inlaid with a deep delicious green, a festive sight in the glare. A hill rose from it to a height he reckoned at four hundred meters. Referring to the Admiralty sailing guide, he decided it was the Cape Verdean island of Boa Vista. Later, a little boat painted in violent African colors went across his bow at a distance of a mile or so. Through binoculars he could make out a shirtless brown man with a red bandana across his head standing behind the wheelhouse. The boat seemed top-heavy and tossed alarmingly in the mild sea. The name *São Martin da Porres* was stenciled across its stern.

At four o'clock, the marine operator broadcast a roll call of the entries. The stars of the race, the big boats, were already closing on Cape Agulhas. Browne's competition was spread westward over several hundred miles. Of the lot, only Preston Fowler was ahead of him, clearing the equatorial doldrums at about latitude eleven south. When the broadcast ended, a weather fax arrived announcing a tropical depression off the horn of Brazil.

Boa Vista passed out of sight before sunset. The moment the sun was down, equatorial darkness closed around him, black on black under the cold stars. Worried about the current and his proximity to land, he stayed late on deck. His mind's eye refused to give up the image of the black and green island. Finally he played the game of refusing the image, trying to force it from his imagination. Eventually he nodded off to sleep. Awakening with an odd but familiar sensation, he discovered himself in tears. The same thing had been happening all the way across the Atlantic. It was strange because his easting had been a particularly invigorating run, spinnaker set and westerlies across the port quarter at seventeen knots. Brilliant autumn weather. But night after night he would go to sleep in perfectly good spirits and wake to feel some old misery slinking away with an unremembered dream.

Finally he put on some Dorsey brothers music to guide himself through the darkness. For whatever reason the old numbers sounded unaccountably sad. The image of the island stayed with him relentlessly until he could almost see it, glowing out on the dark ocean.

In one late dark hour, the mysterious bibliolators came in over the open transmitter.

"A false balance is abomination to the Lord," said a stern female voice, "but a just weight is His delight." The rest was static. Browne went to sleep on deck.

He opened his eyes to a peculiar amber light. There was sand on his eyelids and between his teeth. When he stood up he felt a light salting of the stuff on the deck beneath his bare feet. From every quarter, the horizon seemed to be closing in, visibility eroding at a quarter of a mile or so. The sun was obscured but its glare was all around him. The wind was hot and comfortless. He checked the compass, then went aft to inspect the steering vane. *Nona* was on course in the strange fitful air. Each gust lifted columns of spindrift from an oily, seamlessly rolling sea. Uneasy, heavy-headed, he went below and checked his radar scanner. The beam was reassuring. Half unwillingly, he climbed to his rack and went to sleep again.

His dreams were vivid and sweaty, incorporating a vaguely familiar noise that suggested telephone wires or nights in the country. Opening his eyes, he saw something in motion on the highest step of the companionway. The cabin was darker than usual; something was blotting out the fingers of light that normally penetrated the reinforced cabin windows. Then a moment came in which he connected the noise to what he was seeing and he stood up in terror.

Insects infested the wind. The companionway steps were covered with them. They were spilling like a foul liquor from the higher to the lower steps and had covered the cabin windows. Charging up the ladder, he crushed a million brittle carapaces underfoot. Once on deck, he refused the sight he saw. The things glided down singly like so many paratroopers and in writhing clusters that rolled like tumbleweed and skittered across the main hatch. Each shroud and stay was alive with them, the mainsail and mast crawling.

In his first active, waking moments, he felt the mass of fiddling legs and antennae cover his bare skin. He was briefly unable to control his own panic. As he recoiled, brushing away insects, he became aware of the sound they made.

Browne ran headlong for cover, which the deck did not afford. Frantically he tried to pry the insect bodies from his face. Their mandibles adhered. With his own shrill curses in his ears, he wrapped one arm around the boom, stared down at it and saw it crawling.

All around the boat, as far into the murk as he could see, the surface of the water was smothered, as though the swarm had displaced the ocean. *Nona*'s wake cut a swath through them, churning out creatures and soiled white water. Only when the noise stopped could he see that they had stopped falling. Teeth clenched, shuddering, he brushed himself off. He stamped as many as he could into the deck. Finally, more calmly, he took a bucket to them. He labored for hours to clean the decks and lines and brightwork. For weeks he would find them in unlikely places, sometimes in disgusting numbers. The insects were a little over an inch long, pale yellow and black, with delicate spotted wings folded against the thorax. Holding one spread-winged against a page of his log, he was reminded of a fantastic print he had seen reproduced long before. He thought he must have seen it in a book during his school days. Very distantly, he could remember the book as disturbing, showing things that were outside his experience then and of which he wanted no part.

In Vietnam, the battle-crazy Lurps who lived across the landing strip from Browne's Tactical Air Control base had made a legend of beetles who entered the brain and contaminated the mind. Some of the Lurps had believed so intensely in the beetles that they had succumbed to the infection. That evening, Browne entered the infestation in his log to bring the experience under control:

"1400 GMT, 1300 local, course 130 degrees, wind off the African coast. *Hamseen* or *harmattan* brought a cloud of insects, flying or airborne, covered *Nona* and surrounding sea. Hours cleaning up."

Beyond that he could think of nothing to write. Later, he thought he might sit down to his journal and make a literary event out of it all. Then it occurred to him that not once had he thought of taking out Strickland's camcorder. He put a stick-on memo slip in the log to remind himself to do it in future.

Just before sundown the unwholesome mists cleared and a gentle breeze rose astern. Browne watched the passing of the light with a troubled mind. For the second time since setting out, he was left with his nerves on edge and his confidence shaken.

That night his compass went shifty again. He stayed up to wait for the passing of the navigation satellite to confirm his position and tended his radar screen every hour. Having impetuously come so far east on a favorable wind, he was making scant progress southward, poking along toward the doldrums at their widest point. When he had his satellite bearings he sat down at his navigation station and drew a rhumb line that would take him across the equator at about the twentieth meridian. He felt a measure of irrational dread, as though the wind had brought him to some dark quarter of the ocean.

For hours then he sat awake in the cockpit, lifeline secured. At times he thought himself home with his wife and daughter a room away, but with the din of the insect swarm pressing outside. A few of the surviving vermin still fluttered about the shrouds, visible in the dim masthead light. Dawn came with a fresher wind and feverish colors. It was Wednesday, the day for him to call home. There was no question about it, Browne thought, he had a story to tell.

The prospect of telephoning later that day led Browne to meditate upon his wife. He imagined her voice very clearly and the way she would sound as he described the insects. The thought of her voice aroused him considerably. It might have been that something about the strange Senegalese light inclined him toward obsession. He could not take his mind off her.

Through the day, as *Nona* ghosted along with only the current behind her, Browne waited for the hour of his phone call. Faint gusts of indeterminate direction slapped the listless sea against the hull. Lolling beside the mast in the doldrums' glare, he fell deeper and deeper into the contemplation of Anne, her shape and savor, the contours and tastes of which she was composed. In his tense sleepless state, the desire he felt was restless and uneasy. In spite of himself he wanted to indulge it. He was finding that, at sea, the richest occupations, the keenest sensations, were interior.

It was peculiar, Browne thought, that he could summon up the sensual presence of his wife so vividly. Subversive. In Vietnam, he had spent a great many lonely desirous days but never one so haunted and distracting. Under the desire, he suspected, lay weakness and danger. It went with the weather, the doldrums and the malarial *hamseen*. He began to wonder then just what it was that he should say to her.

33

ANNE WAS standing by the bedroom fireplace when the phone rang. She ran to it.

"Honey?"

"Yes," he said, "it's me."

All along she had planned to ask him to guess what she was wearing, so that was what she did.

"Can you?"

The silence that followed was long enough to be exasperating. She supposed he was embarrassed. She became embarrassed herself. It was all a little silly.

"I found that old black leather miniskirt that I had when we were in the Navy," she explained. "Do you remember it?"

"Sure," he said.

"Do you really? Did you like it?"

"Yes," he said.

"Yes? Yes you did?"

"You were delectable in it," Browne said.

"I still am," she said. "I'm looking at myself right now."

"There's not much I can do about that, Annie. From here."

"Where?" she asked. "Where are you?"

"Well," he said, "according to the last satellite, ten degrees forty minutes north, twenty-one sixty west."

"What?" she demanded. She slid to the floor to read the chart. "What are you doing there? You're in the Sahara."

"It's all water, Annie. As far as the eye can see."

"Good," she said. "So you weren't misinformed."

"What do you mean?" Browne asked.

"Well," she said, "there was a famous movie line. In a Humphrey Bogart movie. About his being in the desert for the waters. And he said he was misinformed."

"Yes," he said, "I remember."

"Are you sure you know where you are? Did you take a sun sight?"

"Yes," he said.

"God," she said, "I wish I was there. I think you're ahead of everyone in your class. You're winning."

"Darling," Browne said, "we're on an open circuit here. I don't want to make things easier for the competition. I don't think we ought to get personal, either."

"I'm sorry, Owen."

"Never mind. But I had a great westerly wind for a while. I had the spinnaker up for a week. I couldn't leave it."

"Shouldn't you be west of the islands?"

"It's all right, Annie. As far as that goes."

"Is it?" she asked. She was trying to sound cheerful. His admonition had wounded her.

"Yes," he said. "Everything's outstanding."

"I'm so relieved," she said. "And I'm so jealous, Owen. I'm going to do all sorts of unruly things. I'm going to get drunk and wear sexy clothes. I'll be disorderly."

"Now take it easy," Owen said. "We're not using procedure and we're not being discreet."

"Screw it," she said.

"You're impossible. You've been tapping the admiral."

"I don't care," she said. "Did you really like my leather miniskirt?"

He was silent.

"I'm sorry, baby," she said. "I was just playing. Just this once."

He let her listen to silence for a moment and said, "Phones at sea are peculiar, don't you think? Unnatural."

"Yes," she said. "They're funny. They're frustrating."

"That's it," he said. "That's right."

"I mean," she said, "in some ways it's like you're right here. As though we're together. And I'm complaining about what you're doing. And you're complaining about what I'm doing. I mean, the old story."

"I nearly call you many times," he said.

"Do you? God," she said, "I wish I was with you! What's it like?"

"The night has a thousand eyes," he said.

"You must call me whenever you feel like it, Owen."

"I don't know about that."

"No?"

"I don't think it's a good idea."

It occurred to her suddenly that he might be angry about something she had left undone. She sat trying to find the reasonableness in what he was telling her.

"Why?"

"We've got to go off the air, Anne. Except for special occasions. It's expensive. It's compromising and we'll be in trouble with the FCC."

"Are you getting enough sleep?" she asked. "Maybe you're not."

She realized that he was right about the marine telephoning. It was peculiar, unsatisfactory and without privacy. It tended to flatten out meaning. Its dead spaces were haunted by suspicion and guilt. Every little unconsidered outburst left echoes to ponder. Its shorthand economies suggested false or pretended comprehension. The tendency was not toward truth.

"This is very expensive," she said after a minute.

"It's Harry's money," Browne said. "But you're right. We'll save the calls for emergencies or public occasions. I'll call you at the Wards' on Thanksgiving."

"Oh, Owen," she said, "I so wish I was there."

"This is silly," Browne said. "We're together, phones or no phones. Like it or not."

To her own surprise, Anne began to cry. If I cry every time he calls, she thought, he will stop calling. Maybe that was best.

"Oh, Owen," Anne said, "I had a letter for your birthday with the boat's papers. I didn't manage to get it aboard somehow."

"Put it out by mail buoy," Owen said.

Mail buoys were an old Navy joke. Aboard ship in the Navy, raw hands were awakened in mid-ocean during the dead of night to look out for mail buoys. They were told it was necessary to watch very closely, since the buoys were hard to see. If the mail buoy was missed, the recruits were assured, no one would get any mail and the lax watch would face the wrath of the entire crew.

"Oh, God," she said. "I wish you had taken my letter. I wish I could write to you. I wish there were mail buoys. Are you sure you're O.K.?"

"Outstanding," Browne said.

34

AT THE EQUATOR, there were starry nights and glass and useless breezes too feeble to dry sweat or raise a hair. Each morning the sun came up on distant ghostly clouds that never changed their shape or bearing — the same clouds, it seemed, steaming on station, day after day. To coax what little air there was, Browne had raised a ghoster jib, a big light sail with a Kevlar luff sheeted to the afterdeck. He spent hours looking over the stern, watching the little mill-pond ripple of the current under his keel. The water was crazy blue, painted, Brazilian.

Once a stormy petrel settled safely on the boom to show him how little wind there was. When he approached it, it fixed him with a wise little eye but never shifted. Out of curiosity he reached his hand toward it. The bird made a quarter turn on its perch and pecked at him. Then it shot off, racing eastward an inch over the surface. As though there were anything for anyone out there.

Browne made a log entry: "Mother Carey's chicken on a fuck-you note."

A not too suitable reflection.

One night he turned on the radio and scanned the dial in search of a few sounds. The clown colors of the sunset had put him in mind of tropical riot, sambas, sibilant Portuguese. What he got was a religious lady on the customary band.

"Many of you have written in," said the grimly English religious lady, "to ask what is meant by God's covenant."

Browne scratched his balls, opened a can of peaches and settled down to listen in spite of himself.

"By God's covenant," the lady said, "is meant the job that we are meant to do. If the boss gives you a job and you do it and are paid for it, then you have kept your covenant with the boss. But if you do not do the job, do not expect the boss to pay you.

"God has a job for all His creatures," the lady went on, "and we must each do ours. For we are either covenant keepers or covenant breakers. Are you a covenant keeper or a covenant breaker? You must think about it.

"If you are not a covenant keeper, then you are in rebellion. I wonder how many of our listeners are covenant keepers. I hope it is very, very many. How lovely it would be if all our listeners were covenant keepers. I hope that none of our listeners are in rebellion."

"Not me," Browne said.

"To be in rebellion," the lady continued, "is to be alone. It is to be insane. For all reality belongs to God."

"I disagree," Browne said.

"We must all remember," the lady said, "what we are told in Hebrews Four: 'For the word of God is quick and powerful and sharper than any two-edged sword, piercing even to the dividing asunder of soul and spirit and of the joints and marrow and is a discerner of the thoughts and intents of the heart.

"'Neither is there any creature that is not manifest in His sight but all things are naked and opened unto the eyes of Him with Whom we have to do.'"

Browne found it curious to consider the dividing asunder of soul and spirit. The dividing asunder of joints and marrow was a sight he knew, familiar to him both from the dinner table and the aftermath of tactical air support. One might think of osso buco but also of someone's arm, impossibly bent, its boiling tubes exposed to flies, its red-mottled white bone to beetles. Hebrews Four, Browne thought, unquestionably had war and sacrifice on its bloody mind.

Overhead the stars were exquisite and, inviting reverence, featured the Southern Cross. Let Him with Whom we have to do, Browne thought by way of prayer, never sunder my spirit from my soul. It certainly did sound like insanity. Let Him with Whom we have to do have nothing to do with me.

When the fax with everyone's position came in, awakening him, he found himself disinclined to read it. It was as though he wanted not to be in a race. Which was not to say, he thought, that he wanted not to win one.

He actually left the fax unread, except for the section about the weather. Not checking it was a little stupid but he was in his own house, in his own kingdom, and he supposed he would find out about the others soon enough. Is this self-confidence or cowardice, he had to ask himself, independence or spite? The church lady's broadcast had put him in a vein of self-examination. He felt as though he might be in rebellion.

At dawn the next day, the same clouds were stretched out in convoy along the eastern horizon. The motionless sea changed with the sky from violet to smoky blue. Browne watched it close over his little wake. When the heat of the day came on, his rebellion took the form of a refusal to patiently endure another stifling day of calm. The silky glowing surface of the water, its cool blue promise, drove him to action.

He payed out a sheet to trail behind *Nona* as a safety line, its end wrapped around a belaying pin. The other end he secured to the mainmast. He left a bar of salt-water soap on the afterdeck. Then he stripped, went forward to the bow and leaned against its aluminum rail for a moment to take a measure of the boat's faint forward motion. In the next instant he took a breath and dived over. The warm, still water closed welcomingly around him. Unresisted, he pushed deep and far. When he surfaced, his head was six feet from *Nona*'s hull. He swam a stroke and put his hand against her skin; he could barely feel her sliding past. Turning over, he swam a few strokes aft, and when the sheet came by he seized it and pulled himself up to the boat's stern ladder. He soaped himself and did it all over again. The satin water, the rush of silence and surface in his ears, the salt on his lips — all made him feel renewed. When he had played the game for a while, he made himself a lunch of crackers, canned crabmeat and vegetable juice, and went to sleep in the cockpit.

By late afternoon, only shifting light had changed the stock-still diagram of boat, attending clouds, and sea. He went swimming again; it was a drill with a rhythm, a good way of staying in shape. He decided he would keep at it through the calms.

Once he broke the surface of the water to find the upper world in unfamiliar shadow. From some quarter of the sky a cloud had come across the sun. Browne swam on his back, squinting at the sky. He felt himself rise on an invisible swell and, looking over his shoulder, saw the ghoster slowly filling, its contours darkening and curving as it puffed out. The boat began to groan; he saw her heave and slide forward, making a sound against the surface like rain in leaves. Then, before he knew it, the trailing safety line was rushing past him. He made an awkward overhand reach for the belaying pin at the end of the sheet and felt it slip through his fingers. In the growing distance, his future life, *Nona* was sailing on alone, leaving him her new wake. Calmly, he swam after the line in strong considered strokes that increased his speed with every kick. After fewer than a dozen, he had caught the sheet; he wrapped it around his wrist and let the boat's strength haul him for a while.

Back aboard, he stood by the transom, looking back at the empty sea where he had made an object. Although the flow of the wake went on and the camber of the sail suggested wind, he felt no breeze against his naked body. In the grip of a sudden notion, he hurried forward and dived ahead of the boat again. This time his heart raced, not with a true panic but with a safer, imagined one. All the same, he swam as hard as he could and when the sheet went by, seized it with both hands and pulled himself home. He did the same thing again and again until he was almost exhausted. There was no sign of the cloud that had obscured the sun before.

Afterward he lay down again on deck, half sleeping, half dreaming of the shore, childish days in the surf, summer birthdays and his parents. In his single true dream, the sky had gone dark and he was swimming in warm water littered with floating straw. He opened his eyes to faded blue. The sun was low. Physically he felt very tired.

He had put his trunks on and was sitting in the cockpit when, on the edge of a vision, a shadow like that of a sail passed along *Nona*'s bow. Leaning over the side, he saw that it was an enormous shark, just under the surface. The thing seemed unseeing and mechanical, barely animate. Once past the stern, it swerved and came alongside the hull again. This time its dorsal fin broached slightly, silently shearing an inch or so of the breathing world. Browne crouched absolutely still to watch its pass. It was perfect, he thought. Worshipful. At home, unlike him.

When the shark was gone Browne found himself discontent. He had never even thought of trying to get the camcorder. When he tried, sitting at his navigation table, to describe for his journal what had happened — his swimming, missing the line, the shark coming — he could not make it turn out right. Nor could he quite manage the thing in memory. Remembering it, he felt both fear and longing, insulted and exalted.

In the middle of the night, when the next false breeze came up, Browne shivered and slaked his peculiar thirst with water.

35

ANNE AND Maggie went briskly down the Academy walks in the November sunshine. Anne was taking Maggie to the chapel, where her parents had been married. Above them loomed the unwashed, oxidizing mass of Bancroft Hall. Strickland and Hersey followed along twenty yards or so behind.

"It's so gloomy," Maggie said.

Because it was Thanksgiving Day there were no midshipmen or visitors about.

"Well of course," Anne said. "Everyone's away."

The plan had been for Strickland to photograph the whole of their visit to the Academy. It had been approved by Duffy although apparently conceived by Owen himself. Somewhat to Anne's satisfaction, it had fallen through. The Annapolis administration would not allow photography on the premises without a number of permits that were not available on the holiday. The film makers were forced to content themselves with an inspection of the Academy grounds in company with Anne and Maggie.

Mother and daughter moved through the gloom of the chapel while Strickland and Hersey huddled in the doorway. From the corner of her eye, Anne watched Maggie inspect the mosaic stained-glass banners and funereal marble shields.

As they went out, Strickland attempted to kid with Maggie.

"What do you think, guy?" he said.

"I don't know," she said stiffly, looking past him. She could not keep from blushing.

"Ch . . chip off the block," said Strickland to his assistant when the women were ahead and out of hearing.

"Which block? Her or him?"

"What's wrong with you?" Strickland asked. "Daddy's girl. We'll want to see that."

"Jesus," Hersey said, looking around the grounds as they headed for the gate, "it's all so fascist!"

"Think so?" Strickland asked.

"Certainly."

"I don't find this place particularly fascist," Strickland said. "I mean, resist the obvious. The Guggenheim Museum is fascist. This is about something else."

"Yeah? What?"

Strickland eyed the athletic fields and the statue of Chief Tecumseh.

"Virtue. Republican virtue. Republican virtue in the water."

"I don't get it," Hersey said.

"Your generation is blessed," Strickland told him.

Ahead of them, Anne and Maggie stopped for a moment on the walk. Anne folded her arms, took a deep breath and looked around.

"It was very glamorous," she explained. "To have a boyfriend at the Academy was, oh, just enormously prestigious. It was to die for."

"There are still girls who would go for it," Maggie said.

"I'm glad to hear it."

"Like greasers," said Maggie, who was in some obscure rage, "who like athletes. Or cops and uniforms."

Anne declined the bait.

"Well, it was considered very desirable," she said. "They were beautiful, you know. We were proud of them."

It made her wonder if her daughter would ever learn what being proud of a man entailed.

"If you went out with a guy at the Academy," Maggie said, "it must have been hard not to marry him. In those days."

"The girls wanted the guys to marry them," her mother agreed. "They were a great catch."

"And did the guys not want to get married as much?"

"I think they probably did."

"I know you and Dad really did."

"Oh yes," Anne said. "Of course, the Vietnam War was on and there was a certain fatality about things."

"Really," Maggie agreed.

"By then, of course, there was a lot of antiwar stuff around too. You had to take a lot of guff some places."

Maggie looked dark. "Did you get like really angry?"

"Some of it was silly," Anne said. "Some of it I'll never forgive the people of this country for."

At the Duke Street gate, Anne directed Strickland and Hersey to Hubie's to feed themselves, with directions to telephone after four. They were not, she explained, to interfere in any manner with the Wards' dinner.

"You probably don't like turkey anyway, right? Hubie's has great crab cakes. You'll enjoy them."

"Would you tell your friends," Strickland said, "that we would appreciate some daylight for our work?"

"I'll tell them," she said. "And Owen's calling in at six, got it? And you be respectful to Commander Ward and Mrs. Ward. Or you'll be sorry."

"Sure thing," said Strickland.

"*Jawohl*," said Hersey under his breath.

At the Wards' house along the Severn, Anne made a quick call to Duffy to get the position reports from the other entries. Then she and Maggie were introduced to Lieutenant (jg) and Mrs. Benny Conley, Jr., who were their fellow guests at dinner. The lieutenant was a tall Afro-American, dark-skinned, with a formal bearing and an open adolescent face. His wife was small, blond and extremely shy. Buzz poured champagne for all the ladies, Maggie included. For himself and the lieutenant, he poured out a measure of Wild Turkey. In the wood-paneled parlor everyone stood for a toast.

"Our ships and men," Buzz intoned. "And women," he remembered to add.

They all, even Maggie, repeated it.

"You must be really excited, Mrs. Browne," Lieutenant Conley said to Anne. His wife, beside him, nodded vigorously in his support. Her name was Joan.

"Yes," Anne said. "And petrified."

"Petrified, hell," Buzz said. "She wishes she was out there."

"Well," Anne said, relaxing, "not right now. I'm happy where I am."

"How about you?" Lieutenant Conley asked Maggie. "Are you a sailor too?"

Maggie's face assumed the scarlet tones of which only her circulation seemed capable. Anne was sorry for her. Teased about blushing, Maggie had once declared, "I wish I could have my blood removed."

She shook her head and looked at the floor. "Not yet, sir. Just an apprentice."

"Well answered," said Mary Ward. Anne saw that Mary had gone almost completely gray. She looked plump and prim, sweet-faced and serene, a prairie preacher's wife. She wore her hair back with a turquoise clip.

When the next round was poured, Anne put her hand over her champagne glass. "Be a sport, Buzz. Give us a shot."

Buzz made much of it.

"I should give her a beer-and-a-ball. That's what these New York Irish girls like," he declared. "A beer-and-a-ball," he repeated, attempting the New York pronunciation. They drank to absent friends.

The Wards had a way of ordering the events. It fell out that Mary took Maggie into the kitchen to assist with the preparations while Buzz, Anne and the Conleys remained in the living room.

"Do you sail?" Anne asked the lieutenant. It was the best she could do at the moment.

"No, ma'am," Lieutenant Conley said.

"Where Ben comes from," Buzz said, "there was neither wind nor water."

"But frequent tornadoes," the lieutenant said. His wife laughed fondly.

He was from Texas, it developed, a pilot like Buzz, assigned to a squadron aboard the USS *Ticonderoga*.

"They both fly," Buzz explained to Anne. "Young Joan, she's no slouch in the cockpit. She's a first officer with Air Chesapeake."

"Well, good for you," Anne said. "You'll be in space together."

It proved the right thing to have said, and they relaxed with her. Joan Conley, who did not at first appear a likely first officer of anything, turned out to be a gravely serious young woman.

Her laughter was nervous rather than humorous and she had a dark fanatical frown with which to discuss matters of principle. Her husband was black and gorgeous, with the manner of a rural Christian athlete, which was what he was.

They must have prayed together, Anne thought. It was easy to picture them doing it. Kneeling, holding hands in front of that Anglo-Saxon-Protestant bookstore Jesus. Should we do it, Lord? Will you bless our love? Are we ready? Is the Navy? How about America? Apparently they had got the word to proceed.

When the turkey was carved and everyone seated Buzz said grace.

"O Lord, for Thy bounty make us truly thankful, these things we ask in Jesus' name. Amen."

While everyone's head was duly bowed, Anne had a quick look at the company. The Conleys were where she expected to find them, deep in prayer. Maggie was sneaking a peek at the lieutenant. Buzz was in his *pontifex maximus* trance. Anne found herself eye to eye with Mary Ward, whose gaze had also been prowling the table. She winked. Mary looked fond.

During dinner, troublesome topics kept emerging and having to be put aside. They began by talking about a series of accidents that had been occurring in the fleet over the past year. Then, since there were three pilots at the table, the question of aviation safety came up. There were carrier-landing stories and stories of stunts gone wrong. Buzz recited his list of commercial airlines one must never, under any circumstances, fly. Then he talked a little about the battles over the Dragon Jaw Bridge. The missiles were the worst, he said, the most devastating antiaircraft weapons in history. But there were a few MiGs too.

"I'm boring you," Buzz said to Anne. "You've heard all this before."

"You're mistaken," Anne said. "You've never talked about it. Not to me."

"Well, I've heard it," Mary said.

"Who flew the MiGs?" Lieutenant Conley asked. "Russians? Koreans?"

"Maybe at first. After a while I think they were all Vietnamese." Buzz took a sip of wine. "You know, you can teach those people to do anything."

The furies of comparative racism threatened to issue forth.

"From plebe year on," Benny Conley said, "I've noticed that trigonometry is culturally biased toward Asian people."

For a moment no one laughed. Then everyone did, except Joan Conley.

"Really?" she asked.

"There are a lot of Vietnamese midshipmen here," Buzz said, to complicate the topic. "Revenging their daddies."

"On whom?" Anne asked.

Urged by some other spectral presence at the feast, Lieutenant Conley brought up *Challenger,* the space shuttle flight that had killed the pretty schoolteacher and all on board.

"Terrible," Mary Ward said calmly.

"Ben and I got into a literary argument after that," Buzz said. "Didn't we, Ben?"

"It was the only time I've known him to be wrong," Conley said.

"Buzz wrong?" Anne asked. "Tell us about it. That's a side of him we've never seen."

"When the accident happened," the lieutenant told them, "I was shocked like everyone else. Then I read about it and I was proud." He pronounced the last word with an almost imperceptible roll of black passion. "Because it was everyone up there. Everyone."

"A black man," Joan Conley explained when he did not go on, "a Jewish woman, a Japanese American, a white Protestant male."

"It was a terrible moment," Conley said, "but a great moment too. I mean an inspirational moment."

"And Ben was much taken," Buzz Ward said, "with the then-President's quotation."

"I have slipped the surly bonds of earth," young Conley recited, "and danced the skies on laughter-silvered wings."

Anne watched the young officer who believed in inspirational moments and found it difficult not to weep drunken tears over him. His wife sat rigidly, lips pursed.

"That poem helped me decide to be a pilot," Conley said. "But my old professor there" — he pointed at Buzz — "insists it's not a good poem."

"I'm afraid it's not," Buzz said. "The pilot in me rejoices. But the English teacher insists it's not a good poem."

"Come on, Buzz," Anne said. "It's a perfectly lovely poem. It's beautiful."

Buzz only shook his head.

"But it's so moving," Anne said. "It is *too* a good poem."

"Negative," Buzz said.

"How can you arrogantly sit there," Anne asked, "with people so moved by a poem and insist it's no good? You really *are* an English teacher."

Suddenly she realized she was disproportionately angry. No one seemed able to tell. They had risen from the table when the telephone rang. It was not Owen but Strickland, asking to shoot in the last of the light. Mary Ward told him to come ahead. Together they cleared the table.

Everyone retreated back to the dining room when Strickland and Hersey arrived. Anne, still slightly drunk, made a mess of introducing the film makers. The project and their presence embarrassed her. Everyone simply exchanged nods.

Addressing the group, Strickland fell into his stammer.

"Why don't you all sit down at the table?" he said finally.

The Wards, the Conleys, Anne and Maggie all resumed their seats. Strickland studied the composition.

"If you all held hands," he said to Anne, "this would look like a séance." He said it directly to her, looking at no one else.

"Come on, Ron," Anne said brusquely, "get on with it."

Immediately she regretted the sound of her own words. She had sounded imperious and familiar. The Wards exchanged looks.

"I'll get some port," Mary said.

"Good idea," said Buzz. "So we'll get a drink while we're looking pretty."

Strickland filmed Buzz's naval toast and the passing of the port. Maggie briefly giggled. Everyone, Anne was convinced, was as strained and stilted as could be and would surely emerge on film that way. Strickland and Hersey spoke softly to one another.

At six o'clock, at what Anne had a feeling must be dead midnight Greenwich mean time, the telephone rang and it was Owen. Mary put his call on the speaker.

"All at home, this is sailing vessel *Nona*. Over."

"Ask him to say it again," Strickland said, "to see if we have sound."

"Whiskey Zulu Zulu one Mike eight seven three, say again, over," Anne said, and he repeated it. Strickland nodded the O.K.

"Our present position," Browne reported, "is six degrees forty minutes south, twenty-one degrees twenty minutes west. Over."

"Well hurray, then," Anne said, "because you're still leading the division."

She read the list Duffy had given her but Browne did not acknowledge.

"I'm going to recite Scripture," he declared.

Nearly everyone laughed. Hersey strained to catch the sound.

"Except the Lord build the house," Browne declared, "they labor in vain that build it. Except the Lord keep the city, the watchman watcheth but in vain."

A few people at the table applauded. Anne glanced at Strickland and noted his cold polite smile.

"That's my Thanksgiving message to the Republic!" Browne announced. He sounded exhilarated.

"How are you, Owen?" Anne asked. "How is everything?"

"Sublime," he said. "How do you like my Thanksgiving text?"

"It's fine," she said in confusion. It had frightened her.

"Tell him it's a worthy text," Buzz said. "But word for word pretty expensive at the going rate."

"Buzz," Anne reported to her husband, "says it's a worthy text. Over."

Anne and Ward looked at each other, grinning uncertainly.

"Are you getting religion out there?" Anne asked brightly.

"I'm getting the southeast trades," Owen said. "They'll do until religion comes along. Over."

Her spirits rose. She told him who was present. She noticed then that Maggie had left the room.

"Greetings," Browne called. "Happy Thanksgiving. Is Strickland there? Let me speak to him."

She felt foolish extending the receiver. Strickland took it with a show of good nature.

"Yes, sir," he said to Owen Browne. "How's the ocean?"

"Are you getting everything?" Browne demanded. "Any problems? Over."

"No," Strickland said affably, "I don't think so. Any instructions?"

Anne kept looking at the Severn, still and cold under the willows at the foot of the Wards' garden.

"I have no idea how all of this looks from your end," Browne said to Strickland. "Just get it all, O.K.?"

"Don't worry, Owen." He glanced at Anne, who kept her eyes on the river. "Just get around, man. Don't forget to take lots of footage. I'm supposed to say 'over,' right?"

"Affirmative, over."

"Right," said Strickland. "Over."

He handed Anne the phone and went to pick up his camera.

"Do you remember what I told you the other night?" Owen asked. "Over."

She glanced around the room uneasily. It was as though he had somehow forgotten, over the absurd distance, that his voice was projected on a speaker. She looked unhappily at the contraption itself.

At the same moment, Buzz hit the speaker's switch so that Browne and his wife might speak in privacy from the other people in the room. Only the thousands monitoring at sea and ashore would hear them.

"Did that go well?" he asked. "Over."

"Well," she said, "I guess so."

"Did it sound pompous and corny? Over."

"A little," she said. "But it's Thanksgiving, right? Over."

"I heard it on the radio last night," Owen said. "Some missionary station. I liked the sound of it. I hope I'm being clear. I find that out here my thinking is clearer. Over."

"It must be wonderful. Do you want to talk to Maggie? Over."

The silence of the sea came back to her. She turned to look for Maggie, who had gone out of the room. Strickland was filming her on the phone, Hersey taking sound. She put the receiver down and went in search of her daughter.

"When did you disappear? Your father's on the line."

Maggie looked up from her book in terror.

"Please talk to him," Anne said.

There was no way out. Trapped in her chair, Maggie let the life and intelligence drain from her face, transforming herself into something coarse, low and unworthy of attention. It was her most effective mode of disengagement. Avoiding her mother's eye, she gave a cruel and foolish laugh.

"No. I don't want to."

"Owen," she said, going back to the phone, "I can't locate her. She's made herself scarce. Over."

"Bless you all," Owen said after a moment. "We'll talk on Christmas. Out."

Anne sat for a moment with the dead receiver in her hand, then replaced it.

Strickland had seated himself at the table and was sipping port. To her surprise, the company were discussing Vietnam. She hurried back into the living room to have it out with Maggie, who had put the book aside and was crying. Anne's anger fled.

"Don't cry" was all she could think of to say. "He's all right."

"What were you in the hospital for?" Mary Ward asked Strickland.

"A lot of things. I had parasites in my kidneys. I had side effects from dengue. Broken bones I hadn't treated. I had just come back from Vietnam."

"I saw your film," Buzz said. "It was shown here."

"Here?" Strickland asked. "At the Academy? That surprises me."

"I think it was," Buzz said.

Joan Conley regarded Strickland as though he were a large lizard on the runway. The film makers left at about seven. Anne, the Wards and the Conleys sat by the fire. Maggie wandered outside, then came in and picked up her book again.

As the Conleys were leaving, everyone but Maggie stood in the vestibule. Buzz and Joan Conley helped the lieutenant on with his bridge coat.

"I don't like that photographer guy," Benny Conley said. "I don't think he's my friend."

"I didn't either," said Joan.

Anne was seeing them out with a bourbon in her hand.

"He has a bad stammer," she explained. "Maybe he's compensating."

"Wonder what he did in Nam," said Conley.

"Made a movie," Buzz said. "Very antiwar. Antimilitary."

Conley nodded in recognition of the type.

"You used to call them peace creeps, didn't you?"

"Not me," Buzz said. "I never called them that."

After the Conleys were gone, Buzz, Mary and Anne went back to the fire.

"How's Teddy?" Anne asked.

Buzz shook his head.

"He's in the hospital," Mary said, "taking the cure. He's in and out."

They looked gloomily into the fireplace for a while. Then Mary Ward got up and went to make her holiday family calls. Anne had another drink.

"How do you think he sounded?" she asked Buzz. "Owen, I mean."

"He sounded all right."

She wanted a little more.

"Sort of rising to the occasion?"

"Yeah," Buzz said. "On his soapbox."

"Right."

"Didn't he sound all right to you?"

"Yes," she said, "I guess so. Did he talk to you before he went? About going?"

"Well," Buzz said, "we talked some when we were out fishing."

"Did he ask your opinion?"

Ward shifted in his armchair.

"Yeah, well, we batted the breeze. Out fishing. I even got him to take a drink . . ."

"Did he ask you what you thought about the trip?"

"We talked about the trip, sure, Annie. We talked about a lot of things."

She laughed at his evasiveness, but her smile quickly disappeared.

"What did you tell him?"

In the silence that followed they both took a sip of whiskey.

"Did you tell him not to go?"

Ward sat up straight in his chair and folded his arms.

"It never came to that."

"No?"

He looked at her in pain.

"Regarding that conversation, Miss Annie, I b'lieve you'll have to ask Owen."

"I see," she said. "Now tell me. Can he do it?"

"Of course he can do it," Ward said. "Certainly he can."

"I mean," she said, "I ask you because I think you know about these things."

"Owen is not about to lose his nerve," Ward said. "Don't you lose yours."

"We both know him, don't we, Buzz?"

"That we do."

His Kentuckian solemnity struck her as amusing, and to his annoyance she laughed. She had not meant to offend him. She stood up and went and poured herself more bourbon. "He's physically brave. And you are too. You both are. But not all men are."

"No," Buzz said.

"How does that work?"

Ward shrugged. "Men are different."

"It's good, I guess. For a man to have balls. As they say. Isn't it?"

"Yes," Buzz said.

"Why exactly?"

"Come off it, Annie," Buzz said. "You know as well as I do."

"No I don't. Tell me."

"All good men have physical courage," Ward explained. "Without physical courage there is no other kind."

"Really?"

"Alas," Ward said.

"But that's not Christian," Anne said. "It's undemocratic."

"Never thought I'd hear that word from you, Annie Browne. What do you care what's democratic?"

"I don't," she said. "I thought you did."

"You do what you can," Buzz explained. "The strong look out for the others."

She stared at him.

"So if you're physically brave, you can cope with anything. Is that it?"

"Negative," Ward said. "You can't have moral courage without physical courage. But you can have physical courage and moral weakness. Anyone who's been around the military knows that, including you."

He grew shy in the luster of her addled admiring smile. She could feel her power over him.

"And you figured all this out over there, Buzz? In the Hanoi Hilton?"

"I was not confined in the Hanoi Hilton," Ward said. "It was known as the Zoo."

They sat in silence until Mary came in.

"We're drunk," Anne told her. "Don't let him kid you," she said, nodding toward Ward. "He is too."

Ward grunted.

"So what am I going to do?" Anne asked the Wards. "Just wait it out? Like before?"

"Affirmative," Buzz Ward said. "Traditional situation."

36

"LIGHT AIR, horse latitudes" read his log entry. He filmed the flying fish. Then he lazed against the mast, reading. He had brought along some published memoirs by solitary sailors to reacquaint himself with the form. As it turned out, he found the books hard going. Except for Slocum, even books that had kept him reading through the night ashore seemed to lose pertinence at sea. The authors all sounded alike. He suspected them of cribbing from each other. The style was that of naval history, British and high-hearted.

They are writing about what cannot be fully described, Browne thought. They reduced things and provided no more than what they knew was expected. It was useless, Browne decided, to speculate about the men themselves. Who knew what they were really like? They seemed not much like him but there was no way to tell. The books gave nothing away.

Browne was used to being where others were not like him. In the past, it had sometimes been possible to find a few kindred spirits. But not out here, he thought, inspecting the horizon. It looked untroubled, perfectly benign. No kindred here.

In his Thanksgiving conversation with Anne, he had lied about the weather. It had been difficult but it seemed to him a little deception was necessary to confuse the opposition. The trades had been intermittent. The boat was not quite so fast as he had hoped.

Seated atop the hatch, he leafed through the stack of books, inspecting the jacket photographs of his memoirists. They were all suitably lean and leathery. Well, he thought, I can do that. Things had their public side and it was not altogether dishonorable to pose. He wanted a book or a cassette of his own. He was sure he could come up with the necessary posture and humorously tough-minded prose.

The sun rose higher and Browne sought the shade of his mainsail with Francis Chichester. As he half dozed the thought struck him of what it might be like to record the reality of things, matched with the thoughts and impressions it brought forth. To find the edge on which the interior met the exterior space. It would not be something of general interest, Browne thought, only of a morbid fascination to certain minds. Something for private reflection that might or might not lend itself to very selective sharing. If he could keep some sense of how things really were, he might retain a little of it over time. The past was always disguising itself, disappearing into the needs of the moment. Whatever happened got replaced by the official story or competing fictions.

Once he had succumbed to the temptation to telephone home via the high-seas operator, in violation of his own instructions. He had been worried about the Thanksgiving business, about the way it had sounded.

"Baby," Anne had said, "you don't have to perform so much. No one expects it."

"I know what people expect," he had told her. "I've read the books and I know the lingo."

"Just be yourself, Owen."

Later that day, the true trades had risen, preceded by their long blue swell. It was as though lies summoned forth the things themselves.

He had put on an Elgar tape, *In the South.* Very grand it was.

When the wind rose again, he decided to rig the spinnaker. He set Strickland's camera in the cockpit to film himself as he did so, passing the jib sheet over the pole. When that was done he took a sponge bath and put on clean clothes in celebration of the bright brisk weather.

His face in the mirror showed a bad sunburn. He had not been shaving and hadn't seen his own face for some time. The sight of it gave him an odd thrill of fear. He stuck a Band-Aid on his nose, put on his windbreaker and a Tacron-9 squadron cap and settled in the cockpit to wait for the next position reports. He kept a notebook by his side.

The wind was steady all through afternoon but Browne found no reflections worthy of his notebook. Voices from the false sea stories he had been reading stayed with him. He could achieve neither the correct attitude nor the appropriate language. It was another case of things not being what they were supposed to be.

Around evening he had another great attack of desire for his wife. After the lust was temporarily taken care of, came loneliness.

She had told him not to perform so much. That people did not expect it. To be himself.

His father had been a professional authority on expectations. He lay back and watched the fluttering telltales.

"What about it, Dad?" he asked aloud. "Can I just be myself then? How about it?"

The very notion of such a question filled him with hilarity. He rolled in the cockpit laughing, imagining his father's voice gathering force for the reply.

"Yerself?"

It was too funny, Browne thought. First the mild and reasonable mode.

"Be yerself, you mean?"

That had been the time of terror, when the pitch changed and the voice ascended sweetly toward the thunderous heights on which it would charge itself with fury.

"Are you inquiring, my son, as to whether your private person will be deemed suitable for the station in life toward which you aspire?"

Browne clapped his hands and laughed harder. He could actually hear the old man's voice.

"Right, Dad. How about it?"

"You?"

The guy went slack, the wind changed, there was a luffing in the main. He heard his father, not enraged but cursing and weeping. That, of course, had been the other side of things.

In the last of the light he put on his safety harness, secured the spinnaker and ran up an all-weather jib. His SatNav position located him at 36°36′ south and 27°33′ west, a formidable combination of treys. He sat up for a while taping preventers, listening to tangos. Eventually he climbed in the rack for some proper z's.

If I have forgiven him, Browne wondered, nodding off on the wholesome swells, why is he out here, waiting for me?

37

ON CHRISTMAS EVE, Maggie came home from a skating party in Darien looking prettily flushed and eager-eyed. There was a boy she liked, one whom, at least on ice, she could briefly manage not to humiliate and terrorize. It was possible for the moment to imagine Maggie happy and Anne was pleasantly surprised. Happiness was the last thing she expected to imagine at Christmastime, which she had been devoutly dreading.

In her despair at the onset of the holidays she had invited Strickland and his crew up, with permission to film as they liked. On Christmas afternoon, just after Anne and Maggie got back from church, Strickland arrived in his Porsche. He brought along a single light, one camera and Pamela, who appeared more thoughtful than usual.

"Where's Hersey?" Anne asked.

"I gave him the day off," Strickland told her. "He's probably in New Jersey. With his girl. Eating squid and cassata."

"That sounds kind of nice," Anne said.

Strickland filmed Anne and Maggie in their church clothes and then shot the tree, a handsome balsam they had driven halfway to Litchfield for. Under it were arranged the day's brightly wrapped presents, and the drill called for them to be opened when Browne phoned in. Anne had even bought small tokens for Strickland, Pamela and Hersey, and a couple of extras in case anyone unexpected arrived. When he put the camera aside and she had changed clothes, Anne gave him a Scotch and took one for herself. Pamela sat broodingly by the lighted tree, chain-smoking without permission.

"I love it," she kept saying. "It's a home-style tree."

Upstairs, on the telephone, Maggie was laughing. Hearing her,

Anne and Strickland looked at one another and smiled. She had always found his smiles troubling. They had a light that could not be shared. In doubt, she fell back on apology.

"I was sorry we couldn't all have dinner together on Thanksgiving. I hope we didn't make you feel like hired hands."

"Don't be ridiculous," Strickland said. "Anyway, we are hired hands."

"How did it turn out?"

She realized that he did not know what she meant.

"The film you took," she said helpfully. "The material."

He laughed. "Oh, the material. The material was fine. Real good."

He had laughed at her, Anne understood, because she did not know what she was asking. She had no idea what his standard of satisfactory material might be. Her suspicions of his good intentions waxed and waned. Since Thanksgiving they had done only one day of filming, at the offices of *Underway* magazine. It occurred to her that she had better discover, as exactly as possible, what he was up to.

As the turkey roasted, they sat and drank in the living room. While Maggie was still upstairs, Anne allowed herself the observation that Christmas was difficult.

"You have your own past Christmases to deal with," she said. "And then your children's."

"I prefer Christmas in a Moslem country," Strickland said. "Christmas in Iran is very nice. Of course under the shah they used to put up decorations. But I think they've knocked that off now."

"You know what?" Pamela asked Strickland. "You're a prick."

Strickland ignored her. Anne pretended amiable distraction.

"I suppose you'd probably rather be somewhere else today."

"I wouldn't say that," said Strickland.

"Good," Anne said. When silence descended she hastened to fill it. "We're at the stage in this house," she explained, "where we still make a big thing of Christmas. Of course everything's different this year, with Owen at sea."

From where she sat Anne saw Maggie appear at the top of the stairs, hesitate and start down. Strickland heard her coming.

"How," he inquired, "except in custom and in ceremony are innocence and beauty born?"

"Please don't tease her," Anne said to him. The image of Strickland as a prick, as something literally phallic, was one she could not somehow put aside.

"Of course not," Strickland said. "Why didn't you go to your father's?"

Anne raised her chin in polite umbrage.

"It would have been too much," she said. "Anyway, Owen's calling."

"The Christmas broadcast," Strickland said. "I wonder what the subject will be."

They sat in the dining room. Anne sliced turkey; Maggie saw to it that the garnishes went round. There was a fine Bordeaux in token of the importer's respect for Anne's father, and Pamela commenced to drink it greedily. She brought her ashtray to the table and carried on with her smoking. When the first bottle was finished she asked for more.

"So you went ice-skating," Strickland said to Maggie.

Maggie smiled. "Yes," she said, "I had fun."

"Good," Strickland said. "You deserve a good time."

Blushing, Maggie looked at her mother and then at the film maker. "Really? Why?"

"Because you know how to have one."

"Why do you say that?" the girl asked.

"I can tell," Strickland said.

Maggie pondered the subject in a brown study.

"God," Pamela said, "I used to love ice-skating." The food on her plate was untouched. She looked at Maggie, frowning through the smoke from her smoldering cigarettes. "It used to get me high."

"Really," Maggie agreed.

"I used to go to Rockefeller Center. This time of year when they had the tree. It was so excellent."

"Pamela's very sentimental about this time of year," Strickland observed. "That's why she came."

"I didn't make him bring me," Pamela said. "He wanted to."

"Relax, Pamela," Strickland said.

"I was bummed and it was Christmas."

"You're welcome," Anne said. "Right, Maggie?"

"Yesterday," Pamela said, "in a truly elegant French restaurant this businessman spewed me with pâté. He wanted to make the guy I was with fight him."

"Oh, dear," Anne said.

"Did they fight?" Maggie asked.

Pamela shrugged. "I left."

"Naturally," Strickland said.

"All this time," Pamela said, growing more agitated, "this idealistic young doctor has been searching the system for me. To help me out. And he still is, like all through the system." She put out her cigarette and began to search for another. "A guy who cares for me."

"Eat your turkey," Strickland told his friend.

After a while she got up unfed. "I think I just want to go watch television. Can I do that?"

"Of course," Anne said. "It's in the back."

"I'm finished," Maggie said. "I'll show her where it is."

Pamela followed Maggie out toward the television room.

"I'm sorry about Pamela. She's having a crisis."

"I'm glad you brought her. It was the right thing to do."

"I figured it was," Strickland said. "How was church?"

"What can I say?" she asked. "We always go on Christmas."

"We should have filmed you."

"The less of that the better," Anne said. "Don't you think?"

"We want things the way they really look."

"Is there such a thing?" she asked. "A way they really look?"

"Well," Strickland said, "there will be."

"How about you?" she asked archly. "Did you make it to church this morning."

"No. But I played racquetball."

Anne got up and walked to the window, looking through the fog over the project roofs toward the railroad tracks and the shore.

"Warm sickly weather," she said. "Aren't you going to film anymore?"

Strickland shrugged. "When your old man calls in."

She turned to him. "You're tired of us," she said. "You must be. And it's only Christmas."

Strickland laughed.

"Please don't laugh at me, all right?"

"I'm sorry," he said. "I'll give you a tip about being a subject. Never worry about anybody being tired of you, or being boring or any of that. Never, never."

"Maybe it's me being tired of cameras."

"There you go," Strickland said.

"Not that a lot else is happening to keep us occupied."

"Filming is kind of boring," Strickland said. "Looking at film is another story. Especially people. I can look at people on film all day. I could look at one person for eight hours. Longer."

She glanced at him quickly, trying to tell whether he was joking. He seemed no less sincere than usual.

Outside it started to rain. A lukewarm wind off the Sound cast the drops against the living room windows. Maggie laid and lighted a fire in the main hearth. Pamela trailed along with a handful of kindling, playing at helping. They had more to drink, waiting. It was only a few minutes until Browne's call was due.

"So what were your childhood Christmases like?" Anne asked Strickland.

"Tell her about your mother," Pamela said.

"They were ordinary," Strickland said. "We were a very small household and not wealthy."

"Ron and his mom," Pamela said.

"I lived with my mother in hotels," Strickland said. "What used to be called theatrical hotels. The kind of places where you might get born in a trunk."

Pamela settled herself by the blaze Maggie had produced and sipped her wine.

"The kids that got born in trunks in those places," she said, "went out with the laundry and never came back."

"It really wasn't as sordid as that," Strickland said.

"Carnival nights," Pamela said. Maggie and Anne stared at her. Strickland looked into the fire.

"What do you know about carnies, Pamela? All you know is from the movies."

Pamela reached out to put her hand around Maggie's shoulder. "I really needed to see someone my own age," she explained. "Even Ronnie said so. Even the shrinks."

Maggie was not usually responsive to such demonstrations but out of social responsibility and native compassion she endured Pamela's embrace.

"For a while," Strickland said, "we traveled with Hill Brothers Great North American Show. So we were indeed carnies. In the twilight of the carny years. For a little while only."

"Wow," Maggie said.

"Wow indeed," said Strickland. "So I can remember your little prairie towns. Talkers. Hey-rubes. Shortchange artists. Colorful stuff. But mainly we lived in theatrical hotels. And my mother worked on stage."

"Doing what?" Anne asked.

"She conducted a kind of seminar on self-improvement." He smiled at their puzzled expressions.

"Were you in it?" young Maggie asked.

"Sometimes."

"He's got some great tapes," Pamela said. "Make him play them."

"Sure," Strickland said. "One time we'll do a memory-lane thing."

When midnight Greenwich mean time arrived there was no call from Owen Browne. Three quarters of an hour later only Pamela was still talking but no one was paying attention. Maggie went upstairs to her room.

"Want to call him?" Strickland asked.

Anne did not want to call him. She did not want to be the one who broke the arrangement regarding the radiotelephone. With no clear idea of what next to do, she excused herself and went into her study where there was a separate line. She kept half hoping that the phone would ring but, quite irrationally, dreading it also. For a few minutes she sat at her desk, waiting. Finally she called Duffy.

"He dictated a statement," Duffy told her. "Guess he doesn't want to give it himself."

"Is it O.K.?"

"Well," Duffy said, "it's serious prose."

"Is it weird?"

"Not at all. It's Christmasy. Except he's got a problem. Do you know what a headstay wrap is?"

"Yes," she said. "Is he showing normally on the transponder?"

"It's being monitored around the clock," Duffy said.

"What position?"

"As of noon, about forty-one south, twenty-eight west."

She stood holding the phone, chewing a thumbnail. "You know," she said, "our arrangement is that I don't call him."

"That's my arrangement too," Duffy said. "The deal is he calls me."

"Goddam it," she said. "I've got the movie people here."

"What do you think happened?"

"I guess he's busy with the wrap. Maybe he forgot to book the call. Maybe he went to sleep."

"Want to hear some of his statement?"

"No," she said after a moment. She was afraid it might be grand and embarrassing. "Not just now. Call me before you release it."

"Get him to read it," Duffy said. "It'll play better."

"I don't care about that," she told Duffy, "but I have to know he's all right. Have someone call him. See if you can get me the weather down there. Call anytime. And tell him to open his presents, if he can find them."

"Right," Duffy said. "Merry Christmas."

Before going back out to Strickland and Pamela she went up to Maggie's room.

"Don't worry," she told her daughter. "He checked in with Duffy so he's all right. Probably busy."

"I don't like it," Maggie said, "when he calls in and Mr. Strickland tapes it."

"Why not?" Anne asked, thinking she knew perfectly well.

"I just don't like it."

Anne had no words of correction or encouragement. "I'm going back down," she said. "You needn't come if you don't want to."

"They are like *really strange*," Maggie said, sounding well entertained this time. It was educational and cautionary, Anne decided, for Maggie to have a look at Pamela, and a kindness appropriate to the time of year. In future she supposed she would have to discourage Strickland's bringing her around. "Is she really my age?"

"No," Anne said.

"I'll come down."

In the Browne living room, Strickland was preparing to film and record the Christmas conversation.

"He won't be calling," Anne told him. "He's busy now. He says Merry Christmas."

"Merry Christmas?" Strickland asked. "That's it? No poems? No quotations?"

"He's got a wrap around the headstay."

"Is that bad or good?"

"Surely you know what that is by now. It's a pain in the butt, that's all."

She brought out presents. Strickland filmed.

"I don't want to open mine now," Maggie said. "I'll wait."

Anne's present was a scrimshaw jewelry box, a polar scene with a whale and a walrus.

"I hope he's O.K.," Pamela said. "I remember that boat. It's real small."

With a firm-jawed formal smile, Maggie left the room. Pamela watched her walk away.

"He'll cope," Anne said.

They sat in silence. Anne made two more drinks. Pamela nodded off on a cushion beside the fire.

"I suppose he had some tough times in the Nam," Strickland suggested.

"Yes," she agreed. "Some tough jobs."

"I knew he did some PR over there. He never told me much about his combat experience."

"He wasn't technically in combat. He was assigned to a Tactical Air Control squadron." Strickland waited for her to continue. "Tacrons," she told him, "are normally part of an amphibious force. They work with carrier-based aircraft. In Vietnam they worked inland. It was all very secret. Still is."

"Was it particularly dangerous?"

"So I've been told," she said, "although not by Owen. I never knew how dangerous."

"So," Strickland said, "no wonder he got bored selling boats."

Suddenly she found herself unable to politely laugh it off.

"I hope you understand this man," she said. "I wonder if you do."

"I've dealt with military achievers."

For a moment his words stopped her cold. "Military achievers," she repeated. "Is that your word for those guys, Ron? That sounds disrespectful to me."

He looked right back at her quite shamelessly.

"I don't want you to get mad at me," he said. "It wouldn't be right."

"Really?" she asked. "But I am. How come it's not right?"

"Because I'm your friend and I like you. And I'm not disrespectful. I'm referring to my own experience. I was there too."

"Don't play veteran, please. You were the press and that was different."

"Hey," he said warmly, "there ain't no false hair on my chest, lady. Not much hair of any kind. Your husband was known to work with the press. And I had a few bad days of my own."

"Tell her about *LZ Bravo*, Ron." Pamela had come out of her doze and was looking at them bright-eyed. She lay across the wide red-print cushion in a fetal position, fists at her shoulders. "Tell about what happened," she said with a lazy smile.

"*LZ Bravo*," Strickland said, "was my Vietnam-related venture."

"I know," Anne said. "I understand it was antiwar. Or whatever they call it now. Critical."

"I had a little trouble after the shooting."

Pamela laughed engagingly. "The guys nearly killed him."

"I made this film," Strickland said. "I was a young man. I had an attitude. We were all competing with the military machismo that prevailed."

"So," Anne said, "somebody didn't like your style?"

"I had no trouble with the men who appear in my film. They didn't like me much but we coexisted. I had nothing against them. I sympathized. When shooting was over I was up in Cu Chi waiting for a ride out, living with the Twenty-fifth Division. I fell in with some tunnel rats. Rather, I fell out with them. They knew me only by reputation."

"What happened?" Anne asked.

Strickland knitted his brows and took a sip of his drink. He spoke with difficulty.

"Tunnel r . . rats were small men. They went into the Vietcong tunnels with miners' hard hats and pistols with silencers. Some of them had switchblades. They were tiny, swarthy predators. They were starvelings. R . . rickety. Hillbillies. Hispanics. Really more like mongooses than rats."

"Rikki-Tikki-Tavi," said Pamela.

"They decided to play a joke on me. So they took me out to a hot tunnel. One in use by the National Liberation Front. It had a bamboo wicker cover over it like a manhole. Down in it there was a stake covered with human shit, a trap. They tied me to it. Left me there all night."

Anne looked into her drink.

"It was a long night," Strickland said. "But it came to an end. As even the longest night must."

"Even the longest night has to end," Pamela agreed.

Anne was chastened.

"So many bad things came," Anne declared, "to so many people. Over there."

"Well put," Strickland said. "And that was hardly the worst. In fact, the tunnel probably wasn't even really hot."

"All the same," Anne said, "it couldn't have been pleasant."

"No," Strickland said. "But I take comfort. I was doing my job. Follow truth too close by the heels, it kicks you in the teeth. Famous saying."

"Yes, I see," Anne said.

"Right," said Strickland. "And I'm still here. Still doing it."

Later, because everyone had been drinking, Anne had Pamela and Strickland stay overnight. Pamela took the guest room, was heard to prowl during the night, but caused no trouble. Strickland slept on a sofa in the study.

Just before they retired Strickland distributed some presents he had brought. For Pamela there was a woolen ski cap from Finland, white with purple trim. She put it on at once and looked very fetching, *gamine* and somehow medieval. Anne got a book of Pre-Raphaelite reproductions.

Anne had presents for them. A sailing calendar for Strickland; for Pamela a bar of scented soap.

The next morning she woke up with a headache and an imperfect recollection of the late conversation. The book Strickland had given her was on the dresser. It had some striking pictures: Millais's *Annunciation*, Holman Hunt's *Lady of Shalott*. They were beautiful and faintly disturbing.

Downstairs Strickland was making coffee.

"So much for Christmas," he said. "Next year in Teheran."

"It was nice to have you."

"Really?"

"Yes. You weren't on your best behavior, though."

"Who, me? I don't get any mellower than that."

"Well, you were nice to Maggie. You were kind to your friend Pamela."

"She *is* my friend," Strickland said. "I try to look out for her."

Anne took her coffee to the window and drank it looking into the fog outside. The trees were black and dripping.

"Why did you tell her that story about yourself in Vietnam?"

"Do you think I shouldn't have?"

"Well," Anne said, "obviously she likes it. She forces you to tell it."

Strickland shrugged.

"It's a terrible story," Anne said.

"She told me her stories," Strickland said. "I had to trade for them with mine."

"Most of the men I know wouldn't tell a story like that," Anne said. "Not to a woman."

"You mean not in front of a woman?"

"No," Anne said. "I mean most guys wouldn't tell a woman that story."

"Most guys wouldn't have to. Most guys wouldn't have been there."

She laughed at his solemn insolence. "Most guys have it easy, you mean?"

"Many do," Strickland said. "There's a lot most guys never find out."

"Lucky for them."

"Lucky," Strickland said, "but nobody cares."

She had to wonder who it was that cared for him.

38

THE SOUTHERN SUMMER, Browne discovered, had light more radiant than that of autumn in Connecticut. Its shadows seemed darker and deeper. Day after day, the sky was luminous. The cool weather and the dry pure air aroused him to a faint excitement. Every night, the dazzle of stars overhead kept him awake and on deck.

His single-handed struggle with the headstay had cost him much sleep and hours of rage and frustration. Now he was tacking south, looking for the big winds below forty. Since crossing the line, he had found no air heavier than twenty knots. Every day the fax reported a stationary front off Patagonia. After a while, the bright intensity of things gave him a headache. He felt as though his personal rhythms were a fraction too fast. He kept starting jobs and leaving them incomplete. The color of the water reminded him of something he could not bring to mind. It had grown a richer blue as he had gone farther south.

One evening, he was on deck listening to the radio when the sky filled with colored light. Curving bands in violet and dark green undulated across the dark blue sky. Bank after bank of purple light radiated from the southern horizon in regular repeated patterns. So orderly were the emanations that they seemed to Browne to be a kind of signal. It was hard to believe that no unitary purpose was behind them.

The aurora reminded Browne of the night sky over the Song Chong valley in 1969. He had seen the most spectacular displays there, tracer rounds in red and green, parachute flares every night. Behind each illumination was some intention, it was being organized and coordinated, but to see it all was to know that things had gone beyond the compass of human will.

Over the radio, as the colored lights ranged across the sky, a man was explaining time: "If we can speak of an absolute future and an absolute past," said the speaker, who had a brusque South African accent, "we can also make distinctions outside the continuum. What is outside and never to be intersected by our lines of event? We call it absolute elsewhere."

The aurora seemed somehow to interfere with the radio signal, so that the lecturer's voice waxed and waned with the throbbing of the lights overhead. Eventually it faded away. The lights were still shimmering when the stars came out. Browne looked up and saw his friends from home, Orion and Canis Major. Sirius burned away.

In the cabin he tried, perversely, to find the missionary station. He had been listening to it with amusement almost every night since crossing forty. This time it was not available.

At latitude fifty south, although the skies were still clear and the air light, Browne secured the hemispheres of his cockpit bubble to the deck. To keep the Plexiglas clear, he washed it with the Clearade he used for his dive masks. He decided to leave the bubble open until the weather changed. The same evening he sought out the missionary station again. Instead there was more mere physics.

"What are we to say," asked the learned Boer, "of particle histories occurring in imaginary time? How can time be imaginary? Yet it can be. For imaginary time works its force on the continuum with the same degree of influence as so-called real time. How can we speak of histories occurring over imaginary time?"

The signal faded out. That night Browne lay in his bunk unable to sleep. Although the pain in his bruised fingers kept him awake, he found rest in the notion of imaginary time. To consider it was like being reminded of something one had always known. It was as though things had a delicious secret side that had been inexplicably forgotten. The trick was to remember it in difficulty, so there was something at the worst of times. If we could experience that, Browne came to believe, we would understand a level of existence at which things were basically all right. He fondly remembered the sound of the broadcaster's voice which seemed pregnant with that experience. Although the savor of the thing kept him from sleep, he could not quite bring it to bear.

39

THE NEW buildings stood in the marshes thirty miles or so beyond Fort Monmouth, on a hummock called Craven's Point. There were five of them, each over thirty stories high, white inside and out, and resplendent with glass. The interiors had tiles and aluminum fittings and an art-deco geometry that suggested both hope and nostalgia. It seemed to Strickland as though someone's lost world, out on the edge of town, might be waiting for a comeback.

The complex was well set on that January day. The newly cleared Jersey ash pits were under fresh snow and the bay ice-flecked. The winter sky itself looked high and white.

On the lobby floor of the principal commercial tower Strickland was shooting the opening of a display of oil paintings. The paintings had marine subjects: tugs, boatyards, docked trawlers, freighters under steam at night. They were really very atmospheric, Strickland thought. They captured something lonely and frightening. The painter was an elderly Lithuanian with a cruel, sensual face, the man whose work adorned Jack Campbell's office. He had been a Soviet seaman who had succeeded in escaping to the States where Anne's father had given him employment. Jack Campbell was a ready supporter of the victims of communism and a collector of marine art. He was also part owner of the bright new buildings whose completion was celebrated with the exhibit. Harry Thorne was among the guests. When Strickland had filmed and recorded all he thought he needed, he sent Hersey back to New York in the van.

It was not easy to catch Anne alone after her father left. For quite a while, his work done, Strickland watched her attended by ham-faced men in dark suits. The men kept bringing her white wine and she kept drinking it. When she found her way to one of the cathedral windows that faced the bay, he went over.

"Sort of like the *Hindenburg*."

"Why's that?"

Strickland shrugged. "The lines of force. The politics. The fact that it's New Jersey."

"Will we crash and burn?"

"I don't know," Strickland said. "Are you enjoying yourself?"

"I like the paintings," she said. "You can't spoil the view. What politics?"

"Of course," Strickland admitted. "There are no more politics."

"My God," Anne said, "does it bother you that these men own real estate? That the artist is a Lithuanian? You're really the last Bolshevik."

"What are you doing later this afternoon?" Strickland asked her. "Are you busy?"

"I'm going home," she said. "Aren't you finished?"

"Not quite," he said. "There's a place down the road I want you to see."

She looked at him curiously. "Really? What place?"

Harry Thorne disengaged himself from another group and came over. He looked at Strickland with what appeared, superficially, to be an affable expression.

"He's everywhere, this guy."

"I'm everywhere," Strickland agreed, "but you've been scarce, Mr. Thorne. Any word from Hylan?"

"According to the paper," Thorne said, "Mr. Hylan is a fugitive. It may very well be true."

"What do you think happened?" Strickland asked him.

"We may never know what happened," Thorne said. "I can't answer for Matty Hylan. But everyone who has a deal with me still has a deal."

"Funny," Strickland said, "the way it all turned out."

"It is funny," Thorne said. "Another thing I notice is that your assistant was taking film of me earlier without notification or permission. I would like that not to happen."

"O.K.," Strickland said. "Sorry."

"It was good to see the captain," Thorne told Anne. He meant her father. "You know we're old friends." Without looking at Strickland, he drew her aside. Strickland watched him address her earnestly at close quarters.

"My driver will take you home," he heard Thorne tell her. "I'll call you. We'll have a conversation."

Strickland brought her another wine when he had her back. "Thorne likes you."

"He's a friend of Dad's."

"He'd like to be a friend of yours."

"He's favorably disposed to me," she said. She was somewhat drunk. "I think that's good. He's a solid guy. A stand-up character, as Dad would say."

"Look," Strickland said, "I need to think about the project. Maybe we should talk. How about taking a ride with me?"

"I ought to get back."

"What for?"

"There's always something."

"C'mon. I brought my car. I want you to help me ponder."

She gave him a brave, distant, troubled look as though she were coping cheerfully with problems that did not remotely concern him. "Where would we go?"

"Down the road a little."

"Well," she said, "I'll give you a ride in Harry's car if you like."

Saying her goodbyes to the thick-necked executives and politicians assembled on the mezzanine, she offered rides right and left. To Strickland's relief, no one accepted. On the way out she stopped in the ladies' on the ground floor. As he waited for her to come out, he glanced up to the mezzanine floor where the party had taken place and saw two hard-faced men looking down the stairs at him.

The driver was the same man who had driven them in New York, his eyes still obscured behind dark glasses. He drove very fast, speeding them across the wastes of central Jersey.

"What's the latest from Owen?" Strickland asked.

"He's in the fifties, northeast of the South Sandwich Islands."

"I hope he's using the equipment," Strickland said.

They sat looking out at the pines and power lines.

"Are you afraid for your film? That it won't look good?"

"Sure," Strickland said.

"Well," she said, "the film is your problem. But I'm afraid too. That makes two of us."

"You don't act afraid."

She looked out the window without answering.

"Has your life changed?" Strickland asked.

"What a question." She looked him in the eye, accepting, he hoped, a somewhat different level of discourse. "My life's all right."

"You know what I wish?" Strickland asked her. "I wish I knew the things in your imagination. I wish I could get you to talk about them."

Anne bent her head and put her hands over her eyes. "God," she said, "you are a peculiar guy. Wherever did they find you?"

They drove for almost an hour before Strickland asked the driver to pull off the parkway. They followed a local road through the pines, toward the coast. At the beach they turned right and headed south toward the glass towers of Atlantic City.

"Ever down here?"

"Never," Anne said.

"Not . . . your sort of place?"

"I have to admit," she said, "it's really not my sort of place. I don't gamble. I don't like taffy."

"We'll see," said Strickland.

He had the driver take them through the streets of the decayed city, among ruined Victorian houses and cinderblock buildings with windowless saloons. There were very few people on the street and, except for the wind, the place lay under a strange silence. The dingy metal sea rolled in as though propelled by a machine. The gigantic casinos along the beachfront and the gray sky looked like painted stage flats.

A few blocks from the ocean they saw what appeared to be a plastic elephant three stories high. On a street called North Carolina Avenue, he had Anne get out of the car and walk with him. Harry Thorne's chauffeur followed them slowly in the Lincoln.

"The first time I ever saw anybody dancing was in that building," he said, pointing to a squat turreted house with a broad veranda. "It was called the Château Dumaine. There was a line of little broads in top hats dancing to 'The Beer Barrel Polka.' The girls were white. The band was black. In a back room there were craps tables and wheels."

"That's the first dancing you ever saw?"

"I was very small," Strickland explained. "My mother took me there."

She laughed. "What for? The dancing?"

"The food," Strickland said. "The food was out of sight. The best steak, the best Italian food you can imagine. We ate with the help."

"I gather," Anne said, "your mother was an entertainer."

"At the time we dined at the Dumaine," Strickland said, "my mother was selling lace. Or Meissen china. Or furniture — early American knockoffs. The place was owned by a friend of hers."

"Oh," Anne said, "but you said carnivals and hotels."

"We lived in the Chalfonte on the Boardwalk then. Sometimes there were fashion shows there and my mother would deliver the commentaries. She always sounded very . . ." Strickland bore down on the word, trying not to blow it: ". . . High class. That was the term people used. Especially here. In this town."

"So she was educated."

"Skidmore, class of 1925. Or so she told me. Her father was a Methodist minister. Or so she told me. Sometimes she made things up. I never checked her out. I mean, she was Mom."

Anne laughed, and for a moment Strickland was sure that she might take his arm. She didn't.

He showed her where the old Atlantic Club had been and the Sea Breeze and Clothilde Marsh's interracial brothel.

"My mother went there for bridge," Strickland recounted. "Clothilde Marsh had a lesbian girlfriend called Ernie, her own Alice B. Toklas. With them in the place was a very light-skinned black man they called Doctor Leroy. God knows what he did there. Every week Mom and Clothilde and Ernie and Doctor Leroy played a couple of rubbers of bridge. She always had bridge games going."

"And you went there too?"

"I made drinks for the bridge players."

"And did you talk to the girls?"

"I hardly ever saw the girls. They weren't allowed near Clothilde's bridge game."

"And then you grew up and made a movie about prostitutes."

"Yeah," he said. "Funny. Want a drink?"

She frowned. "Not around here."

"We'll go to a casino. We'll have a quick one."

At the entrance to Bally's no one made any trouble about the car when it parked to wait for them. Strickland led Anne across the spangled lobby toward the bar at the edge of the casino floor.

"About what you expected?" Strickland asked when they had their drinks.

"Let's have our drink and go," she said. "I can take the carpet colors but not the cigarette smoke."

"Have another drink," Strickland said. "I want my snake-eyes bet."

"I'll have one more and then I want to go."

She stood up a little contentiously. Definitely an Irish relationship with alcohol, Strickland thought. Her intoxication had a rowdy, slightly dangerous quality that pleased him. At the same time he understood that the seductiveness he had thought to see might be an illusion. He led her down the steps to the casino.

The dice tables were nearest the bar and fairly uncrowded. Out among the slot machines, several thousand dull-eyed, emphysemic proletarians pumped away in a hereafter of mirrors. Strickland kept a lookout for someone he might know at the craps tables. A number of the people he had met making *Under the Life* came down to Atlantic City, although not usually on winter afternoons. The cocktail waitresses, the security, the pit bosses, took a fraction of a second to notice Anne Browne. She was agreeably out of place there.

At one table a broad-shouldered, short-necked man in a good suit was picking up the dice for a come-out roll. The man had a flushed, pushed-in face and looked like an ex-fighter or a crooked cop or an actor who played one. There were half a dozen other players at the table. Strickland put a fifty on the table and said, "Aces." The dealer took his money.

"What are you doing?" Anne asked. No one answered her.

As they watched, the old pug rolled snake eyes. Strickland put his drink down in disbelief.

"Did you win?" she asked.

Everyone at the table looked at her, except the dealer and the man who had rolled.

"It pays thirty to one," Strickland explained when they were in the car on the way out of town. "It's a dumb bet. Really irresponsible."

"So you won fifteen hundred dollars?"

"I bet it for you," he told her. "It's yours."

She laughed that away. She seemed alert and sober.

"Really," Strickland said. "I should buy you something. What would you like?"

"How wicked. What will you buy me?"

"Hey," he said, "you name it."

"Well," she said, "how about a new waffle iron? How about a rowing machine? An inflatable boat?"

"You're not supposed to make fun of a winner," Strickland told her.

On the drive along the Garden State, Anne asked him who his mother's friend had been.

"His name was Phil Hassler. He owned half of the Dumaine and he was a kind of movie producer."

"What kind of movies?"

"It was a scam," Strickland said. "It's a long story."

But she persisted and he told her how Phil Hassler had done it.

"He starts out with a flick. Some kind of crazy Dutch sex-education movie. A training film for Bulgarian midwives. Some artifact he's acquired. Remember, this is back in the forties and fifties. Has to have something to do with sex."

Strickland paused, closed his eyes and drew breath.

"Then he drives into some shit town where there are lots of rednecks and Catholics. He finds a crummy falling-down theater. Tells the owner he's some kind of mogul. He was mogul-like, Phil."

"I'll bet," Anne said.

"Money's no object," Strickland continued. "Only thing is he has to have the place for a couple of nights. To measure something or test something. Some rebop. The theater owner needs to believe this. Then Phil brings in his cruddy Dutch pregnancy picture. He blitzes the shit town with the horniest possible advertising and fake reviews: 'Dirtiest foreign porno movie I ever saw!' 'My eyes bugged out of my head!'"

"Didn't people object?"

"But of course," Strickland said. "He makes sure all the preachers see the advertising, but too late to close him. Figures it close. By show time there are twenty thousand jerkoffs screaming to pay ten dollars to see the goddam thing. He runs it around the clock. He'd hold it two days if he could. By the second night the cops would close the theater but by then Phil had emptied the till and was on his way to the next shit town."

"Didn't he ever get arrested?"

"Usually the theater owner got arrested. But occasionally Phil got picked up. Of course there was always an out for him. Remember that these things were not actual pornography. So the line would be: 'Your honor, this movie instructs the young and prevents unhealthful practices! It's hygienic! It's educational!' This was known in the trade as 'the square-up.'"

"And that's how you got into film making?"

"Not really," Strickland said.

He thought that she might fall asleep on the drive back but she looked quite animated, lost in thoughts the nature of which he could not imagine. She kept a half-smile that might have been booziness or amusement at his tales or anything, for all he knew. Her hand was on the seat by her side and for the longest time he wanted to put his own on it, just touch her. But of course the excursion and the stories were not appropriate to such a move. Presently he felt foolish and bitter.

"The square-up," she said at one point along the road. "I like that."

When they got back to Craven's Point it had been dark for hours and the empty white buildings were ablaze with light. The high flat on which they stood was completely deserted.

"I seem to have this need to tell you the story of my life," Strickland said to Anne.

"Yes," she said, "I see that you do."

Getting out, he peeled off the top bill from the roll he had won at the casino and thrust it toward the driver. Without even glancing at Strickland, the driver shook off the tip with a barely perceptible shrug. He was still wearing the dark glasses.

When the limousine pulled away Strickland found himself alone with the glowing towers and the lights of Asbury Park across the flats. It was a cold, dangerous place to be. He walked deliberately across the frozen mud to his car and then stood beside it, looking down a dark bank into the soiled marsh. The roll was still in his hand, new bills, crisp hundreds. He took the money in his right hand and fanned out the bills like a dealer and tossed it all into the darkness.

40

THE EVENINGS grew shorter and faded no darker than cold blue. He felt as though he were stalking the wind. The absence of it seemed unnatural. One morning it occurred to him to call up Duffy.

"Where you been?" the publicist asked him.

"Can't you see me?"

"That's a blip, Owen. We like to hear your voice. I like to tell Annie I talked with you."

"How is she?"

"She's a rock, man. A tower."

A tower of ivory, Browne thought. "Don't I know it," he said. "By the way, we're supposed to use a standard procedure on these calls, Duffy. You're supposed to say 'over' when your transmission is over. When you're signing off you say 'out.'"

"I don't know whether I should tell you this, bro, but your sponsoring organization is in bad shape. Listening to the news?"

"I get the BBC," Owen said, "once in a while. Over."

"There isn't going to be much left of the Hylan Corporation."

"Tough," Browne said cheerfully. "That doesn't mean much out here."

"You don't care," Duffy informed him, "because you're gonna win regardless. You're gonna win it for the little guy."

"Am I?"

"Affirmative," Duffy said. "The fat cats fade but the little guy goes on and on. That's the angle."

"I like it," Browne said.

"Yeah," Duffy said. "It's a good one. Little boat, big ocean. Unquenchable spirit. What's money?"

"I hope you're being paid," Owen said.

"Hey, what do I care?" said Duffy. "I'm in it for the story."

"How's your wife?" Owen asked.

"Better," Duffy told him. "You're neck and neck with Fowler and Dennis. They're not getting any more wind than you are."

"Good," Browne said.

"So," Duffy asked, "how the hell are you?"

"I always dreamed of being here," Browne said, "and now I am."

"And it's terrific, right?"

Far off on the horizon, Browne thought he saw an instant of reflected sunlight. He could not imagine what could be out there to catch it. He let Duffy's question go unanswered.

"Do you want to provide a quote," Duffy asked, "or am I authorized to invent one?"

"I'd like to get it right," Browne said. "I'd like to do it justice."

"Think about it," Duffy said.

"The quality of light is extraordinary," Browne said.

"Don't forget the pictures."

"I have no regrets," Browne said. "I'm where I need to be and they should all know that."

"Whatever you say, Captain."

"It's like the edge of things."

"Really? Are you feeling O.K.?"

"Yes, it's a different dimension. A little faster, maybe. There's a quickening. It's good," he assured Duffy. "It's really good."

"That's great, Owen," Duffy said. "Stay with it."

Since they had closed Duffy's office at Shadows, he worked out of what had been a realtor's office on the twentieth floor of the old Saint George Hotel in Brooklyn Heights. Although it overlooked sedate brownstones and the harbor, the place always reminded Duffy of the boiler rooms from which he had supervised telephone sales campaigns during newspaper strikes.

It took Duffy less than fifteen minutes to whip up a handout. When he was done he phoned in a digest of it to one of his cronies on the *Daily News*.

"It's the fulfillment of a lifetime dream. Out on the edge the pulse quickens, the light takes on a new dimension. He'd rather be out there than anywhere else."

"Jesus," said the *Daily News* man, "he's a fucking wordsmith, ain't he?"

"The client is introspective," Duffy told his reporter friend. "He's definitely a thinker, this guy."

41

ONE MID-WINTER MORNING, Anne awoke in a state of some confusion about the night before. At the end of her day's writing she had stayed downstairs to read. The book was Minna Hubbard's memoir about crossing Labrador. She had been drinking a Sangiovese alongside. Anne found that she could not remember having dinner, nor could she account for a missing second bottle of the wine. Neither could she remember coming upstairs to bed.

Later in the morning, she recalled a film she supposed she must have watched in bed. Bits and pieces came back to her. It had been something she never would have endured sober. There had been murder and lyrically pornographic scenes in which a greasy-haired, unshaven man in a leather jacket and lifter's gloves slapped an undressed, slack-mouthed blonde and called her a bitch. She had turned out to be a killer.

That day Anne decided to stop drinking. It followed hard on her excursion to Atlantic City with Strickland. When she called the local Veterans' Hospital to volunteer as an aide, she found herself not required. She had done years of hospital work during the Vietnam War. As a poor substitute she started early morning exercise classes at the Y. The classes began before dawn at a desolate building in a dangerous part of town. On the bulletin board over the sign-in sheet someone had put up an amusing Larsen cartoon called "Aerobics in Hell."

Often, in the late afternoon, she got blue. Sometimes she thought about going riding but the trails were icy and the nearest stables closed for the winter. She began writing more for *Underway*, sentimental pieces about nature or sailing with children, drawn from her own childhood adventures or outings with Maggie. They made her cry when she wrote them and embarrassed her in print. Magowan was no help; he published everything she wrote without comment.

At certain times Owen's absconded presence obsessed her. She had imaginary conversations with him, laughed and teased him, argued, sometimes bitterly. She entertained fantasies of telepathy. At other times, she was surprised at how remote from her life he seemed. When she tried deliberately to imagine his voice and manner she could not always bring them into focus. Early on in the voyage, tracing his progress on the chart in her study, she liked to think she was sharing his days and nights at sea. For weeks she was really off with him; people were amused at her abstractedness. It had been thrilling at first, his becoming a man of uncustomary skies, other stars, impossibly far horizons. Though she had never learned to love *Nona*, she thought fondly sometimes of the cabin that lodged him, how it would smell, of being in the bunk with him.

But after the holidays she found herself resisting the image of him at sea. When she entertained his presence, it was unlocated. In the middle of the night, she would wake up and think of him in the roaring forties and fifties and imagine some lapse in seamanship or fit of absentmindedness and be filled with anxiety. It had turned out not to be like the war. They were not young anymore. Then she had been proud in the teeth of the world. Now, entitled to conventional, respectable pride, she found her only security in dread, as though her fear were his ransom.

At one point she tried taking up religion. She wanted it back in her life, to practice it earnestly, energetically, the way she had as a kid. The eleven o'clock Mass at Annunciation was always filled with families in their Sunday best and she felt out of place. She knelt alone and recited formal prayers for his safe passage.

The exercise classes nourished her physical vanity. After a couple of weeks, still sore and newly abstemious, she felt trimmer and brighter. She tried on old breeches and bikinis she had once despaired of and antique miniskirts like her leather one from the sixties. Abstention from alcohol gave her vivid dreams. Occasionally these were euphoric, sometimes frightening, often sexual. A doctor wrote her some Xanax; the drug seemed to make her dreams even more spectacular and emotionally unfamiliar, as though they were drawn from the stuff of someone else's life. Sleeping and waking, the notion of being lost, of having wandered out of the right life, kept turning up in different guises. She imagined mirrors in which she could not find herself.

One fantasy she had deliberately indulged involved sailing the world with Owen and collaborating on a book. After he had been gone a few months, the idea took odd turns that made her anxious or angry. Every day she hated the soiled suburban winter more. She turned away, superstitiously, from the sight of calendars. Sometimes she dreamed of sailing alone.

Unbidden, unplotted fantasies also prowled the margins of her concentration. One was based on a dream and involved negotiations over an antivenom kit of the sort sports outfitters sold. In it, she found herself in conversation with a kind of louche salesperson who appeared to be encrusted in armored scales, part condottiere, part lizard. The other seemed to come from parochial school martyrology. She was chained behind a cart, or more elegantly behind a chariot. The image had come either from some obscure actual martyrdom or from Technicolor movies. Never had she been so taken with the processes of her own mind. She supposed that, for her, consciousness had mainly been a synonym for being awake and a tool with which to discharge responsibilities. Self-observation made her feel more and more like going to sea herself.

Every day she entered Owen's position on the master chart in her study, as reported by the VERC Global Positional System. Since the race had begun, she discovered that at least half of their competitors were following daily courses set by assistants ashore who had the best and latest shoreside equipment and the best weather information. She regretted bitterly their not doing things that way, because it would have engaged her energies.

Duffy called regularly from the office they had given him in Brooklyn. Although Anne had come to rather like Duffy, she often left his calls unanswered. He always began by asking her about the film and Strickland.

"He hasn't called for a while," she told Duffy a week after she had given up wine. "Maybe the money's not there. Maybe he's changing his mind."

"He got a lot of money up front and a good deal on rights," Duffy assured her. "That won't happen."

"He always sounds so casual about it."

"Never mind casual. He's in too deep."

"Good," she said, "so am I."

Anne thought that Strickland might be feeling awkward about all that he had told her. She always tried to receive his confidences, ugly as they were, in a sympathetic spirit. Sometimes, pondering them, she found it hard to look at him. Inwardly she would imitate his stammer and cold quick laughter. It was plain that he wanted to shock her and then to be forgiven. As in most situations, she found her attractiveness useful. She felt it provided a certain security.

You had to pity the man's early life, she thought. It was all confusion — no religion, no father, a scandalous mother. If he was sometimes frightening, it was because he had been so often frightened. Almost a handicapped p . . p . . person. The sense of her politely philistine Catholic education was that weak men, flawed men, often made good artists. It gave them another sort of power, not necessarily benign.

Imagining him hog-tied over the hole in Cu Chi, she was driven to silent, guilty laughter. She raised a hand to her mouth. It had served him right. How terrified he must have been. How he must have needed something. But all he had was style.

42

THE FIRST iceberg Browne had ever seen appeared to him in the middle fifties around eleven o'clock on a summer evening. He had sighted a distant glint at first light and suspected ice. Rather than get closer, he had immediately changed course, set his radar alarm and headed due east. The weather was still clear, with only a single mother-of-pearl band of clouds low on the northern horizon. His westward heading put him on a beam reach in about twelve knots of apparent wind. For days Cape Town had been promising advancing depressions and winds of force 7, so he stayed with his basic sail plan: main plus genoa on a spinnaker pole. With possible ice in sight, he reset the steering vane and took the helm. He had trouble staying awake. Once, secured to his lifeline, he even dozed off on his jury-rigged outdoor toilet, only to be awakened by the cold on his private parts. An absurd story for the great world there, earthy and ingratiating.

Late in the day, he had gone below to catch the weather report and somehow fallen asleep again. It was after that, when he came wearily on deck, that the tower of ice confronted him.

The ice at first appeared to Browne as a steam tug, like the ones his father-in-law owned at Outerbridge Reach. The tug had polished brightwork and gilt lettering on the wheelhouse. The colors, he thought, were ones popular at the turn of the century, colors that were obsolete today. Each color represented a certain quality. A kind of blue might stand for honesty at the same time it suggested someone's eyes. Some of the old tugmen were deep in Masonry.

Browne stared at it, sleepy and amazed. Only gradually, as his vision adjusted to the special brightness of the Antarctic light, did all the embellishments fade away. Then he saw how incredibly complicated the actual colors were and how the shapes were unknown to geometry, beautiful but useless in any sort of measurement. It seemed to Browne that others had remarked on the protean nature of sea ice. He thought Shackleton might have been one. It was a principle known to adventurers.

In spite of the danger, he went below to get the camcorder. So equipped, he brought *Nona* around and made another pass at the berg, watching the water ahead of his bow. But even as he filmed he knew that he had failed to record the ice's mystical, Shackletonian quality. How to photograph a psychological principle? He had to be content with a banal observation.

"This is your flat-topped Antarctic berg. It's the first one we've seen and we hope it's the last."

He could think of nothing more to say. Well, he thought, I'll see the film and I'll remember.

He stayed awake at the helm during the short night. When the sun rose again the sea was clear. There was nothing he could do but set the self-steering again and hope that the radar might give him some warning. The same morning he checked his satellite position against a sun sight and located himself at fifty-six degrees forty minutes south, nine degrees fifty minutes west. He kept his northeasterly heading, waiting for the winds.

He had stopped reading. In Vietnam, at the worst of times, he had been able to read himself clear out of the war, into history or else out of it, depending on the point of view. Now, with plenty of time, he somehow lacked the patience. And about music he had found that it was necessary to be careful. Certain music produced a confusion that was hard to resolve. The best entertainment, Browne discovered, was his own thoughts. And then, as a kind of puzzle, there was the radio.

The day after he had seen the iceberg, Browne managed to locate the missionary station again. The reader, who sounded like an English-speaking African, announced that a dramatization from Genesis would be broadcast at twenty hundred Greenwich mean time. Browne decided to celebrate. In order to keep his thoughts clear, he had been fasting, living mainly on unheated, undiluted consommé. To accompany the broadcast, he undertook to prepare a homely feast: frankfurters southern-style from his *Fannie Farmer Cookbook*, with canned tomatoes, chopped onion, thyme and oregano.

Browne's feast proved a disappointment. He had spent the afternoon trying to clear his generator's fuel injectors; when he turned to in the galley, his hands were still fouled with diesel fuel. It was extraordinary the way the stuff managed to contaminate the ingredients of his proposed meal. Finally he gave up on it and opened a can of corned beef instead. He ate the corned beef with saltines and settled down to listen to the night's drama.

The missionaries' radio play was about Isaac and his family. Jacob was played by a young Canadian. Isaac sounded like an elderly southern white man. Esau was played, somewhat humorously, by an African. Rebekah was played by a young woman with a sweet clear northwestern voice, which reminded Browne of a woman from Oregon he had once known. It was apparent that there was some doubling up. Isaac was also Laban. Rebekah was both Rachel and Leah.

A narrator, who might have been the English lady Browne had been listening to before, reminded the audience of how Isaac had been spared sacrifice and of his adventures among the Philistines in the land of Gerar. She pointed out that even in today's world, travelers must be careful to protect their loved ones.

"How many of our listeners," she asked, "have been sojourners, have been among those of some other nation? How many have feared for their safety? Do we know," she inquired, "how we shall behave when our loved ones are threatened?"

Browne wrapped the remaining corned beef in foil, turned on his Kempar heater and wrapped himself in a dry Navy blanket on his bunk as the dramatization began.

"Oh, that red pottage," said Esau, "that red pottage smells so good to me. I am faint with hunger."

"Would you like some?" Jacob asked. He sounded honest enough, a wholesome North American. "Then sell me your birthright."

Esau seemed to consider the offer in a stage whisper.

"I am afraid I going to die. What good is some old birthright to me?"

Browne thought he heard voices rising all over Africa. No! Esau!

"Then Jacob gave Esau bread and pottage of lentils," recited the English lady, "and he did eat and drink and rose up and went his way." She paused. "Thus," she proclaimed severely, "Esau despised his birthright."

The scene shifted to the tent of old Isaac. Rebekah spoke to her son in the voice of that daughter of the pioneers whom Browne had known in Bremerton so long ago. She instructed Jacob to kill the goats and she would cook them up the way the old man liked it. Then young Jacob would bring the meal to him and Isaac would bless him before he died.

The girl of whom Rebekah reminded Browne had been the daughter of the captain of the USS *Pollux* out of Bremerton. It was she who had asked Browne to sail with her around the Queen Charlotte Islands. Out of fidelity to Anne, he had not gone. Then he had lied about sailing the same waters.

"But, *Mother*," said Jacob in a slightly epicene tone, "brother Esau is hairy! My skin is smooth. Father might feel my arm. Then he'd say I was a deceiver. He'd give me a curse instead of a blessing."

Rebekah's reply was sweet as country water. She sounded more resigned than conniving, like someone doing what she had to do.

"Upon me be the curse, my son. Only obey my voice."

So of course Jacob did. Any boy would.

There was one line that caught Browne's particular attention because he had often heard his father use it: "The smell of my son is as the smell of a field the Lord has blessed."

Later, when Esau found he had been displaced from his father's blessing as well as his birthright, his anguish was unsettling. The actor's voice trembled terribly. Who knew, Browne thought, over there in Africa, what his life was like, what things he'd seen?

"Have you only one blessing, Father? Please bless me, Dad. Bless *me* also." But he was out of luck.

"And Esau lifted up his voice," declared the stern English lady, "and wept."

Browne listened to all of it, huddled in the blanket. He was unaware of the tears that coursed down his cheeks. Isaac let poor Esau know that he was basically on his own. Then Jacob went to work for Laban and Laban deceived him, substituted Leah for Rachel, extorted his labor. Then he returned and simple-hearted Esau welcomed him and miracles ensued.

When the dramatization was over, the lady returned.

"When Esau came in from the field," she asked the public, "was he really starving to death? I hardly think so. Wasn't he only being greedy after a day in the field? Listeners will remember how he despised his birthright. Wasn't he a thoughtless young man?"

The English lady allowed that many listeners would feel sorry for Esau because of the way things turned out for him. She admitted it was only natural to do so.

"But what are we to think of Jacob's behavior?" she asked. She paused again for general reflection. "Didn't he act wrongly? What do listeners think?"

Jacob's behavior was absolutely unjustified, the lady maintained. It was wrong of him to impersonate Esau. She made no comment regarding Rebekah.

"What are we to think of this story?" the lady asked. "What message does it hold for us?"

"Good question," Browne said from his rack.

"Its message," the lady replied, "is that of God's almighty will. Never forget that God is strong. What is God's is likewise strong. The will of God binds the world and everyone in it. There is no setting it aside. There is no pleading against it."

Browne stirred in the bunk, his teeth set in rage.

"When we say that our God is a fortress," the lady declared, "we proclaim His strength. Would a weak God be worshipful? Would a weak God be worthy of love?"

In spite of the tender emotions he was experiencing — the self-pity, the loneliness, the disappointment — Browne found himself compelled to admit that a weak God would not be worthy of love. As for the English lady, she had no doubts whatsoever.

"Certainly not!" she declared vigorously. "The weakness of a little child is moving," the lady said. "We have all seen sick, unhappy children. There are millions of them today. We pity them. We help them. This does not mean that we are worshipers of weakness. Almighty God is our all-eternal father, the Lord of Hosts and stronger than the strong. Almighty God makes provision for the weak in His mercy," the lady went on, "as provision was made for Esau. But his weakness and heedlessness were not blessed. They were forgiven but not forgotten. There was no covenant with Esau.

"Doesn't all of nature proclaim the great strength of God? Can we not see the strong plants forcing their way through the earth? Can we not see our strong cattle thriving and providing for us? Don't we rejoice in the strength of our young men? Whom would listeners prefer for a son? Esau? Or Jacob?"

Browne considered his daughter, the only child close to his heart. She was without guile. There were many things he wanted to explain to her.

"I think they should prefer Jacob," the lady declared. "Just as Rebekah did. In preferring Jacob, Rebekah anticipated God's will. She was its instrument."

Browne pondered the admission into which he had just heard the Christians trick themselves. They were talking to Africa, engaging primary process. You had to come a long way, he thought, to the margins of the world, to get the message straight. Of course, the woman was absolutely right.

"When God had made His covenant with Jacob, Jacob was raised up into Israel," the lady concluded. "It is easy for God to raise man to His purposes when that is His almighty will."

During the white night, the glitter of distant ice beguiled his mind's eye and denied him sleep. Around one in the morning, he started up the engine to charge his batteries and found one of the starboard fuel tanks contaminated with algae. His other tanks, it turned out, were fine but the injectors were glutted now with an animal-vegetable-mineral jelly that took him hours to clear away. Eventually, he was able to hook up and charge.

Wiping the scum off his hands, Browne considered God's will, how hard it was. Toward morning, he climbed into his bunk. For a long time he lay awake. His mind was racing and it struck him suddenly that there might be some form of false thought, notions that had their origin outside the brain and even outside ordinary reality. He went to sleep trying to work it out.

Sleeping at last, he dreamed. In the dream, he was swimming with difficulty, his chin raised awkwardly for breath. In reality, Browne was a strong and skilled swimmer. There was turmoil in the water behind him and he was paddling away from it. There was a gray sky and an angry voice. Browne knew that his father was behind him, drunk and enraged. It was some kind of swimming lesson. He woke up breathless and terrified.

Something had happened in life to suggest the dream, Browne

thought. Then he was aware of the noise. It was a rending, the kind of sound that could be made by tearing open a taped package but ten times magnified. It was not the ordinary noise of bulkheads creaking, although he heard that as well. In the galley, hanging pans rang together. He climbed out of his bunk. *Nona* was rolling in heavy seas. The wind had come with a vengeance.

Browne hurried up the companionway and opened the hatch to see the gray sky of his dreams looming above a scattered ocean.

43

LATE ONE snowy afternoon, Anne took tea with Harry Thorne at his apartment on Seventy-first Street. The tones of the living room ranged from creamy white to tan. There were pale Chinese vases full of fresh flowers and a Raphael Soyer ballerina above the mantelpiece. Outside, whirling flakes softened the confining geometry of the East Side streets, obscuring the lines of shaded, lighted windows across Park Avenue.

"What kind of tea do you like?" Harry asked. "Irish tea?"

Anne, who would have preferred Irish whiskey, smiled bravely and tried to remember how long she had been on the wagon. There were cucumber sandwiches. An unsmiling West Indian woman in black and lace poured the tea.

The apartment had been decorated by Thorne's late wife. It was his pied-à-terre, he told Anne, for evenings at the opera and the theater. He had changed nothing.

"It's beautiful," she said.

Harry seemed to be assessing the sincerity of her opinion. His eyes were bright. At first he had appeared cheerful but she shortly saw he was upset.

"The man I bought this place from," Harry declared, "was well known. He believed in maxims."

"Maxims?"

"This place was hung with maxims. Proverbs. Fables. Little tales of wisdom. Framed. Out of books. Out of Bartlett's. About the only book he owned."

"I see."

"Once I got a look at his corporation's prospectus. Each section began with a maxim. That was the mark of the guy."

She laughed.

"Ask me if he went broke," Harry said.

"Did he?"

Thorne did not really answer her. "Very soon," he said, "we are going to see bad news in the papers. Bad news for us. Things are worse than we understood."

Anne had become impatient with the fortunes of the Hylan Corporation. Sometime after Hylan's disappearance she had begun to think of that whole corporate world as one that might be all behind them. Her dreams now were of a life of sailing and writing.

She half listened as he talked about damage control and gutter politicians and the gutter press. He himself had done nothing wrong. He was indifferent, he told Anne, to the insinuations of snide reporters and the attitude of the fool in the street. It was her faith he valued. And Owen's. They must continue to believe in him.

In their other meetings he had always seemed so tough, cool and humorous. Now his eyes were lustrous, like those of a man who carried some humiliating wound. His passion intrigued her although she could hardly follow his words.

"Did you know him?" he asked her. It took her a moment to understand that he meant the absconded Hylan.

"My brothers know him," she said. "I rarely met him because his operation was in Boston." She paused and saw that he was waiting for more. "He spoke at Maggie's grammar school graduation."

"And did she have a crush on him?"

Anne laughed as much as she dared.

"Not at all. The kids all thought he was a boob. The nuns told them to overlook his bad manners."

"The nuns took his money, though."

Then he was off on Hylan the Son and Betrayer. And Boston, and everyone at Harvard Law. She drank her tea and nodded.

Finally she said, "You ought to tell me how this affects Owen."

"You're going to know everything," Thorne said. "The two of you will be all right. I know you. I know your people. I was in the Navy, you know, same as your husband. You have nothing to fear." He kept staring at her as though poised between fondness and some kind of rage. "Would you like a drink?" he asked her suddenly.

At the point of declining, she felt an impulse somehow to give way to him. To allow him something and assuage all that emotion. The idea of a drink was welcome, too.

Thorne served the drinks himself. Scotch from a decanter. Sipping hers, Anne savored the tawny glow of the lamps and the bright apartment and the dark, heavy-browed elegance of the unhappy man across the room from her. Drinking it, she soon missed her clear head and regretted the wasted days of self-denial. In spite of that, the drink made her feel better. Owen, she thought, what things have you left me to?

"Ever been to Ireland?" he asked her.

She shook her head.

"No? I'm amazed. It's beautiful. How about Newfoundland?"

It was flattering that he had remembered her background. She had never been there either, but Harry had.

"Austere," he told her. "We had a lot of Newfies go to Boston, you know."

"Right," she said. "Relatives of mine."

"They went to Southie. Disappeared among the Irish there."

"Yes," she said, "that's me."

"I sold papers on the docks up there," Harry said with a hard grin. "I was the only Jew some of those guys had ever seen. The only thing they knew about Jews was Father Coughlin. You probably don't even know who Father Coughlin was."

"I've heard of him," she said. It made her blush because she knew well enough. Her grandfather had been a great contributor to the Shrine of the Little Flower.

"Boston was a tough town for a guy like me, Anne. But I'll tell you what — I love it. If I had time I'd keep a place on Beacon Hill."

"They say living well is the best revenge," Anne said.

"That's the only kind of revenge I want," Thorne said. He said it so violently that his jaw trembled slightly. They both looked at the beige carpet. Thorne cracked his knuckles.

"We're trying to salvage the recreational side, Anne. Originally I was sure we could do it. Now it's a little uncertain."

"In which case," she said calmly, "there won't be any dealerships. Or a new line of boats."

"I'm not kidding myself anymore," Thorne said. "I see now the kind of losses we're going to take. But I also see more clearly what can be saved."

"You have to take care of Owen, Harry. You owe it to him."

Thorne smiled at her directness.

"I asked you here for two reasons, Anne. One, so that you would hear everything first from me. And two, to tell you that we can provide for you and Owen."

"How?"

"What would you like?"

"The boat," she said at once, "and a cash settlement if Altan and Hylan go under. We'll be writing a book."

"How expensive is that?" Harry asked good-humoredly. "Writing a book."

"Not very," she said. "Not for us. We'll probably live on the boat." Her heart rose up. She found herself speaking her dreams. "We'd like the equivalent of his past two years' salary and commissions."

Harry kept watching her and nodding as though in recognition. "You're a cool one," he said.

"You know me, Harry. I'm like my father."

"Don't be silly" was his answer. She thought he must know whereof he spoke. "Down the line Owen will find a valued place with us. If he wants."

"He's a good man," she said.

"He's a lucky man too," Harry said. "Don't worry, we'll take care of him."

"What about the film?" Anne asked suddenly. "Will it go ahead?"

Thorne looked at her blankly. "What, that Strickland guy? Who needs him?"

"I'd like it to continue," she said. "It might be good for us. If we write something."

Harry laughed. "Be kind," he said, "if you write something."

She left the building high on the whiskey and the notion of freedom. As long as they had some money and the boat, the whole Altan business was beside the point. The fact was they had been wasting their lives. She had been bored sick without knowing it. Owen had been right about the race. It had opened up life.

Thorne's chauffeur had double-parked the Lincoln several car lengths from the canopy at the Seventy-first Street entrance. Making her way through the falling snow, Anne happened to glance up the block and recognized Strickland's van parked fifty feet or so beyond the limousine on the far side of the street. She hesitated for a moment and walked toward it. Halfway across the street she recognized the man himself behind the wheel. He was alone in the van. When she came up he rolled the window down.

"What are you doing here?" she asked him. "Were you filming?" Strickland regarded her with his thin-lipped stare. He looked disheveled and weary. "What's the story on you, Ron?" she asked. "Sitting out in the weather."

"Maybe you can figure it out for both of us," Strickland said. She stood beside the van for a moment, eye to eye with him. "You look happy," he told her. "Pleased with yourself."

"Just drunk," she said. "Anyway, what's the matter with happy? What's the matter with pleased?" She laughed at him. "I mean, what *are* you doing here?"

"Call it research," he said. "Call it background."

"Are you following me around?"

"His car's waiting," Strickland said. "Where are you going?"

"I'm going home," she said. "Get off my back." On her way to the limousine, she turned in the street and called to him. "You are truly a heartless man. And you know nothing about me."

"You're mistaken," Strickland called back.

She paused, took a confused step toward him, then turned again and got into the Thorne limousine.

On the road back, in spite of everything else that had happened, she kept running the last exchanges with Strickland over and over in her mind. She should never have turned after walking away, should not have spoken again. She had lost a trick.

She realized that the thing had always been more complicated than they could ever have imagined. What had appeared to be a race was war, life stakes for everyone. Owen was at sea. Ashore she was beset, outmaneuvered, of questionable morale.

I must be careful, she said to herself. I must understand what is required. She had always heard it said that it was necessary to know what you wanted. She thought she might have a difficulty with that but hoped it might not matter.

As usual, as they sped through the snow, her driver kept his dark glasses on.

44

OVER THE AFTERNOON, the wind kept rising; by sixteen hundred hours, his indicator clocked it at thirty-six knots apparent. Browne distrusted the indicator. Opening the sliding panel of his plastic hemisphere, he peered through the freezing rain. It was very hard, even with much experience, to judge the speed of the wind you ran before. Finally, although the barometer was falling steadily, he decided against reducing sail. He had come south for the big winds and it would be necessary to live with them.

More and more, he was coming to dislike the bubble that protected him. Closed, it clouded over, obscuring his vision. The confinement made him sick. When the panel was open, following seas flooded the cockpit well, and the constant rain had a gruel of ice in it.

Nona still held her lead although the race, at that moment, seemed a distant notion. He was sailing on main and headsail — a number-three genoa poled wide. It was a strategy derived more from his reading than from experience but it worked for a while. Increasingly he was aware of aspects of the boat's performance he had not noticed in lighter air. For days he had been hearing a curious rending sound beneath the cabin sole. In gusts, she kept turning to weather, losing speed as the autopilot labored to bring her back around. It made him reluctant to leave the helm. Another problem was that no amount of trimming could make the main set right. Its perverse luffing and flapping drove him to distraction. Eventually he got out of the cockpit and crawled forward along the hatchtop, hitching his harness to a jackline.

At the foot of the mast, he rose slowly to his feet and embraced it, peering up the shaft toward the swirling sky. He stayed there for a long time, eyeing the luff of the mainsail until he was dizzy. The sail was slack and its camber uneven. In the south forties he had loosened the backstay to give the mast a slight forward rake. Now, in harder weather, he decided to tighten up.

Easing back along the cabintop, he looked out at the soaring black waves and wondered if he were not dealing with force 11 seas or even higher. But when he got back to the cockpit his elegant anemometer read forty-seven knots, which was a mere force 9. Somewhere he had read that waves were always about three fifths the size they appeared.

On deck, the icy rain fell from every direction. Hunched up and partly blinded, he pulled on his canvas gloves and tightened the stay with the hydraulic jack. Then he winched up the halyard, trimmed the mainsheet and cleated it in the cockpit. He wore oilskins over his wool-lined foul-weather gear.

By evening the wind was still increasing. The sea was gathering itself up in towering masses that rolled from the horizon, trailing ghostly wands of foam. The sight of these enormous rollers and their fragile, attendant spindrift hypnotized Browne. He had never been out in such a sea before and never heard such wind. The boat felt as though she were gliding, airborne. The sky overhead was prison gray. He understood that he was about to experience the true dimensions of the situation in which he had placed himself.

45

SHE SPENT a cold gray afternoon trying to write. Around three she tried lighting a fire under the piece with a little Pouilly-Fuissé. It was reminiscence, about a solitary hike in Dominica she had taken one spring break years before. The island had been sumptuous, gloomy and sinister. Its mountains were shrouded in small rain. The people were secretive, their patois inscrutable. At every bend in the trail she had sensed menace and surveillance. She had done a lot of whistling in the mist on that one. Later on, others had told her about the dangers of walking alone there, but she had sensed them all along. She considered them an acceptable price for the private pleasure of the island.

Around five, she heard a car in the driveway and turned to see Strickland's van parked there. She finished the wine in her glass and waited for him to appear at the door, but for nearly fifteen minutes no one came. Just as it was dark, she heard him rap on the kitchen door that opened to the back garden. She stood up to the sight of herself in one of the hall mirrors. Its frame was gold, topped with a rampant eagle. She was wearing jodhpurs and slippers with a navy blue shirt. She looked pale; her hair was down. She brushed a strand from her forehead.

Straight-backed, stiff-gaitedly she walked into the kitchen and saw Strickland through the glass. His graying, thinning hair was wet with rain. There were pouches under his eyes; otherwise his face was all dark angles, mean, deprived. She had never looked at him so forthrightly. She unlocked the door and stepped back and folded her arms. He came in and wiped the rain from his eyes with the arm of his sweater.

"Hi," she said coolly. "What's up?"

Strickland opened his mouth and began to speak. Words failed him. He stood in front of her, struggling with his jaw until she could stand no more of it. She put her hand out and covered his lips with her fingers. She was astonished to have done so. Having done it, she closed her eyes as though she were waiting for a wave.

As he took hold of her there was an instant when she might have hit him, caught him on the jaw with her left elbow. She very nearly did. Then there was the wet wool and warmth and the taste of his bitterness, watchfulness and humor. It turned out to be what she wanted.

"I knew you would come," she said a moment later.

"You knew it," he said. "And I knew it."

"Since when?" She could see her own face in the pane of the kitchen door as he ran his hands over her. At first she tried to make him stop by holding tight to him. It was not the way.

Strickland took his time answering. "Since day one. Since that island."

"Steadman's Island," she said helpfully.

"That's the one," Strickland said.

Upstairs, undressing, he removed a thin chain from around his neck on which a tiny ornament was hung. Anne found her own avidity embarrassing. It was as though he had hardly to breathe on her. They kept it up for what she might have sworn was an hour.

"Christ," she said when he had indeed come, "you fuck like a god." She was laughing. Her words echoed blasphemously in the empty house. I must be drunk, she thought.

"No, I fuck like a musician," Strickland said. "I've been told that."

46

LISTENING to the wind, Browne recalled that, with luck, noise was the worst part of certain experiences. Lashed within his bubble, he struggled with the helm. For hours it had been blowing over sixty miles an hour. His own intermittent headway was off the scale; sometimes it exceeded fourteen knots. Surfing down the crests brought on a double vertigo. Each slide promised to bottom out in nothingness itself, each stalling of the rudder brought him the sickening impotence of an unresponding helm. In each trough his bow dug deeper into blue water, the vessel shuddering as though scalded as she tried to rise. He felt he was riding the edge of a green wall that closed off possibility, thinly balanced, accelerating and about to fall. Spinning out, every minute.

The wind sounded as though things had stopped putting up with him. When their patience was expended, Browne considered, things had the forbearance of an insect and the same random energy. At first he had shouted back at it all, ready to sing along. At first it had sounded familiar — the good old thrashing main, school of liberty, cradle of the race. After a while, when it had compelled his closer attention, he heard the stone annihilation, the locust's shriek magnified from the abyss.

"Christ, that my love was in my arms," he said.

The gale whistled in his slackening shrouds like incoming fire. He laughed in despair. He could imagine the long-legged crabs of Fiddler's Green rosining up their bows for him. He felt warm, sweet and powerless, a morsel, a portion. Above all, alone. Also the wind, for all its fury, was not the only sound he heard. There was a worse sound below that made him prefer it.

The sound from below was nasty indeed. He could not remember when he had begun hearing it. Just beyond the doldrums, probably, in the rising of the southeast trades. There was something human in its nastiness, a squeal, a squawk. It sounded like the gutter, like an obscene threat, a New York objection. Plastic. Listening, he clenched his teeth.

Its whine suggested loud vulgar language and cheap macho menace. Bad workmanship and sharp practice. Phoniness and cunning. Fucking plastic, he thought, enraged. It sounded like a liar burning in hell. Plastic unmaking itself.

That was what it was. And of course he should have known. He had been seeing the crazes and having trouble with the locker doors. Like a little tin soldier in a paper boat, he thought, biting his lip, headed for the drain. He was riding a decomposing piece of plastic through an Antarctic storm.

"You bastards!" he shouted, trying to outdo the wind. "What have you done to me? You fucking filthy swine!"

It was hard to force himself down into the cabin where the whine was loudest. It reminded him of the kind of dirty laughter it was sometimes expedient not to hear. You are not called *Nona*, bitch, he told the boat. Fake bitch. You have no name. But she was not even a bitch. Just plastic.

He sat down at the navigation table and started going through the chart drawers in search of the boat's design drawings. He had not seen them for months. The first document he laid hands on was the rough copy of a brochure he had written himself. He stood up and, holding fast to the overhead rail, got to read his own prose.

"Altan Forty! Master-crafted! A seasoned winner in the newest design! All the elements of the precision-designed racer — attainable! Affordable!"

They were his own words. And of course he had approved the boat. More than that: in imagination he had invented a perfect boat for it to be. It had been salesmanship by ontology, purveying a perfect boat for the perfect ocean in an ideal world. The very thing for a cruise to the perfect island, the one that had to exist because it could be imagined. He had been his own first, best customer.

With every gust the fiberglass screamed. The urgency in the sound was genuine and he understood that, under sail, she could not stand up to the weather any longer. He went on deck and, laboring furiously with the cockpit open to black sky and rain, dropped the main and genoa and raised a storm jib. He brought the boat to a close reach, virtually hove to, a humble penitent posture.

Below again, he had to strip the boards of the cabin sole with a crowbar to reach the mast step. The devilish, spiderwebbed craze patterns across its surface were worse than anything he had imagined. The makers of the boat had simply piled on extra fiberglass underneath. With each tightening of the stays, Browne realized, he had been driving the mast step down and bending the hull.

Clinging to the overhead rail, he began to smash the bulkhead cabinets with his crowbar. They were his own work, poor quality, of the cheap material he had bought to replace Dolvin's obsessive masterpiece. He had a proper use for them now. When he had stove in the lockers attached to the main bulkhead, he saw that there too the glass was crazing. So it was no wonder, he realized, that his shrouds were slack, since the chainplates were secured there. All the secondary bonds were giving way.

Again and again, Browne brought his crowbar down on the shiny, cosmetic cabin fittings of his worthless boat. "What do you do for a kid with a terrible laugh?" he remembered the woman in Connecticut saying. It was an odd thing to recall in his rage. He remembered her voice so clearly he could hear it in the cabin. His thoughts raced.

Res sacrum perdita. He could not remember the origin of the phrase. Sold our pottage, overheated the poles, poisoned the rain, burned away the horizon with acid. Despised our birthright. Forgot everything, destroyed and laughed away our holy things. What to do for our children's terrible laughter?

He lowered the storm jib. With all sails down, the boat was pitching relentlessly. Browne lay across the cabin sole, his legs braced against the bulkhead, trying to buttress the mast step with the ruins of the floorboards. He jammed the fragments of his cabinets against the angle between the hull and the main bulkhead. Every few minutes he had to turn away from work to retch over a bucket.

The suffering plastic ground on. It was like a last, terrible

laugh. There is a justice here, Browne thought. He had been trying to be someone else. He had never really wanted any of it.

The tie-rods he found behind the liner were not stainless steel
rod but appeared to have been rigged out of galvanized wire. It
made him laugh to see the way they had stretched because it was
like a practical joke. Like a cartoon in which some furry creature's flying machine deconstructed itself element by element until the poor thing was left about to fall, humorously embarrassed
and terrified, naked and unsupported over emptiness. Flightless
furry me, Browne thought.

Drenched with sick sweat, he hammered the slats into place.
Gradually he realized that the noise in the cabin had diminished.
With the sails down, the pressure eased; the boat was relieved of
her misery. He went on deck and felt ashamed to face the gale.

When the wind shifted to southwest, he put out a storm drogue
and started northeasterly with the wind on his quarter. The
drogue kept his speed down but he had to stay at the wheel to
keep the course.

Hours later, the wind eased and he raised a storm jib again and
went below to rest. Sleep eluded him in spite of his fatigue. Sickness came and went. Petty hallucinations assailed him. He found
himself absurdly concerned with appearances. Everyone must
have seen the poor set of the main. Anyone could have found him
out, exposed his lack of knowledge and experience. It had all
been pretending, he thought, as far back as memory. He was at
the root of it. He was what raised the stink at the heart of things.
There would always be something to conceal.

The sleep that finally came was shallow and thirst-ridden. In
dreams, he was trying to overcome his father's loony drunken
scorn with quiet logic. It was necessary to be patient because his
father was highly intelligent and knew no limits and was capable
of saying anything.

But reasonableness had been the strategy. There was always
a chance you could surprise him and strike a spark of approba-
tion. You had to stage an ambush to wring a good word from
him.

Half waking, Browne felt the peculiar anxiety with which he
had always awaited his father's laughter. If I'm not careful, he
thought, thrashing in the bunk, he'll have me laughing too.

Browne thought he heard that little bubbling up of humor in the throat that preceded one of the old boy's amusing sallies. His heart fluttered, in fear of embarrassment. Then he heard the voice itself, dry and theatrical, heartless.

"Everybody loves you when you're someone else, son."

That was a good one, Browne thought.

47

SHE WOKE to gulls. Steadman's Island. Outside the warm bedroom in which the two of them lay, the sky was winter blue. They were naked under a huge down comforter of the same color.

She turned over and put her face against Strickland's shoulder, put her hand across his chest and ran it down his belly. She was remembering the night he had walked in on her. Late that night when they were making love, he had urged her down on him. He had done so silently. It had all been very unfamiliar. He came, she swallowed. And he had said, "Good for you, baby."

It had been as though she were someone else altogether. Every smell and sensation had been strange. His voice had sounded unlike any voice she had ever heard.

This morning, nestled against his side, she thought back on it and shivered. When she raised her head to look at him he seemed to be still sleeping. Both his eyes were open just a fraction and she could see a sliver of his flat, cold gaze. He looks phallic, she thought. Yes, a prick, a snake. She laughed silently and put her open mouth against his ear.

In the next minute, she heard a crash against the side of the house. A shadow passed across the daylight. "Shit," she whispered, and pulled the down blanket over their heads. Strickland woke up.

"What's happening?"

"We're hiding from Mr. Baily."

"Who the fuck is that?" he asked impolitely.

"Mr. Baily is the propane man," Anne explained. "He's changing our propane tanks so we won't freeze to death. But we don't want him to see us."

"I'm hip," Strickland said.

It struck her as funny and she kissed him as they huddled under the spread. The wall shook as Mr. Baily, outside, rammed the replacement tanks into place. When they heard his truck start up, Strickland got out of bed.

Anne stretched and felt herself sore in unfamiliar places. She pulled the pillow over her head. Strickland was standing at the window, looking out at the winter light.

"Nice place," he said.

"I always thought I liked it. Now I don't know."

"I spoiled it for you? That what you mean?"

"No," she said. "That's not what I mean."

"Last time," Strickland said, "I thought you went very well with the place."

"Last time I did."

"What are you talking about?" he asked her. "You're the same."

She watched him pick up what appeared to be a small medallion on a chain that he had set down on the dresser. When he slipped it around his neck, she beckoned him over.

"Show me."

He sat down on the bed to let her see the thing. Leaning on an elbow, she took it in her fingers to examine.

"It's tiny," she said. On the chain was a minuscule human figure with an agonized expression. It seemed to represent a man assaulted by a winged monster of some sort. "Am I seeing what I think I'm seeing here?"

"It's the god of d . . discomfort." He laughed and began to stammer.

"Seriously. What on earth is it?"

"Mayan," Strickland said. "From the Grijalva. It's a guy tied to a stake. A captive. There's a vulture on the stake and it's eating his eye."

"It's horrible," she said after a moment.

"Come on," Strickland said. "It's exquisite. Look at it."

She let it fall against his chest and looked up at him.

"I do love you, you know."

He stood up and went back to the window to pull a T-shirt on. "Yeah, well. It's only rock and roll."

Anne sank back and pulled the spread around her, trying to see it as rock and roll. Maybe, she thought, I can make a friend of him.

"I don't know what that means," she said. She had no idea what she wanted, finally. It was a brutal business.

Strickland kept looking out of the window and did not reply. All at once she was lonely and frightened. Her remorse felt like mourning. It would be necessary to put all life aside and deal with the man presently in her bedroom and protect herself. That made her feel cold. She pulled the spread closer. On the wall across from her bed was the yellow flowered wallpaper she and Owen had hung together two years before.

"What do you want me to do?" he asked. "Promise you no regrets?"

"No," she said. Was she wishing her husband dead? Maybe she was wishing them both dead, Owen and herself. Maybe they both should have died long before, in 1968, in Bu Dop. Bu Dop was a heartless name for your generic Vietnamese hamlet. Her life seemed to be disappearing before her eyes. "No," she said, "that would be impossible." After a moment she asked him, "What will it be like?"

He laughed and again began to stammer. "Like with everybody," he managed to say. "What happens to everybody will happen to us."

"What's that?" she wanted to know. But he did not answer. Presently he went out to the kitchen. Anne stayed in bed under her comforter. When he came back later, he brought two cups of tea.

"What will we do?" she asked him. She was still naked, wrapped tight in the quilt. "Will we go on filming?"

"Sure," he said. "That's what we do. That's how we make our way through life."

"Everyone's going to see it."

"See what?"

"You and me," she said. Strickland looked thoughtful. He shrugged. There was something on his mind. "It will come out in the film," she insisted.

"Not unless I want it there, Anne."

"People will see it."

"They'll see what we want them to see."

"They'll see us."

"What are you," Strickland demanded, "a fucking mystic? You think the camera never lies?"

"I think it will be apparent," Anne said.

Strickland only laughed. "Don't get so French about it. It'll just be a movie."

They sat in the sunny room drinking tea for a while.

"Take it by the day," he said. "Can't you do that?"

"Not really," Anne said. "I tend to live for the future. Of course," she added, "I don't really believe in the future I live for."

"Same here," Strickland told her.

48

HE CLEANED UP the cabin as best he could. He was very tired and it was difficult to concentrate. His arm was sore; he assumed he must have fallen at some point during the gale. The radio was still functioning because there was news from Cape Town and a report on the race that had the competition spread out in a broken line to the west. Fowler and Kerouaille were nearly neck and neck in the fifties, riding the same weather that had driven Browne. Dennis, Rolf and Cefalu were to the northwest, less than a hundred miles apart. Held's boat had sustained serious damage in the forties. His and another American entry were heading in company for the coast of Argentina. Browne was fascinated to realize that in one period of thirty-six hours, he had covered nearly four hundred ten miles.

He was steering northeasterly, sailing a broad reach on the port tack under a marbled mackerel sky. The wind was stiff but serviceable; it filled the belly of his sails and played the worthless fiberglass below like a cheap harmonica. He had fashioned tie-rods to hold the craft together out of spare wire and turnbuckles. But he knew that the next big blow would dismast him and beat the boat to death.

In the aftermath of the gale, he found himself meditating on the race's circularity, its notions of flight and pursuit. A game, if you could stand the incessant motion, made a perfectly decent life. Games were all that made things serious or gave them form. To be a serious person, it was necessary to embrace one.

Browne took comfort in his reflections, although he supposed the race was lost to him. Sometimes anger kept him from sleep and spoiled his appetite. He rarely ate or slept.

Once he spent a day that was rewarded with a night, although a brief one. He thought it delicious to see the sky go dark. There were no stars. To his bemusement, Duffy was on the line to him.

"How's tricks, Captain? Where you been?"

Browne regretted having responded to his call sign. He had no idea of what to say. I would have won if the boat had been good, he thought.

"I've had high winds," he reported. "I've made good time. Over."

"Are you O.K.?"

"Outstanding," Browne said.

"I'm supposed to remind you to keep filming."

I could say, Browne thought, that I was anywhere on the planet except for his transponder tracking me. I could be free of them all.

"I will."

A stratagem for silence occurred to him.

"Look, I have a problem. Over."

"What's that, Owen?"

"My fuel injectors are blocked. I'll have to clean them before I can charge the generator. I may have to go off the air for a while."

"Is that like a major problem?"

"No. I have gas. It'll be all right. Over."

"What should I tell the public?"

Browne could not keep from laughing.

"Are you laughing?" Duffy asked. He sounded as though he wanted to laugh too but was prevented by some caution.

"Tell it to get some sleep," Browne said. "Out."

Hours later, he dug Buzz Ward's crumpled letter from under the boards.

"No one knows how he will react to being alone," Buzz had written. "There are different levels of it. My opinion is that we are much more alone in a human situation that is utterly alien to us than when alone at sea or lost in the woods or something of that nature. The point is to keep solitude from becoming a prison. The old saw that 'stone walls do not a prison make' is valid."

Encoffined in his grinding fiberglass walls, Browne waited out the short night. Just before dawn, the boat's power failed briefly and the masthead light went out as he was watching it. The light's going out seemed to be a part of a process that was outside randomness.

He took up the letter again, in the beam of a flashlight.

"In 1970 and '71 we had fourteen months in solitary without light. After a few months I found a hole from which I could see daylight and even sometimes people. They were local rural people, Tonkinese peasants, mainly elderly for some reason. They came to barter with the guards — some kind of scam. Often they stopped to shoot the breeze and rest. Watching them, I would think: How sane they are and how little they expect from life."

With the return of light, he thought how strange it was that he had so doubted his abilities as a single-handed sailor that he had been reduced to lying about his experience. In the end he had managed perfectly well. He might have won if the boat had been good.

For some reason, in his desolate quarter of the globe incoming messages multiplied. An Australian voice explained the Doppler effect for the benefit of students for a radio officer's certificate. An instructor who might have been Asian American held forth on the history of spectroscopes:

"Early instruments employed a combination of electrostatic and magnetic focusing whereby ions were sorted specifically according to their mass."

Not useful. Then there was a mad ham in South Africa, Zulu Romeo Alpha one Juliet five six three, who had bestowed upon himself the handle Mad Max. Max was apparently a teenager who traded worldwide for all sorts of collectibles. He broadcast over two assigned frequencies, voice transmission on one, Morse code on the other. Browne could catch only one end of the conversation. In Morse, Mad Max had an able, subtle fist: his pauses resonated, his dots and dashes rhymed, his silences could be downright sarcastic. His voice was a husky boy soprano with a South African drawl. Sometimes he sounded frantic.

"I have a set from India's sunny clime! I have an ivory set from Thailand, the western game but the rooks are elephants with tusks. I have a mahogany set carved on Devil's Island by a convict. Dreyfus? Monte Cristo — Cuba's finest cigar. I have a Persian set, Kaz, the original game still played up the Khyber. I've got a set out of walnut as well. Coconuts? I've a loverly bunch of those!"

He also went in for impossible jokes, available to Browne only in fragments.

"It wasn't the feather or the ten shillings, yer honor. 'Twas the mean low cunning of the bastard."

He seemed part pitchman, part voluble, greedy child.

At sunrise, when Browne went up on deck, there was a pale blue shimmer over the northeastern horizon. Staring at it, he saw something inexplicable.

In the center of the glow was what appeared to be an inverted mountain range. Peaks hung upside down like stalactites, their points barely touching the surface of the sea, thickening to a central mass a few degrees above the horizon. It was as though an upside-down island hung suspended there.

He stood for a long time staring at the strange sight. The inverted peaks were delicate and beautiful, flashing ice colors as the sky lightened. He turned the boat toward them. After about thirty minutes the sight vanished. But where the line of ice had been, a single petrel soared on the wind, ranging ahead of the boat at a constant bearing, as though it were leading him on. Impelled by some urgency like hope, Browne steered his vessel after the bird's passage.

49

STRICKLAND stood with the telephone to his ear, watching Pamela Koester attempt to open a bottle of no-salt vegetable juice. Her first efforts to twist the cap off having proved unavailing, she had begun to bang the top of the bottle against the side of the refrigerator. Each blow was harder than the last. Her eyes took on a cold fanatical cast. The tip of her tongue protruded from one corner of her mouth. Strickland intervened. Without putting the phone down, he walked over to Pamela and took the juice away from her. He had his partner, Freya Blume, on the line.

"We can proceed with the film," Freya was saying happily. "We seem to be provided for."

That morning a number of people connected with the Hylan Corporation had been indicted, including Hylan himself. No charges had been lodged against Harry Thorne.

"Good," Strickland said. He wrapped a dish towel around the juice cap, gave a sharp twist and handed the open container to Pamela. Pamela threw her head back and drank greedily. "Because I have a few subjects lined up."

"As counterpoint, you mean?"

"Yes. As layoff coverage. I think we'd like to hear from some boat people. We got some pithy commentary from those guys on Staten Island. We might have a little more of that."

"Honestly," Freya said, "do you know what those guys are talking about? Can you make it comprehensible?"

"I don't know," Strickland said. "Maybe it doesn't have to be."

All day he had been trying to reach Altan's former chief designer, a man named Fay. When he had left yet another message on the man's machine, he saw that Pamela had succeeded in spilling juice all over the tiles of the kitchen area of his loft. He shouted after her.

"Can't you clean up after yourself? Don't be such a child."

He went into the main loft space and saw her huddled on cushions near the great window, leaning sulkily on her fist and looking down toward TriBeCa.

"I didn't pay my maintenance this month," she said. "I'm really worried."

"What about your dad? Maybe while he's preparing for death he'll think of you fondly."

"His mind," Pamela said, "has been poisoned against me."

Pamela's recent social ascent had led her to a position as a hatcheck girl at the Marabout Club, the young new year's most dashing. It had slipped away when she was discovered attempting to steal a Caius College, Cambridge, scarf from one of the club's prominent customers. Pamela felt particularly ill-used, since she had not coveted the scarf for herself but as a gift for a new boyfriend.

"Don't look at me, Pamela," Strickland said. "I don't believe I'm suited for nurturing."

"I know that."

"These are lean times for me. I'm not from Hollywood."

"I understand," she said. "Can't I stay here for a while?"

"I'll loan you the money to pay your maintenance. If guys are harassing you, leave town."

"I will," she said. "In a couple of days I'll go to the Cape. To Provincetown."

"And you'll hang with your junkie friends up there and get in deeper."

"It's the only place they'll take me in," she said. "It's like home."

"All right," Strickland said. "You can stay here today and tomorrow. I have to go out later." He sighed. "I'm so tired," he said, "of seeing people fuck up."

"Really?" she asked. "I thought you couldn't get enough of it."

"I guess I've finally had enough. Maybe I'm losing my nerve. Maybe I'm getting old."

Pamela studied him. "You look sort of old."

"Thanks a lot," said Strickland.

"But happier," she added. "You look happier lately."

"What are you talking about?"

"I don't know. You look sort of up. Where do you have to go out to?" she asked.

"Out on the job. Up to Connecticut."

"To Brownes'?"

"That's right."

She looked at him sidewise. "Are you fuckin' her? I bet you are!"

"Mind your business."

"But, baby," she cried, "what about us?" For a moment Strickland thought she was serious but she let forth a burst of her chattery ersatz laughter. "Can this really be the end?"

Informed all at once by a burst of unsound energy, she went to the bulletin board where he had fastened a few dozen pictures of Browne and his family.

"Let us have a lookitchere," Pamela crooned, imitating a pimp's drawling manner. "Lessee her one mo' time." She held a picture of Anne at arm's length, inspecting it under one of his pole lamps. "Hey, she's a honey, Strickland. She's old but she doesn't look it. She'll never look old."

"Under forty," Strickland said.

"She should be ashamed of herself," said Pamela. "At her age. With a cute little daughter. And a really excellent husband. Fucking a mean, street kind of guy like you."

"I am not," Strickland said, "a street kind of guy. Put the picture back."

"Afraid I'll get it dirty?" Pamela asked. "With my ho's hands?"

Strickland turned away from her to look out of the window. It was a gray, drizzly morning.

"Boy, I wouldn't be fucking you if I had a husband like Owen." Strickland turned in amusement. "Wouldn't you?"

"Hell no," said Pamela. "I'd be true."

"Women do seem to like him," Strickland observed.

"Fuckin' right," Pamela said warmly. "He's real."

"I suppose I don't get it."

"That's right," she said. "Because you're a carnival-type person and he's a high-class guy. She's got her brains in her pussy."

"You seem to feel very strongly about it."

"You don't know what love is, Strickland."

"Everyone says that."

"You're a seducer," she told him. "You got 'em fuckin' before they can turn around."

"There's a place for seduction, Pamela. Sometimes people have to be told what they like."

"You're like a hot handful of pistachio nuts," Pamela said. "That's my image of you."

"Go home," he said. "Put the picture back. You take too many drugs. You've been under the life too long."

She walked back to the wall, singing to Anne's picture:
"Go tell mah babee sistuh
Don't do what ah have done —"

In Strickland's film *Under the Life* there was a sequence in which Pamela belted out a few giggling choruses of "The House of the Rising Sun."

"So what are you gonna do, Ron? Run off with her?" She pinned the photograph neatly back on the wall. "What?"

"I don't know," Strickland said.

"Crazy for love," Pamela said. "Who woulda thunk it."

Having finished the vegetable juice, Pamela began drinking red wine. Strickland joined her in a glass.

"You know," he said, "there's a level on which she's never been got to."

"You can do it," Pamela said, "if anyone can."

"I'd like to," he said quietly. Pamela looked at him and shivered. "What's the matter now?"

"You're a freak," she said.

Strickland sighed. "My dear Pamela. Who took you in? Who taught the cultivated world to love you? Who understands?"

"You," she said.

"Exactly."

She turned to him with the kind of sneer that had teeth at the edge.

"A freak. Out of the carnivals. You're an *attraction*. Just like your mother."

"Well," Strickland said after a moment, "Moms was a strong joint."

When Pamela went out, he worked at his monitor through the

afternoon. At around four, Fay returned his call. They talked about boats and whether Fay would appear in Strickland's film.

"No sir," Fay said. He had a somewhat military style. "I would have to pass up that opportunity."

"Well, tell me this," Strickland said. "What beef do the Finns have? Has Owen got their boat or not?"

"I can give you my theory on that."

"Yes?"

"Well, I think Matty probably planned to sail their boat in the race and mass-produce the design in the Far East. Then he couldn't pay the Finns. He didn't want to pull out of the race. So when they did the knockoff in Korea or Taiwan or whatever, he took the first one off the line."

"To sail that one instead?"

"Sure," Fay said. "It's a fast design, he might have won with it. Then he would have put it into production with all the race publicity. That's essentially what Browne's hoping to do. In Matty's, shall we say, absence."

"What kind of boat is it?"

"I'm sure it's well designed. How it's made is another story. Sometimes they cut corners."

"Browne likes it a lot."

"Well," Fay said, "Browne's an asshole. Sorry," he added, "I don't mean that. He's a salesman."

"Do you think it's unsafe?"

"Uncomfortable is more like it. A cheap boat will knock you around a lot."

"Browne would know if it were unsafe, right? And not go?"

"Unless he's more of a salesman than I think he is."

"What about Mr. Thorne?"

"Harry doesn't know any more about boats than Owen Browne tells him. These days Owen Browne is his fair-haired boy. Harry's busy."

Strickland succeeded in getting back to work for a while, cutting footage of Browne and his preparations to the music of Erik Satie over WNYC. The news that evening was of terror. Bombs were going off in comfortable, progressive European cities, causing power outages and loss of life. It was the anniversary of something.

Strickland was due in Boston the next day for an appointment with the Public Broadcasting people there and he had been attempting to persuade Anne to go with him. She kept declining because Boston was too near to Maggie's school for comfort. That evening, sipping wine, boiling an egg for dinner, he could not keep from telephoning her.

"I was in New York today," she said. "I thought of coming to see you."

"Why didn't you? Come to Boston."

"I couldn't," she said. "I'd be crazy. Just come back to me."

Come back to me, she had said. Strickland repeated the words to himself. He could not believe she was saying them to him. It made him dizzy.

"B . . baby," he began. They laughed together over his stammer. It reminded him of when she had laughed at him in the street.

"Poor sweet," she said. "Poor tied tongue."

"I want you to do crazy things for me," he told her. "I'll do the same for you. I want you to dress up for me. I want you to cut your hair."

"God," she said, "I love your saying that." Hearing her, Strickland laughed to himself. "How shall I cut my hair?" she asked.

"Short," he said. "Short as you can." He smiled at the anxiety he sensed there.

"For disgrace. What shall I wear?"

"Silk. Skin. Something visual. So we can see where everything is."

"And who pays for these clothes, boss?" She called him boss in imitation of Hersey. "Will you buy my clothes now?"

"I'll do anything," Strickland said.

50

BROWNE FOLLOWED the petrel until it disappeared beyond the black, foam-crested waves. Over the daylight hours he kept watch for the strange inverted towers he had seen at dawn. The weather turned gray and threatening.

That day's sky was too overcast for a sun sight and the navigation satellites out of range. His on-deck thermometer registered an air temperature of seven degrees Celsius. The surface of the sea was a little above two. The wind was steady from the west at ten knots, whipping aside patchy fog. Once he spotted a small floating berg a few miles off. He kept to an easterly course.

In mid-morning Browne heard his call letters recited by the frenetic Mad Max. He assumed that Max had volunteered to patch a telephone call through. Disinclined to chat, Browne had just about decided to go off the air, pleading the generator. He logged Max's signal but did not respond. Shortly thereafter, Whiskey Oscar Oscar, the high-seas operator, called out from the Jersey marshes. WOO had another call from Duffy.

"We got a minor problem with all you guys," Duffy said. "You're off the map, so to speak."

Browne asked Duffy what he meant.

"Some Basques blew up the satellite receiver. They're not getting your transponder signal."

"Basques?"

"Basques," Duffy said, "Colombians, Armenians, who knows? It was a capitalist invention, they blew it up. So you'll have to call in with a position report every twenty-four hours. Let us know if you get in trouble, because we can't see you."

He asked Duffy how long the thing would be down.

"The company isn't giving out much information, Owen. They

don't want to say exactly where their receivers are or what they'll do. Our information is, up to a week."

Browne was silent. Then he said, "My injectors are still giving me trouble. Tell them I may be off the air a while."

"I told them," Duffy said. "Is everything else O.K.?"

Browne assured him that everything else was fine. He decided not to respond to any further transmissions. Let invisibility be matched with silence, he thought.

Continuing east, he saw no more of the peaks. He concluded they must have been some trick of the southern horizon. Of ice, thin light and fog.

During the night, he happened on the missionary station again. A broadcast in a language unfamiliar to him was suddenly concluded by the voice of the Englishwoman whose narratives he had listened to weeks before.

"We now conclude our lesson broadcast in Tagalog and shall broadcast in English starting at seventeen hundred hours Greenwich mean time. We shall then broadcast the same lesson in Cantonese at twenty-two hundred hours Greenwich mean time, in Korean at zero hundred hours and once again in English at zero four-thirty. Our next Tagalog broadcast will be heard at ten hundred hours GMT."

Browne put a can of chicken broth on the galley stove. It was the first nourishment he had taken in twenty-four hours.

"I wonder," the lady asked, "how many of our listeners are tuning to our broadcasts while at sea? Our mail indicates that we have many listeners who are serving on shipboard. Many listeners are employed in the petroleum industry. Others are fishermen. I wonder how many of our listeners remember that our Lord's first disciples found their employment as fishermen?"

Pouring out his broth into a coffee cup, Browne found himself listening to radio-drama effects that weakly replicated the very sounds of the sea that beat about his wounded vessel.

"Listeners may remember," the lady said above the rising sounds of wind and sea, "that when our Lord was pursued by His enemies, Saint Matthew tells us that He went by ship into a desert place apart. When the multitude came to Him they were sent away satisfied — satisfied in spirit and in body as well, fed

by His miraculous abundance. When they were gone He went off
by himself to pray."

Great day in the morning, thought Browne, this has got to be
taped! He was overcome with hilarity. I'll dine out, he thought,
on this one. There would be loaves and fishes.

Since there was no time to attach the recording unit properly,
he simply put a mike beside the speaker and switched it to Record. The lady described the amphibious apostles setting forth
upon Gennesaret. Grinning, he clung to the overhead bar, clutching his cup of broth, crouching over the radio.

"But the ship was now in the midst of the sea," the lady said
breathlessly, "tossed with waves, for the wind was contrary."

He imagined himself listening with his wife. They would laugh
together.

"And in the fourth watch of the night Jesus went unto them,
walking on the sea."

"Fantastic!" Browne said. There, complete with special effects,
with tame whistles and a pussycat's roar so unlike the thing itself,
mighty J.C. went strolling on the briny — the hoariest, silliest
miracle of all.

"They were troubled," the lady declared.

Browne spilled a little broth in his high spirits.

"They cried out for fear," she said.

Browne did a silent mouthing imitation of the disciples crying
out for fear.

"But," the lady continued, "straightaway Jesus spake unto
them, saying —" Here the lady's voice was interrupted by that of
an actor. His was the North American voice — fruity, resonant
and epicene — a beach-blond, Aryan, California Jesus.

"Be of good cheer; it is I; be not afraid."

Browne thought he would die of laughter at the pious, bogus
style.

Peter, preternaturally amazed straight man, was portrayed by
an African actor — perhaps, Browne thought, the same one who
played Esau. Conned again.

"Lawd, if it be Thou, bid me come unto Dee on de water." A
moment of dialect comedy.

"And He said —" breathed the lady.

"Come!" intoned the self-satisfied American voice.

Browne laughed and laughed. But in the voice of the African actor, shouting next, "Lord save me!" — when the wind was boisterous and he was afraid and beginning to sink — there was something rather sad. Something honest and desperate. In his own boisterousness, Browne was inclined to foolish tears.

"Lord save me," he repeated.

"O thou of little faith," asked the cool J.C. reproachfully, "wherefore didst thou doubt?"

"And when they were come into the ship," declared the Englishwoman, "the wind ceased."

Afterward, Browne put his broth aside unfinished and lay in his bunk. Why on earth, he thought, broadcast such pointless, foolish, unconvincing stories over thousands of miles of empty sea? He found that he could not put the question out of his mind.

It was amusing to consider the personalities behind the voices. The English lady with the fussy, overpunctilious diction. Who was she, and what was her life? A smarmy American, an African, a complacent Torontonian. Alone with them on the ocean, Browne sometimes found it difficult to remember that they were not inventing the stories they enacted. He discovered at some point during the hours of darkness that he was still weeping. People were sentimental about religion.

Unable to sleep, he kept thinking about the story. Very sweet, he thought, but after a while he decided there was something sinister about filling the air with false promises. Homely as these little presentations were, a sly skill underlay them. People were vulnerable. In certain circumstances it was hard for the mind to resist examining them over and over.

Slavery, Browne thought — we are enslaved to these strange stories. Hidden voices, bought and paid for, endlessly repeated them. Out on the ocean you had no option but to listen and recognize and ponder as though you had the other half of the dollar bill. They kept making you recognize yourself on their terms. It kept a man from being free.

Concealment was a constant theme. Someone was always being played for a fool. The very process of telling the stories was a game of withholding. Every narrative was reversible and had its outer and its inner side. They were all palimpsests.

They start the stories for us, Browne thought, but we have always known the endings without knowing it. They lead us to water and they make us drink, if it really is water and not wine. Again and again these demands for blind trust. Jump, leap and He may or may not be there. And you — spread-eagled over the ocean — may or may not fall and sink when the wind is contrary. When the wind is boisterous and the sea so big and the boat so small. Endless games. Deception without end, infinity to one, all against all. And on the wind, amplified through the stratosphere, stories to give it form. To keep us absolutely fast in the ice and darkness. Stories like false dawns. But ice, darkness, boisterous winds, and false dawns were all true things that had to be lived out.

If we didn't have the other half of the bill, Browne thought, if we didn't know the end of the stories, we might actually begin to understand. The stories only reinforced our ignorance.

Then suddenly Browne thought: Christ (walking on the water!), what about the stormy petrel? Because in Joshua Slocum, circumnavigator and master of hallucination, a connection was made between the stormy petrel and the story he had just heard. Quickly, but with all the calm he could muster, he sought among his books until he had found both his King James Bible and his copy of Commodore Slocum's *Sailing Alone Around the World*. He remembered quite clearly that at some point old Slocum had traced the origin of the petrel's name to the same lame miracle, Simon Pedro Pescador shuffling off across the deep. In his impatience, Browne could not find the reference in Slocum, although he was sure it was there.

Of course, he had seeen a petrel that morning. Connections were always being invited. Also he remembered the petrel he had seen in the doldrums. They lived so impossibly far from every appearance of hope, on Providence itself, it seemed. Mother Carey's chickens, a sailor had to feel for them. Scattered broadcast from her apron was the grace, the corn, littering the remotest latitudes.

If I were to entertain for the moment, Browne thought, a notion of some strange causality that might apply only on the ocean — why a petrel? Why that morning?

He put the books aside and lay back. Why should there be

petrels at all, he thought, if not for some purpose? What was the need? What message in all those wings? Why petrels? They weren't beautiful. To occupy the emptiness? On behalf of what? Because we're out there, for us? For me?

The tape recorder clicked off. He started rewinding it to listen but at the last moment became afraid of what he might hear.

51

STRICKLAND sat watching his Central American documentary in a studio in Cambridge, Massachusetts. Vultures were on the screen. Startled, they scattered from the corpse of a burro. The tracery of their plumage as they rose and their spread wings made the composition suggest the blossoming of some fatal flower.

Good, thought Strickland. He glanced secretly through the darkness at Clive Anayagam, the PBS producer who had expressed interest in the film. Anayagam, a rotund south Indian, fidgeted in his seat and blew into his fist. One seat away, Anayagam's assistant Mary Melish watched in sober silence through her aviator specs.

To Strickland's intense annoyance, Anayagam laughed his way through most of the film. The figure of Mary Melish seemed to exude a quiet satisfaction that Strickland imagined must bode badly for him. He was suddenly struck with the notion that his film had failed utterly in all that it set out to do. For a moment he could not even concentrate on what that had been.

When the lights were on, Anayagam turned to him and giggled. "Very good. Very subtle. Un-American."

"Are you sure that's good?" Strickland asked politely.

"Yes, it's good, good," the producer said briskly. Anayagam wore a checkered shirt and knit tie. He had white hair and eyebrows, and full cheeks. These, together with his manner, gave him the appearance of an English country squire — less the windburn and whiskey coloring. He looked at Strickland, twinkling mischief. "Are you sincere, I wonder?"

"I don't know what you mean by sincere," Strickland said. "The film reflects the reality of the situation there."

"Truth is beauty," Anayagam said. "Don't you think?" He turned toward Ms. Melish and Strickland half expected him to wink at her. "In film I believe that truth is beauty," Anayagam told him.

"Seems reasonable," Strickland said.

"You have a penetrating vision," Anayagam said. "You're a veritable fucker."

"Thanks," Strickland said.

"You know what the law of rape says?" Anayagam asked playfully. He addressed the question first to Ms. Melish and then to Strickland. "It says that penetration, however slight, is sufficient to complete the offense."

"Is that right?" Strickland asked.

"Penetration," Anayagam repeated, "however slight."

They went out of the screening room to the adjoining corridor. Chairs with red leatherette cushions and tubular arms and legs were lined against the purple wall. A framed San Francisco Mime Troupe poster hung opposite them.

"The Grecian urn in Keats's poem depicts a rape," said Anayagam in a droll manner. "Yet we say: Truth is beauty. And of course it's true."

Strickland courteously showed him a smile.

"Some of your subjects, Mr. Strickland, may feel violated when they see your film."

"Maybe. But they'll recognize themselves."

"You're political, Mr. Strickland. That's against the temper of the times."

Strickland began to stammer. "It f . . falls where it falls in my shows."

"Shows? Is that what they are?"

"That's right," Strickland said.

"You're a showman?"

"Yes," he said.

Anayagam chuckled. Everything amused him. "A dangerous sort of entertainment, eh?"

"That's the best kind," Strickland said.

When Anayagam withdrew, he was left alone with Mary Melish. "He really likes it," she said.

Strickland studied her briefly. She was a tall handsome woman with sharp blue eyes and a long jaw.

"Does he? Will I get paid?"

"I'm sure you will, Ronald. What do you want, praise? Are you insecure or something?"

He had a room at the Sonesta, overlooking the Charles and the Boston skyline. It was very late when he came in. Ray's *They Live by Night* was on WGBH and he watched it with the sound off. Frame for frame, he decided, it was the best film in the world.

When the movie was over, he lay back on the bed in the flickering light of some nature short and thought about his own work. No one, he thought, could ever accuse him of trimming. He had never changed a frame to suit a soul. Although gold was honorable he had never whored after money or even purchased cheap recognition. He had always declined to sentimentalize but it did not seem to him that his work was without feeling. People who wrote about his work, if they understood it, assumed the facetious and knowing manner of the insulted.

He thought of himself sitting in the dark waiting for the fat man's approval and was ashamed. But there was no other way to do it. In spite of his pride he had accepted the attendant humiliations.

The trouble was, Strickland decided, that his work was too much like things. People required their illusions. They wanted to be inspired and he had nothing for them. He had only the news they wanted not to hear. Demystified, things were disappointing.

On the other hand, he thought, perhaps that was not the trouble. Perhaps the trouble was that things had some aspect he could not perceive. Sometimes he suspected they must. Sometimes he almost hoped for it. The other aspect of things might be routinely visible to the average asshole in the street, a personage upon whose inner life Strickland had long speculated. Then his own insight might be the result of some minor mutation, like the ability of the color-blind person to see through camouflage. It might be that he perceived in relief and reversed all signifiers. Thus his impatience and his penetration and readiness to fuck, all the consequence of what he failed to see. A great many careers were based on misperception. Most people had no idea what they were looking at and would pay any fool to tell them.

Above all, he thought, you had to stay in charge and ensure that your definitions prevailed. His unquiet mind and thick tongue had taught him the arts of silence. Untended silence was anarchy, potentially anyone's, an unacceptable free-for-all. He knew how to work the silences, the white noise and dark frames. Anyway, he thought, *vissi d'arte.*

In spite of philosophy, Strickland's doubts frightened him. It was his job to look clearly into the dark. But if you look into darkness long enough, he wondered, will it not look back into you? If his nerve failed him in the dark, he was sure to fall. He imagined an impossible circumstance, that he had long ago gone blind. Imagining his own blindness, he heard the telephone. Anne was on the line.

"I thought you'd be awake," she said.

"I was."

"Did you hear about the satellite?"

"What satellite?" he asked. She sounded cheerful enough.

"The GPS — global position system. The monitor in Switzerland was bombed."

"Bombed?"

"By Armenians, I think. Or Kurds. All the boats in the Eglantine are off the screen. So we don't really know where anyone is."

"Permanently?"

"I can't quite make it out. I think temporarily. The Coast Guard guys at Avery Point say it could be up to a week."

"But," Strickland said, "it doesn't make any difference, does it?"

She was silent for a moment. "Not really."

"Everyone's all right, yes? Owen's all right?"

"Yes," she said. "As far as we know, everyone's all right. Owen's out of radio contact. Generator trouble."

"Are you worried?"

"No," she said.

"Well, I'm coming down," he said. "I'll be there as soon as I can."

"It's O.K.," she said. "I just wanted to get in touch or something. With you."

"I'm on my way."

"But I'm home."

"On my way," Strickland said.

At Logan he got a commuter flight to New Haven and took a cab from there.

She was bathed and dressed when he arrived. She still smelled of soap. They sat in her downstairs study and she got them both coffee as though it were a polite call.

"It's not that I'm worried," she said guiltily. "I happened to be thinking about you."

Strickland put his cup and saucer aside, took Anne's from her hand and led her up to the bedroom. She came along smiling gravely.

"What are you doing?" she asked, teasing him.

They made love and he went to sleep. Awakening to the quilts and paisley and suburban birdsongs, he had no idea where he was. She came in and sat down on the bed beside him.

"Glad you came," she said. He was gratified by her sweet spacey smile. After a moment he realized that she had taken a drink.

"Are you O.K.?"

She smiled the wider. "I'm tense."

"You said it was all O.K."

"Yes," she said, holding the smile. "I'm not worried about Owen. I'm sure he's fine. I'm just tense."

"O.K.," he said. He kept an eye on her as she walked to the window. "I just hope he's filming. Owen, I mean."

She looked briefly frightened. "I'm sure he's doing what you wanted him to. He's a neat photographer."

Strickland sat up, wondering if she was about to cry for her husband on the sea.

"If you're not worried," he asked, "why are you tense?"

There were no tears. She seemed in control.

"I must be feeling guilty," she said. "That must be it."

"I see."

"You know," she said, "I have to ask myself if I love him."

"How do you have to answer yourself?"

"Well, I do," she said matter-of-factly. "Of course I do."

Strickland edged up against the sunny wall and put a pillow behind his back.

"I really don't know what that means."

"You don't know what love is?"

"The word covers such a range of behavior. I really don't. I mean," he added, "it's an alibi." He shrugged.

"I've been his wife for twenty years," she said. "We lived through Vietnam. I never had another guy. We grew up together."

"Some people," Strickland said, "might call that a codependency problem."

She laughed. He got up still naked and brought her beside him on the bed. He saw her frown, thinking of the unguarded window.

"Maybe it is. Are you trying to help me or something?"

"You've been out of the fucking world," Strickland said. "You've been playing household nun for that guy."

She pulled away from him and stood up.

"What on earth do you mean?"

"Don't get mad," Strickland said. "I'm jealous. I'm entitled."

"What do you mean, household nun?"

"Ah," Strickland said, "the two of you — you've been hiding from life, for Christ's sake. In your pretend world. Running off to that island."

"We got by."

"You got by like a couple of fucking children. Juvenilizing your life. The guy was doing a number on you, understand?"

"No," she said.

"I say yes," Strickland shouted. Seeing her stare at him, he spoke more coolly. "You're a fantastic woman. You're too good for him. He's this dorky fucking citizen, for Christ's sake. A stiff. A stuffed shirt."

"I don't want to hear that," she said. "I love him."

"Well," he said, "*that* is what I don't want to hear."

She sat down on the bed and looked at him sadly.

"I have feelings," Strickland said. "I'm an artist, right? Anyway, I make movies."

"But I do love him," she said.

"If you're going to use that kind of diction," Strickland said, "I can't help you."

"Twenty years is a long time, Ron."

"Sure," he said. He shook his head in disgust. "For God's sake. He kept you out of circulation. Exploited you. You've been married twenty years because you don't know anything about the opposite sex. Neither of you. And because you don't know anything about the opposite sex you've stayed married."

"I wish," Anne said, "I knew as little about it as you do." She went out and downstairs and he heard her pouring a drink. She came back with a glass of wine.

"You really never had another guy?"

"No," she said.

He thought she was avoiding his eye. "In twenty years you never got it on with another man until me? I'm sorry, but I don't believe it."

"It's true," she said, looking at him directly. He saw immediately that it was. Her arrogant innocence amazed him.

He reached out from the bed and took the glass from her hand.

"You shouldn't drink all that," he said. "Not by yourself. Not without me."

He drank the wine and held his breath, suddenly bemused, as though he were just another fellow like his patron and quarry, the average asshole in the street. All at once he was afraid of losing her.

52

THERE WERE no petrels in the cloudy dawn, but Browne brought his boat about and headed east for where the peaks had been. He felt distinctly in rebellion. About midday, after hours of running before the wind, he saw them again, right side up this time, ice towers that formed the spine of a volcanic island. He made a cautious circuit of the place, checking bottom all the while. The heights rose to a snow-covered central peak of two hundred meters or so that extended jagged arms around both ends of the island. Browne suspected there might be a central caldera beyond the spires. Small glacial valleys saddled the line of hills. When his boat passed close inshore, cold winds rushed down from the canyons and set his mainsail luffing and rattled the unsteady mast in its step.

Approaching nearer the island, he saw that below the snow line there were hummocks of coarse yellow grass. Some dark green, thick-fleshed plant seemed to cover certain hills. He thought he could make out a few scarlet spots that might be gentians in bloom. There were purple stands of saxifrage but no trees at all. The rollers were almost within his hearing; he could imagine the sound of them. Sometimes he thought he heard the screaming of birds echoing off a canyon wall. He saw a flight of cormorants just outside the wave line.

By the end of the day, Browne was still sailing around the island he had found. The dusk was many hours long, with shadows so extended that it seemed the planes of the visible world could not contain them. The sea turned inky black and the sky a breathless blue. That evening Browne heard his call sign repeated over and over again in a hoarse adolescent voice: "Whiskey Zulu Zulu one Mike eight seven three." He made no reply.

The idea of invisibility made Browne feel as though he might be able to sleep. For a long time, though, he could only lie staring at the overhead, transfixed with cold anger. At some point he had a sense that the wind had reversed. It seemed desperately necessary that he liberate himself somehow from the humiliating race. Eventually, out of exhaustion, he lost consciousness for a while.

The next day, studying his island's contours through binoculars, Browne saw birds everywhere. There were gulls and petrels of every variety, shearwaters, albatross. One of the black rock beaches was so crowded with king penguins that he had mistaken their seething mass for foliage at first glance and their yellow crests for flowers.

He suspected that the caldera formed a lagoon which might be somewhere open to the sea. The only coast with an approachable strand appeared to be on the west side. But the beach there, such as it was, had been pounded out by enormous rollers driven by the prevailing winds that made any kind of anchorage impossible. The leeward shore of the island was a wall of sheer black rock, bluffs over a hundred feet high at their lowest point, priestly black and remote, a fortress. The Island of Invisibility gave nothing away.

After a few days his rebellion assumed a routine. During the brief periods of darkness he would head just off the wind with only a storm jib up, sailing away from the island. With first light, he would come about and head back toward the peaks. Every day, winds permitting, he got a little bolder and approached the shore more closely, feeling his way in on the sounding device. There seemed to be no bottom anywhere.

The high-seas operator at Whiskey Oscar Oscar kept him apprised of the race into which he betrayed himself. The positioning satellite was still down. Fowler, Kerouaille and Dennis had already passed him during his northward excursion. Others were gaining. At his chart table, he made a game of calculating where he might have been if the winds had held, if the boat had hung together, if the world had been different from what it was. He might well have made over two hundred fifty miles a day down in the south fifties. Three weeks of that would have borne him most of the way to Australia. He marked his imaginary daily positions on the chart, the road not taken.

Studying the positions, he found himself imagining log entries to go with them. The weather had been constant enough throughout the area, the winds consistent, predictable stuff for that time of year at that latitude. All of it, together with the droll gallantries and plagiarized meditations, might have gone into the book he had imagined writing. The book of a stern, steady man, a man for long solitary passages.

Browne was moved to consider the differences between the man he might pretend to be in a book and the one he actually was. The differences, it suddenly occurred to him, were everything. He might spend his whole life considering them. He sharpened a pencil with a Buck knife and took up a spare notebook:

"Two hundred and eighty miles today," he wrote, "in a near gale." Just to see what it might look like. He could not bring himself to set down the name *Nona* anymore.

"I'm in excellent spirits in spite of dark weather, minor injuries and my faulty generator."

He could sense his father rejoicing in the discovery of a lie.

"Out of the night that covers me,
Black as the Pit from pole to pole . . ."

So the trite, brave anthem, beloved of the old fool. But the night covering Browne's father had been hell itself, so black that in it he had ceased to be a man at all.

"I remember the night," he told the old man. "I remember your drunken screams there. I remember your smiling, unlucky face."

He was the captain now. The master of his fate, an inherited rebellion. Somehow he had cut himself with the Buck knife. He washed his wounded hand in the galley sink. The cut was deep. He had to spend nearly an hour dressing it. Later on he found that he had cut a tendon and could not bend the finger at the outermost joint. It was his left index finger.

He took up a new notebook and sat down again. What more might be in the edifying book? With "Invictus" as its epigraph. Something absurd for ardent children. Onward, upward, away from Dad's night. He had to admit it might have been good to have won. To have served himself and his country, to have done a decent, simple thing well.

Carefully, he examined his imagined positions on the chart. All the stories were embroidered, so it was said. Sailors privately ridiculed each other's accounts. No one had ever brought the truth ashore. It was not to be had.

The stern, steady man — a man not altogether unlike Browne — who had made the speeds indicated by those fictional positions would experience predictable weather. Above all, Browne thought, he would experience conventional emotions and suitable reflections. The stern, steady man's log would read like dozens of others and his memoir would imitate the form. Indeed, the man or his publisher might employ a hack to agreeably ornament his narrative.

But if the man were not in fact so stern and steady — if he were in rebellion and his positions fictional like Browne's — he would face a few dilemmas. As a game, Browne began to put himself in the position of a man given to subterfuge, a man who might fake his positions all the way around, as he had once humorously imagined doing. A not so stern and steady man who might not sail around the world but say he did.

It would be necessary to work backward. Instead of determining longitude and latitude by comparing the real and calculated angles of his sightings, he would have to start with the position and extrapolate both angles in the *Nautical Almanac*. Some very fancy figuring would be involved. It would be an absorbing game and a demanding one, a game of time and space. The perfect entertainment for Absolute Elsewhere. Playing would require some difficult impersonation. He would have to impersonate the individual he had spent his whole life earnestly not becoming.

It could all be looked at as philosophy, Browne decided — as a question of reality and perception. Everyone had to believe his informing story. Everyone had to endure his own secret. That was survival. Survival made him think fondly of the island he had found. If he could only find an anchorage, he might rest there, in a safe secret harbor.

53

STRICKLAND, Hersey and Jean-Marie were guests at the Inn on Steadman's Island, the only off-season hostelry in the island's tiny town. Strickland was staying there for propriety's sake, in a gesture at preserving Anne's reputation on the Island where she had spent her summers since childhood. Hersey had brought film equipment to accommodate Strickland's possible notions. Jean-Marie had come along with Hersey. She disclaimed knowledge of ever having been on an island before, playing excessively dumb, to annoy Strickland.

On arriving, the film makers had been compelled to share the inn with a party of dissolute construction workers who drank, cursed and occasionally subjected Jean-Marie to mild sexual harassment. After the second day, the construction workers had packed up and gone home to Bridgeport. Leaving, they had complained loudly. The vacation housing market was collapsing, they announced. Their employers had been ruined.

"Degenerates," Jean-Marie said. "Good riddance."

On the third day it rained. Strickland spent part of the morning playing three-handed hearts with the young students. Hersey did accent routines.

"Zee nine of spades," he would declare in a portentous *gitano* quaver, "eet ees zee card of death!" He would repeat the line whenever it struck his fancy. After a while Strickland threw his own hand in.

"I'm going up to the house."

"Should we come along?" Hersey asked.

"I'll call you if I want you," Strickland said.

Jean-Marie went to the rain-streaked window and looked after him.

"I wonder if he hits her," she said.

Hersey dealt for the two of them. "Hits her? The guy's in love."

"In love?" she repeated. "That coldheart?"

"He's a romantic," Hersey said, "believe me."

Jean-Marie turned from the rain.

"We gonna get paid or what?" she asked her boyfriend. "Because that company is in bankruptcy, that's what I hear. The boat company."

"He's been taken care of," Hersey said. "He'll pay us out of his pocket."

"Really?"

"Anyway, I'd work for him free," Hersey said. "As long as I could."

Jean-Marie stared at him. "Wow!" she said.

Hersey picked up his hand and examined it. "Once again zee nine of spades," he wailed. "Zee card of death!"

At the house, Strickland found Anne in the living room going over Admiralty charts. There was a glass of white wine beside her chair.

"You're starting early."

"I know it," she said.

He came up beside her chair and ran his hand along her cheek and beside her ear, brushing back her hair. She had cut it very short to please him. The clothes she put on when they were together, her lingerie and what she wore to bed were all chosen to suit his taste. When he touched her face, she inclined her head against his hand slightly. The hand had been curled in a three-quarter fist and he relaxed it.

"I take it he's still off the air?"

"Yes," she said. "I wouldn't mind hearing his voice."

"Well," Strickland said, "anyway, they'll soon have that thing back up."

"Avery Point says it's unlikely all the transponders will be transmitting."

"Then," he said, "we'll still have our element of mystery. Christ, I hope he wins!" He sat down in a wicker rocking chair, shoved himself fore and aft a few times and got to his feet. "The goddam company goes under and he goes ahead and wins it."

Her impatient smile put him on his guard. For a moment he had the sure sense of her slipping away. It had never mattered all that much before. He had always watched women cure themselves of him with the detachment of a philosopher. All things passed.

"We should film," he said, pacing.

"God," she said, "I dread it."

"Why's that?"

"For God's sake," she said. "The home front? Me waiting faithfully? Are you kidding? I don't know a lot about documentaries, but surely there's an authenticity problem."

"Good point," Strickland said. "Still, I want more of this island."

When the rain stopped, he summoned Hersey and Jean-Marie and they staged some chores for Anne Browne to perform. Some grocery shopping. A visit to the island hardware store.

The clerk at the hardware store was a grossly overweight man in his forties with a youthful but pustulous face who wore unbuttoned plaid flannel that exposed his belly and T-shirt. He was something of an extrovert and ready for discourse with the camera. When Anne had made her purchase and gone out, he recorded his attitude toward Browne's voyage.

"Wouldn't catch me out there in one of them little boats."

"No?" Strickland asked. "Why not?"

"Hell," he said with a giggle, "that's dangerous. Life is sweet."

The image of a fat, leprous clerk declaring life sweet seized Strickland's imagination. Over time it would become a catchphrase for the film makers and they would toss it back and forth incessantly.

"Hey, life is sweet."

Strickland would show the footage in which the clerk uttered it over and over again. Hersey and Jean-Marie took to exchanging glances behind his back. In New York, he showed it to Pamela a number of times. She variously laughed and cried.

When they were through filming Anne at her workaday tasks, Hersey and Jean-Marie stashed their equipment and went for a walk. Strickland and Anne went back to the house. Anne had another drink.

"I must have looked loaded," she said.

"Maybe. We'll see."

That night in bed she talked about Owen.

"He believes in all those things people used to believe in. Before people were like you. Like us."

"Precision bombing," Strickland suggested as he ran his hands over her. "Surgical strikes. All the good old stuff."

Bad cards, he was thinking. I'll never come through. This bitch has got my brains, my blood.

"Virtue," she said. "Navies."

Somehow things turned ardent. Afterward, she replaced the amulet around his haggard neck. She kissed him.

"My sparrow," she said drunkenly. In the light of the bedside lamp she examined the little carving yet again.

"It's so small. How could anyone have carved it without a magnifying glass or something?"

"They were very mysterious," he said. Indeed, he thought, it was a wonder, and he would never part with it. The captive's features, minute but precisely carved in the exuberant, faintly comic Mayan manner, expressed unmistakable agony.

"I call him the Sufferer," Anne said. She took it in her fingers.

"That's good," Strickland said. "Who did you decide he was?"

"I don't know," she said. "An informer? A voyeur?" He watched her regard the little figure without mercy. "A lying witness?"

"No," he said. "A truthful one."

54

Six hundred yards off the south shore of Invisibility, Browne's depthfinder suddenly gave him a reading of one hundred twenty feet. He had been tentatively edging toward the shore all morning in unusual light air, wondering if he could find a temporary anchorage. Seconds earlier, the bottom had been beyond measure. He brought his bow across the wind, lowered the main and dropped anchor in about ninety feet. When the hook dug in, he payed out scope as she drifted slowly downwind. He imagined a ledge of lava below, an outcropping of the island ahead.

For the first time since arriving off the island, he had a quick glimpse of sun in a dappled, March-like sky. The showing was over before he could get out his sextant. Off the southern point, the smoky seas were pitching restlessly as though they missed the wind's authority. Scanning the shore that morning, he had seen glistening in the unaccustomed sunlight what looked like a passage through the volcanic wall. Immediately he had started cautiously toward shore.

Satisfied for the moment with his anchorage, Browne cast a weather eye on the distant horizon. There were not many signs to watch for. At any time the wind might shift and resume its full force and there would be no warning breeze or change in pressure.

He got his inflatable Zodiac dinghy out of storage, pumped it up, attached the outboard to its mount and secured it to the stern ladder. For his exploratory trip, he brought along a diver's face mask, a marlinspike and an antique lead-line with leather depth markings some Campbell progenitor of Anne's had hauled from Newfoundland.

It was strange to pull away from his boat and watch her roll at that uneasy anchorage. Her fouled hull and battered rigging aroused no forgiveness in him. He felt glad to be leaving her. Set free.

He made a zigzag course in, checking for rocks, looking for bottom. Here and there he put out the lead-line; each time it sank taut. Random winds of surprising force blew down from the island, turning the Zodiac's bow aside, showering him with icy spray. Eventually he made out the channel quite clearly. In the next cove, two sea lions were drawn up on the rocks in what appeared to be astonishment, watching him. He passed swimming penguins that shot through the water like miniature dolphins. Predatory black gulls came out to meet him. There were eyes everywhere. When he drew closer to shore, the sea lions fled.

The passage in the rock was about forty feet across at the surface. The water, though full of kelp, was amazingly clear and he could see at a glance that there was clearance for his vessel. The channel seemed to widen with depth, as though it had been a cave in the lava, an underwater tunnel with its roof either worn down by the sea or blasted out by men. It would do in any case. He gunned the outboard and motored into the bay he had discovered.

The place was plainly a caldera. Around it, the blasted ridges had been worn smooth by time. Over it, beyond the screeching of the skuas and the whine of the outboard, hung an enormous silence. There was snow on the ridge line and dark autumnal vegetation lower down. The surrounding peaks cast deep cold shadows.

He could not resist shouting once. His own voice surprised him but its answering echo made him feel, for a moment, in possession of the place. When the wind rose, it too resounded in the crater and its sound was very strange, music out of stone.

Back aboard *Nona*, Browne decided to come into the bay under sail, in spite of the perverse winds. The alternative was to tow the boat in with his dinghy on a slack tide — a process that, when he imagined it, made him feel out of control. He hauled up the anchor and set off under a light jib, the dinghy bobbing along behind.

"All right, lady," he told the boat. He thought *Lady* would make a good name for her. It would be pronounced in the New York style, with veiled but apparent contempt. I'll rename her, he thought as the island's winds rattled in his sail and its walls bore down on him, for my secret purpose, in the book, the film.

The bad winds were merciful and he cleared the passage and dropped anchor in the middle of the crater. He could see rocky bottom forty feet below. Late that evening the obscured glare of the sun disappeared beyond the surrounding ridges and Browne lay down on his rack. Lying at anchor in the bay felt so different from the open sea that he was restless. Boiling an egg for a sandwich, he turned on the single sideband. That night Melbourne would not oblige him. Eventually, on thirty megahertz at the even hour, Whiskey Oscar Oscar reached out, broadcasting the name and call sign of each entry in the race. Browne zeroed in on the top end of the band. Soon he heard the cheerful, Gallic lisp of Patrick Kerouaille.

He had to fiddle to get the reply. He heard: "Zero four hundred Zulu time. Over." He thought it must be when the satellite system would resume tracking. By Browne's Rolex, the most expensive thing he owned after his house, it was eleven hours or so until nineteen hundred GMT, "Zulu time." Thereafter he would be plotted in New York. He lay down to think about it. For some reason, something Ernest Shackleton had said came into his mind. Shackleton had been a boyhood hero of his, a figure of the vanished world he had childishly thought he might inherit, instead of rebellion. Of course the world had changed many times since Shackleton, and even since Browne had read of him in the old books, in the old gatehouse, on winter Sundays.

"A man must shape himself to a new mark directly the old one goes to ground."

That night, under cover of the brief darkness, he climbed the mast and removed the transponder before it could reveal his existence and position.

55

THAT WEEKEND Strickland talked her into driving down to Atlantic City in the rain. He claimed to have another project in
mind. Fretful, hung over, she went along. She found herself nursing a weak Bloody Mary for nearly an hour while he checked
them into Bally's. A music video played against a giant screen on
the crimson back wall of the bar. Cab Calloway in a yellow zoot
suit was cakewalking through a dance set that resembled the New
York Street in an old movie. The beat was contemporary and
relentless.

"What am I doing here?" she asked him. "It's so ghastly."

"Consider it a field trip," he told her.

There was boxing at the hotel that afternoon and he wanted to
see one of the fights on the undercard, a bout between two mid-
dleweights. He had been following the fortunes of a fighter from
Providence called Joey Azzolino, whom he referred to as a guinea
psychopath. Azzolino was matched against a Philadelphian
named Underhill. After the fight they were going to a party to see
some of the people who had been in *Under the Life*.

The fight took place in a welter of obscene cries, blood and
spittle. Half drunk, she found it easier to take than expected.

"You liked it," he insisted afterward. "You liked seeing those
guys whacking away at each other. It got your blood up."

"Maybe so," she said. She felt distracted and confused. "I used
to fight when I was small. I used to like it."

Their room was small but clean, commanding a few square
miles of serried, rain-dull ocean. The theme was a milky beige,
vaguely organic and sensual. Mist raced by outside. In the oversized mirror, she got to inspect herself gross and full of bread, a
drink in one hand, a lipstick in the other. The sight gave her a

quick vision of her future as a blowsy middle-aged reveler, all booze and beige hotel rooms. A former wife and former mother easing into forlorn, privileged self-indulgence, bloated and shrill. By the bathroom scale, though, her weight was a reassuring hundred twenty-eight. Penalties might be suspended.

When they went out, she was dressed to please him, shorn and tightly encased.

"Like a woman of mine and not some other guy's," he said. The voice he said it in was strange. She thought he might be doing an impersonation.

The revelers convened in a cloud-bound apartment in another hotel. The ratty city behind the hotel strip was partly visible below — yellow beer-sign lights, traffic signals, motel flashers. Inside, hundreds of people were jammed together; men and women smelling of oil and leather, blacks and whites in equal numbers. A sound system was blaring James Brown.

They encountered a man called Junior, whom she vaguely remembered from the film.

"I say, my friend," Junior said to Strickland. "I say, my man Ron."

He was tall, very dark and round-faced. He began explaining it all to them in a careful sibilant diction.

"What it is," he explained, "the woman is drawn to the strong. Whatever's strong draws the woman's nature, the force is central, you know what I'm sayin'? Be natural like the tide, like the phases of the moon." He addressed himself to Anne and Strickland in turn.

"The male is substance, the female has the fluid quality. The fluid is sweet, is drawn by substance. The substance stands, the nectar flows. The substance is warm and strong, the tide is of the moon. Be soft, curving, burns by reflected light."

"Good Lord," Anne said.

"Woman will always turn from the weak to the strong, be the nature of forces, the way of thangs." He carefully pronounced the word "thangs" as though to indicate its distinction from things in general. His voice hung just below the baseline of the music in the room.

"Female finds completion in the male, the syrup in the branch, the honey in the rock. So all thangs turn to the light. See what I'm sayin'?"

"I'm so bombed," she told them. "It's wasted on me."

"I'm hip," Strickland said.

They were separated. Anne found herself talking to a man who claimed to play with Lester Lanin's orchestra.

"I remember you," he insisted to her. "It was Scottsdale. Sure it was."

"I've never been there," she said.

"Sure it was. It was the country club there. I remember your frame, man. I remember your eyes."

"Why are you calling me 'man'?" she asked him.

"You were there with your fiancé. You told me, 'We'll get in trouble.'"

"Oh gosh," she said. "A whole life I've never lived."

"Sure it was, sure it was," the man insisted.

Eventually she found Strickland in conversation with a pale fat man in a tuxedo, who turned a glittering smile on her approach.

"Have a heart," she said. "Let's go."

"To what do we owe the pleasure?" the man in the tuxedo asked her. "What brings you to Jersey? You his project?"

"She's a f . . friend," Strickland said. "Not a . . . project."

"Sort of a friend," Anne told the man. "An ex-project."

"An ex-project?" inquired the man. He turned to Strickland. "Is she kidding?"

"I never know," Strickland told him.

56

DURING THE NIGHT there was a single hour when the sky cleared and the southern stars appeared to him in their cold alien courses. Scorpio was entirely visible beside the Southern Cross so he tried getting a fix on Antares. He kept losing it and finding it again. Each tremor of the shoulder set him wandering among the constellations. Eventually he brought the right star to the horizon. As a young man, he had been good at celestial navigation; he had known the names and aspects of more stars than anyone.

Without much confidence, Browne calculated his position at approximately forty-nine degrees south, nineteen degrees east. Neither the Admiralty nor the Hydrographic Office charts showed an island there.

When it was light, he had some juice for breakfast and sat down at his navigation table. Taking his night's sighting as a starting point, he awarded himself thirty knot winds and an average speed of a little over nine knots. At that rate he would make around two hundred fifty miles a day, seventeen hundred fifty miles a week.

Marking the next day's false position filled him with dread. It seemed to matter less that it was false than that it marked time unlived. After that he found the work quite easy. Once he had picked a mark to represent dead reckoning, he worked out a calculated sextant angle in the almanac together with a true one. A false true one. Then he entered the figures and plotted an intercept and a line of position. It was agreeable to work at anchorage, seated at a steady table.

It took him all day to work out a week's worth of positions. Logging them, he realized that he would have to invent weather for each position, and not only weather but little incidents to accompany the entries. Wraparounds and broken poles, parted stays and chafed halyards, reefs, sheared bolts and jammed winches. And of course there would have to be suitable reflections — not the freakish notions that haunted unsound minds but helpful and healthful insights to inspire happy strivers everywhere. He would be fashioning a counterworld in which to locate his improved self. At the same time he would have to live secretly in the actual world as the man he had become.

Browne surprised himself — not only with the ease with which he worked out false angles and positions but at the fluency with which he was able to invent convincing details for the imaginary future days he was constructing. It was much easier than attempting to record even the roughest outline of truth. He felt as though he had happened on a principle of existence. He became more and more elated. With a swift and lively imaginary week's sailing behind him, he felt a sudden urge to take command of the new island. There were still a few hours before nineteen hundred Zulu. He put on his arctic foul-weather gear and went out on deck.

The sun was thirty degrees above the ridge line, in an edge of clear blue. A massed bank of bitter black clouds had occupied most of the sky. The wind was variable, alternately icy and mild. He took his camera, a marlinspike and the dive mask, climbed into the dinghy and cast off.

He stepped ashore on a shingle of flint that shifted beneath his boots. Not far away, on the ocean side of the island, he could hear great waves crashing and the hiss and rattle of their retreat over stones. The unsteady wind carried a chaos of birds and a chicken-coop stink. He trudged on over the flint, sliding and stumbling toward firmer ground. The disc of the sun glared on the water and the peaks of ice. Browne put his sunglasses on.

It was hard humping to the ocean side, over a quarter-mile spine of delicate, razor-sharp black lava that was riddled with fissures, hollows and fossilized bubbles. The rocks looked to Browne like a mold from hell, a maelstrom frozen at a stroke. The going was dangerous. Once he fell and cut his hands.

The nearer sand on the ocean shore was black and soft as dust and he sank sometimes to the ankles. Advancing toward the breakers, he at first felt a sense of liberation. *Thalassa*, he was thinking, repeating the whispered word as he labored over the beach. When he was nearer, the murderous force of the great waves was plain. They threw themselves against the stones with much brutality, seeming to double their strength after cresting and accelerate on the final roll. You had only to watch their coming in to feel the dizzying, suffocating force they contained. Each breaker cast up a thin cloud of debris, so that going closer to the water, Browne felt not only icy spindrift on his face but pebble shards and dirt that soiled his eyes. It made him remember that he was not one of the Ten Thousand and that the ocean was his prison and not the road home. The sight of it made him sick so he stretched out and retched on the sand.

Lying there, he became aware of the birds. It was the smell of them, he thought, that had made him sick and not the ocean. There were thousands, right at the edge of the soft sand on which he lay. They had black button eyes and yellow crests through which the sun and the spray made rainbows. He stood up and walked over the sand toward them.

Penguins surrounded him like wheat. The ground was slippery with kelp and guano and the landscape stank to heaven. The crowd of penguins gave way to make a path for him. Their clucking calls filled his ears, echoing off the rocks until they made a silence. It was a droll scene, he thought, the Protestant formality of the birds on their icy stone island with a black sky overhead. But the sun's upper limb shone from an edge of sky as though reflected in an index glass. Everything is measurement, Browne thought, everything I see. The sun's rays lit the penguins' crests to a thousand colors.

Ahead of him, along the penguin shore, were white shapes in the sun's glare. Ice, he thought at first. Coming closer, he saw that the white shapes were not ice. What they might be confounded him. At first they seemed meaningless and without form; closer up, they assumed a geometry with which he was somehow vaguely familiar. For a moment his attention was distracted by the sight of a young penguin besieged by skuas. The penguin was alone within a circle of disaster ten feet in diameter. No other bird came nearer. It was eyeless although it stretched its neck and strained to face the sky. One leathery flipper was raised in comic rage at things. The other hung bloody and truncated at its side. Overhead, skua gulls were wheeling. Every minute or so, a skua would descend screaming from the wheel to tear flesh from the dying bird. Browne stopped for a while to watch, then turned away and put the back of his arm across his eyes to protect them from the glare. I want a missionary woman now, Browne thought, to make a story out of this. Mother Carey tending her chickens, God's sparrows falling aslant his gaze. Creatures for sacred inscrutable reasons denied flight are brought piecemeal into the sky as meat.

The white shapes, Browne saw presently, were the bleached bones of whales. Hundreds of bones were strewn along the beach just beyond the rollers. Penguins wandered among them like the citizens of a town. He walked faster, bracing for balance with his marlinspike.

There were fin bones like skeletal wings, head-high pelvic bones and mandibles full of peg teeth the size of fists. Cages of five-foot ribs were piled like the tiers of a stylized prison to a height beyond reach. The field of bones stretched to the end of the cove, a mile in the distance. They were clean and dry. Their contours were natural and pleasurable. At first Browne was shocked, as though he had stumbled on some kind of sordidness or scandal. But the beauty of the scene, the order and grammar of the bones, put his mind at rest.

He walked patiently around the next point and saw what appeared to be black towers rising from the beach. The towers proved to be huge vats raised on three metal legs. The rocks here and the scattered bones were all burned black as though by fire. It seemed that the cauldrons had burned out of control.

A few hundred yards from the shore was a black metal shed. Browne went closer and saw that it was covered with graffiti. He stopped and stared uncomprehending at the shed's walls, unable to assign any meaning to the scrawled words.

ONIONHEAD. HOBB. TREMAGISTER. SEVEN SPIRITS.

There was a trident and the tricolor flag of some nation which Browne, who knew his flags, failed to recognize. There were semaphore characters, together with drawings of genitals and odd smiling faces.

One of the island's freak winds came up and rattled the metal roof of the building and played one curving wall to the tone of a musical saw. He was aware of darting figures on the ground. Rats, he thought at first, seeing a gray-brown blur. But when he had a closer look he saw that the creatures were not rats but small flightless birds that looked like plucked penguins. He thought they were called rails.

There was a stick covered with flaking white paint on the ground and he picked it up. He wanted to write something on the wall, to leave something there. The paint on the stick was long dry and there was nothing to write with. Be true to the dreams of your youth, he thought. He traced that, word by word, on the black wall with his white stick, although it left no mark at all.

BE TRUE TO THE DREAMS OF YOUR YOUTH.

Inside the shed, the droning of the wind in the metal frame was deafening. The pitted metal floor was burned black too. An empty bottle of Australian brandy stood in one corner.

When he went out of the shed, he noticed another structure he had not seen before. It was a square house of two stories, tucked out of the wind's reach behind a hill. Beside the house was a fenced-in area that might have been a dog pen or, in some other place, a garden. The protecting hill was unnaturally round and grown with tough yellow grass. He walked toward the house, up stony, invisibly slanting ground. At close regard, it appeared to be made of wood that had seared to the color and consistency of charcoal but somehow remained upright.

The house's entrance faced the lagoon in which he had anchored. There was a charred porch that somehow supported his weight. The door was missing and he was just about to pass inside when a flourish, a bright flash like a banner, caught his eye. Looking toward the ocean, he saw a languid curve of colored cloth. The wind had a bright silk dress, gusts filled it like a sail and gave the appearance of flesh. Then he realized he was seeing a woman there. When it disappeared, he could almost remember a face, a frowning blue-eyed look.

Inside, the first room was in deep gloom, its unglazed windows nailed and boarded. Fungi grew along the walls and years of spiderwebs in every corner. The naked doorway he had entered through admitted the only light. Two of the strange little birds clattered out of the shadows, startling him. He thought the place should smell of ashes but it had the same odor as the foul wind outside. Thick gravel dust sanded his steps.

His eyes had been dazzled with an Antarctic glare and it took him a little while to adjust to the half-light. When he had, he saw a second room beyond the first. The connecting door was ajar. Behind it was a hallway from which a flight of stairs ascended to the upper floor. What light there was seemed now to be above him, but at the top of the stairs he found himself in darkness. Immediately before him was yet another door. Light was visible beneath it. He was surprised by the notion that he had been in a similar place somewhere before.

He opened the door to see an empty window open to the sea. Framed in it was the half-disc of the same setting sun that he was certain he had watched on the horizon hours before. It was impossible, he thought, as though the sun hung out of time. Browne grew frightened. He drew his breath carefully. How can it lurk there like that, he wondered, like a jack or a joker? He was reminded that he had taken liberties with time and located himself falsely. These are the interstices, he thought.

Slowly he became aware that part of the room was in shadow, unilluminated by the vagrant sun. It was a vast high-ceilinged room. In one shadowy corner was what appeared to be a high-backed old-fashioned Cape Cod rocking chair. It was piled with what he thought were quilts. Among the stack of quilts he thought he saw braided human hair. His anxiety was replaced by sexual excitement.

A febrile rush made him shiver. The pulse under his collarbone beat hard. He felt a dizzying pressure behind his eyes. At the same time, he was stirred to sudden emotion, a dear, bittersweet longing and a sense of expectation. He suspected he was not alone.

"Who is it?"

The close air was suddenly fragrant. There was a wind chime. Browne had the sense that an old game was in progress. The players were familiar and affectionate but there was an edge of conflict or pursuit. He heard mocking, sprightly music. Panic, Mozartean strains.

"Who is it?" he asked again, smiling.

The sound of his importuning voice hung in the air. The first land crab of twilight scuttled across the floor. He felt called upon for gallantry or wit. Believing that there was a woman in the room with him, he began to proclaim his undying love.

At some point, he thought she tried to warn him she was more coarse and lascivious than he understood. He paid no attention. He cried; his hands described figures in the air. The shadows, the faint music, all suggested she was less nurturing than he required, more carnal. Shameless. Free.

He decided it was only an illusion of the light, of sensual shapes and things that lingered in any old room. Drafts composed themselves into female whispers. The wind was always full of voices.

"Midshipman Browne."

"It isn't anyone," he said.

Browne was certain that no one was there. He looked cautiously at the sun that hung so strangely in the window, at the edge of the sky. Its suspended motion furthered illusion. He spoke to the persuasive image that he had mistaken for a wife, who seemed to want him to stay.

The deasil was sacred. It was an old principle of the sea. He moved his extended palm from horizon to horizon in a clockwise motion. Perfect order. It was always necessary in determining the relative motion of bodies to hold their courses in mind. Clockwise was sound.

He thought of himself heading around the world, congruent with the sun and stars. All that whirl, so much true and apparent motion.

"Look what connects me to them," he told the illusionary woman. He referred to his wife and daughter.

There were bone hooks fastened to his flesh, inserted under the muscle so that he could swing free. Hide lines bound him to a pole, the central pole, the axis of the world. He swung around, in the ancient deasil motion, at varying angles to the blue horizon, supported by the trusty hooks beneath his ligaments. The line groaned as it turned on the bit. He himself sang in the grip of the hooks, glad to be there, exhilarated by the dips and turns. The rational, algorithmic Sun Dance. Such was love.

I'll make my fortune on the Japan Ground, Browne thought, bring my pretty ones silk and amber. Many before him had thought the same.

All at once Browne was certain that he was alone after all and that he had better get out of the familiar house. It was difficult to isolate and address hallucinations, which were part and parcel of sailing alone. It was hard sometimes to distinguish them from the genuine insights which only the sea provided. Sometimes you had to take the bitter with the sweet.

In the next cove, he found more bones and another familiar sight. An ancient steam windlass coiled with rusted wire lay on the rocks together with a welter of ventilator tubes, riveted funnels and iron boilers.

He started back then. Coming in sight of the ash house, he stopped for a moment and looked anxiously at the single window on the second story. He wanted to see someone there. Yet he was afraid of seeing her. That was typical of him, he thought, to be afraid of what he wanted.

That made him consider all that he had learned about himself. From a certain point of view, Browne thought, there were things about himself he hardly dared reflect on. Can it be, he thought, that everyone has this much to conceal?

It was difficult, and every day had its secrets. Every hour had some unsuitable reflection. The longer everything stretched on, the greater the weight of subterfuge. It was necessary to live and then to justify, to balance the calculated and the true. It was necessary to experience life correctly but at the same time compose it into something acceptable.

He stopped and turned back toward the house. He felt truly exhausted, ready to fall asleep on his feet. How restful it would be, he thought, if he could put himself to one side and put things on the other. When he looked at the horizon again, to his great relief the sun was down.

57

ONE DAY Thorne's office called to say that Harry had consented to go on camera for Strickland's film.

"Seriously?" Strickland asked Joyce Manning. "What made up his mind?"

"Frankly, Ron," Joyce said, "I think he's always been curious about your operation. He told Duffy he'd personally pay you off."

"Sounds ominous," Strickland said.

Harry came alone to the Hell's Kitchen studio. "I wanted to have a look," he explained. He did not seem favorably impressed. They talked movies.

"I have friends in the picture business," Thorne told Strickland. "They take a lot of shit from highbrows. But they're very good at what they do."

Strickland was taking his own sound. When he had tested the level, he aimed a camera at his guest.

"Really? What is it they do?"

Thorne laughed humorlessly. "You might say they anticipate popular taste. Across the country and across the world. I think that's pretty good."

"Your friends in pictures used to manufacture popular taste," Strickland said, "when they owned all the tools. Now they're just gamblers."

"You seem to know all about it."

"Everybody does. People in that business don't know from one season to the next what will sell for them. It's a pseudo-rational process. They're medicine men. If it rains, they say they did it. If not, they blame someone else."

"But it appears," Thorne said, "that you couldn't cut it out there."

"I took my business elsewhere. I found other things to do."

"Really?" Thorne asked. He took his glasses off and squinted at Strickland with a hard smile as though it were easier to see him that way. Strickland kept filming. "Less trivial things, maybe?"

"Maybe."

"I suppose you think Hollywood films are trivial. A lot of them are. Documentaries are more serious."

"We try."

Thorne watched him with what seemed to be myopic pleasure at the filming process.

"The guys in L.A. make a lot of trivial pictures about trivial things. Maybe that's bad. Other people make trivial pictures about serious things. Like the Vietnam War. They trivialize what's important."

"Who," Strickland asked, "me?"

"Who knows," Thorne said, "maybe even you. A man risks his life and you look for small significances."

"Small significances," Strickland said, "are neat."

Thorne put his glasses back on and settled into a chair.

"Some people go out and do things," Thorne said. "They put life and reputation on the line. Others seem to see their role as following after. Checking up. With a flashlight. Looking for cracks."

"Or a shovel," Strickland said, "looking for bullshit." He did not stop filming. Thorne laughed amiably.

"What I'm saying," Thorne said, "is there's a difference between people who actually do things and people who find fault and poke holes and make judgments."

"It isn't true," Strickland said, "that I don't do anything. A film is something."

"Not one of your films, Strickland. A film of yours is just an attitude about something."

Reflecting on the notion, Strickland put his camera aside and turned to the window to check the declining light. On the street below he saw the Brownes' sedan draw up against the curb opposite. Anne got out, looked at her watch and locked the car.

"That has its uses, I guess," Harry Thorne was saying. "Opinion making is important. That's why I was advised to hire you. I think now I was ill-advised. I think it was a waste of time."

"You're probably right about that," Strickland said, watching the street. Anne came straight for the street door of his building. She seemed not to notice Thorne's Lincoln, parked near the corner of Eleventh with its driver at the wheel. "You would have been better advised to get a different man."

"It was Matty," Thorne said, and shrugged. "Originally. Then Anne. She wanted the film. Anyhow, I think we've reached the parting of the ways."

The downstairs bell rang. It would be necessary to go down and let her in. There was opportunity enough to turn her away.

"Excuse me," Strickland said. "I'm expecting company."

"I'm leaving," Harry assured him. "My people will be in touch. Do you have anything for me to sign? A release?"

"You don't mind signing a release?"

Thorne seemed pleased with himself. "Glad to have my thoughts on record."

He put his coat on and they went out and got into the scrofulous, graffiti-ridden elevator. Strickland started it down.

"Too bad it didn't work out," Strickland said.

"Yeah, too bad," Harry said.

She was standing square in front of the elevator, framed very nicely when Strickland opened the door. She smiled guiltily, all confusion, and blushed becomingly. It was genuinely embarrassing. Glancing at Harry, Strickland saw his quick gasp and equally quick recovery. He seemed to understand the situation readily enough.

"Harry," she said, "good Lord, what are you doing here?"

"Anne," Harry said smoothly. "Nice to see you." He hurried by her to the curb outside. His car came abreast upon the moment.

"God," Anne said, riding up with Strickland. "I never expected to see Harry."

"Yeah," Strickland said, "he happened by."

"God," she said. "I think he knew, don't you? I think he knew about us."

"I wouldn't think so," Strickland said. "You were discreet."

"I was?"

"Sure. Quite matter-of-fact."

"I don't know about that," she said. She got out of the elevator with her arms folded, looking at the floor.

The shamefaced posture touched him but he was pleased at her humiliation. He meant no vital harm; his lust was to capture, not to kill. Sometimes he had the fantasy there was some wound he might inflict that could make her into a creature more like himself. For company's sake. So as not to be lonely.

58

AT NINETEEN HUNDRED Zulu time, Browne sat hunched by his radio, waiting. In the same moment, at the Southchester Yacht Club, they were attending the monitor, waiting for his signal, in vain. By nineteen-thirty Zulu, the reaching out would begin. Borne by Whiskey Oscar Oscar, by Kilo Oscar India on the cypress cliffs of Marin, by Whiskey Oscar India on the Florida Gold Coast, on the hour and the half hour, all the concerned souls in the other world would start singing him home. He waited, smiling, with his lie coiled, ready to spring it into space.

At nineteen-seventeen, on 21.390 megahertz, he heard Mad Max's frenetic fist.

"CQ DE ZRA1J563, CQ DE ZRA1J563." Over and over again.

Max was CQ-ing the entire planet to advertise his antic presence, inviting discourse. Browne decided to give him a thrill. He tapped out his call sign and the bitch's name, *Nona,* on Max's frequency. Max was delighted.

"JLY GD RARE DX EXCLT SPR," he exclaimed. Which Browne understood was Anglo–South African ham for jolly good unusual and interesting long distance transmission excellent super.

Max inquired the weather, as custom decreed. Browne glanced at his most recent weather fax to see if it would indicate conditions at the false coordinates he was about to claim. He had decided to claim approximately fifty-three south, forty-eight east.

Mad Max was impressed. "SPR DX." He thought it formidable transmission. "QRX?" He was inquiring into the intelligibility of his signal. Browne sent him a numeral five for excellent and asked in turn for Max's location. Max was in Pietermaritzburg, Natal. He asked Browne to mail him a DSL card, the post-card memento that hams exchanged to commemorate their rare DX. Browne readily agreed. Then he gave Max the telephone number of Duffy's office and asked Max to patch him through. Equipped with the number, Max radioed one of his rare DX pals in New Jersey. The ham in Jersey patched the signal to Duffy's phone. In an instant the worried publicist was on the line. Back in the world, Browne thought, but not of it.

"RNDZVS ON 29.871 MZS," Max broadcast. At the rendez-vous, on 29.871 megahertz, Browne found an exasperated Duffy.

"Jesus Christ, chum," Duffy was saying, "where the hell you been?"

"My tanks were contaminated, Duffy. I couldn't charge my batteries. I just got it squared away."

In the simplex transmission they could talk to each other easily.

"We thought you sank, babe. Your dingus isn't sending signals."

"I can't be the only one."

"You're not," Duffy said. "Cefalu and Dennis are down too. We haven't heard from Dennis. Where are you?"

Browne gave him the false position.

"You're leading, then. Is everything O.K.?"

"Everything's fine."

"Can you dream up something for the press?"

"I would hesitate to dream," Browne said.

"Well, we don't want to seem strange or unusual, chum. And how about calling your wife?"

"Should I?"

"Definitely," Duffy said.

"I will, then."

"Maybe we should start preparing the world for a winner. When do you figure on clearing Cape Horn?"

"I'll let you know. It's bad luck to guess."

"All right, buddy," Duffy said. "Keep up the good work."

"I will," Browne said.

Later Max started sending BTs — dah-dit-dit-dit dah, dah-dit-dit-dit dah, dah-dit-dit-dit dah. It was the Morse equivalent of a stammer. He was thinking of what to say next.

"STNDBY FOR HLS," he tapped suddenly. Browne tried to remember what HLs were.

"INTERROGATIVE HLS?"

"HA HA HA HA," Max wired. HLs were laughs.

Browne sighed and sent him a roger.

"HEAR ABOUT MINIATURIZED TRNSMTTR?"

Browne waited.

"FOR PEOPLE WHO LIKE SMALL TALK."

"HL," he told Max.

"YOUR CALL STATESIDE LIKE TWO SNAKES FIGHTING."

Browne was taken with the image. He waited.

"CALL WAS POISON TO POISON."

"HL," he sent back.

"ONE HORSE TO OTHERHORSE AT RACECOURSE."

Browne waited the beat.

"CANT REMEMBER YR MANE BUT YR PACE IS FAMILIAR."

"HL," Browne replied. The puns continued for some time. Browne interrupted the next wave of BTs with a sign-off and closed down. He fell to the work of imaginary positions, devising himself eastward, figuring the angles until he grew tired. The fatigue that settled down on him was considerable. He stood up, put on his fur-lined jacket and went on deck for air.

One minute the lagoon was very still, the next a sudden wind from the peaks would race across its surface, addling the reflected sky. Leaning on the rail, Browne had a sudden recollection of himself speaking to the press in the offices of the Joint Public Affairs Office. His manner had commanded an unaccustomed silence. His words, deliberate, grammatical and clearly spoken, had deepened the attention of the room. He had felt transfigured by his own forthrightness and the reporters had sensed his honesty. He could no longer remember the nature of the information he had been providing the press or whether it had been misleading or not. He remembered only the appearance of rectitude that had surrounded him.

I am neither that person, Browne thought, nor the person remembering that person. There had been something like a death.

He went back down to the navigation table and looked with loathing at the almanacs. Browne thought he could take no more of it. It was too hard for him. He went back on deck.

The trick was to take pleasure in knowing what was true and to deprive the rest of the world of that knowledge. That was the power suggested in the Bible stories. The power of command over reality consisted in being party to its nature and possessing the knowledge exclusively. All at once Browne understood that such power would always be denied him.

"I can't do it," he said aloud. His voice echoed powerfully off the surrounding rocks.

When he was certain he could not get back to work, he prepared to go ashore again. It was late evening and the sun was low. He climbed into the dinghy and set off westward in the lagoon, hoping to find the house he had seen the day before. When he had gone a few miles and it failed to appear, he backtracked. Eventually he landed in a bay that resembled the one he had seen behind the house. One bay looked very like another here. Walking along the shore, he found the mouth of a clear stream and followed it inland.

The stream was fast, running over black rock and through small meadows of coarse yellow grass. A short distance from the shore it curved and widened to a pool and he went beside it and looked into the water. He was surprised to see salmon in the pool, struggling upstream. He could see them clearly in the fading light — enormous, ponderous fish, their bodies gray and scarred. They held their own against the current and it was possible to imagine them gaining the odd fraction of an inch.

The sight of the salmon moved Browne to tears. He thought he had never seen creatures of such gravity. They had won out over time and the ocean. They had survived everything and come home. Browne thought he would give anything to be in their condition.

Ahead, the stream cascaded down from a three-tiered bluff some ten feet high. Browne followed a path beside it. When he had gained the rise, he heard the crashing sea and saw the house of ashes.

On the way to the house he tried to remember where he had

seen salmon before. On the Pacific Coast, he thought, in similar polar light. He could have spent hours watching them.

This time he walked confidently up the porch and through the downstairs rooms. There seemed to be more blackened furniture in the place than he had seen before. On the wall was a faded needlework sampler of Gothic letters in a language he could not understand. Turning, he saw a flash of reflected light. A peeling, shattered mirror was bolted to the wall. Approaching, Browne saw a face in the glass. The face was dark brown and bearded, wild-eyed, like a saddhu's. Or a dervish's, Browne thought, the face of a man in the grip of something powerful and unsound. He raised a hand to his beard. The figure in the glass did the same.

"I can't believe it," Browne said, laughing. He saw a flash of white teeth in the brown face. The little mirror in the head aboard his boat had been deceiving him.

He went upstairs and opened the door and found the room where he had stood before. A scrimshaw tusk lay on the floor. He heard a scuttling in the shadows and saw that crabs had gathered in the dark part of the room. A carapace cracked underfoot and he stepped back. He believed he had been told that rails and land crabs preyed on each other's eggs. The rails by day, the crabs by night.

"Where are you?" Browne inquired.

With the delicacy of an acrobat and the cunning of an engineer, one of the land crabs was easing itself down a leg of the old rocking chair. It touched one extended claw to the rocking bow while the other clutched an edge of the seat until its armored weight was balanced for the leap. Then it rattled down to the floor and hurried off, like a cavalier dragging his sword behind. Browne walked up to the chair and examined the rotting quilts and horsehair that he had taken for a human figure. Mistaken a crab's nest for his wife.

"Johnny Plowboy," sang the hard-hearted woman of the shadows. "Johnny Never-Should-Have-Seen-the-Ocean."

He presumed it was some old song, drawing him into things he wanted no part of.

"Look there away," sang the crab wench.

Browne wanted to invoke the honest, well-spoken young man

he had taken himself for. The role of the information officer was difficult. There were worlds to explain. Something was trying to direct his attention toward the window. Browne stood his ground. He was afraid he might see another face to match his own. Tricks of the mind and of the eye, Browne thought. He had hardly slept for days.

"Look there away," she said. He thought of a thin woman with watery blue eyes, wailing.

Finally, broken-willed, he consented to turn, dreading the thing that might confront him in the window. There, in place of the declining sun, he saw innumerable misshapen discs stretched in limitless perspective to an expanded horizon. It was a parody of the honest mariner's sighting. Each warped ball was the reflection of another in an index glass, each one hung suspended, half submerged in a frozen sea. They extended forever, to infinity, in a universe of infinite singularities. In the ocean they suggested, there could be no measure and no reason. There could be neither direction nor horizon. It was an ocean without a morning, without sanity or light.

On this ocean, Browne thought, goodbye to almanacs and hope in Stella Maris and the small rain down. This is a game beyond me. A diver, he felt as though he were breathing from an emptying tank. His windpipe contracted in its greed for the thin stream. His gasps went unrewarded. He knelt down on the floor of the house. He felt the suspension of hope and wished for it back. He regretted lying.

For a moment he thought he might undo the deception. I'll go home, he thought, before I take a crab's nest for a wife. Before a thin ghost is all the wife I require. Then he was certain it was too late for that. He was a new man with a new fortune.

59

THERE WERE daffodils on the lawn of the Southchester Yacht Club as Strickland made his way to Captain Riggs-Bowen's office. Songbirds were tootling in the locust trees. Inside, he recalled the perfumed booze and hornpipe ambience that had informed the place the previous autumn.

The captain brewed Typhoo tea on a hot plate. He wore a white Irish fisherman's sweater and a maroon and gold ascot, the first ascot Strickland had seen in years. On his desk were tiny flags, the Stars and Stripes and the white ensign of the Royal Navy. Framed on the wall behind his desk was a document displaying the harps and anchors of the equally Royal Irish Yacht Club.

Captain Riggs-Bowen took his tea with evaporated milk. Strickland had lemon.

"Well," the captain said heartily, "he's out in front, your man. You must be pleased."

"We are," Strickland said. "We're pleased. We hoped you might comment on the race. For our cameras."

"I'm tempted," Riggs-Bowen said. "But I won't as yet."

"How do you think he's doing it?"

"Interesting question. I *do* wonder."

"His boat must be better than you thought."

"Umm," said the captain.

"Wouldn't it be that?"

"I'm confounded, Strickland. At a loss. We'll have to find the answer in his logs. We'll want to look closely at those."

"Why?"

Riggs-Bowen looked innocently out at the spring day.

"Well, because there we'll find the secret of his success." He turned to Strickland with a confident smile. "Won't we?"

"When it's over — will you appear for us?"

"When it's over, yes. You may have a more sensational film than you imagine."

"You're behaving like a man with a secret."

"You're wrong. I don't know anything you don't."

"Well, you've seen the reports he's been sending. Can you sort of piece things together?"

"His reports are rather colorless," Riggs-Bowen said. "Lacking in detail. His speeds are erratic. It's hard to tell what's going on."

"I wonder why. When he's so articulate."

"I do too," Riggs-Bowen said.

Strickland watched him, waiting for more.

"I don't think he enjoys life," the captain continued. "I don't think he even enjoys sailing. Some of them, you know, they go out there to suffer."

"I guess he's sort of a philosopher."

Riggs-Bowen laughed. "Is that his wife's opinion?"

Strickland kept his eyes on the tea.

"She worships him," he told the captain. "Thinks the sun rises and sets on the guy."

"Lucky man," said Riggs-Bowen.

Walking back across the club lot to his car, Strickland felt oppressed by the sweet spring weather. Driving to Anne's, he had an attack of despair. It seemed clear to him that no reasonable person would care remotely about the race that Matty Hylan had conceived or about the pilgrim, Owen Browne.

He parked discreetly downhill from the house, hiked up and let himself in through the kitchen. She was upstairs in the bedroom, dressing.

"Ron?"

"Right."

He poured himself a shot of Scotch and went into the living room. On the mantel was a picture of Owen as a newly commissioned ensign, virtually draped in Old Glory. Somewhere along the line, Strickland realized, he would have to do something with flags and navies.

"Where did you park?" she asked from upstairs.

"Miles away," he said. "Not that anyone around here cares."

He took his drink up. She was lying on the bed in jeans with a folded newspaper beside her. He thought she seemed preoccupied and tense. For the first time in days he stammered in her presence and, just for a moment, thought he detected her impatience.

"I . . . went to see Riggs-Bowen. Thought I might get him to go on for us."

"Will he?"

"No."

"Too bad," she said.

"It is too bad. He's a real package. He's got this happy-to-be-a-prick attitude."

"That you admire?"

"I think it's unbecoming in a man who doesn't drink."

There was a Winslow Homer show at the Metropolitan Museum and Strickland decided they should go to see it. Running up the museum steps with him made her feel briefly like a schoolgirl with a day in town. She was amused to find he was a member of the Metropolitan.

As they made their way to the gallery in which the Homers were on exhibit, he held her hand. His grip felt somehow fateful. The moment she saw the seascapes on the wall, she drew her own hand away in surprise.

"How about this stuff?" Strickland asked her.

The oils in the first room depicted the ocean crashing ashore at Prouts Neck.

"Well," she said, "at least I can tell what it is."

"Kindly don't play the philistine."

"Want to give me a lecture?"

"Sure," Strickland said. He took her by the elbow and marched her to the largest painting. It showed four female figures standing on rocks beside a swollen sea. "The ocean is in its place. The force of nature barely contained. The women are frozen by its power. Late nineteenth century, Eros and Thanatos, the Red Universe. Full of subverted morality. See it there?"

"I guess so," she said.

In fact, she found herself quite able to see what he said was there. She was an old intimate of the ocean.

"Look at the women," he said. "They're out of equilibrium.

Facing in different directions, as though they're hearing different voices."

"Is that really there?"

He began to stammer again. "Of c . . course it's there. It's in the composition." A well-dressed Latin American couple in front of the next picture glanced at them.

"Are you angry?"

Strickland laughed in frustration. "Of course not," he said.

"You're right," she said, studying the picture. "I see it."

By the time they had done all six rooms, the ocean was crashing behind her eyes. The muted Maine colors belonged to a world now lost to her. She felt herself wrapped in a shawl like the women in the first painting, standing stricken beside the water.

Afterward, she made him take her to the cafeteria for wine. They sat in the glass-covered atrium, listening to the fountain. Strickland looked displeased.

"I liked the pictures," she pointed out. "I saw what you wanted me to see. What's the problem?"

"I don't know," he said. "Successful work annoys me."

"Winslow Homer probably had a very unhappy life, Ron. Look at the bright side."

"It's no good," Strickland said. "He had a long and satisfactory life. He died rich in honors. Having done what he set out to do. It's enough to make you fucking weep."

"Aren't you successful enough?"

"Nah," Strickland said.

Anne finished her bad Chablis.

"What gets me," Strickland said, "is how he can take something as boring as water and make it swing that way."

"Water isn't boring, Ron. The ocean is not boring." She glanced about the museum café, still half afraid of being seen by some friend or acquaintance of theirs. "What's the Red Universe?"

"Oh," he said, "you know. Nature. Red in tooth and claw. Christ!" he said savagely. "A turn of line. A shade of light. And he does it. So close to nothing at all."

She watched him give his wrist an elegant turn. The sudden curve of his forearm, the thrust of his strong graceful hand in a checkered cuff, aroused and repelled her.

"Ron," she said, "you do the same. Your films do."

"Ah," he said, "but I'm saddled with people and their silly bullshit. If only I could eliminate the human factor."

It struck her as wonderfully funny. She took his hand and pressed her pursed lips against his knuckles.

That evening, in his loft, they smoked marijuana and it was pleasant for a while. During the night she awoke in desperation. She had been dreaming of Owen; her sense of him was intense and immediate. She was suddenly panic-stricken at the presence of the impossible man beside her. The confusion made her feel as though she were losing not only consciousness but identity. Her mind drifted over landscapes of desire and memory. She experienced flashes of shame and absurdity, laughed and cried. In the gray morning light, she felt herself exhausted, thirsty, lustful, pursued by more notions than her mind could safely contain. She thought it must be the drug.

Seeing Strickland awake, she said, "He's coming back, Ron. I've got to prepare."

He turned over in bed.

"Don't be ridiculous."

"Yes," she said. "I do."

He put his arms around her. She lay still.

"Look, that's the past," he said. "It's over."

She was touched at his urgency. At the same time, she realized she would be far freer with Owen than ever with him. He was really out of the question.

"You have to stop saying that," he commanded her. "You have to stop thinking it. You've wasted enough of your life on that guy."

He was far too much work, she thought. Too much hassle. She was too old for it, and there was Maggie.

"We have to go on living," Strickland said. "Remember that."

She agreed absolutely. Somehow, she thought, he failed to understand that this was the problem. She rested against him, giving him her body as comfort for the moment, wondering what he thought he wanted. Did he really believe in hope, this sufferer? In happiness?

60

DURING THE WEEKS sailing north, he applied himself to his logs. The false one he filled with suitable reflections. In the true one, he described what he had seen ashore. Sometimes he thought of himself as headed for the Azores. He had periods of great elation. Northward, the weather was superb and he spent each evening out on deck watching the stars. Meteorites illumined the black subtropical sky. In imagination, he continued to work himself around the world, keeping his businesslike false log, sending position reports through Mad Max.

Max tried to keep him entertained in Morse:

"HEAR ABOUT NUCLEAR PHYSICIST WHO HAD TOO MANY IONS IN THE FIRE? SWALLOWED URANIUM AND GOT AN ATOMIC ACHE!!"

"HL," Browne radioed.

Presences addressed him over the sound of the wind and the luffing of the sails. The voices they employed were all vaguely familiar. Most of the time he knew no one was there.

"Monitor your thoughts," he would instruct himself. The words were on the wind: "Remember everything."

Sometimes he thought it might be possible to explain it all away. Any excuse might be accepted if he did not claim to have won. Then he might go back to the life he had left. The problem was that the life he had left seemed more and more unsatisfactory. There was no passage in it.

One day he found himself a few hundred miles east of Tristan de Cunha, crossing the fortieth parallel. His reported location was far away, in the central Pacific. In his doctored log, he entered the weather he was experiencing because it was so pleasant. The ocean was a deep dark blue and the sky a few shades lighter.

There were flying fish in dozens. A stand of towering cumulus clouds lay to westward, in the direction of the island.

In the warm sun again, he felt an overpowering nostalgia for innocence and the truth. It was hard to believe that they were lost for good. In the evening he saw a petrel. That night he listened in on the missionary station.

"Therefore snares are set round about thee," the English lady informed her listeners, "and sudden fear troubleth thee.

"Or darkness that thou canst not see and abundance of water cover thee.

"Is not God in the height of heaven? And behold the height of the stars, how high they are!

"And thou sayest, How doth God know? Can He judge through the dark cloud?

"Thick clouds are a covering to Him that He seeth not; and He walketh in the circuit of heaven."

So Browne knew that things had found him out, down to the deepest level of his dreams. He thought of the shadowless beach, skuas descending out of the sun. The snares were like land crabs whose bustling caused hallucination. The fear was the loss of reality, never quite retrievable once your share in it was put aside. The appearance of stars was a deception.

Max sent more HLs.

"SI SI SAID THE BLIND PERUVIAN WHEN HE REALLY COULDNT SEE AT ALL."

Copying the message, Browne experienced a sudden insight. He called for a voice rendezvous on 29.871 megahertz.

"Whiskey Zulu Zulu one Mike eight seven three, Whiskey Zulu Zulu one Mike eight seven three, this is Zulu Romeo Alpha one Juliet five six three, over. Yowsa yowsa." Max was in his carnival barker's mode.

"Zulu Romeo Alpha one Juliet five six three," Browne said, "Whiskey Zulu Zulu one Mike eight seven three. I have a question, Max. I'm going to make a guess, over."

"Go ahead, over."

"I'm guessing you're blind. Am I correct? Over."

"Affirmative," the youth said.

"I knew it!" Browne said triumphantly.

"Thanks very much I'm sure. How? Over."

"I know more than I know," Browne explained. Then he felt badly about sounding so enthusiastic. "How old are you?"

"Sixteen," Max said, "over."

"Always blind?"

"Negative your last. Blinded at age eleven. Cycling. Over."

The idea of young Mad Max, in conversation with the world from his own darkness, seized Browne's imagination.

"Know what a basso profundo is?" Max asked. "It's a deep-thinking fish. Know what's a rapscallion? It's a door knocker shaped like an onion. Over."

"Very good."

"Like those? Over."

"Yes, they're excellent. Really funny."

"Good," said Max. "Play chess? Over."

"I know the moves."

"Just know the moves? That's it? Over."

"Yes, that's pretty much it."

"Got a girlfriend? Over."

"Yes I have."

There was static but he made out the word "picture."

"Yes," he said. "I have a picture somewhere. Salted away."

Somewhere, salted away, he had a picture of Anne.

"Max," Browne asked, "why do you collect chess pieces if you can't see them?"

Max was becoming alarmed.

"Whiskey Zulu Zulu one Mike eight seven three, do use procedure. Over."

"Why chess pieces?"

"I like chess," Max said. "I like nice pieces. Over."

"And coins?"

"Coins are smooth. They have edges. They have grooves. Over."

"Listen," Browne said, "we've got to keep in touch."

"In touch," cried Mad Max. "I get it. Out."

Later, Browne discovered that with a little instruction Max could be made to function like a *Nautical Almanac* and help to construct position lines. Once, in his impatience to forge ahead

370

on the logs, he kept the boy awake for a twenty-four-hour period. He regretted it.

"Sleep is important," Browne told Max. "You're lucky."

"Everyone sleeps," Max said.

"Not me," Browne told him.

After a few days of contacts, Browne began to speculate aloud about whether Max would ever be able to see again. Max broke off communication for a while.

"I can only broadcast on the QT," Max explained the next day. "It's my 'rents. They don't want me talking to you."

He had learned to call his parents 'rents from talking to teen-age hams in America, many of whom were also blind.

"I understand," Browne said.

But the next day he approached Max again.

"Listen, I want you to patch a call for me."

He gave Mad Max his phone number in Connecticut. Max patched the call through his friend in New Jersey. Browne heard his wife's voice. There was music in the background that sounded like progressive jazz. He found it impossible to imagine her life. Without a word, he closed down his transceiver.

On deck one evening, he found himself wondering again about going back. He had just listened to Duffy ramble absurdly about public appearances and promotional trips. Browne ended the transmission, affecting a malfunction.

He was not at all in the vein for traveling with secrets. His time was occupied in learning to live a life of singularities, in which no one action or thought connected certainly with any other and no one word had a fixed meaning. There was an art to it. Singularities had their satisfaction but they put a great burden on concentration.

Singularities were the most fun at night when they could be observed among the stars. A man might undo and reorder entire constellations. Stargazing kept the voices at bay, and the crab-borne hallucinations.

One night, rich with shooting stars, Mad Max sent him a co-vert message.

"It is better to travel hopefully than to arrive."

"Roger your last," Browne replied.

How beautiful, he thought, and how true. The most familiar saws took on lustrous new meanings when examined in the light of singularity. By that principle, hope existed as the opposite of possibility. Perfection was always close to nonexistence.

He became preoccupied with blindness. On another starry night he found himself wishing he might forget the order of stars, an illusion that distracted from singularity. Might he be better off blind? Yes. Yet, he thought, if he were blind, the black interior of his skull would sprout stars. There was always the vacant gaze, ever in search of something shiny to reverently bend itself upon. Always the need for a fix.

"I wish I were blind," he said prayerfully. He meant free. He cocked an ear to the wind as though expecting an answer.

61

THE SIGHT of Thorne's Lincoln in the driveway gave her a thrill of hope. She could not keep herself from wanting to be thought innocent. Thorne came to the door with his hat in his hand but his somber expression sent her hopes scurrying.

"Please come in," she said.

He thanked her formally and followed her inside. At first he refused even coffee. She practically had to beg him to accept a cup.

"Owen's doing very well," he said coldly. "We're pleased."

"Yes," she said. "We're very proud of him around here."

Thorne did not smile.

"When we spoke earlier I told you that he would be taken care of by our organization."

"Yes, Harry."

"It still goes. Our corporate difficulties are coming under control, you might say. So you won't have to worry about anything. You can enjoy the fruits of his . . ."

"Adventure," she suggested.

"Right," Harry said. "I think you know that the world of boats is not my world. They're not something I know much about."

She nodded. "Yes," she said, "I know that."

"We all want him back, right? We'll take care of him. Everything possible will be done."

"I appreciate it."

"When we spoke earlier — I tried to explain myself."

"Harry," she said, "I understand completely. We're really very grateful."

"Good," he said, "good." He put the coffee aside. "This documentary of our friend Strickland — it's got to terminate. I know you have a special interest in it." He composed himself into a posture that was a parody of concern and smiled coldly. "It's really not going to do anyone any good. Believe me."

She felt her face reeking of blood and looked at the floor. The polished oak, the woven Spanish rugs, all the artifacts of her domestic life embarrassed her beyond measure.

"This guy Strickland," Harry went on softly, "he's a dog. In my estimation."

She tried to say something to fill the silence that followed.

"Really," Harry asked, "is he gonna help us? Is he gonna help Owen? No. So we're going to pay him off and have him take his business elsewhere."

"That's your decision to make."

He managed to behave exactly as though she had not said a word.

"You know," he said, "I'm a fantast. Maybe the word is fantasizer. I get carried away with my impressions about people. People to me are a source of wonder. I think maybe I like them." He smiled at his own ingenuousness. "I idealize them."

"I see," she said. She felt flayed.

"Lucky for me I have a sense of irony. I used to think my business was built on my skill as a judge of character. I should think again."

"Harry," she said, "you deserved better from everyone involved."

"You know what?" he asked. "I'm not the only one."

62

It was three-thirty in the morning when they got back to Strickland's loft. The day before, Anne had given a press conference at the yacht club. She believed that Owen was about to pass Cape Horn, hundreds of miles ahead of the competition. Strickland had filmed her performance. In the evening they had gone to Da Silvano for dinner and then to a party at Rex. The people at the party were various of his allies or enemies. A singer of Strickland's acquaintance had stood and given an impromptu recital. Pamela had gotten sick.

Strickland spent half an hour after their return reviewing footage on the monitor. When he came into the bedroom he found her beside the round window with an empty glass. He took it from her. The speakers were blaring a tape of sixties hits she had ordered while drunk through a television ad the week before.

"I can't take more days like this," she told him. "I just can't."

"You were great," Strickland said. "I'll show you if you like."

"No thanks."

"You ought to see it. I was proud of you."

"Please," she said.

Strickland went to the window and looked out down Eleventh Avenue. "I don't appreciate being treated like a secret vice, you know."

"I understand," she said, "but I don't know what I'm going to do now."

"It'll be tough," Strickland admitted. "You'll have to get through all the happy horseshit."

"As you said, I'll have to go on living."

"You make it sound hardly worthwhile."

"It's late," she said. "We should talk tomorrow." She stood uncertainly by the foot of the bed.

"What's wrong?"

"Nothing," she said. "I just wish I were home."

"Somehow," Strickland said, "I knew that was it."

"Don't take it personally. It would just be handier." She went around the bed and sat down on it with her fists together in her lap. "There'll be more and more to do."

"I'm feeling," Strickland said, "as though you're chilling me out."

"He's coming home, Ron."

"Have you spoken to him?"

She shook her head.

"Do you want to?"

"I'm afraid."

"Of what?"

"Christ," she said, "that he'll know. That he'll sense something."

Strickland grinned with displeasure.

"Do you seriously propose to take up where you left off? You won't be able to. Believe me."

"I have to. If I can."

"You're out of your mind. You're not that kind of hypocrite."

"Oh yes I am," she said.

He laughed. "You're not thinking. You can't do it."

"Sorry," she said, "but I have to."

She watched him struggle to speak. "To coin a phrase," he managed to say, "you can't do this to me."

"Oh, c'mon," she said, and shook her head dismissively. "Look, your kind of life is not for me. I'm much too square, Ron. I don't belong with you."

"You must be kidding."

"Ron," she said, "I adore you. I do. I always will —"

Strickland interrupted her. "Please don't say it."

"But," she went on, "it's hopeless." She looked at him with a forlorn smile. "Impossible."

"Why?" he asked.

The feeble, stricken question sobered them both.

"But you know why as well as I do."

"You're mistaken."

"Look," she said, "the party tonight . . . I mean, you go

through that crowd like you're at a museum. You react in the same way. I don't have that kind of detachment. I find those sessions very . . . hard."

"What the hell are parties to me, Anne? Do you think that silly shit is what I'm about?"

"No, my dear. But all the same."

Strickland came and sat down next to her. It was an action unlike him.

"Do you not see," he asked, "what a great team we could be? What things might be like for us together? How much fun we could have?"

"Fun?" She looked at him in wonder and laughed.

"I realize that sounds distressingly frivolous. I just don't know how else to say it."

"I'm sorry," she said.

"I travel the world, Annie. I know that's what you've been wanting to do. I mean, I don't mean to be a kid about it. I thought we might have a chance at a decent life."

"I understand," she said. "I do."

"But you don't care about a decent life?"

She laughed silently. "I have no ambitions," she said, "on that level."

"I can't let you go back and be a doormat for that fucking boring man. It offends me. It's against life."

To keep him from saying more, she put her fingers against his lips, as she had on the winter evening months before.

"Enough talk," she said. "Enough trouble."

He let her gentle and flatter him into making love. Wanting to satisfy him, she applied herself. She could feel him trying to excel, to impress her and bind her to him. Her own pleasure made her feel affectionate and uncritical, almost hopeful that they might somehow go on. But in the dark she knew better. When he had gone to sleep exhausted she lay awake and cried because it was the last time.

Throughout the week that followed she kept the answering machine on her telephone and did not return his calls. She knew that eventually he would come. On the Wednesday, she had lunch with Duffy across from the railroad station in Saugatuck. They talked about Owen's return.

"Getting him on talk shows is not a problem," the publicist explained. "I like the idea of getting *you* on. Like the week before he arrives."

"We don't have anything to sell yet," she said. "Later on we'll have our video. And his book."

Duffy looked perplexed. "I think Owen's gonna need a rest, frankly. He's sounding sort of spacey. Don't you think?"

"I don't know," she said. "We haven't spoken."

"You haven't?"

She shook her head.

"Well, the world won't wait," Duffy told her after a minute. "We gotta strike while the iron is hot."

In their common Irishness, she and Duffy affected a relaxed manner in each other's presence which ironically underlined the increased discomfort both felt.

"How's the moviemaking?" Duffy asked. He skimmed one of his handouts as he asked the question.

"It's O.K. We're set for the last scene."

"Gonna miss being a star?"

She watched him sidewise. "How do you mean, Duff?"

"Oh, I just mean — will you miss the attention?"

"It'll be fine," she said. "The world will take up the slack."

When they parted in the station parking lot, she called after him.

"Ask Owen to call me. We've had enough silence, I think."

"Sure thing," said Duffy.

She heard nothing from Owen. On Friday, she took Strickland's call. She found herself missing him dreadfully.

"I feel like a kid," he told her over the phone. "I'd appeal to your sense of irony if you had one."

"Oh, but I do," she said. "We have to tough it out."

"If it was a good cause," Strickland said, "that would be one thing. I mean, I hate to be egotistical about it, but why me and not him?"

Because, she thought, in my love for you I make you part of myself. What I decide to endure you will endure also and we will be together in that. She did not think it bore explaining, certainly not over the telephone.

"You mean, why him and not you, Ron."

Nevertheless, she agreed to see him the following weekend. She decided to have him come to Connecticut, to *her* life. They met in a clam house on a salt marsh outside Westport. The dining room had a view across the open water of the marsh. A night heron walked the tidal flat outside. The Chardonnay they drank was the first alcohol she had taken since their last night together.

"I know better than you," Strickland told her. "You have to believe me."

"Ron," she said, "you surprise me. Do you really expect to be happy? Don't be such a child."

"I don't know what it is," he said. "I can't explain it."

They had something of an argument in the parking lot. They had come in two cars but Strickland insisted on going home with her. He followed her along I-95, driving so erratically she was certain he would be stopped. At the house, he pulled into the driveway behind her. She let him come inside and then began to worry about his being on the road. To keep things on track, she began to lecture him.

"We're going to call it quits," she said. "We might as well get in practice."

"If you think I'm walking away," he said, "you're crazy. You're going to change your mind. I'm going to make you."

"You don't know me very well, Ron. If you did you wouldn't say that."

"Sorry, but I owe this to myself. I owe it to us. I'm not taking any walking papers."

"Don't be so proprietary."

"I have a right."

"No you don't! And don't push me around."

"I will be goddamned," he said, "if I let you disappear into mediocrity with that asshole! In this stupid suburban bullshit. Like some fatassed Navy wife."

"That's what I am. That's all."

"Bullshit! Nonsense!"

"You're getting in the way of serious business. It was fun. It's over. I have a job to do."

"Don't play the cold-hearted bitch with me. I don't buy it."

"You're kidding yourself, Ron. Believe me, I can be a cold-hearted bitch with the best of them."

"I'm going to keep you from this disaster. I insist."

She had been avoiding his eye. She turned and looked at him.

"What I don't understand is why you're so angry."

"I can't help it," he said. "The whole thing rocks me."

"Yes, me too," she said, "but I'm ending it anyway."

"I can't."

Strickland looked as though he were on the edge of control. She began to feel oppressed by him.

"Can't? Grow up."

He began to stammer. She looked away.

"I'm willing to wait," he said finally. "I will."

"No," she said. "I won't. I won't give you hope because there is none. I'm sure of that."

"This whole grip-of-fate bullshit — it's ridiculous."

"Look," she said, "I can handle him. I can handle life with him. You I can't handle."

"You put your finger on it!" he said. "That's the bottom line. Now you got the idea!"

"Maybe so," she said.

"Then don't be suicidal."

She stood in the middle of the living room, folded her arms and shook her head.

"You have only one crack at it, Anne. You have only one life."

She laughed. "Sure," she said. "Life is sweet."

He hit her across the face with the flat of his hand. He brought the hand up from his side and caught her across the cheekbone, snapping her head back. She backed away in astonishment.

"I'm sorry," he said. He followed her into the downstairs bathroom and stood behind her as she looked in the mirror.

"I lost it," he explained.

Anne examined her blazing cheek and felt along the left side of her upper lip.

"I guess it's not serious," she said.

"Sorry."

"But I didn't like it much," she told him. "You better not do it again."

They went back out to the living room. She looked at him and at the door.

"Well, I can't put you on the road in your condition. You can stay in the guest room."

"Come on," he said. "I lost it for a minute."

"I'm not receiving you tonight. Sorry."

"All right," he said. "O.K."

"Funny thing," Anne said. "I grew up with my old man and three brothers — the only girl. They were sort of basic guys. Nobody ever put a hand on me. I've spent twenty years married to an officer type and it would never occur to him to strike me. Nobody ever did. Not until I started hanging out with you sensitive artistic souls. Now I get clobbered."

"We're temperamental."

"Really? Well, I'm not used to it. So don't."

"You know I love you. You know that, don't you, babe."

She hurried past him, then turned and pointed silently to the guest room. Upstairs in the bedroom, she locked the door and went into the medicine cabinet for her Xanax. With the tube in her hand she sat down on the bed and poured the tablets out on the spread. There were twenty-five. The last thing he had said sounded in her mind's ear.

"I love you . . . You know that."

Vain words, a sad little song. She put one pill aside and, one by one, replaced the rest in the tube.

63

ONE BRIGHT blue morning, Browne felt himself unable to pursue the fiction of lines. Ceaseless singularities had obviated all connections. For weeks he had been trying to organize reality into a series of angles. Alone, in hiding, he had the sense of constant scrutiny.

His actual location was north of Ascension Island. His official one was in the far Pacific. He had mastered the mathematics involved and filled every available space with calculations. The sunny, windy weather was fine for sailing; the mast held firm. Over the radio, Mad Max was trading coins in Morse. Max no longer responded to his call sign. Browne had frightened him away.

His nights still teemed with old voices; the crab woman's was only one. He was incapable of sleep. Sometimes his father offered ironic English counsel:

"Give them every assurance, son. Deliver what you can. It's the only way."

It's all up, Browne thought, all over with me. In spite of the bad boat, he had faced down every aspect of the ocean. They would have to give him credit for that. He had never stopped wanting to prevail and go home. It was only that he was tired of imaginary lines. The one abyss he could not cross was wider and deeper than he had imagined. Its horizon was not relative.

That morning he tossed his parallel rulers on the chart table and went on deck. The day was so brilliant that he could imagine making port: a white city. Its domes and tapered spires would be welcome after months of savage geometry, chopping the cup of sea and sky into imaginary angles. Of pretending to locate himself in space and time as, little by little, he was reduced in scale and duration, and singularity erased all reference points.

In the cathedral square, Browne thought prayerfully, he might kneel and walk on his knees across the cobblestones of the plaza and strike his brow against the lowest step of the temple until the blood flowed. Until sleep came, an end of calculation.

What's this, Browne's father said, religion? Unctuous religiosity in extremis? That's for women, my son. For little Juanito, swart Maria and your lady mum.

In port, bougainvillea. Red tile roofs and mandolins. In the cool cathedral square he would offer his humiliations to the Holy Spirit. In the soft spring evening, watch and pray.

Everything is relative, Browne thought, but a joke's a joke. Another man might have done it — have taken the prize and spent the rest of his life in secret laughter. God, he thought, it's truth I love and always have. The truth's my bride, my first and greatest love. What a misunderstanding it all had been. He could no more take a prize by subterfuge than he could sail to the white port city of his dreams.

So it had been in the war. Things had turned out strangely. The order of battle, the hamlet evaluation reports, the Rules of Engagement, were dreams. Truth had been a barely visible shimmer, a trick of the mind that confounded logic and caused words to cast odd shadows.

Browne experienced his reflections with welcome clarity. His state of mind seemed to mirror the weather. The sky was as clear as creation morning. The sea was true blue. He could not help but watch for petrels or pelicans. Nothing came.

He stood clutching the mast with one arm, facing the wholesome wind. He was thinking it would be wonderful to have back the man he had once been. The honest innocent drone who had never seen the blue forties or heard the crab songs. Unattainable. Then he reflected that the man he had once been had never been satisfactory. In any case it was too late. The lie had been told and sustained. It was horrible, Browne thought, to have to lie with complete precision. To employ the godly instruments of rectitude — compass, sextant, rule — in lying. It eroded the heart and soul.

He supposed there would always be something to conceal. It was a difficult situation for one so in love with the truth as he had become. He felt ready to do anything in order to be reconciled.

Mad Max was on the line. Browne knew his fist and listened in.

"REPEAT ZULU 1800 DESCRIPTION PLAYBOY CENTER-FOLD AUGUST 1989 OVER."

He thought of the boy's darkness. The whole world in hiding.

There was a way to resolve the real and apparent aspects of things. Refusing the option, he put both arms around the mast and it swayed with his weight. So clumsy, while the world before him was perfect, absolutely in balance.

If he moved toward resolution, those few truths he had retained would be forever lost. Some of them were worthwhile. He had not been such a bad sailor after all. He had not given in to fear or storms; he had looked into the terrible light. The lie had been only a game. No one would ever know.

He had to wonder to whom the truth might matter. Anne and Margaret were the ones he loved most. It was a shame that they would never understand how it had all come out. Maggie was, down deep, a good and clever girl; she might live long, seeing the clouds, looking into the night sky. His regret for her was sweet and sunny, rose hip and honeysuckle, a broken promise on some summer down the road. Too bad, but the lie had broken the covenants. He had made himself unworthy of his own predicament and the truth was no longer his to convey. It had to be served alone. Single-handed, he thought, I'll make myself an honest man.

Browne went below and from the cabin's squalor retrieved the diver's weight belt he had brought along. He had thought it a useless encumbrance. Now it would come in handy. He made a final entry in his log.

Then he went up and sat on the afterdeck and put on the belt. Pulling himself upright, he stood bent-backed along the rail and looked wide-eyed at the wake that trailed behind. All at once a surge of hope rose in his breast. He had learned so much. He felt filled with illumination. It seemed suddenly as though he might go home after all and tell the tale and take life as it was. He nearly unclipped the belt and let it fall. Living, he thought, affords the only truth there is.

But when he had taken only a single step toward the helm, he saw how false it felt. A single step was so charged with ambiguities. A single word, the smallest gesture, was a compromise. The thing itself, the pure reality, was always unavailable. Every act betrayed it. Every whimper, every fidget, every argument defamed the truth. He would never be satisfied. He would always be ashamed.

And jumping, stepping into space, he had to wonder if something might not save him. Somehow he had always believed that something would. He had never realized how much he had believed it. Be out there for me, he thought. Stay my fall.

Nothing did. He saw the wind-whipped surface of the water. He felt the warm surge of it around him. The sky overhead was flawless. Here, he thought, is deeper than Gennesaret.

He struggled to turn and raise his head and saw the rudder holding firm as the boat, imperfectly surviving, left him her wake to swallow. Then the ocean smothered him.

64

AT A leaded battlement window above the river, Thorne received the first news of Browne's deception. *Nona* had been picked up derelict the week before. The man on the line was calling from Brazil.

"Are you sure of this?" Harry asked him.

The man assured him that the evidence lent itself to no other interpretation. Browne had been preparing two logs — one genuine, one spurious. He had never gotten much beyond the Cape of Good Hope. In the end he seemed to have gone over the side. His late entries were altogether irrational.

"As of now," Harry asked, "who knows this?"

The man was a Miami admiralty lawyer named Collins, a consultant to the marine insurance business.

"As of now," Collins said, "you, me, Duffy and the lady. Also her friend. The guy that's making the movie."

"Strickland. He's there?"

"At the same hotel."

Thorne was silent for a moment. "What about the Greek?"

Floating abandoned, *Nona* had been taken aboard by a Panamanian freighter called the *Eigea*. Captain Diamantopoulas of the *Eigea* had examined the logs and called Duffy, whose telephone number appeared in the margins.

"We don't know what he knows. Obviously he reads English. Anyway, his ship's at sea. En route to La Guaíra."

"Is your phone secure?"

"Negative."

"Fucking mess," said Harry sadly. "Tell Duffy to call me."

In the small hours of the morning, Duffy called. He sounded less than sober.

"Sit on it," Harry told him. "Understand?"

"Harry, what else would I do?"

"We have to do something about Strickland."

"It's up to her, Harry."

"Quite right," Harry said.

He had taken to spending some of his insomniac nights at Shadows. The place had grown on him. Through the heavy lancet window, half obscured by ivy, he could see the moonlight on the Hudson and the great brooding shape of Storm King Mountain against the luminous night sky. In one corner of the oak-paneled room stood his reading chair attended by a Tiffany lamp. His books lined the wall beside it. There was a fire in the grate. That evening he had been reading a history of the Venetian republic.

The ironies, Harry thought, might be satisfying had he been a bitter man. He tried not to be one. The last measure of Matty Hylan's perfidy had come to light: banks purchased with junk bonds making loans secured by worthless boats. Cooked books, forged storage receipts. He himself had survived it all. Every division of the Hylan Corporation he directly controlled had weathered the crisis. No allegations of dishonesty had been proved against him. Sunday supplements and the slick yuppie press had run his most unflattering pictures, sinisterly lit from below. They had mocked his good causes, his cultural pretensions and his diction. Even his dead wife's memory had amused them. In the end, they had proved nothing against him. His attorneys were reviewing areas of defamation.

The truth was they had wanted him dead. They had wanted him smashed to a pulp on the sidewalk like his old friend Sam, disgraced and out the window. They had wanted to jerk off and moralize over his corpse and turn his life's work to laughter.

In the end, all his most jaundiced suspicions had been confirmed, all his trust confounded. False friends and *Schadenfreude*, cheerful lies and bad intentions had all been made plain. The time of reckoning was at hand, when the foxes would have their portion and the common laughers their reward. There was a last laugh available for him, if he wanted it.

But laughs were easily come by, Harry thought. What he had wanted for once was not to laugh. To be reduced to reverence, to be worthily impressed, to be edified even, by something human. And now this.

In the firelight of his riverine fortress, Harry shook his head over the Brownes. So elegant, so intelligent, and finally a pair of flakes. It had been naïve of him to fall for the old white-shoe routine, but of course he had always been a sucker for it.

His lost regard for Anne embarrassed him. He could imagine her laughing at him. Indeed, considering her background, he could imagine the worst. He knew her father well. Hardly a surprise that Jack's daughter turned out to be a superannuated, angel-eyed colleen with a round behind and heels to go with it. As disillusionments went, it was survivable.

Enough to make a just man fall back on religion, Thorne considered. His old friend Sam had been a scholar, betrayed by books, confused by explanations. Of course there was more to faith than commentary and explication.

Punishment had come to her. You had to wonder about the scene down in Brazil. The new widow, her husband dead and disgraced, her stuttering boyfriend, the clever prick. Some godforsaken equatorial port. What would he talk her into? He might have a promising film there if he could finance it.

Of course a film was not desirable. It reflected badly. Moreover she should realize that the relief fund he had established when *Nona* was found was no longer viable. No one wanted to contribute to the relicts of a chiseler. He might provide something for her himself, privately, if the film was dropped. If she had the self-respect to ease herself from sight. On the other hand, she might realize that, properly advised, she could do well from a film, if she was whore enough to profit from her own family's humiliation. It remained to be seen.

The idea of putting something aside for her appealed to him. Lest they should dare imagine, he thought, that he, vain suitor of excellence, hoped to profit by their argosies, their fancy dancing. When the dawn colored the sky above the mountain, he got up and went to bed.

65

THE HOTEL stood beside a river called the Cachoeira; her window commanded the squalor of the port. Police klaxons, exhaust fumes and the fragrance of hibiscus drifted up from the streets.

"Don't you see it?" Strickland demanded. He was drenched in sweat because there had been a power outage. Thunder sounded over the deep green peaks to the north. "It's an incredible story!"

"What is that to me?" she asked. "What good is it to Maggie?"

"The story here is more important than a couple of people."

"In your world maybe. Not where I live."

"Look," he insisted, "it's a way of coming to terms with it."

"I don't want your advice on coming to terms."

"You talk as though it were none of my business."

"It isn't," she said. "Not really. It's not you going through it."

He stood in the open balcony doorway mopping his brow.

"I want to be here for you."

She simply put up her hand and turned away, cutting off his words, blocking out the sight of him.

"You're wrong," he insisted softly. "You'll regret it all your life if we don't finish this."

Clear-eyed, she looked out at the gray sky.

"My responsibility is to my daughter. It's my job to protect her now."

"It is not your responsibility to stage a cover-up. It's not your responsibility to lie."

"I did this to her," Anne said. "I caused it all to be. I lost her her father, letting him go."

"Anne, that's utterly crazy."

"He was sick at heart. I talked him into being a goddam hero instead of helping him cope. I played around."

Strickland rolled his eyes heavenward and smote his brow.

"I think God punished me," she said.

"What are you? Some shawlie in the hills of fucking Skibbereen? Get straight."

"I can't give her her father back," Anne said. "But I can keep the world from making him a figure of contempt."

"This is wrongheaded," Strickland told her. "Look, the world will find out. You know it and I know it." He smiled grimly. "I mean, it's too good to conceal. A thing like this will surface."

"I know how it would look in your hands."

"You talk as though I were your enemy."

"You were *his* enemy. Don't say you weren't."

"I was in a state. Involving you." He stood back and folded his arms as though surprised. "That's true enough."

"You mocked him. You encouraged him to try and explain his dreams."

"I told him not to go," Strickland said. It had just occurred to him. "I bet that's more than you did."

"Did you?"

"I did. In the boat at South Street. I got a feeling."

"Well you're right," she said. The dreadful night before his departure came back to her. He would not have gone if she had only spoken up. "It's more than I did."

They stood in silence for a moment.

"Sorry."

"Oh, it's all right," she said. "I know how cruel you can be. That's why I can't let you go ahead."

"I suppose," he said, "I suppose I have to infer from this conversation that things are over between us."

She looked away.

"Sorry to hear it," Strickland said. "But that's life, right?" He looked out over the tin roofs toward the mangrove banks of the river. "So I won't say anything about what you might owe *me*." He walked over to where she stood and put his palms together.

"Let me explain something to you, Anne. It may look to you as though Owen is a figure of contempt. You may think that the world will despise his memory and that my film will somehow further that." He shook his head and showed her his bleak smile.

"You're so wrong! Can't you understand? What he did — it's what everybody does."

She looked at the ceiling and folded her arms. "No, I can't understand, Ron. I can't follow your reasoning. I never could."

"Everybody trims, Anne. Everybody fakes it. Of course they do. We all try for the reach. Believe me, I've been putting the movers and doers on film all my life. They're all fakes, one way or another. It's the c . . ." He fought for the word. "Condition."

Strickland grew encouraged from her look.

"In a way he was a true hero, Anne. Not as some hyped-up overachiever but as an ordinary man. He reduced his problems with life to that diagram — the sky, the ocean. For Christ's sake, don't you see it?"

"It was a simple lie!" she shouted. "He would have lied to us."

"I have a feeling you're wrong," Strickland said. "I think he would have told you everything."

"I wouldn't have accepted it," she said. "I wouldn't!"

"My dear Anne. Of course you would have. You would have forgiven him."

"Do you really have so high an opinion of him now?" she asked coldly. "You didn't used to."

"I don't have to see you go back to him now," Strickland said, "so I'm on the level."

She bit her lip and looked away. Strickland sat down on the bed and watched her.

"You know, his problem was really his honesty." He shook his head and rubbed the back of his neck. "Some men would have faked it and spent the rest of their lives laughing. Not our Mr. Browne."

He watched her for a moment, then shrugged.

"You should be proud of him. He wasn't a great sailor. But he was an honest man in the end. Annie," he asked, facing her opaque scrutiny, "are you hearing me at all?"

"Yes," she said, "I hear you."

"I'll tell you something else, my love. My former love, in your case, although not in mine. I really am an artist. I mean to the extent that it means anything, if it means anything. I do try."

"I suppose you do," she said.

"This I swear to you, Anne." Standing up, he raised his right hand. "Any audience that sees my film will understand what I've said. If you will let me work. If you will let me tell the story, I will compel them to understand. Now do you comprehend what I'm telling you?"

"Sure," Anne said. "I get it. The square-up."

66

THAT NIGHT she slept on sedatives, awakening to her grief and crashing rain. It took her nearly an hour to notice that the old-fashioned, legal-size manila envelope that contained the log sheets was missing. Before calling anyone, she sat trying to imagine what had happened.

Strickland had a key to her room. The sliding bolt on the lock had sheared in half and could be opened by anyone with a key. She called Collins, the lawyer, and Duffy. As they sat in her room pondering what next to do, the town's electricity failed again, putting the air conditioning and the lights out of commission. Duffy opened the shutters.

"Some goddam nerve," he was saying.

Anne paced the floor.

"I can't believe he did it," she told them.

Later the hotel desk called to say that an envelope had been left for her. The envelope contained the logs, with a note from Strickland. She told Collins immediately, before reading the note.

"Anne," it said, "I have a responsibility to Owen, to myself, to all the other people in the world — even to you and Maggie. This is one you ought not to win. Love R."

She sat and reread it, blushing with rage. He had copied the logs in the hotel office. Later Collins determined that he had gone to the marina and taken all the exposed film he could find from the boat. Then he had flown to Salvador, Miami and home.

"That no-good son of a gun," Duffy said.

"Of course," Collins told them, "it was his film. He provided it to Mr. Browne."

"It belonged to me," she insisted. "To us. We could have gotten the Brazilians to hold it."

"Ma'am," Collins said, "I'd say he got the jump on us."

That afternoon she engaged one of the taxis in front of the hotel to take her to the marina where the boat was being held. On the drive they passed a burning cane field and Indian cattle grazing under swarms of flies among ruined vines. The earth was blood red, the vegetation fleshy. Everything was death and fecundity. The taxi's radio played softly insinuating music.

A black Brazilian sailor in whites and spats patrolled the gate of the marina, carrying a carbine. He swung the metal barrier aside and motioned the taxi through unchallenged. They followed a winding asphalted road that led down to the water through groves of sea grape and coconut palms. Where it ended, two long docks stretched into the bay, lined with the pleasure boats of the rich. The air carried a scent of teak and suntan oil, but the day was stormy and there was no one in sight. Palm fronds tossed uneasily. The bare rigging of the moored boats whistled and jingled in the wind. She had the driver wait.

Nona was off by herself, moored by the harbormaster's cabana at the north end of the marina. The sight of her caused Anne a swelling of grief because for a moment she was sure she would see Owen aboard. The boat's contours suggested his presence.

Drawing nearer, she saw that the mast was sagging badly. A litter of turnbuckles and wire lay across the cabintop. The sails hung slack and unsecured. She tossed her shoes on the dock and stepped aboard over the bow rail. The warm fiberglass deck underfoot increased her sense of moving in his traces.

She ran her hand along the salted surface of the mast, then leaned on a stay and looked out toward the open sea. The water, light green under a heavy gray hot sky, was flecked with dirty whitecaps. For a while, at first, she had indulged an unlikely hope that, having fallen overboard in some unsound mental state, he might be rescued. Now, in sight of this feverish green ocean, she felt certain he was dead. Months of solitude had impressed his living presence on the boat. That was what she had been feeling.

She paused for a moment on deck and then went down into the main cabin. It seemed to her that the interior still held a sullen male smell that suggested violence. She felt it was more than just imagination. She found the innumerable fiberglass patches around the mast step and the splintered bulkheads.

On the flight back to New York, she had nothing to drink but cried unashamedly. The other passengers were mainly Brazilians on their way to Miami. The Brazilians were young, chic and good-humored; many of them appeared to be gay men. A middle-aged lady seated across the aisle from Anne watched her cry, approvingly. Back home, sitting alone in her living room in Connecticut, Anne decided to get some advice regarding Strickland and the film in his possession. That night she called her father.

67

"So," Pamela said, "it turned out *really* interesting. They were like doomed."

"They put it all in one boat," Strickland agreed.

He was just back from Brazil, having spent a night in Miami en route. The two of them lounged side by side across the great bed, which was covered in a quilt and piled with notebooks. It was an hour or so before dawn and they had both been drinking.

"And you like found love."

He looked at her in dull exasperation.

"I bet you're not so cynical now," Pamela said, "about love and all."

"It definitely makes the world go round."

"But it's all over, right?"

"All over."

"She hates you, I bet. I bet she hates herself too."

"No doubt," he said.

"But you're sitting pretty. You have like this *superb* movie."

"Not yet," said Strickland.

"I bet it will be *so* good."

"The potential is there. There's very little on the stuff he shot out on the ocean. The best stuff is him. And the logs."

"Hey, you can do it, Ron!" said Pamela.

"The logs are astonishing," Strickland mused. "I have to find a way to get them in. I mean, he quoted Melville. 'Be true to the dreams of your youth.' He wrote that in."

"Wow," she said. "The dreams of your youth?"

"Melville!" Strickland exclaimed. "*Moby* fucking *Dick*."

"Yipes."

"It's all there," Strickland said. "I think. But I don't know if I can pull it off."

He slept briefly, then got up to run the tape again. The blue of the ocean was marvelous. The Owen Browne who appeared on the monitor was a different entity from the tame Connecticut citizen who had set out from South Street. The man on the monitor had blazing eyes and a lupine grin. At first Strickland thought it might actually be another person. The quality of the sound was poor and he could hardly understand a word of Browne's occasional monologues. What little he could make out led him to conclude that Browne had been speculating on weighty matters. The Big Picture.

He began to think about which section of the logs to match with which footage. This would entail a limited degree of deception, since the association between the words and pictures would be arbitrary and imposed from without. It would be in a good cause. While he was deliberating the phone rang. Freya Blume was on the line.

"You may have some legal problems," she told him. "Widow Browne is claiming the tapes as her property. I think she's going to sue you."

"She's out of her mind. I mean she's actually gone bonkers. Maybe I can still talk her around."

"Better watch it."

Freya had seen difficult times, to say the least, and Strickland was inclined to trust her instinct for trouble.

"Coming into Manhattan?"

"Yes, this afternoon," she said.

"Come for dinner. I'm going to make duplicate tapes. I can do it on my television. I'll give you a set."

It occurred to him then that he ought to make duplicates of his copy of Browne's log books. The security of his building was generally good. Nevertheless.

He took the logs and set out for the nearest copy shop, which was at Forty-seventh and Eighth. When the logs were copied he stopped at a grocery to buy penne and mozzarella for dinner with Freya. He was thinking of penne primavera.

Walking west again, he thought he might as well put the duplicates in his storage locker and get it over with. He walked as far as the river.

In the block between Eleventh and Twelfth avenues, a stretch limousine went past him at high speed and someone in the limo seemed to whistle at him. It was a peculiar New York moment. When he got down to the storage building beside his garage on Twelfth Avenue, two young men were engaged in a shoving match.

"You guinea prick, ya!" one of the young men said.

"You no-good Irish asshole," replied the other.

They were in his way. Both men were smiling foolishly as they quarreled and seemed to have been drinking. Strickland steered a wide course around them, entering the building through the garage entrance. The gasoline smell of the first level of cars brought back to him some childish recollection. He tried to bring it up to consciousness. Long-finned, chrome beauties lined up in a carnival parking lot somewhere. Some field on the edge of a smoky copper town out west on a muddy spring night. A film he had never made, never would.

A middle-aged security guard with a sick pale face and long oily hair stood by the steel door that connected the garage to the storage rooms. The guard simply walked away as Strickland approached the door. It was unlocked. There was no one at the lobby desk to sign in with.

The light in the elevator in which he rode to the next level was defective and the space was lit only by its red emergency sign. The door was slow to open. He got out into the narrow corridor short of breath. Banks of storage lockers stretched to within a few feet of the spongy cement ceiling. There were flaking sprinklers overhead and bare-bulbed lights in wire housings. It was impossible to walk facing forward; he had to ease sideways, clutching the envelopes that contained the logs, to avoid the filthy locker doors. Passing down the first corridor, he felt irritated and depressed, then increasingly anxious. It occurred to him that the logs contained the essence of things. Behind him in the cement room, the old elevator rattled into action. At the first turn of the tier he stopped and looked both ways down the silent rows. The left-hand corridor ended at a blank brick wall. The aluminum sign indicating section numbers was missing and for a moment he could not remember which way to turn. The elevator door rang in the distance. People came out of it. He was momentarily relieved.

Strickland shambled toward his storage locker like a child lost among the attractions. A great sadness had settled on him. It had to do with the woman and the film; he understood that much. Stress and the pains of love. It would be necessary not to drink too much, to exercise and concentrate the empty hours in work. The work would have to make up for a great deal. In his anxiety, he clutched the logs, together with the cheese and pasta, close to his body. A ghostly telephone rang somewhere in the building.

For a moment, Strickland paused in his passage. Regret and longing ached in his throat. They did not suit him. Apparently, he thought, it would be worse than he could ever have imagined. Never had he contrived so strenuously to impress anyone, to beguile and entertain. Certainly he had never sought to be understood before. Quite the opposite. Now, having had her beside him, a companion, bending to his wit and lust and will, he could not forget what it was like. For the first time in his solitary life, Strickland felt himself alone.

"Dumb bitch," he muttered softly. Immediately he was aware of other voices on the same floor. They seemed to converse in malignant whispers.

At the river end of the building, the storage spaces were larger, divided into sections by metal walls that were scratched with graffiti. Each section was a few feet off the main corridor, approached through a tiny three-sided room. The spaces were protected by a single heavy metal door secured with a combination lock. Strickland hurried on, feeling vaguely frightened and not altogether well. It occurred to him that the security provided was inadequate. When he got the logs out, he decided, he would go to a bank and rent a safe-deposit box. He had never stored anything so at risk before. The distant telephone stopped ringing.

Finding his cubicle, he stood just outside it without switching on the light. The logs were clutched under one arm, the groceries under another. Two men were coming down the corridor; one of them was softly whistling a one-note ditty between his teeth. Strickland experienced an impulse toward full flight. He stayed where he was.

The first thing Strickland noticed about the two men who came up to him was the smell of alcohol on their breath. Even before one reached up and switched on the cubicle light, he knew they were the pair who had been shoving each other out on Twelfth Avenue.

One of the men had thick black hair, brush cut with a lock down the back. Although Strickland had no way of knowing it, the man was called Donny Shacks for his gallantry with the ladies. The second man was fair; confronted with his long lashes and huge irises, Strickland was reminded of his own phrase: "the eyes of a poet." The poetically-eyed young man was called Forky Enright, from a nasty incident at a New Jersey picnic. They were with an out-of-town local.

"Open it, you fuck," Donny Shacks said to Strickland. Forky seized the logs from under his arm.

"You drunken moron, give me those!" Strickland shouted.

"Open it," Donny Shacks repeated.

Strickland bent to open his locker. It was empty. He straightened up again. He was angry and alarmed.

"Those aren't worth anything!" he explained. Forky smiled and began to sing. Donny Shacks looked up and down the corridor.

"Ireland was Ireland before Italy got its name," Forky sang plaintively. "Ireland is Ireland and Ireland it remains!"

Strickland stared wide-eyed at the minstrel, who sang louder still.

"We're all Roman Catholics! We all go to Mass!

And all you guinea bastards can kiss my Irish ass!"

Donny Shacks reached up and switched out the light.

"Help!" Strickland shouted, without much conviction. "I'll call the p . . p . . p —" He failed to get the word out.

One of them punched him in the face. Strickland flung himself forward in a rage. He had been raised by a woman of genteel pretensions, and violence, although he had experienced a fair amount of it, always opened new and terrifying doors in his psyche. He was resolved to fight for the logs. Only at the last minute did he see the shadow of the implement coming at him. Just in time, he raised his clenched, embattled fists in a defensive posture and felt half a dozen of his knuckles shatter like Christmas ornaments under the blow. It was a baseball bat, hence the land from which no film maker returned. He dived and covered up and took one bad blow at the back of his ribs and a lesser but painful blow across the spine. Most of the others were glancing, aimed generally at his legs, because Forky was quite drunk and out of breath. Donny Shacks had broken Strickland's nose with the first punch.

"P-p-p-p-p . . . pop? P-p-p-p . . . poop?" Forky stood over him in the darkness, leaning on the bat, sputtering like a half-wit. "You better not say cops, you fuck. You was gonna say police? You better not, you fuck, you."

"All right," Strickland said from the cement floor. "Take it."

"You got no fucking respect," Donny Shacks said to him. "That's the trouble with you."

When they were gone, he struggled to his feet and found that he could neither straighten out his back nor close one of his hands. His pain felt serious. He stepped over his splattered grocery bag and slowly dragged himself down the ramp that led to the garage. When he got in sight of the street and saw the traffic, he leaned against a guardrail and shouted.

"I'll make it anyway! I'll make it! Anyway!"

The strange thing was that although the garage section was active, with dozens of people coming and going, no one paid the slightest attention to Strickland. Bloody-faced, bent double at the waist, cursing, his crippled, broken left hand supported as in supplication by his right, he made for his car under the unseeing gaze of busy passers-by. It took him prodigies of effort to release the lock of his car and get the door open. Safely behind the wheel, he passed out briefly.

Reviving, he felt irrationally responsible for his own appearance. He wanted not to walk the streets and be ignored. Painfully steering the car with the heels of his hands, he drove down the ramps and pulled up in front of the cashier's station.

The attendant in the booth was the same Latin youth who had been on duty when he returned from Central America. When he handed over his monthly rate ticket, the young man did not return it. Instead, he picked up his clipboard and went out to frown down at Strickland's license plate.

"You can't park here no more," the boy told Strickland.

"What are you talking about?"

The youth, incensed, grew immediately hot-eyed. "What I said, man. You can't park here no more. 'Cause the space ain't available."

Strickland looked at him for a moment and said, "I see." There was no use in arguing.

Wearily and carefully, in the same heel-handed style, he drove across Twelfth Avenue and east on Forty-sixth Street, to park illegally in front of his loft building. He went in slowly, putting one foot in front of the other deliberately, bent-backed. He regretted alarming the pedestrians hurrying by and understood their situation. Not half a block away, three men had been shot down dead for interfering in a duly arranged murder.

Upstairs, he found Pamela chatting with Freya Blume. They were talking about furniture. Both women rose to their feet when he came in.

"What on earth?" asked Freya.

Strickland leaned against one wall and managed to speak. "I think I want a bath."

"You need a doctor," Freya said in a quiet frightened voice. "What happened to you?"

"Oh God," wailed Pamela.

"I need a bath," he repeated. "That's all."

But when he was in the bathroom with the tap running, he realized he could not manage it. He went back into the loft living room, sat down in a ratty armchair and looked out the window on the late spring evening. He still could not straighten out his back.

"I can't let it go," he told the two women. They were still on their feet, staring at him. "But I don't know if I can do it now. But I've got to try, understand?"

"Roosevelt Hospital," Freya said to Pamela. "Roosevelt–Saint Luke's. We'll take him in a taxi."

"I have my car," Strickland told them.

"The guys from the lab came and got the film," Pamela said. "I let them in."

"What guys?" Strickland asked. "What film?"

"The stuff from Owen's boat. The UPS guys. They took it to the lab."

"I never sent it to any lab. It was just videotape. I was going to copy it."

"But these guys took it. It was on the marked ninety-minute spools. It said 'Browne' on it and they just sort of picked it up. All the stuff that had 'Browne' on it, they took."

He got painfully to his feet, walked into his cutting room and saw at once that all Browne's tapes were gone. But it was worse than that. He had been keeping most of the original sound track from his film in a handy cabinet to make his own retransfer. The cabinet was marked BROWNE SOUND. It stood open and empty.

"My sound," Strickland said. "They got my sound."

"Go to the police," Freya told him.

"They've got my sound," he said. "They've got the logs. They've got the tape."

"Get a lawyer."

"I will," Strickland said. "Definitely." All the footage he had taken of the Brownes ashore was secure in a laboratory vault. Most of it was silent now, and there were no tapes from the boat to match with it, and no logs. "But I don't think it will help."

Almost certainly, he thought, salvaging a film from the remnants would prove beyond him. Such a thing would require vast ingenuity and measureless labor. At the same time, he was not at all sure he could keep himself from trying. He would have to sit in the dark and look at the mute dummy of the film that he had lost, and at the woman also. He might spend a lifetime.

"No," he said, "I don't think so."

He would fail, Strickland thought. There would never again be the old nonchalance of the hand.

"Come," Freya said. "We'll drive you."

"Oh God," said Pamela.

"You should call the police now," Freya said as they hobbled toward the door.

"Right," Strickland said. "The insurance."

"What next?" she asked.

"I don't know if I can do it now. But I've got to try."

"Oh baby," Pamela said. She looked fond and somewhat happier.

"I've got to get out of here. Set up somewhere. Maybe I can still do it."

In pain, he stopped. They held him upright.

"God," he said, "my hands are killing me." One of them was especially swollen. He swallowed hard. "Or maybe . . . maybe I should just look for another number. Maybe it's a nonstarter. Bad karma."

"Really," Pamela agreed.

"Anyway," he said, "I can't stay here."

"Why not?" Freya asked.

He began to wheeze. They thought he was laughing.

"I think I've lost my parking space," he told them.

68

WHEN THE MOVERS had taken up the last rug, Anne unfolded a beach chair and sat smoking in the middle of the bare white living room. The impulse to smoke again had come upon her early in the summer, out of nowhere but irresistible. Upstairs, she could hear Maggie weeping in her stripped bedroom, sitting on the floor with her back against one wall, clutching a bear. Seeing that clearly in her mind's eye, Anne closed her eyes and brushed her hair back from her forehead. Her hair was finally growing in longer.

She had found a house for them outside South Dartmouth, Massachusetts. It was an old house of the sort she favored, colonial, with a view of Buzzards Bay. There, Maggie could transfer to day school and live at home. Anne could prepare for the race. She planned to get under way during Maggie's first year at college. Everyone had given up trying to talk her out of it.

Except for the smoking, she was sober. She had taken to going every night to an Alcoholics Anonymous meeting at the Congregational church. Most of the other alcoholics in the meeting were men. There were soft pink suburbanites and a few proletarians.

Men seemed wary of her. It might be the wounds somehow visible, she thought, or it might be simply that they thought her hard. So she presently would be. Her sense of humor had become rowdy and somewhat unpresentable. Bitter, a little cruel. She was forgetting her schoolgirl good manners. Above all, she had become impatient.

In an old half-discarded briefcase she found the note she had forgotten to give to Owen. It had been mislaid in the confusion when he had been setting out. In it she had quoted from *Romeo and Juliet*:

My bounty is as boundless as the sea,
my love as deep; the more I give to thee,
the more I have, for both are infinite.

She could not imagine transcribing such sentiments.

The stories about Owen's voyage were coming out, in spite of her precautions. Captain Riggs-Bowen, who prattled endlessly about discretion, was a loose-lipped showoff who could not keep from seeking credit for what he thought he knew. It was all ironic and she supposed Strickland had been right after all. The fact was that he had understood. Who would have thought it?

No doubt, she thought, his movie would have been fine. She heard rumors through the magazine that he was still trying to piece something together. The world's curiosity was well whetted. If it ended up on television, there was nothing she could do. But surely it would be easier not to go through all that. To be recognized everywhere and pitied, philosophized about, eyed year after year? No. Things were bad enough as they were. There were more important concerns than one smart guy's career and the state-of-the-art movie.

She had inferred, from a dark remark of her father's, that they had stepped hard on Strickland. She had not intended him injury but she did not pursue it. If true, it was one more thing to regret and be ashamed about.

In the grip of some confessional impulse she had inflicted the whole story on Buzz Ward, Strickland and all.

"I'll be goddamned," he had said.

She had said, "That doesn't sound like absolution."

"It's not," he had said. "Hell, no."

Loyalty was honor itself to Buzz. In spite of everything, though, she felt he had in part forgiven her. He knew the turns things took. But perhaps it was wishful thinking on her part.

In her disorderly way, she remembered that unburdening as a nearly comic scene, and she had to wonder if one day they might not laugh about it together. Sex was absurd. Love was absurd.

One of the worst things was that sometimes she could not think of Owen as dead. She was pursued by a nonsensical nightmare image of him pinned to the horizon, outside of time and motion, suspended undead over the sea, the Dutchman. In that manifestation she could neither clearly recall nor forget his face.

She put her cigarette out in the coffee can that was serving as an ashtray. Upstairs, Maggie turned in her sorrow. The sound echoed through the empty house.

In her contemplation of pain, Anne found herself returning again and again to Owen's mad logs. His idea of himself as a Sun Dancer particularly impressed her: him spinning, hooked, at noon, on the axis of the world. Now hearing Maggie's foot on the stairs, she thought of it.

"Are you almost ready?" she called.

The girl did not answer at first. Anne turned to look and saw her daughter staring out a window toward the shore. Her teddy bear was thrust unsentimentally beneath her arm. She had a crazy false smile.

"I'll be so glad to be out of here," the girl declared.

"You must think of the good things," Anne said. She knew that saying it risked a pointless argument for which Maggie would have a thousand times more energy than she. But they were at the point of leaving. It was as though the last minutes of the house required respect and reason.

"The good things," Maggie said with a laugh. "That's really funny."

Maggie had constructed a four-line poem about her father that began: "Liar liar liar." Her mother had continually to beg her not to recite it. She had read the logs.

Grieving, Anne watched her daughter's ghastly pretense of saturnine amusement. With her high forehead and her honest gray-eyed look, she was so like him. How could either of them, Anne wondered, ever imagine they would put anything over on the world?

Feeling a little faint, she lit another cigarette.

"You mustn't say that, dear."

"I know," Maggie said. She spoke as though she were party to a private joke. Her eyes were brimming.

"Maybe you should have another look around the house," Anne said to her daughter. "Just to make sure you have everything."

"I've looked and looked," the girl replied. They faced each other in the empty room. "Maybe *you* should, Mom."

Anne found herself wandering listlessly through the blank

rooms. One had been the dining room, another the study Owen had made for her. She went into the sunny kitchen.

"God," she said aloud, "I can still smell that jerky."

In her race, Anne thought, jerky was an item she would do without. Suddenly she found herself wondering if some of the food she had packed for him might have gone bad and poisoned him and caused his mind to go. It very often happened, when she turned the voyage over in memory, that she discovered derelictions and occasions for guilt.

She made her way back to the living room and stood behind the beach chair. She had known that leaving would be hard. It was important that she cope, she thought, for Maggie. Somehow she could not resist an attempt at comforting words.

"Mags," she began. It was a false start. "Mags, you must not judge harshly."

Helpless, she watched her daughter's face give way.

"One day," Anne said, beginning again, "I hope you'll understand the kind of man your father was. He risked his life. He risked his sanity. He experienced everything. Very few men have ever done what he did. Very few men test themselves that way."

Maggie turned away with a low moan. It was expressive, Anne understood quite well, of contempt and exasperation at her mother's self-deception.

"One day you will, Mags."

Maggie ran through the front door and into the street. Anne started after her, afraid for a moment that her daughter might go headlong down the hill, toward the tracks, the highway, the Sound. But Maggie was only running to the car. She huddled with her bear in the passenger seat.

Watching Maggie through the window, Anne remarked on how changed she had been in a year. She looked almost a grown woman, clinging to the ridiculous bear. I should have made her leave it, Anne thought.

Someday, one way or another, Maggie would come to terms with it. Until then she would suffer in confusion. Anne had to hope it would harden her, pretty guileless creature, Owen's daughter, to survive the lovely illusions she would certainly embrace, the broken promises ahead.

For the race, Anne would be sailing a boat built in Wisconsin to her specifications, financed partly by her brothers, partly by the publisher of *Underway* and partly — she had discovered — by Harry Thorne. As the widow of a cheat, she had not even asked for corporate sponsorship. Everyone had been outraged, at first, at the risk. She had had to explain again and again that it was absolutely necessary, that it was a risk that must be taken. She was convinced that expiation was required and that their honor could be restored if she went to sea. There, she half believed, she might somehow find him and explain. The ocean encompassed everything, and everything could be understood in terms of it. Everything true about it was true about life in general.

Anne slept very little and accepted her wakefulness. She had learned to value the sunrise and the lightening hour before dawn. One morning she had lain listening to a white-throated sparrow chanting in the single living elm across the street. Everything seemed obviated in its plainsong. There were many around the house in South Dartmouth and she looked forward to that. She hoped land would be sweet to her when the voyage was over. She hoped to treasure the first landswell. She thought she saw a model for herself in the order and simplicity of the sparrow's call.

She folded the chair and took it with her into the street and let the teak door swing shut behind her.

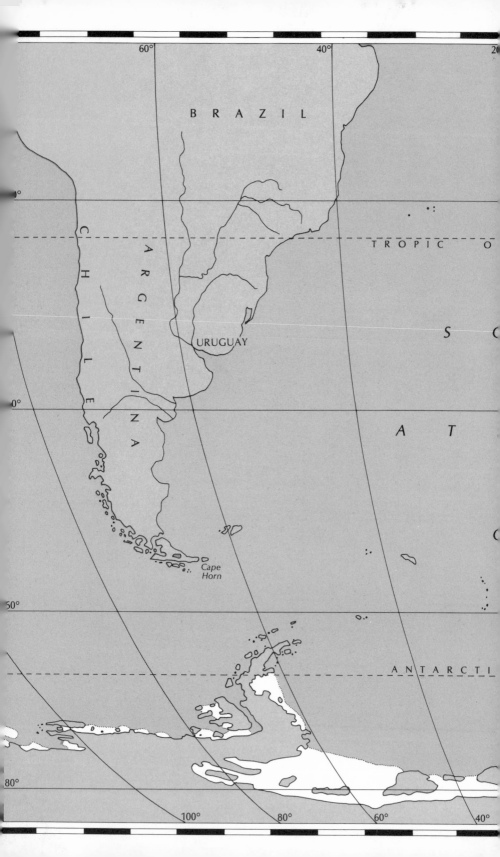